the
further
adventures of

SHERLOCK HOLMES

THE WHITECHAPEL HORRORS

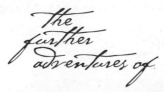

SHERLOCK HOLMES

THE WHITECHAPEL HORRORS

EDWARD B. HANNA

THE FURTHER ADVENTURES OF SHERLOCK HOLMES:
THE WHITECHAPEL HORRORS

ISBN: 9781848567498

Published by
Titan Books
A division of Titan Publishing Group Ltd
144 Southwark St
London
SE1 0UP

First edition: October 2010
10 9 8 7 6 5 4 3 2 1

Names, places and incidents are either products of the author's
imagination or used fictitiously. Any resemblance to actual persons,
living or dead (except for satirical purposes), is entirely coincidental.

Visit our website:
www.titanbooks.com

What did you think of this book? We love to hear from our
readers. Please email us at: readerfeedback@titanemail.com,
or write to us at the above address. To receive advance
information, news, competitions, and exclusive Titan offers
online, please sign-up for the Titan newsletter on our website:
www.titanbooks.com

A CIP catalogue record for this title is available from the British Library.

Printed and bound in the USA.

"To Sherlock Holmes she is always the woman. I have seldom heard him mention her under any other name. In his eyes she eclipses and predominates the whole of her sex." — *A Scandal in Bohemia*

For Marcia, *the* woman in my life

Foreword

Edward B. Hanna was a dedicated bibliophile. He had thousands of books on hundreds of subjects, not the least of which was the work of Sir Arthur Conan Doyle.

He was most in his element surrounded by the written word and steeped in history. In the later years of his life he researched and wrote in the privacy of his study with his patient cat, Mystère, distracting him only to remind him that it was dinnertime.

Always the harshest critic of his own work, he constantly wrote, rewrote and destroyed his work. He spoke of his book subjects to no one, saying that when shared he lost interest in his subjects.

When Hanna completed *The Whitechapel Horrors*, he revealed to his beloved wife that the ending surprised him. Hanna had a certain conclusion in mind when he began the book, however, the writing of the tale of Mr. Holmes and Dr. Watson took on its own life. It is fair to say that in the composition of this work the characters became alive for Hanna and created their own destiny.

I hope that you find enjoyment from *The Whitechapel Horrors*.

Leigh Hanna
March 2010

Prologue

&

"Somewhere in the vaults of the bank of Cox & Company, at
Charing Cross, there is a travel-worn and battered tin dispatch-box
with my name, John H. Watson, M.D., Late Indian Army, painted
on the lid."

— *The Problem of Thor Bridge*

O ne of the first official acts of Mr. Ronald F. Jones upon taking up
his new position as director and general manager of London's
venerable Claridge's was to inspect the contents of the safe in his office.
There were two surprises.

The first was an unopened *basquaise,* or flat, long-necked flagon of
very old and equally fine Armagnac, a Reserve d'Artagnan, if the faded
label was to be believed.

The second was a thick leather portfolio, also very old and once very
fine, with the initials *JHW* embossed in faded gold leaf in the center.

The presence of the Armagnac has never been explained; it had been
there when Mr. Jones's predecessor arrived many years before and, as

far as he knew when queried, when *his* predecessor arrived many years before him.

The leather portfolio was more easily explained. It had been left in the care of Claridge's management by a gentleman who had been a permanent resident for as long as even the oldest staff member could recall. He was a retired surgeon by the name of Anstruther who, being a childless widower and the last of his line, had no family, and being quite elderly, had outlived all of his friends and contemporaries.

It seems that Mr. Anstruther had little faith in banks, having lost a sizable part of a large inheritance during the Great Depression, and no trust in the legal profession, upon which he blamed most of the ills of the world ("First, kill all the lawyers," he was fond of misquoting Shakespeare). Therefore, he chose the strongbox of Claridge's, which he considered the second safest depository in all of England. Banks could fail, Britain could lose her Empire, but Claridge's? Claridge's would remain unchanged, untouched, untroubled for as long as that other great monument to the English race and Western civilization, the Tower of London. And since its vaults were otherwise occupied, Claridge's safe would simply have to do.

But then one day old Mr. Anstruther died, and the worn, cracked leather portfolio remained quite forgotten until the occasion, several years later, when Mr. Jones took up his new position.

Having more pressing matters on his mind at that time, it was not until a number of months had passed and Mr. Jones once again had occasion to rummage through the contents of the safe, that the presence of the portfolio (and the Armagnac) came to mind. The temptation to open both came upon him, the portfolio because he was curious, the Armagnac because it had been a particularly arduous day. But one just doesn't break the seals of a bottle of old and rare brandy on a whim or without proper occasion, especially since it had remained undisturbed in its sanctuary for how many years? Its very presence, though known to few, had become as much a part of Claridge's as the marble and mahogany and gleaming brass of the public rooms, and though there was little likelihood of a rightful owner returning to reclaim it, or of some hidebound traditionalist writing an indignant letter to *The Times*, good form and Mr. Jones's integrity demanded the bottle be returned undisturbed to its place of rest. Besides, if the truth be known, he was really partial to cognac.

The portfolio? Ah, well, that was another matter.

The topmost document was a letter, a sheet of heavy foolscap yellowed with age, bearing the logotype of Cox & Company, Charing Cross, London. It was dated July 30, 1929, and was addressed to Mr. Elwyn Anstruther, F.R.C.S., Harley Street. At first reading the brief contents were uninteresting, disappointing, a dry and formal communication from banker to client.

Dear Sir:

I have to inform you of the unfortunate death, on the 24th instant, of Dr. John Hamish Watson, an honored client of Cox & Company of many years standing.

It had been Dr. Watson's custom, from time to time, to entrust to our safekeeping various notes and records of a confidential nature, the contents of which I, naturally, have no knowledge. It was his wish, as expressed in a letter of instructions to this firm, that upon his death the folio, hereunto attached, was to be delivered over to Dr. Ian Anstruther of London Hospital and Queen Anne Street whom, upon inquiry, we learned to have passed on these several years since.[1] The late Dr. Anstruther was, I believe, your father.

Accordingly, upon consultation with the firm's solicitors, and having determined you to be the only surviving son and heir of said Dr. Ian Anstruther, Cox & Company deem it will have acquitted itself of its responsibility by delivering over to you the aforementioned file.

If, sir, Cox & Company may be of any further assistance, you have only to communicate with the undersigned at the firm's offices in Charing Cross.

I remain, sir, et cetera, et cetera . . .

There was a brief postscript at the bottom of the page:

I call to your particular attention that at the behest of the late Dr. Watson, included in the document attached hereunto, none of the contents of this file may be publicly revealed until the year 2000, or until such time as fifty years shall have passed from the date of his death, whichever comes later.

Inside the folder Mr. Jones found a thick sheaf of unbound manuscript paper, yellowed and somewhat brittle to the touch, the top sheet containing a dozen or so lines set down in a neat but spidery hand. Mr. Jones gasped, scarcely believing what he read. There were two names that seemed to separate themselves from the jumble of other words on the page and leap into sharp focus – two names from long ago. Both were remembered with awe, one with something approaching reverence, the other with utter horror:

Sherlock Holmes. Jack the Ripper.

EDITOR'S NOTE

The following account is based primarily on notes compiled by John H. Watson, M.D., near the end of his life, and which, as has been related, ultimately found their way into the safe of Claridge's. The editor has tried to remain faithful to the material throughout; however, it must be appreciated there were instances when that proved to be impracticable. Because of a scarcity of detail, a conflict of dates (undoubtedly the lapses of an old man's memory), and, as is the case in several instances, the unaccountable omission of certain established, widely known facts, it has been necessary on occasion to resort to other sources, as noted in the footnotes and bibliography. Obviously Dr. Watson never got around to organizing the notes relating to this matter in any but the most desultory fashion. It is most likely that he never intended to. Much of the information contained in the material is of such an extremely sensitive and confidential nature it is surprising that he ever reduced it to writing at all. But knowing of his reputation for discretion and great integrity and the fact that he had always respected the confidences shared with him by his friend, Mr. Sherlock Holmes, it must be assumed that his motives were noble, for no other assumption is acceptable. It may well be that he simply could not bear to take to the grave secrets relating to the most notorious murderer of all time. Whatever his reasons, one thing is certain: Had any of the contents of this file been revealed at the time the events occurred, or even for a good while thereafter, it would have not only ruined the reputations of several well-known, highly placed individuals, but almost certainly would have brought about the fall of the government then in power. Indeed, it may well have caused the downfall of the British monarchy.

PART ONE

"Horror ran through the land. Men spoke of it with bated breath, and women shuddered as they read the dreadful details. People afar off smelled blood, and the superstitious said that the skies were a deeper red that autumn."

— From a contemporary account

One

ℰ♪

"It is not really difficult to construct a series of inferences, each
dependent upon its predecessor and each simple in itself."
— *The Adventure of the Dancing Men*

"Aperfectly marvelous, gruesome experience," observed Sherlock
Holmes brightly as he and Watson wended their way through the
crowds streaming out of the theater into the gaiety and glare of the gaslit
Strand. "I cannot thank you enough for insisting that I accompany you
this evening, Watson. Rarely have I been witness to a more dramatic
transformation of good to evil, either onstage or off, than our American
friend has so ably portrayed for us."

He pondered for a while as they walked, his sharp profile silhouetted
against the glow of light. It was the first of September, the night was
warm and clinging, the myriad smells of the city an almost palpable
presence. London, noisy, noisome, nattering London: aged, ageless,
dignified, eccentric in her ways – seat of Empire, capital of all the world;
that indomitable gray lady of drab aspect but sparkling personality –

.was at her very, very best and most radiant. And Holmes, ebullient and uncommonly chatty, was in a mood to match.

"I have no doubt the author was telling us," he said after a time, "that we are all capable of such a transformation. Or, should I say transmogrification? – such a wonderful word, don't you think? – capable of it even without the benefit of a remarkable chemical potion; that we all, each and every one of us, have the capacity for good and evil – the capability of performing both good works and ill – and precious little indeed is required to lead us down one path or the other. While hardly an original thought, it is sobering nonetheless."[2]

But if he found the notion sobering, it was not for very long. He was in particularly buoyant spirits, having just the previous day brought about a successful conclusion to the amusing affair concerning Mrs. Cecil Forrester. And if his hawklike features seemed even sharper than usual, the cheekbones more pronounced, the piercing eyes the more deepset, it was due to an unusually busy period for him, one of the busiest of his career, when case seemed to follow demanding case, one on top of the other, with hardly a day between that was free from tension and strenuous mental effort. Though the pace had taken its toll insofar as his physical appearance was concerned – he was even thinner, more gaunt than ever, and his complexion a shade or two paler – it did nothing to sap his energy or weaken his powers. It was obvious to those who knew him – Watson in particular, who knew him best – that he not only thrived on the activity, but positively reveled in it, was invigorated by it. As nature abhorred a vacuum, he was fond of saying, he could not tolerate inactivity.[3]

Still, Watson was glad to have been able to entice him away from Baker Street for a few hours of diversion and relaxation. Left to his own devices, Holmes would have been content to remain behind, indeed would have preferred it, cloistered like a hermit amid his index books and papers and chemical paraphernalia, the violin his only diversion, cherrywood and shag his only solace.

Several theaters seemed to be emptying out at once along the Strand, and the street was rapidly filling with even greater throngs of gentlemen in crisp evening dress and fashionably gowned women, their laughter and chatter vying with the entreaties of the flower girls and the urgent cries of the newsboys working the crowd.

"'Ave a flower for yer button'ole, guv? 'Ave a loverly flower?"

"Murder! Another foul murder in the East End! 'Ere, read the latest!"

"Nice button'ole, sir? Take some nice daffs 'ome for the missus?"

Holmes and Watson elbowed their way through the crowd with increasing difficulty, conversation made impossible by the press and clamor around them.

"Here, Watson, we will never get a cab in all this. Let us make our way to Simpson's and wait for the crowds to dissipate."

"Capital idea, I'm famished," Watson shot back, dodging a pinched-faced little girl with a huge flower basket crooked in her arm.

Holmes led the way, stopping momentarily to snatch up a selection of evening newspapers from grimy hands. Then the pair of them, holding on to their silk hats against the crush, forced their way through to the curb and navigated the short distance to the restaurant, gratefully entering through etched-glass doors into an oasis of potted palms and marble columns, ordered, calm, genteel murmurings, and starched white napery.[4]

It was not long before they were ushered to a table, despite several parties of late diners waiting to be seated; for the eminent Mr. Holmes and his companion were not unknown to the manager, Mr. Crathie, who ruled his domain with a majesty and manner the czar himself would have envied. Shortly after taking their places, they were served a light supper of smoked salmon and capers, accompanied by a frosty bottle of hock.

Conversation between the two old friends was minimal, even monosyllabic, but there was nothing awkward about it or strained, merely a comfortable absence of talk. Small talk was anathema to Holmes in any case, but the two had known each other for so long, and were so accustomed to each other's company, the mere physical presence of the other was enough to satisfy any need for human companionship. Communication between them was all but superfluous in any case, their respective opinions on almost any subject being well known to the other. And besides, throughout most of the meal Holmes had his face buried in one or the other of his precious newspapers, punctuating the columns of type as he scanned them with assorted sniffs and grunts and other sounds of disparagement occasionally interspersed with such muttered editorial comments as "Rubbish!" "What nonsense!" and, for variety's sake, an occasional cryptic and explosive "*Hah!*"

Watson, well used to Holmes's eccentric ways, resolutely ignored him, content to occupy his time by idly observing the passing scene. The captain and waiters, on the other hand, could not ignore him: An untidy pile of discarded newspapers was piling up at his feet, and they were in somewhat of a quandary over what to do about it. Holmes, of course, was totally oblivious to it all.

"It would seem," he said finally, laying aside the last of the journals with a final grunt of annoyance as their coffee was served — "It would seem that our friends at Scotland Yard have their work cut out for them."

"Oh?" responded Watson with an air of disinterest. "What are they up to now?"

Holmes looked at him quizzically from across the table, an amused smile on his thin lips. "Murder! Murder most foul! Really, Watson! Surely you are not so completely unobservant that you failed to take note of the cries of the news vendors as we left the theater. The street is fairly ringing with their voices! 'Orrible murder in Whitechapel,'" he mimicked. "'Sco'ln' Yard w'out a clue.'"

Watson made a face. "Well, I hadn't noticed, actually. But surely, Holmes, neither bit of information is hardly unusual. There must be a dozen murders in that section of the city every week, and few if any are ever solved: You above all people must be aware of that. What makes this one any different?"

"If the popular press are to be believed —" He broke off in midsentence and laughed. "What a silly premise to go on, eh? Still, if there is even a shred of truth to their rather lurid accounts, this particular murder contains features that are not entirely devoid of interest. But what intrigues me more, Watson — what intrigues me infinitely more at the moment — is your astounding ability to filter from your mind even the most obvious and urgent of external stimuli. It's almost as if you have an insulating wall around you, a magical glass curtain through which you can be seen and heard but out of which you cannot see or hear! Is this a talent you were born with, old chap, or have you cultivated it over the years? Trained yourself through arduous study and painstaking application?"

"Really, Holmes, you exaggerate," Watson replied defensively. He was both hurt by Holmes's sarcastic rebuke and just a little annoyed.

"Do I? Do I indeed? Well, let us try a little test, shall we? Take, for example, the couple sitting at the table to my left and slightly behind me. You've been eyeing the young lady avidly enough during our meal. I deduce that it is the low cut of her gown that interests you, for her facial beauty is of the kind that comes mostly from the paint pot and is not of the good, simple English variety that usually attracts your attention. What can you tell me about the couple in general?"

Watson glanced over Holmes's shoulder. "Oh, that pretty little thing with the auburn hair — the one with the stoutish, balding chap, eh?"

"Yaas," Holmes drawled, the single word heavy with sarcasm. He examined his fingernails. "The wealthy American couple, just come over from Paris on the boat-train without their servants. He's in railroads, in the western regions of the United States, I believe, but has spent no little time in England. They are waiting – he, rather impatiently, anxiously – for a third party to join them, a business acquaintance, no doubt – one who is beneath their station but of no small importance to them in any event."

Watson put down his cup with a clatter. "Really, Holmes! *Really!*" he sputtered. "There is no possible way you could know all that. Not even you! This time you have gone too far."

"Have I indeed? Your problem, dear chap, as I have had occasion to remind you, is that you see but do not observe; you hear but do not listen. For a literary man, Watson – and note that I do not comment on the merit of your latest account of my little problems – for a man with the pretenses of being a writer, you are singularly unobservant. Honestly, sometimes I am close to despair."

He removed a cigarette from his case with a flourish and paused for the waiter to light it, a mischievous glint in his eye.

Watson gave him a sidelong look. "Very well, Holmes, I will nibble at your lure. Pray explain yourself!"

Holmes threw back his head and laughed. "But it is so very simple. As I have told you often enough, one has only to take note of the basic facts. For example, a mere glance will tell you that this particular couple is not only wealthy, but extremely wealthy. Their haughty demeanor, the quality of their clothes, the young lady's jewelry, and the gentleman's rather large diamond ring on the little finger of his left hand would suffice to tell you that. The ring also identifies our man as American: A 'pinky ring,' I believe it is called. What Englishman of breeding would ever think of wearing one of those?"

Holmes drew on his cigarette and continued, the exhalation of smoke intermingling with his dissertation. "That they are recently come from Paris is equally apparent: The lady is wearing the very latest in Parisian fashion — the low decolletage is, I believe, as decidedly French as it is delightfully revealing — and the fabric of the gown is obviously quite new, stiff with newness, probably never worn before. That they arrived this very evening is not terribly difficult to ascertain. Their clothes are somewhat creased, you see. Fresh out of the steamer trunk. Obviously, their appointment at Simpson's is of an urgent nature, otherwise they would have taken the time to have the hotel valet remove the creases before changing into the garments. That they are traveling without personal servants can be deduced by the simple fact that the gentleman's sleeve links, while similar, are mismatched, and the lady's hair, while freshly brushed, is not so carefully coiffed as one might expect it to be. No self-respecting manservant or lady's maid would permit their master or mistress to go out of an evening in such a state, not if they value their positions and take pride in their calling."

Watson sighed, a resigned expression on his face. He smoothed his mustache with his hand, a gesture of exasperation. "And the rest? How did you deduce all of that, dare I ask?"

"Oh, no great mystery, really. The man's suit of clothes is obviously Savile Row from the cut; custom made from good English cloth. It is not new. Ergo, he has visited our blessed plot before, at least once and for a long enough stay to have at least one suit, probably three or four, made to measure."

"Three or four? You know that with certainty, do you?"

Holmes, who was fastidious in his dress and surprisingly fashion conscious, and the possessor of an extensive wardrobe now that his success permitted it, allowed a slightly patronizing tone to color his reply.

"Formal attire would usually be a last selection; an everyday frock coat or 'Prince Albert' and more casual garments for traveling and for weekend country wear would customarily be the first, second, and third choices."

Watson looked pained, but he bravely, perhaps foolishly, continued: "You said he was a railroad man. How do you come by that, eh? And your conjecture that he is waiting for an urgent appointment, a business engagement, you said – and with someone beneath his station? How do you arrive at those conclusions?" He snorted. "Admit it, Holmes: pure guesswork, plain and simple!"

"You know me better than that," Holmes said, casually dabbing at his lips with a napkin. "I never guess." His lips puckered in a prim smile.

"Well then?" said Watson impatiently, drumming his fingers on the table.

"It is manifestly clear that the gentleman is waiting for another individual because of his repeated glances toward the door – anxious glances which suggest that the other party is not only eagerly awaited, but of no small importance to the gentleman in question. That it is one individual and not more is supported by the obvious fact (so obvious, Watson) that the gentleman and lady are seated at a table for four, and there is only one other place setting in evidence. These conclusions are all supported by the additional observations that the man and his charming companion – his wife, I dare say, from his inattentive manner – have yet to order from the menu despite being at table for some considerable time, and the wretched fellow is well into at least his third whiskey and soda – with ice, I might add," he said with a slight curl to the lip, "further evidence he is an American, should any be needed."

"As for the rest –" Holmes stubbed his cigarette out and continued: "That the man has a well-stuffed leather briefcase on the chair beside him suggests an engagement of a business nature. Why else would anyone bring such an encumbrance to a late evening supper? As for the engagement being with someone beneath his station..." Holmes sighed and gave Watson a somewhat patronizing look. "Really, Watson, this is getting tiresome. Obviously, our friends over there are wealthy enough to dine at the Ritz or the Cafe Monico. Why Simpson's, as good as it is, with its simple English fare? Hardly what a wealthy American tourist or business magnate would choose unless he had good and sufficient reason to do so – such as not wishing to appear in a highly fashionable restaurant that caters to the *crème* of society with someone unsuitably dressed or of a lower station."

Watson raised his hands in a gesture of surrender. "Enough, enough; I should have known better than to doubt you. You have my most abject apologies. Now, for God's sake let us get the bill and find our way home. I am suddenly very weary and want only my bed."

Holmes chuckled and snapped his fingers for the waiter.

As they threaded their way toward the entrance minutes later, Watson had to step to one side to avoid colliding with a man rushing headlong into the restaurant: a short, round individual with a large mustache, who after a hurried glance around the room made directly for the table occupied by the couple in question, profuse with apologies once having arrived. He was carrying a bulky briefcase and was dressed in a sagging dark business suit, not of the best cut or material. His voice, which could be clearly heard over the hubbub of the restaurant, had a decidedly middle-class accent – *lower* middle class. Watson shot Holmes a sidelong glance to see if he had noticed. He need not have bothered: Holmes's face was a mask of perfect innocence. There was just the glimmer of a smile, the mere hint of a smile on his thin lips, nothing more.

"We have a visitor, Holmes," said Watson as their hansom clattered to a halt in front of their lodgings. There was a light in their sitting room window, the shadow of a human form in evidence.

"I am not totally surprised," said Holmes laconically.

"You were expecting someone at this late hour?"

"No, not really. Nor am I surprised someone is here. H-Division, in all likelihood." Without a further word of explanation he bounded from the cab, his eyes bright with anticipation, leaving Watson to settle the fare and follow.

Two

SATURDAY, SEPTEMBER 1, 1888

"It has always been my habit to hide none of my methods,
either from my friend Watson or from anyone who might take
an intelligent interest in them."
— Sherlock Holmes, *The Reigate Squires*

Mrs. Hudson was waiting for them just inside the front vestibule by the staircase landing when they entered, but Holmes rushed past her with barely a nod, bounding up the stairs two at a time.

"Yes, yes, I know, Mrs. Hudson," he called as he ran. "Thank you, thank you kindly. No time for how-d'ya-dos."

Watson followed at a more leisurely pace. "A good evening to you, Mrs. Hudson. Apparently we have callers. How good of you to see to their comfort. Thank you so very much indeed."

The long-suffering Mrs. Hudson, so used to their irregular ways and the odd callers Holmes received at even odder hours, shrugged in resignation and returned to her kitchen for her nightly glass of hot milk (laced with a circumspect spoonful of whiskey) before finally retiring, she fervently hoped, for the night.

Watson, upon reaching the top of the landing, found Holmes in the front room, their common parlor, with two men, one having just arisen from the settee where he had been seated, not terribly comfortably, with teacup in hand. The other, the heavier of the two and the better dressed, had been anxiously pacing in front of the window but was now by the door, shaking hands with Holmes. It was obvious what they were, if not who they were, for while their faces were new to Watson, intuitively he was able to identify them at once: the way in which they carried themselves, their aura of authority, if not to say officiousness, was to the practiced eye identity enough – as obvious signs of their profession as actual signs around their necks would be.

"Ah," said Watson before Holmes had a chance to make the introductions. "H-Division, I presume."

Holmes shot him an amused glance. "No, dear fellow: CID, as it happens." He made a gesture of presentation. "My friend and colleague, Dr. Watson, gentlemen. Watson, this is Detective Inspector Abberline and Sergeant Thicke."[5]

It was the higher-ranking Abberline (for his aura of authority was just that much more in evidence) who came forward to shake hands with Watson, while the other man, Thicke, was occupied juggling his teacup, desperately looking for a place to set it down.

Abberline was a soft-spoken, portly man with a high brow and heavy whiskers who looked and sounded more like a bank manager or solicitor than a policeman. He favored Watson with a quizzical look.

"Dr. Watson is not totally incorrect," he said. "Both Thicke and I have been temporarily assigned to H-Division on an especial duty, the very matter that brings us to you at this late hour, in point of fact."

"Please make yourself comfortable, gentlemen," said Holmes. "I see our Mrs. Hudson has provided you tea. May I freshen your cups? No.

Well then, help yourself to cigars if you like. You will find them in the coal scuttle by the fireplace there. I won't tempt you with a brandy or whiskey, seeing as you are still on duty."

With a flick of the tails of his coat, Holmes plopped himself down in his favorite chair and tented his hands in front of him. "Now, pray tell me how I might be of service."

Abberline took the proffered chair and waved away the offer of tobacco while Thicke gratefully resumed his place on the settee, teacup still balanced precariously, and peered over toward the fireplace with a bemused expression, no doubt trying to fathom why any sane individual would want to keep his cigars in a coal scuttle.[6]

Abberline began speaking immediately: "Good of you to see us at this late hour, Mr. Holmes. Believe me, if it were not a matter of some urgency, I would not have troubled you. Lestrade assured me that not only would you not mind the intrusion, but, to the contrary, would receive us graciously, as I have indeed found to be the case."

"Ah, my good friend Lestrade," said Holmes with a faint smile and noncommittal tone, concealing his somewhat low opinion of the man's professional skills.[7]

"Yes, it was he who suggested that I come to you. You are known to me by reputation, of course − the assistance you have rendered to the Yard in the past is well known to us all, as is the fact that your unofficial status and your − shall we say, um, unorthodox methods − can sometimes bring about more satisfactory results than we in an official capacity can achieve."

Though scarcely effusive with praise, this was an astounding admission coming as it did from a professional police officer, and it was one that was obviously made with some difficulty. Holmes enjoyed every word of it, but his facial expression betrayed none of his feelings. While hardly a modest man, it would have been foreign to his nature to gloat, yet he was far too forthright to indulge in false humility. He merely nodded politely, then shot a warning glance at Watson, who seemed to be having difficulty containing himself.

Abberline cleared his throat and continued: "We have a most dreadful mess on our hands at the moment, Mr. Holmes, a horrible mess, and frankly I am at a loss as to how to deal with it. I don't mind admitting to you that as things now stand, the matter would appear to be beyond the capabilities and resources of the Metropolitan Police."

Watson could restrain himself no longer at this admission. "What refreshing candor from a Scotland Yard man," he said, smiling broadly. "You are to be congratulated, Inspector. You fellows usually show great reticence in admitting half as much." He gave Holmes a wink. "Something to do with this Whitechapel business, I would wager."

Abberline turned toward him in his chair, his expression a mixture of mild annoyance and surprise.

"Why, yes, Doctor, it is indeed the Whitechapel affair that brings us here. However did you guess?"

"Guess? Dear chap, I don't guess. Just look at the two of you: Your boots and trouser bottoms are covered with mud — that distinctive brownish-blackish muck you will find only in the mean streets of the East End. A spattering of the stuff is even on the upper legs of your trousers and on your hats over there. You must have been crawling around in it half the night, noses to the ground, I shouldn't wonder." He snorted. "Obviously called out to investigate the murder of that poor woman, eh?"

Abberline and Thicke both peered at Watson with expressions bordering on admiration.

"Damn me, but that's observant of you, Doctor!" Thicke exclaimed. "Your powers of observation are most impressive."

Watson preened his mustache and stole a glance at Holmes. "Oh, elementary really. Nothing much to it when you have the knack."

Holmes smiled ruefully and rendered Watson a little bow from his chair, then turned back to Abberline.

"Please continue, Inspector," he said, his tone and look implying that he would appreciate the absence of further interruptions from Watson.

Abberline sat back, his face resuming its anxious expression. "Dr. Watson is, of course, correct. We have spent the better part of the day and evening in the Whitechapel district trying to come up with something – anything at all – that would give us a clue to this heinous crime. I tell you, Mr. Holmes, I have never come up against anything like this before. It's the most horrible thing I have ever seen. Without doubt, the most horrible, vicious thing."

Thicke, from his place on the settee, nodded woefully in agreement.

Holmes leaned forward in his chair with anticipation, his eyes glinting fiercely in the light of the table lamp.

"Perhaps, Inspector, I can prevail upon you to begin at the beginning," he said softly, enunciating each word with great care. "Leave nothing out, I implore you."

Abberline nodded, sighed deeply, and began:

"Of course it is in all the newspapers, as I am sure you have noted. The sensational press are falling all over one another in their efforts to report the events, and there is scarcely a street corner in London that isn't emblazoned with a news vendor's broadsheet upon which the word *murder* is prominently displayed." He took a deep breath before continuing. "For a change, the newspapers are correct, I fear. The headlines are no more sensational than they deserve to be. The latest crime, Mr. Holmes, is as hideous and as dreadful as they say it is. Indeed, even more so, because the Fleet Street crowd haven't printed the worst of it!"

Holmes raised his eyebrows but said nothing.

Abberline shook his head. "Oh, I know, I know. Violent death is no stranger to Whitechapel or to Spitalfields. As I don't have to tell you, the Spitalfields district is populated with the very lowest of the low: the poor and the very poor and beneath them the utterly destitute – the dregs of society, as they say. Why, crime – crime in its most violent forms – is a way of life there. And life is so cheap, they'll slit each other's gullets for a sixpence and think nothing of it."

Holmes nodded.

"The Evil Quarter-Mile, they call it," Abberline continued, "and so it is. We have got eighty thousand people packed into the space of a few small acres, most of them unemployed, uneducated, diseased. Many of them surviving like foul dogs from day to day on what scraps they can find in the streets. Most of them without a shred of decency, without even a modicum of self-respect, let alone respect for others. Death is an everyday occurrence, and welcome it is to many! Hardly a day passes when somebody isn't found floating in the Thames. We pay the river boatmen a shilling a body to bring them in. And many of them are murder victims. They'll kill each other over a pair of shoes or a piece of bread! Or over nothing at all. Believe me, our chaps have their hands full over there."

He paused and tugged at an ear. "But of late there has been something new, which is why we" – he nodded toward Thicke – "have been temporarily assigned to the East End, along with a dozen or so other chaps. During the last several months there have been a rash of murders that are distinctly out of the ordinary, that don't fit the usual pattern – unusually vicious crimes, all committed with a knife, all perpetrated against women, and all of the women being 'unfortunates,' as they're called – common prostitutes with hardly a copper coin to their names. In other words, Mr. Holmes, these murders don't appear to have any motives, none at all. They appear to have been committed for the thrill of it! The sheer bloody thrill of it, if you'll pardon my language."

Holmes interrupted: "You speak of the murders of that Emma Smith woman last Easter Monday and, what was her name, Turner or Tabram, who was found a fortnight ago with, how many? – thirty-nine stab wounds?"

Abberline nodded his head. "Yes, those are the ones. And there have been others as well. You've been keeping up with things, I see."

"It is my business to do so, Inspector," Holmes responded.

"Yes. Well, we didn't have a clue for either one of those homicides, not a single clue. And not a reliable witness either – one that would come forward, in any event. At first we thought some soldiers from the nearby Tower garrison or the Wellington Barracks were responsible for the Tabram murder, because the wounds appeared as if they could have been made with a bayonet. And we even made some arrests, but the two lads we had as suspects turned up with ironclad alibis and we had to let them go. And now this... this latest one."

Abberline removed a pocket notebook from his coat and flipped through the pages, finally coming to the section he was looking for. He cleared his throat.

"At three forty-five on the morning of Friday the thirty-first of August – yesterday – Police Constable John Neil, number 97-J, of H-Division, while in the course of his normal rounds, did come upon in Buck's Row, the body of a woman lying in the street." Abberline put the notebook aside and continued in a normal speaking voice. "At first he thought she was just another derelict, unconscious from intoxication – God knows, a normal sight in Spitalfields. He reported he smelled the reek of gin. By the light of his bull's-eye lantern he could see that she was lying on her back with her eyes open and staring. Her skirt was pushed up to her waist. He felt her arm and it was still warm – 'warm as a toasted crumpet,' he said. So he tried to get her to her feet. That's when he saw that her throat had been cut, and the blood was still oozing out of it. Then he looked closer. The windpipe and gullet had been completely severed, cut back to the spinal cord."

"My word," whispered Watson.

"Funny how the mind works sometimes," continued Abberline. "Neil told me that his first thought was 'Well, here's a woman who's committed suicide!' Can you believe that? He actually started looking around near the body for the knife she did it with. Then it came to him. She had been murdered.

"Well, as you can imagine, he started up, half expecting to find the murderer lurking in the shadows, the body being still warm and all. He was in the process of making a quick search of the immediate vicinity when he spotted the lantern of his mate who was walking the adjoining beat" – Abberline glanced in his notebook – "Police Constable Haine, number – Oh, I don't know what it is, but he's also assigned to H-Division. And just about the same time, another constable by the name of Misen came on the scene. It seems that two passersby on the street came upon the body just before PC Neil – a George Cross and a John Paul, both market porters on their way to work – and they had run to fetch help and came upon Misen patrolling in the next street. Neil must have come by not a minute or two later. Well, in any event, Neil called to Haine to run for the doctor. Fortunately, there's a surgery close by, and within a quarter of an hour, no more, a Dr. Ralph Llewellyn was on the scene. He made a cursory examination of the woman, confirmed that she was indeed dead – though how she could be anything else with her throat slashed ear to ear, I don't know – then ordered the body taken to the mortuary adjoining the local workhouse."

"A cursory examination, you say?" asked Holmes.

"Yes, that's right. A more thorough job was performed later at the mortuary. The light was so poor in the street, you see. Only the one gaslight on the corner, and the constables' bull's-eye lanterns. Don't know how he could have done more under the circumstances."

"So there was no search of the area for a weapon or footprints or anything at all that could have been tied to the crime?" Holmes asked.

Abberline shook his head. "No, nothing of the sort. Except, as I said, the first quick look-around that Neil conducted right after discovering the body. Not ideal conditions to find anything."

"And when daylight came?"

Abberline looked embarrassed. "Well, of course a search was made the next morning, but nothing was found. As for footprints or suchlike, bless you, Mr. Holmes, but Buck's Row is paved with cobbles. And the muck in the street, as Dr. Watson has so astutely observed on my boots and trousers, was by then so churned up by so many footprints, it would have been useless, quite useless, to even try to isolate the one pair that might have been of any interest to us."

Holmes looked at him with hooded eyes. "Then the area was not cordoned off?"

"Well, not until after I reached the scene several hours later. And by then, well..."

Holmes shook his head sadly. "Please continue, Inspector."

"Well, of course we knocked on all the doors facing Buck's Row and questioned everybody who resides in the vicinity, but most of them were asleep, or so they say, and heard nothing. But you know those people, how suspicious they are of the official police. They're not likely to share any information with us, even if they did know something." His voice trailed off. He was noticeably tired and was having difficulty organizing his thoughts.

Holmes prompted him gently: "The body? It had been taken away?"

"Ah, yes. As I said, the body was ordered sent to the mortuary by

Dr. Llewellyn, and it was there that a more thorough examination was in due course undertaken. And that's when we discovered the real horror of the crime."

Abberline paused to wipe his brow with a handkerchief taken from his sleeve. Holmes and Watson waited expectantly, not making a sound. Only the ticking of the clock could be heard, and the hiss of the gas lamp.

"It was like this," Abberline said finally. "Dr. Llewellyn returned to his home to get a few more hours of sleep and his breakfast, while the body was stripped and prepared for autopsy. This was done by two inmates of the workhouse to which the mortuary is attached – two regulars, I might add, who have often performed the same service and are well acquainted with the correct procedures: a Robert Mann and a James Hatfield," he said, referring once again to his notebook. "The lads earn an extra bob or two lending a hand, as it were. You know, doing the dirty work.

"It wasn't until they were in the process of undressing the body to prepare it for the doctor that the discovery was made."

He paused. His voice sank to a hoarse whisper. "She'd been gutted, Mr. Holmes, gutted like a fish!"

Three

SATURDAY, SEPTEMBER 1, 1888

"It has long been an axiom of mine that the little things
are infinitely the most important."
— A Case of Identity

They were at the mortuary within the hour. A hastily summoned
four-wheeler conveyed them through the night to the slums of
the East End, although the cab's jarvey was most reluctant at first to
take them.

"Ye must be daft, or think I am!" he said from his box, shaking his
head obstinately. "I'll not be goin' there, not at this hour of the night.
'Tis bad enough in the daytime!"

It took a flashing of police credentials and a most impressive display
of Sergeant Thicke's official manner to change the man's mind. It did
not change his humor. He lapsed into a sullen silence for the duration of
the trip, a silence frequently punctuated by venomous over-the-shoulder
glances, which expressed his feelings far more eloquently than words.

The ride was not a very long one, the East End of London being separated from the West End more by birthright than distance. It is a squalid, miserable place, a place not so much where one lives as survives, but not always and never easily.

The jarvey, jaw firmly set, pulled up in front of the Whitechapel station of the underground railway, near Brady Street.

"Ye'll 'ave to 'oof it from 'ere, gents, Metropolitan P'lice or no. I'll not be taken yer lot any further, and that's me last word!"

Watson paid him double the fare anyway.

The mortuary, located in Old Montague Street, was but a short walk, but it is a walk into a London few respectable Londoners even knew existed. The area of the East End known as Whitechapel, though in close proximity to the lofty sacred precincts of St. Paul's, is a low and hellish place, and the few adjoining acres called Spitalfields, which they had now entered, is the lowest level of that hell. No more than a quarter-mile square, the darkened narrow streets and alleyways of Spitalfields contained the worst of London's slums and the very lowest form of humanity. It had been fifty years since Charles Dickens had described the district in *Oliver Twist*, yet little had changed for the better, and not even someone with his powers of description could prepare the unwary for the worst of it. Spitalfields was a place that penetrated the soul with feelings of repulsion and dread.[8]

The stench from the streets was all but overpowering, a witches' brew of smells: the familiar odors of poverty — garbage, excrement, boiled cabbage and decay, stale beer, cheap gin and unwashed bodies — was intermixed with the stink of coal gas which permeated everything, and the gagging vapors from the slaughterhouses and tanneries and small, run-down factories that were scattered about the area.

They walked quickly, eyes to the ground, detouring when necessary around the occasional small clusters of vagrants, misshapen lumps sleeping huddled in doorways or against the building walls.

Their arrival at the mortuary was almost a welcome relief; the smells there were merely of formaldehyde and lye, strong and gagging but somehow cleansing to the nostrils. Still it was no place for those with delicate stomachs or sensibilities.[9]

The darkened room into which they were ushered had bare brick walls that were whitewashed once but were now coated with grime and lampblack. What illumination there was came from wall sconces that seemed to give off more smoke than the sickly light, dancing eerily on the ceiling.

The center of the room was taken up by several rectangular wooden tables, only one or two of which were bare. The others were draped with sheets of a rough material under which the lumpy shapes of cadavers reposed. Off to one side were a half dozen or so wicker baskets which at first glance in the dim light appeared to contain small bundles of dirty laundry. They contained the bodies of infants, the day's collection.

The four of them, Holmes and Watson and the two policemen, were escorted directly and without ceremony to one of the tables located at the far end of the room. A lantern was brought and the sheet pulled back.

"She be identified as one Mary Anne Nicholls," said a gravelly voice from the shadows, that of a mortuary worker. "Polly Nicholls, she be called, forty-two years old, mother of five, prostitute. Only known address be a doss-house at number 18 Thrawl Street."

The four of them stood around the table as if transfixed. The face they looked down upon was that of a homely, coarse-featured woman who appeared far older than the stated forty-two years. Her eyes were open.

"Hold the light higher, please, someone!" ordered Holmes, his voice sounding unnaturally loud, even strident.

The wound at the woman's throat grinned grotesquely in the flickering light. The blood had been wiped away so the lesion was plainly visible. The windpipe and gullet had been totally severed, cut right down to the spinal cord. On the left side of the neck, about an inch below the jaw, there was an incision almost four inches long starting at a point immediately below the ear. On the same side, but an inch below, was a second incision, which ended three inches below the right jaw. The main arteries in the throat had been completely cut through.

"What do you make of these wounds, Watson?"

Watson bent lower over the body. "From the manner in which the carotid arteries are severed, I would say it was done with an extremely sharp instrument, very sharp indeed. And see here: There are no jagged edges, no torn flesh around the throat. A very neat incision. It could have been done with a razor, or a sharp flensing knife of some sort, or even a scalpel, heaven forbid."

"Mr. Llewellyn, the surgeon," said Thicke, holding a lantern by Watson's shoulder, "he thinks it could have been a cork-cutter's blade or a shoemaker's knife."

"I am not all that familiar with either." Watson shrugged.

Holmes pointed to the right side of the woman's neck, just under the ear. "The point of entry, you think?"

"Hard to say. Perhaps." Watson looked closer. "Yes, I think you are right. It would appear to be."

"Now, look at the bruises here on the face, on the side of the jaw, and on the other side as well. What does that suggest to you?"

Watson took the lamp from Thicke and held it closer. "Yes, I see what you mean. They could be bruises made by fingers, perhaps — by a thumb and forefinger, as if she were held from behind with the assailant's hand tightly over her mouth, to suppress a scream no doubt."

"Precisely! To suppress a scream and at the same time to pull her head back and bare her throat. Excellent, Watson! And which bruise would you say was made by the thumb?"

"Well, it is impossible to say for certain, but if I had to choose, I would say the one on the right side of her face, this one here. It seems the bigger of the two."

"Excellent again!"

"What difference could that possibly make, Mr. Holmes?" asked Inspector Abberline.

"Why, it suggests that our assailant was left-handed, Inspector. It would be quite natural for a left-handed person to grab his victim with his right so as to leave the dominant hand free with which to wield the knife."

"Oh, I see. Yes, of course."

"That is, unless," said Holmes, "the assailant did not accost her from behind, but – unlikely though it may be – did so facing her, in which case our man is right-handed after all."

Abberline sighed heavily.

Holmes pulled the covering down farther, baring the woman's torso.

"Good God!" exclaimed Watson.

Even though they had been forewarned by Abberline, the extent of the mutilations to the woman's lower body was horrifying. Holmes and Watson had both seen many corpses over the years – Holmes had been a student of anatomy with what Watson once referred to as "an accurate but unsystematic knowledge" of the subject, and Watson, as an army surgeon, had beheld many terrible wounds – but neither of them had ever seen anything like this. Nor had the two veteran police detectives, if the tightness around their mouths was any indication.[10]

A deep gash, starting in the lower left part of the woman's abdomen, ran in a jagged manner almost as far as the diaphragm. It was very, very deep, so deep that part of the intestines protruded through the tissue. There were several smaller incisions running across the abdomen, and three or four other cuts running downward on the other side.

"We identified her from the stencilings on one of her petticoats,"

Thicke said. "Lambeth Workhouse markings. The only personal articles found in her possession were a broken comb and a piece of broken looking-glass. She hadn't a farthing to her name."

The expression on Holmes's face was grim, his features strained. "For God's sake, cover her up," he said, his voice almost a whisper.

He groped in his coat pocket for his magnifying glass and proceeded to examine the woman's fingernails, first the right hand, then the left. After several minutes he arose from his crouched position and shook his head. "Nothing," he said, "not a thing. One would have hoped to have found a hair or a sample of blood, even a fragment of torn skin or flesh, but there is nothing!"

He stood looking down at the woman's body for a long moment as if his gaze alone would extract the information he sought.

Finally Abberline spoke: "Is there anything else you wish to see?"

Holmes shook his head. "No. We are finished here, I think. Let us leave this dismal place."

It was almost dawn before Watson and Holmes returned to Baker Street. Both were tired and somewhat disheveled from their labors, the distinctive mud of Spitalfields now caking their shoes and trouser bottoms.

After leaving the mortuary, despite the lateness of the hour and lack of light, Holmes had insisted upon a visit to the scene of the crime. As anticipated, the visit was unfruitful. Holmes could do little more than ascertain where the body was first discovered, and "take the lay of the land," as he put it. Buck's Row, where the body had been found, was much like any of the other mean streets of Spitalfields, a narrow, gloomy passageway lined with rows of ramshackle tenements smelling of rotting garbage. One end of the alley let out into Baker's Row, the other into Brady Street.

"If it were me," said Thicke, "I would 'ave made straightaway for

Brady Street and thence for the underground station at Whitechapel Road. Easy to get lost in the crowd there."

"You have as good a chance of being right as wrong," responded Holmes, "inasmuch as there were only two ways our man could have gone."

"Of course we questioned everyone who lives in the alley," Abberline said. "No one saw or heard anything, which is what you might expect them to say – to us, in any event. Although Thicke here is well known by the locals, and is probably trusted by them more than most of us. They would talk to him if to anyone."

"And none of them heard anything?" asked Watson.

"No," replied Thicke, shaking his head. "The closest would have been Mrs. Green, who lives down there just a few doors away, and she said she didn't 'ear a thing, not a blessed thing, even though she was awake. Couldn't sleep, she said. I know 'er; I think she'd tell me if she knew something. Mrs. Emma Green is 'er name, a decent sort really."

Holmes shrugged. "Me for my bed, gentlemen. There is nothing to be learned here."

Abberline would not leave it at that, however. "Do you not have any thoughts at all, Mr. Holmes? Or suggestions?"

"Only one, I'm afraid. Wait for the next murder."

Watson and the two policemen stared at him.

"Oh, there will be another one, have no doubt. Have no doubt whatsoever."

The first gray light of dawn was filtering through the window draperies when Holmes finally climbed into his bed, his once-immaculate evening clothes an untidy pile in the corner by the dressing table. No sooner had he pulled the covers over his shoulder than there was a light tap at the door and Watson stuck his head in.

"Forgive me, Holmes, but there is one thing I fail to understand."

"Only one? How simply wonderful for you," Holmes said sleepily.

"Last night in Simpson's – you recall?"

"As if it were only yesterday."

"That American chap sitting at the table across from us. You said he was in railroads, I believe."

"Quite so."

"However did you know that? You never did tell me."

Holmes yawned. "Oh, that. Why, I overheard him say so, old fellow."

Watson stood there. "Good night, Holmes!" he snapped.

"Good night, old fellow."

Four

SUNDAY, SEPTEMBER 2-SATURDAY, SEPTEMBER 8, 1888

"Her cuisine is a little limited, but she has as good an idea
of breakfast as a Scotchwoman."
— *The Naval Treaty*

Watson awoke shortly after noon to find tea waiting for him in the front room, brought up with the Sunday newspapers by Mrs. Hudson, who had heard him stirring. Holmes was nowhere to be found.

"Gone these few hours since," announced Mrs. Hudson as she shook her head disgustedly. "Don't ask me where, I don't know. I never know where he goes or when he'll be back. Hardly pecked at his breakfast, and such a nice one too. My best Sunday table with kippers and eggs just like he likes them, and that marmalade he favors — costs a pretty penny, I can tell you. And him? He gulps some coffee down and is off! Hardly half a cup!" She shook her head some more and actually waggled a finger at him. "Out till all hours of the night, the both of you! You're as bad as he is, sometimes!"

Watson stood there like a shamefaced schoolboy.

"I expect he'll miss his dinner too!" she said accusingly, as if it were Watson's fault.

"I don't know, I'm sure, Mrs. Hudson," he mumbled. "No doubt he'll do his best to return in time."

She sniffed. "Well, I have my church meeting to attend and I won't hold up dinner, so if he's not back in time for it, he'll just have to go without. Now, drink that tea before it gets cold, and there's fresh scones there under the warmer, and try not to get crumbs on the floor!"

"Yes, Mrs. Hudson. Thank you very much indeed."

"And the two of you tracked mud in last night," she charged as she exited the room, closing the door on the last few words of her parting sentence. "All over the stair runner, it was!"

"Sorry, Mrs. Hudson, I assure you," he called to the closed door as he attacked the tea and scones.

The remainder of the afternoon was spent with the newspapers, which were full of the Whitechapel murder and fairly screamed with the horror of it all. The leader in *The Star*, lurid as it was, was more restrained than some, and far more accurate than others:

A REVOLTING MURDER

A WOMAN FOUND HORRIBLY
MUTILATED IN WHITECHAPEL

GHASTLY CRIMES BY A MANIAC

A Policeman Discovers a Woman Lying in the Gutter with Her Throat Cut – After She Has Been Removed to the Hospital She Is Found to Be Disemboweled[11]

London's popular press could be forgiven for indulging in sensationalism in this particular instance, for it was indeed a sensational occurrence. Victorian England had never experienced such a horrible, vicious crime. Such a thing was virtually unknown, unthinkable. Murders were indeed committed, but generally in connection with a robbery or as a result of a personal dispute. But rarely was the victim a woman, even of the lowest order. No Englishman would treat a woman so cruelly. If this kind of depravity existed at all, it existed on the Continent – in Germany or France or Italy. That was to be expected of foreigners, after all. But to have such a thing happen on home soil was simply without precedent. The public, highborn and low, was deeply shocked, and the popular press accurately reflected that view.[12]

The day was waning, the shadows deepening, and Watson was dozing over the cricket scores when Holmes's footstep was heard on the stairs at last. Watson awoke with a start as the door crashed open; Holmes cast him the briefest of dark glances upon entering.

"I should be both eternally and internally grateful for a good stiff one, if you would be so kind," he said. "The day has been entirely fruitless."

Watson bestirred himself and crossed over to the tantalus and gasogene as Holmes made for his room, removing his suit coat.[13]

"What have you been about?" Watson called over his shoulder as he fussed with the drinks.

"I have been about totally frustrated is what I have been about," Holmes shouted irritably. He emerged a minute or so later in his favorite dressing gown, and took the whiskey and soda that Watson handed him, nodding his thanks and sipping appreciatively.[14]

"It would seem that for once our friends at the Yard are not alone in being confounded," he said. "I tell you, this maniac, whoever he is, may just as well be a ghost as a living creature, for all the spoor he has left behind him. No one saw him, no one heard him, no one knows a thing! We have a murder without a motive – a singularly brutal murder, I might add – we have four people who came upon the victim within minutes, perhaps even seconds of the crime, we have only two directions in which the murderer could have gone, and we have nothing! Absolutely nothing!"

"You have been back to Spitalfields?"

Holmes plopped himself down in his favorite chair, crossed his legs Indian fashion, and gazed into the empty fireplace. "I have been to Spitalfields, I have been to the district police station, I have been to the local settlement house, to the local workhouse, to several doss-houses, and even to a few 'houses of joy' would you believe?"

"Holmes!"

"I have spoken to police constables, publicans, ladies of the street, missionaries, derelicts, teamsters, and jarvies, and just about everyone else you could think of short of the lord chancellor, and for all the good it has done me I might as well have frittered away the day as I see you have done."

Watson ignored the barb. "You have seen Abberline again?"

"No," he said disgustedly. "To what purpose? He has nothing, poor fellow. God knows he is trying hard enough. A good man, that – far better than most." High praise, coming from Holmes.

"So, what's your next step?"

Holmes brooded for a minute before answering, then shook his head violently as if to rid himself of depressing thoughts. "My next step? Why, a good wash-up and dinner! If I am not mistaken, that is Mrs. Hudson's footfall upon the tread, and she most assuredly is accompanied by a leg of mutton, if the smells emanating from the kitchen are to be credited. And I, dear fellow, am famished!"

For all his protestations of hunger, Holmes ate very little that Sabbath meal; he merely pecked at his food, listlessly moving it around the plate, deep in thought. And when the dinner service was cleared away, he moved to his chair by the fireplace and spent the evening brooding, in one of his brown studies, not even looking up when several hours later Watson finally left the room to retire, quietly wishing him a good night.

The next morning, a bright and sunny one, Watson awoke at his usual hour to find Holmes once again already gone. This time Mrs. Hudson was at least able to impart the news, when she arrived with the breakfast things, that he had left hurriedly, in summons to an urgent telegram, that he was carrying his battered Gladstone bag, and that she overheard him tell the cabby that his destination was Paddington Station. "And when I called after him to ask what time he wanted dinner served, he shouted back, 'seven-thirty next October.' Now, really!" She shook her head and moved toward the door. "Oh, he said to tell you to be sure to take notice of the mantel."

Watson went there at once, where he retrieved the note Holmes had left for him. It took a moment to decipher the hurried scrawl:

W —

Off to the countryside for a few days.

Looks to be an interesting little matter.

If nothing else, I shall enjoy the comforts

and diversions of a country manor.

H.[15]

The "few days" turned into several more. It was late Friday evening before Holmes returned from the countryside, a glow in his cheeks and, for once, in good humor. He declined to go into the details of the case, however, and even refrained from telling Watson where in the countryside he had been.

"His lordship insisted upon total confidentiality, and I gave him my word. Can't say as I blame him, though he is hardly the first old fool with a young wife and a randy groundskeeper. But it is nothing that would interest you, dear fellow, I assure you. Merely a sordid little case of blackmail, a simple matter after all. It just took a while to sort out. A pretty house, though, with quite a lovely park. Unfortunately, the food was abominable. The lord of the manor is a vegetarian, would you believe: one of those rabid antivivisectionist fellows. Professes to despise all blood sports, and even chases behind the local hunt in his trap, ringing a cowbell and bellowing quotations of that Oscar Whatshisname chap.[16] Won't allow meat or fish at his table. Not even an egg for breakfast! God, what I would not do for a good thick cut of roast beef. Is it too late to dine at Rules, do you think? Oh, I see that you have been at table already. Pity, that. Well, perhaps tomorrow, if you have no other engagement. Yes, Rules tomorrow: something to which we may look forward!"

But it was not to be. It was shortly after seven A.M. when the two of them were awakened. There stood Mrs. Hudson on the landing, in robe and slippers and old-fashioned mobcap, the unmistakable uniform of a telegraph boy behind her in the shadows. "Most urgent it is, the lad says. Is it bad news, do you think? Oh, heavens, it must be at this hour!"

"Calm yourself, Mrs. Hudson, dear lady," Holmes said, patting her on the arm. "Back to your bed now, and mind the stairs. No, no, don't trouble about breakfast. A shilling for the lad, Watson, if you would be so kind. Make it two, seeing the earliness of the hour."

Holmes turned up the lamp on the side table and tore open the flimsy envelope. A mere glance at the telegram was all that was needed.

"Quick, Watson, into your clothes! The devil's afoot!"

Five

Saturday, September 8, 1888

"You know my method. It is founded upon the observation of trifles."
— *The Boscombe Valley Mystery*

It was a wild dash through the nearly empty streets of a gray-streaked London, the clatter of the horse's hooves loud against the cobbles, Holmes banging on the ceiling of the hansom cab with his walking stick, urging the driver on to even greater feats of recklessness. Fortunately there was little traffic at that hour to impede their progress.

"Faster, man! Faster!" Holmes shouted. "In heaven's name, faster!"

Watson, who had been handed the telegram as soon as he was bundled half dressed into the hansom by Holmes, was trying unsuccessfully to make out its message by the feeble light of the coach lamp, but the jouncing and buffeting of the speeding conveyance made it impossible.

"Great Scot, Holmes!" he shouted to make himself heard over the clamor. "Will you not tell me what has happened?"

"Surely you've guessed!" Holmes shouted back. "There's been another murder in the East End!"

"Good Lord!"

"That's from Abberline," snapped Holmes, gesturing to the crumpled message in Watson's hand. Once again he called up to the driver, "Faster, man! Can't you go faster!"

Watson, for one, devoutly wished that he could not, for the coach was swaying alarmingly as it was; he could keep his seat only with the greatest of difficulty: His hat was knocked askew at almost every turning, and he found himself gripping the side strap so tightly that his hand hurt from the pressure.

"When did it occur?" he shouted to Holmes as he resettled himself in his seat after a particularly wild swing around Oxford Circus. "Does the telegram say?"

"Barely an hour ago, from what I gather. Fortunately the post office was at its most efficient. I'm thankful for that!"[17]

"Does Abberline give any details?"

"No," came the shouted reply. "The telegram says merely, 'Come in haste. Another Whitechapel outrage.' And then the address, Twenty-nine Hanbury Street."

"Hanbury Street? Not all that far from the site of the last murder, is it?"

"No, not all that far. A short stroll away; a half mile, perhaps."

They then lapsed into silence, each wrapped in his own thoughts as the hansom sped through the city.

Familiar streets and landmarks flashed by in a kaleidoscopic blur as the daylight grew stronger, and the relatively few pedestrians at large turned to stare in alarm as the coach hurtled past: Oxford Street into Tottenham Court Road into High Holborn into Newgate, past the towering dome of St. Paul's into Cheapside, Cornhill, Leadenhall, Aldgate – their progress from the West End of London to the East End was made in what must have been near-record time. It ran the course not only of the city's streets but of its social and economic groupings as well, for while the two ends of London were mere miles apart geographically, they were poles apart in every other aspect. Their journey took them past mansions and palaces of the titled and wealthy, the sedate homes of the merely affluent; past shops filled with finery and all manner of delicacies, through lower-middle-class neighborhoods, shabbily genteel, into poor working-class districts, grimy, grim, and colorless.

The hansom took a particularly violent turn as it rounded into Commercial Street from Aldgate, the horse veering wildly to avoid a lumbering brewer's dray: Both of them were knocked sharply to the side. The jarvey now was forced to slow his horse; the streets were getting narrower, the traffic heavier. They rode on in tense silence: The jostling ride made conversation difficult in any case, and the scarcity of information made it pointless.

The sky had brightened considerably in the meantime, but still the day promised to be a drizzly-gray one. Visibility was such that it was just possible to make out distinctive features of the buildings they hurried past. Holmes leaned forward expectantly in his seat, peering onward.

"Ah, we are almost there," he said at last. "If I'm not mistaken, there's a bevy of 'bobbies'[18] milling about up ahead."

Watson, too, spotted the police picket in the distance. Obviously, the street leading to the scene of the crime had been cordoned off, and despite the early hour, small crowds of onlookers stood off to one side, straining to catch a glimpse of whatever it was that had caused the police to converge on the neighborhood in the first place.

The hansom jolted to a halt at the corner of Commercial Street and Hanbury: A rope barricade across the intersection would permit them to travel no farther. Holmes pushed open the doors and bounded from the cab.

"Pay the man, Watson! I promised him a sovereign if he didn't spare his nag!"

The group of helmeted constables at the barrier had turned upon the coach's arrival, and a large sergeant with a cavalry mustache and proud bearing sauntered over, barring Holmes's path.

"And where might you be going, sir?"

"My name is Holmes. Show me to Inspector Abberline at once, if you please. I'm expected."

The policeman's attitude changed at once. "Mr. Sherlock Holmes? Yes, indeed, sir! This way, sir. Mind your topper goin' under the rope. Bagley! Escort these gents to Inspector Abberline, then report back 'ere. Smartly now, none of yer dawdlin'! An' do up your butt'n, for God's sake!"

In appearance, Hanbury Street was not very much different from Buck's Row, the site of the earlier murder: It was forever in shadow. Narrow and dark, the sun's rays rarely ever reached its recesses, and the brooding tenements that lined both sides of the street seemed shriveled with cold. They were dilapidated affairs, three-storied brick structures for the most part, with shops on the ground floor and flats above. A few contained boardinghouses on the upper floors: doss-houses, as they were called, reeking dormitories with rows of beds at four pence a night. Holmes and Watson picked their way through rotting garbage to where a small circle of police officials in civilian clothes was gathered in front of an open doorway at number 29. The doorway was located alongside an empty storefront which, as indicated by a weathered sign over the darkened window, was at one time occupied by a barbershop, N. BRILL, HAIRDRESSER AND PERFUMER the sign said in fading block letters, while other, smaller advertisements in the storefront window extolled the virtues of VASELINE and BRYLCREEM hair dressings.

The squat shape of Abberline separated itself from the other forms as Watson and Holmes approached.

"Well, Mr. Holmes," he said by way of greeting, "your prognostication was entirely correct. It would seem that you have your other murder."

"Which provides me with scant satisfaction," said Holmes tersely. "The particulars, if you please."

Without further preamble the police inspector quickly presented him with the salient facts. It did not take him long, for the facts were threadbare and few. The body was found in a rear yard by a lodger, a yard located behind the building they now faced. It lay there still.

"You are certain it was done by the same hand, are you?" Holmes asked, peering through the open doorway that presumably led to the site.

"See for yourself, sir. There cannot be two such devils stalking the streets. It's our man, all right, make no mistake." With a gesture Abberline directed them through the door into a passageway. Dank and smelling of urine, it extended through to the rear of the building to another door which opened onto a small courtyard in the back. There were three stone steps leading down. At the foot of the steps, alongside a low wooden fence enclosing the yard, lay what appeared to be a bundle of rags. In the gray light it took a moment or two for their eyes to adjust and for them to realize that it was a body they were looking down upon. It was that of a fully clad woman sprawled on her back, her legs drawn up with her feet flat on the ground, her knees turned obscenely outward. Her clothing was badly disarrayed and pulled up over her waist, exposing the lower portion of her extremities. She was horribly mutilated.

After only the briefest of glances at the terrible sight, Holmes looked around him with an almost casual air, scanning the yard and the surrounding rooftops as if the dead woman were incidental. The sense of urgency and extreme excitement that he exhibited all the way from Baker Street was now nowhere in evidence. Instead, he displayed a cold, analytical air, calm and self-contained, almost disinterested.

"Watson, this is more in your line," he said, gesturing toward the body at his feet. "I would value your opinion. In the meantime, I'll just take a brief stroll." He then wandered off, examining the ground as he went, like a man who had just dropped his last coin and would go without dinner unless he found it. Several of the police detectives exchanged looks. There were incredulous smiles on the faces of more than a few.

Watson pushed back his hat and went to work.

It was a good quarter of an hour before Holmes made his way back. He had roamed around the yard for a brief period of time and then disappeared back through the passageway into the street, where he was observed walking up and down, peering into doorways, searching the gutters, poking into crevices in the pavement with his stick, and occasionally bending down to peer at one thing or another at his feet. Watson, in the meantime, had completed his examination and was standing by the body, wiping his hands on a handkerchief, when Holmes returned.

"Your men have already searched the street, I perceive," said Holmes to Abberline somewhat coldly.

"Yes, of course. We scoured the area thoroughly," replied Abberline. "Twice, in point of fact. The lads have even sifted through the rubbish and have searched the alleys and doorways. I can tell you, Mr. Holmes, that except for what is before you, we found nothing – nothing that can be tied to the crime, in any event."

"Nothing," repeated Holmes half to himself with a sigh. He then fixed Abberline with a keen, penetrating gaze. "Inspector, has it not occurred to your minions, whose foot sizes do them credit, that the very act of seeking out evidence can, if not accomplished artfully and with some care, obliterate that which they seek?"

"Sir?" said Abberline, taken aback and clearly failing to comprehend.

"If I did not know better," continued Holmes, "I would be prepared to swear that the Brigade of Guards has paraded through here this morning." He shook his head. "Wherever there's the smallest patch of mud in the street, I see the unmistakable imprint of a policeman's boot. It is as if your fellows went out of their way to leave their mark so as to prove their existence." He smiled thinly. "I will say this for them, they're a well-shod lot. Only one seems run-down at the heels insofar as I can ascertain: a pigeon-toed chap, a bit overweight, who goes by the name of Bagley, I believe."

Abberline looked at him open-mouthed.

Holmes removed his hand from his pocket and held it outstretched, a small, glittering object in his palm. "Popped a button, I think you will find."

"Oh, for heaven's sake," muttered Abberline, taking the object from Holmes, who then turned without another word and walked over toward the body.

"Now then, Watson, what can you tell me?"

Watson took a deep breath. "Well, Holmes, it's at least as horrible as the other. More grotesque, if anything."

Holmes walked carefully around the body, barely glancing at it for the moment, devoting his attentions instead to the ground around it, scrutinizing every inch slowly and carefully. Apparently satisfied there was nothing to be found, he turned his attentions to the body itself, that of a plump, well-proportioned woman in her mid-forties, with what had once been dark good looks now ravaged by drink. The woman's face, bruised and smeared with blood, was turned to one side, the tongue protruding slightly from between the teeth. Her throat had been cruelly sliced: The head was almost completely severed from the body.

Holmes's eyes narrowed and his lips compressed into a thin line. Chin in hand, he gazed at the sight intently.

Watson got down on his haunches and pointed. "Her throat wasn't merely cut, Holmes; it was slashed, just like the other. And as far as I can tell, it, too, was from right to left. The entry wound is here, you see, and the angle of it suggests that her chin was raised unnaturally high, consistent with being grabbed about the mouth from behind and her head pulled back."

"Yes, I see." He looked around him. "She probably led the way through the passage from the street and he took her unawares as they entered the yard."

"It was done with a very sharp instrument," Watson continued, "a thin, narrow blade. I would say that it was done with great strength, a vigorous stroke. Yet the man knew what he was about; there is no frenzy, no wild, misaimed slashing indicated. The wound at the throat is very precise, and the cuts here and here (he pointed with a finger) are well calculated. But that's the least of it." He inhaled deeply. "As you can see, there are frightful mutilations of the abdominal region. She's been virtually disemboweled."

Holmes stroked his chin. His eyes had a hard, unnatural look to them.

"That's not the whole of it, Holmes. Not by half."

"Well?"

"It would seem that several organs are missing."

Holmes looked at him sharply. "Missing?"

Watson returned his gaze. "A kidney has been removed, and the uterus as well, and I don't know what else: We will have to wait for a proper autopsy. Holmes, I tell you, I don't know what to make of this; I have never seen anything like it."

Holmes pursed his lips and stood silently, looking down at the body. When he finally spoke, his voice was low and husky; his eyes burned fiercely. "I will have this creature. I will have him, make no mistake."

Watson stood up and massaged the back of his neck. "There's not much more I can tell you at this point. As I say, the autopsy may reveal more. But one thing's for certain – one thing I have no doubt of whatsoever." He patted his pockets for his cigarette case. "He would seem to have no small degree of anatomical knowledge. He's no stranger to *Gray's Anatomy*, I'll wager. He knows what he is about."

"A medical man, you think?"

Watson shrugged.

"Well," said Holmes, "it's too early to make a judgment. And there's far too little evidence upon which to base it in any event. Let us not make the mistake of jumping to conclusions."

Watson nodded. "Yes, of course."

Holmes turned to Abberline. "Has an identification of the victim been made as yet?"

"Yes. She's apparently well known in the vicinity. Her name is Annie Chapman or Annie Siffey – most people know her as Chapman. 'Dark Annie,' they called her. As you know, it's not unusual for this class of woman to be known by two or even more surnames: They often adopt the name of whatever bloke they happen to be living with at any given moment. At this particular moment Dark Annie was living without a man, and she had no permanent address, but she usually dossed down right here in number 29."

"A streetwalker?"

"Oh, yes – part of the time, at least. But for all that, the people we questioned who knew her said she was a decent sort."

Holmes pointed with his walking stick at a small, square white cloth spread out on the ground at the foot of the body. "What can you tell me about that?" he asked.

"The handkerchief? That's Inspector Chandler's. He was first on the scene." Abberline went over and carefully lifted a corner of the handkerchief. Beneath it, neatly laid out in a row, as if part of an elaborate ritual, were two brass rings, a few pennies, and a couple of farthings. "Hers, probably," he said. "The rings were apparently wrenched from her fingers, the coins taken from her pockets. Chandler left them just as he found them."

"Ah, a paragon, this Chandler, an absolute gem! I must meet this man."

"That's him, right there." Abberline motioned him over, a tired, rumpled man in a houndstooth inverness and brown derby.

Holmes looked at him keenly after the introductions were made.

He was obviously exhausted from being up all night; his face was drawn, his eyes empty. He was a man who had suffered shock and was emotionally drained.

"You were the first to arrive, I am told," said Holmes. "How very fortunate for the rest of us who followed. Would that you could have kept the herd at bay."

Chandler smiled grimly despite himself. "I'm somewhat of a student of your methods, Mr. Holmes, and realize the importance of leaving things undisturbed as much as possible until a thorough search has been made for clues."

Holmes rewarded him with a look of mock pity and patted him on the shoulder. "You will not go far in the Metropolitan Police, I fear. They must think you a dangerous radical."

He smiled. "Merely a harmless eccentric, I believe. But I am not alone in my views. Many of your methods are winning growing acceptance by my colleagues, among them Inspector Abberline here. Oh, we are scoffed at by some of the older chaps, the so-called graybeards, who have little patience with scientific detection. But the younger ones that are coming into the department now are more open to new ideas, so please, Mr. Holmes, don't tar all of us with the same brush."

"I will reserve opinion as to that," replied Holmes archly. "Now, as to this sorry business, what can you share with me?"

"Quite by accident I arrived on the scene within minutes of the body being discovered. I'm on nights at the Commercial Street Station and was making a tour of the area. It was shortly after six A.M., and I had just rounded the corner into Hanbury Street when I encountered three men running toward me, shouting. At first I thought it was one man being chased by the other two, and that the three of them must be the worse for drink. Then I thought it must be a house on fire, they were that agitated. Then they were upon me and shouting, 'Murder! Quick... it's horrible...' I tell you, Mr. Holmes, I have never seen anyone in such a state as I did these three. Well, as they led me the way back along Hanbury Street toward number 29, I tried to piece their story together." He slipped his notebook out of his coat pocket.

"Two of the men, it seems – a Jack Kent and a James Green, both of whom work at Bailey's Yard just up the street: It's a case-maker's shop – saw the third fellow, an old porter by the name of John Davis who lives in number 29, come stumbling into the lane with his trouser belt in his hands. He was so upset and befuddled, they said, he could hardly get a word out. Finally he was able to make himself understood enough for them to realize that something was very, very wrong. So they let him lead them back through the passageway there and followed him right here into the yard." Chandler massaged his chin. "Well, they took one look and ran, didn't they? And that's when they came upon me."

"It was just after six, you say?"

"Yes, that's right, just a few minutes after. When I came upon the scene, the entry into the passageway – that door opening out onto the street – was open and a crowd was already starting to gather, but not one of 'em would dare step into the yard proper, they were that frightened. That you can be sure of. Like everyone, they're curious about dead bodies, but not up close they're not."

"So you couldn't have come along too much after the act had been committed?"

He scratched an ear. "Well, as to that I don't know. I'm no medical examiner and I don't pretend to be an expert in that area. But I sent for one straightaway: the divisional surgeon, actually – Dr. Phillips. And of course I arranged to have a telegram sent to Inspector Abberline here, knowing he was in charge of the earlier murder that was just like this one – the Nicholls murder. And I sent back to the Commercial Street station for more men to cordon the area off and keep people out. And then – well, then I started my search for clues and such."

Holmes shook his head approvingly. "It appears you have done well."

Chandler shrugged and glanced around the yard. "Well, as to that, I don't know. If I missed anything, it wasn't for the lack of trying. But I've been all over this yard with a fine-tooth comb and haven't come up with much, just a few of her poor possessions that were scattered about – and this."

He pulled out his wallet from an inside pocket, removed a slip of paper, and handed it to Holmes. "I found it lying on the ground right near her head. It isn't much, but it might tell us something."

It was a fragment of a bloodstained envelope bearing a regimental crest and postmarked London, 20 August 1888.[19] There was a portion of a handwritten address, but only the letters *M* and *Sp* were still legible. There were also two medicinal pills wrapped carefully in a slip of paper.

"Excellent!" said Holmes. "You are to be congratulated. Is there anything else?"

Chandler removed his hat and scratched his head. "Well, yes, but I don't really know if it has anything to do with this affair, you see."

He led Holmes over to a cold water tap in a corner of the yard. Nearby, on the ground, lay a leather apron, saturated in water.

Holmes knelt down and examined it. "What makes you think it's not related?" he asked, turning it over with his stick. It was the kind of apron a butcher would wear, or a worker in a slaughterhouse.

"There's no sign of blood on it, you see," replied Chandler. "And it looks like it has been in water for quite some time. Notice how supple the leather is. It would take quite a lengthy soaking to make it so. It may have been here for days."

Holmes looked at him with new respect. "I see I've not misjudged you, Inspector. An astute observation on your part, one that most would miss."

"I confess that I certainly would have," said Watson, who had followed them to the tap and was peering over Holmes's shoulder.

Holmes shot him a sardonic glance. "Oh, no, not you, old fellow."

Abberline kicked the ground with a foot. "What bothers me is that there are no signs of a struggle. As you can see, there is no proper paving here, just a patchwork of stones and earth. If the woman put up any sort of resistance, you would expect to find some indications of it. Yet, the ground doesn't seem to have been unnaturally disturbed. She must have come here with him voluntarily, or even brought him here. Certainly, she was not dragged by force."

Chandler nodded in agreement. "No question about that. Living here, she no doubt knew the yard well and probably used it with her men friends more than once. As for the ground around the body, I examined that straightaway, as soon as there was light enough to see by. And there was nothing, I assure you, not a sign to be found."

Holmes glanced up at the windows of the surrounding buildings looking down into the yard. "No one heard anything, of course?"

Abberline shook his head. "My lads have been through all of those buildings, Mr. Holmes. We have questioned everyone who was in residence last night – everyone within sight of this yard. And of course we've questioned the residents of this building – all sixteen of them. Only one individual admits to hearing anything out of the ordinary, a man by the name of Cadosh who lives next door. He said he was in the yard behind his house – the yard that adjoins this one – at precisely a quarter past five – relieving himself no doubt – when he heard a woman's voice sharply say no followed by the sound of something falling against the fence. He thought nothing of it at the time, he said. Didn't give it a moment's notice. Just turned right around and went back to bed. Said he hears much worse most nights."

"I shouldn't wonder," muttered Watson.

Holmes looked up sharply. "A quarter past five?" he asked. "You say he was certain of that – most precise?"

"Yes, absolutely certain. He said he had just heard the brewer's clock strike the quarter hour."

"That's helpful," Holmes said. He pondered for a moment. "You examined the fence?" he asked, taking the few steps necessary to bring him up to it: A low wooden wall, made up of rough boards crudely nailed together. It formed a border on three sides of the yard, the rear of the house itself forming the fourth.

"I ran an eye over it, but I can't say it's been examined closely," admitted Chandler. "You'll have noted those bloodstains on the boards just above where she is lying, but there's nothing else as far as I can tell."

Holmes whipped out his lens and spent the next several minutes conducting an examination of the fence, concentrating most of his attention on the top edges of the jagged, unpainted boards and on the bottom of the boards where they met the ground. Completing his task finally, he stepped back and placed his hands on hips, shaking his head. "No, not a thing."

Abberline spoke up: "I have had a man examine the ground all along the fence on the other side, and there is nothing there either. No footprints, no sign of anyone vaulting over."

Holmes nodded. "I doubt if he made his escape this way. He must have used the passage and walked right out through the door, calm as you please. A cool fellow, this."

Chandler agreed. "That's my guess. Yet our men haven't been able to find anyone who saw a stranger about. Of course it was very early in the morning and still was dark, and most people would have been in their beds."

"Yes," said Holmes tonelessly.

Abberline referred to his notebook. "As I have said, we've interviewed everyone who lives in the immediate vicinity, or has legitimate business here, and we have a fairly complete list of those whose business would have had them up and about at that hour. We've cross-checked it, of course. No one that we've been able to question saw anyone who looked the least bit suspicious or out of the ordinary: Not a soul. No one who didn't belong, no one who wasn't known, no one who acted strangely."

Holmes looked up with a strange smile on his face, an almost gleeful grin that took the others quite by surprise. Turning abruptly, he slashed the air with his stick and stamped his foot on the ground. "God, but this fiend is a wonder! He is a wonder indeed!"

At that point there was a clatter in the passage and two uniformed constables entered the yard, wheeling a litter. Abberline acknowledged their presence and turned wordlessly to Holmes, a questioning look on his face.

Holmes shrugged. "I'm finished with her. Are you, Doctor? Yes? Well then, I see no reason why the body shouldn't be removed, Inspector. As you see fit."

Gingerly, the body was eased onto the wheeled contrivance, covered with a scrap of canvas, and taken away. Holmes stood off to one side, looking on quietly. He then turned and started pacing up and down, deep in thought, his walking stick on his shoulder like a soldier's rifle. The others observed him silently.

The windows looking down into the yard had filled with curious faces throughout the morning as the sky had brightened. Obviously, an opportunity was not to be lost, and entrepreneurial spirits among those who owned the buildings had been doing a brisk business renting out places at the windows to journalists and the morbidly curious, including several who, one would think from their shabby appearance, could put their shillings to better use. Holmes suddenly became aware of their presence for the first time. He stopped and looked up in annoyance, and then swiftly turned and made for the passage leading to the street.

"It would seem that we are making spectacles of ourselves," he said dryly to no one in particular. "Perhaps we should adjourn to a less public place."

He led the way through the door into the dark passage and was almost to the street when a thought occurred to him and he stopped abruptly, causing the others who followed to pile up behind.

"I nearly forgot. Has this hallway not been examined? Yes? Well, I take it no one shall mind if I have a look. Inspector Abberline, would you be so good as to order one of your men to fetch some bull's-eyes?"

Chandler spoke up from the rear. "We've already searched here, Mr. Holmes. I assure you, there was nothing to be found: only rubbish, as one might expect."

"Nevertheless, I would like a quick look. Some light if you please."

Lanterns were brought in short order and the others stepped aside as Holmes, on hands and knees, spent the next ten minutes crawling the length of the dank passageway, poking into every corner and cranny.

He finally emerged into the daylight with the knees of his trousers covered in filth, a glint in his eye, and something tenderly clutched between thumb and forefinger. He held it up for the others to see, his thin lips turned up in a triumphant smile.

"Observe, gentlemen! Our elusive phantom has taken human form. And it would seem that he has more than one disgusting habit. He smokes!"

Several of the policemen in the group looked at him with undisguised astonishment, more than one concluding that he had taken leave of his senses. But Abberline and Chandler rushed to his side and peered closely at the flattened cigarette stub he was holding in his fingers. Holmes took out his pocket magnifying glass and examined the object with something approaching ardor.

Abberline was the first to speak, making no effort to disguise the strong notes of skepticism and impatience that crept into his tone. "How can we possibly know it's the killer's, Mr. Holmes? It could have been anyone's, and it could have been lying in that hallway for days, even weeks."

Holmes shook his head. "The tobacco is still quite fresh: The cigarette was discarded quite recently. Fortunately, the owner did not grind it underfoot, but merely crushed it with his toe, and he could have taken only two or three puffs, because the fag end is quite long, almost complete. As to your first point, Inspector, we certainly don't know it is the killer's, I grant you that. But in the absence of any other tangible leads, it is a line of inquiry I shall gladly follow."

Chandler, in a tone of voice containing more than a hint of doubt, joined the conversation: "There are many smokers present among us, Mr. Holmes. You yourself are one, I believe, as is Dr. Watson, whom I observed smoking a cigarette a short while ago. Surely, it could belong to any one of us."

Holmes gave him an indulgent smile. "Not Watson's brand," he replied tersely. "His bears the imprint of his tobacconist, Bradley. Nor is it mine, since I have not yet indulged this morning. As to the possibility that it belongs to one of your colleagues in the department, Inspector, unless the Home Office has granted the Metropolitan Police a handsome increase in emolument that has escaped my attention, I should be very much surprised if many policemen could afford the price of these. It is a custom Turkish blend, I do believe, and the paper is of the finest quality. It is not a common brand you will find at your corner tobacconist's; I doubt if they're obtainable for less than seven and six the hundred."

Both Abberline and Chandler considered this new information. Chandler scratched his ear thoughtfully. "I don't know. Even if you're right, such a trifle doesn't tell us much."

"My dear Inspector Abberline, my method is based upon the examination of such trifles. It has long been an axiom of mine that it's the little things that are infinitely the most important. Whatever this 'trifle' may or may not tell you, it tells me volumes. It tells me that the man who smoked it is someone of substance, a gentleman of refined tastes with the wherewithal to indulge them. It tells me that he was present at this location less than twenty-four hours ago, probably less than twelve. It tells me he was in somewhat of a hurry, for he took only two or three puffs. And that he tarried at all to do even that tells me that he is addicted to tobacco and is no doubt a heavy smoker. I would venture to say that he knows the district well and is no stranger to it, otherwise it is unlikely he would have found his way to this particular doorway off this particular street by sheer happenstance. It is, you will agree, a rather unsavory address and a good bit off the beaten path. Shall I continue?"

At a loss for words, the two policemen shook their heads. They both seemed considerably chastened.

Holmes bowed politely. "I would suggest, gentlemen, that you might gain some profit in having your men scour the streets between here and the major thoroughfares around us for other specimens of this cigarette. I should pay particular attention to street corners normally frequented by cabbies. It is possible that our friend hailed a hansom at some point; it is most unlikely he would have ventured far on foot. We may find he has left us a trail to follow.

"In the meantime, I shall hold on to this for the moment, if I may," Holmes said, tucking the cigarette carefully into an envelope he had taken from his pocket, and then into his wallet. "I believe it may have even more to tell us once I have had the opportunity to examine it at greater length and submit it to chemical analysis."

"You are welcome to it, of course," said Abberline. "I've heard you're an authority on the diverse varieties of tobacco, Mr. Holmes, but still —"

"No, Inspector," he interrupted, quietly and matter-of-factly, "I am *the* authority." With that, he turned away, leaving the two policemen with jaws agape.[20]

Six

SATURDAY, SEPTEMBER 8, 1888

"It is a capital mistake to theorize before one has data. Insensibly one begins to twist facts to suit theories, instead of theories to suit facts."
— *A Scandal in Bohemia*

Watson emerged from his bath wrapped in dressing gown and towel to find Holmes, still occupied with his chemical apparatus, hunched over the cluttered, acid-stained deal table in the corner, test tube poised over Bunsen burner, totally oblivious to the pungent odors issuing forth from his efforts. He had been thus engaged since their return from Whitechapel over an hour earlier, hardly pausing to remove his suit coat, which was still draped untidily over a chair where he had flung it. When Watson returned from dressing ten minutes later Holmes was gone, a thin blue layer of haze the only sign in the room that he had been there at all.

It was not until considerably later in the afternoon that he reappeared, his expression troubled and thoughtful. His only response to Watson's questioning look when he walked through the door was a shake of the head and a curt wave of dismissal. Clearly he was in no frame of mind for questions or conversation. He fell into his chair, placed a finger to his lips, and lapsed into deep thought.

When he finally did speak some little while later, it was in a quiet, subdued manner, his words hesitant, uncertain – so uncharacteristic of him as to cause Watson to look over in surprise, his attention gained as readily as if Holmes had shouted.

"This is most disturbing," Holmes murmured, shaking his head. "Most disquieting. I cannot credit it at all."

"You've been unable to discover the origin of the cigarette?" asked Watson.

Holmes gave him a contemptuous sidelong look. "To the contrary, all too easily. I had only to visit three tobacconists in Belgravia before ascertaining the manufacturer. It was Grover's, of course."

"Good Lord!" Watson looked at him with widened eyes.

G. Grover, Tobacconist, conducted a highly successful trade from a fashionable shop in Buckingham Palace Road not far from the palace itself, a discreet plaque over the door proclaiming, BY APPOINTMENT TO HRH THE PRINCE OF WALES. Largely as a result of the prince's patronage, Grover's had an exclusive clientele that included many of the most prominent names in England, among them peers of the realm, of course, and individuals highly placed at court and in government.

"As I suspected," said Holmes, "the cigarette is made from a particular blend of fine Virginia tobaccos with an almost imperceptible touch of Turkish. Chemical analysis reveals that it is cured with brandy, would you believe – unusual in a cigarette tobacco. All very easy to trace, of course, as was the cigarette paper, which is manufactured exclusively for Grover's use. This specific blend was identified by their manager immediately – he hardly had to look it up to confirm it: It's prepared especially for one client, and one client only."

Watson leaned forward in his chair expectantly. "And that would be?"

But Holmes did not reply. Instead, he gazed pointedly up at the ceiling, and for a moment Watson wondered if he had even heard the question. Finally Holmes drawled: "I think it would be best, old man, if I kept that knowledge to myself."

Watson was startled by Holmes's response, his curt, even cutting response – and more than a little hurt. It was rare for Holmes to keep anything from him, to deny him at least a civil reply, no matter how delicate the question or ticklish or touchy the matter at hand. But more than that, his remark had been made in such an offhand manner, in a tone so aloof, so patronizing, that had it come from anyone else it would have been grossly insulting. As it was, Watson did take umbrage, did feel some resentment. Color rising in his cheeks, he looked down at his hands to cover his confusion.

An awkward, embarrassed silence fell between them, and Holmes rose from his chair and moved about the room. Such moments were rare in their relationship, but they did occur, as they are bound to in any relationship, no matter how friendly or close. Clearly Holmes regretted his abrupt manner; was distressed, disconcerted by it. If he could not share the information with Watson, whom he trusted above all others, and whose feelings he would not hurt for the world, he should at least provide him with an explanation.

"Forgive me, dear chap," he said at last, "but we are in very deep waters here, and it would not do to jump to false conclusions and bandy names recklessly about, even in the privacy of these rooms. I could be on a false track, there could be any one of a number of explanations for that cigarette to be where it was. I must ask you to bear with me for the while until, until..."

His voice trailed off and with a faint gesture of futility he let the sentence hang in midair. He returned to his chair and burrowed deeply into it.

Watson, after a while, got up to shut the window. He felt chilly all of a sudden. Holmes had always shared his confidences with him, even in the most sensitive of cases. If he felt he could not confide in him in this matter, it must be very, very serious indeed: Far more serious and sensitive than anything Watson could think of. He remained at the window, gazing out at the street below.

"Well, never mind," he said quietly, feigning a nonchalance he did not feel. He looked over his shoulder at Holmes with a puckish little smile. "I mean, after all, it's not as if you refused me the name of your tailor."

Watson did not know how long he remained at the bow window, how long he gazed unseeing at the passing scene beneath him, but the shadows in the street had lengthened considerably when a familiar, slight, unprepossessing figure, dodging through the traffic, caught his eye.

"You've enlisted the aid of the Irregulars, I see," he called to Holmes.

Holmes looked up from his ruminations in surprise. "Why, yes. Earlier this afternoon. However did you know?"

"Here comes their urchin-in-chief, in all his unwashed glory."

Holmes laughed. "Oh. For a moment I foolishly entertained the thought that you had deduced it."

It was only a matter of seconds before the slamming of the downstairs door and the loud trample of footsteps on the stairs heralded the arrival of the unsavory and insignificant Wiggins, the leader of the nondescript band of street arabs that Holmes was amused to dignify as the Baker Street division of the detective police force. The boy burst into the room not only unannounced but without even the nicety of a tap on the door: A dirty face with large shrewd eyes, an unruly mop of hair, and a slender frame enveloped in a cast-off coat several sizes too large. His was not so much an entrance as an explosion, but the cloud of dust which in Watson's eyes seemed to accompany the event was surely only illusionary.[21]

"Wiggins!" barked Holmes sharply. "You must knock before you enter!"

Wiggins looked from Holmes to Watson and back to Holmes again, an insolent but not entirely unengaging grin spreading across his face. He sniffed violently and wiped his nose with the back of his sleeve.

"Wh'ell I begs yer pard'n, I'm sure, guv," he said, his words weighted with exaggerated sarcasm, "but yer did tells me not ta tarry, an' I din't, did I?"

Holmes's mouth twitched. He bore no small amount of respect (and if the truth be known, affection) for this enterprising survivor of the streets, and despite himself, the scowl on his face gave way to an indulgent little smile.

"Why, so I did, Wiggins, so I did; and so you didn't. But in the future you need not take my instructions so literally as to forget the niceties."

Wiggins cocked his head to one side and gave Holmes a funny look. "Come again?"

Holmes laughed outright. "All right, Wiggins, come in. But next time you must knock, and no excuses. Now, what have you to report?"

The boy sniffed loudly again. "H'its a foine pickle, Mr. 'Olmes," said Wiggins. "The 'ole of Whitechap'l is in a panic, an' 'at's no lie. Da streets is fairly buzzink w'iv da news of da murder. An' da stories going about? Yer wouldn't credit the 'alf of 'em, you wouldn't."

"I dare say. And what can you tell me that I would credit?"

Wiggins scratched the side of his head vigorously, causing Watson to hope that whatever was residing there did not become dislodged.

"Wh'ell, dere's talk of a killer, a demon o' some sort, stalkin' da stweets w'iv a 'atchet. Some sez 'e's a Jew w'iv a wild beard down 'is chest, an' some sez 'ees a butcher fwom da slaughter'ouses w'iv a le'dder h'apron, an' some sez 'ees a toff fwom da West H'end out to kill all da 'ores..."

"All the what?" queried Watson.

"Da 'ores, da 'ores — you know, da lydies o' joy, da prost-ee-toots!"

"Oh."

"Wh'ell h'anyw'ys, h'its h'imposs-ee-bul ta figg'r, dere's so much, ah, so much, watcha-callit goin' about."

"Rumors?"

"Yeah, 'ats h'it — roomers!"

"Well, Wiggins, let us see if we can separate rumors from fact, shall we?"

Wiggins scratched again, this time deep in the folds of his coat. "H'ide wyger h'its a Jew w'iv a ledd'r apron, t'ats me guess!"

Holmes waggled a finger. "We must not guess, Wiggins. What we need is hard information. Now, tell me, did you or any of the other lads find anyone who actually saw anything? Someone who, for example, may have run into this, this 'Dark Annie' person in the streets before she was murdered?"

Wiggins's shrewd eyes narrowed and he nodded his head. "Wh'ell, I t'inks I did. 'Ard to know, but I t'inks I did."

Holmes leaned back in his chair and closed his eyes, and the tips of his long, slender fingers came together in front of him.

"Tell me," he said quietly.

The story that Wiggins now laid before them could, for all intents and purposes, have been given in code or some foreign tongue, for his cockney accent, heavily laced with the slang of the streets, required intense concentration to decipher, at least on the part of Watson, who more than once was tempted to stop him to get clarification. But he let the boy tell his story uninterrupted, knowing full well that Holmes, with his thorough knowledge of a wide range of regional accents and dialects (and his uncanny ability to mimic many of them), understood him if not always perfectly, at least adequately.

This, then, was Wiggins's story:

As instructed by Holmes, he and his confederates spread themselves out among the public houses, soup kitchens, and other popular gathering places of Whitechapel, fading unobtrusively into the background to learn what they could. Following Holmes's strict instructions to the letter, they refrained from asking questions outright, which might have called attention to themselves, but merely listened and observed. Then they regrouped to share what information they obtained: As luck would have it, it was Wiggins himself who came up with the most promising lead.

There was a man in one of the local pubs, The Britannia, in Fish Street Hill, who maintained he saw Dark Annie at around 5:30 that morning, shortly before her death. Wiggins was unable to learn the man's full name, but several of the other patrons of the pub called him "Dick" or "Dicko." Apparently he was a regular at the pub and was well known in the neighborhood. Wiggins said he seemed very upset over the killing because he knew Annie well and claimed to have been a friend of hers. As a result, he was somewhat the worse for drink, and his story was rambling and disjointed and not always completely coherent.

Dark Annie was not alone when this fellow, Dick, claimed to have seen her. She was with another man, a "mark" whom she had apparently just encountered in the street, for they appeared to be haggling over price as Dick approached. He said he overheard the man ask her, "Will you?" and she replied, "Yes."

As he came closer to the pair, the man made an effort to hide his face, an act which called attention to himself all the more, resulting in Dick's being somewhat more observant than he would have normally been. He was dressed as a gentleman, a "toff," as Dick described him to his listeners in the pub. He wore a deerstalker, probably brown, and a long dark coat, and he carried a small satchel of some sort, made of shiny leather or a similar material. He was of average height and he had a mustache. The two words Dick heard him speak confirmed he was a gentleman because the words were spoken in a cultured, upper-class accent.

That was the sum total of Dick's description of the man. Because of the poor light in the street, no more could be seen. And nothing more was heard. Dick continued on his way, and that was the last he saw of Annie Chapman.

Dick did say he passed another woman coming from the opposite direction at the very same time, and that she also would have seen the man Annie was with and could confirm the story, but Dick had never seen her before and didn't know her name.[22]

Having completed his account, Wiggins stood quietly waiting for a reaction from Holmes, who said nothing at first but continued gazing up at the ceiling. Finally, he did speak:

"Describe the man again, exactly as you heard our friend Dicko tell it."

"H'average 'eyght, dressed like a toff, brown deerstalker 'at − lyke I sees youse wear some-da-tyme − an' a long cloak or coat, an' 'ee 'ad a tickler and a −"

"A what?"

"A tickler − you know, a mustache."

"Yes, of course."

"An' he carried sometin' like a Gladstone bag, but mebbe smaller, like wot I seen da doctor 'ere carry some-da-tyme."

"A medical kit bag?"

"Aye, h'at's ryght. Made out of ledder, mebbe, or 'Merican cloth.'"[23]

"And this mustache, this, ah, tickler − he was quite certain about that?"

"Aye, h'at's ryght."

"What kind of mustache was it, did he say?"

"'E said it wore a milit'ry mustache, but da lyght was bad an' da bloke tried to 'ide his face, an' Dicko, 'e din't get a clear look. But it wore a milit'ry mustache, that much 'e could tell."

"Upturned or drooping?"

"Huh?"

"Was it turned up at the ends, or did it droop down?"

Wiggins rolled his eyes. "Luv a duck, guv, I don' know."

Holmes pulled at his chin and thought a minute. "He didn't see the man's eyes?"

"No, 'e said 'e din't. 'Is 'at were pulled down."

"And he saw nothing else?"

"Well, one t'ing. 'Ee sez 'e caught a flash of da bloke's collar when 'e turned lyke. It were funny, 'e sez, 'cause it were diff'rent."

"Different? In what sense?"

"Well, 'e sez it were a wery 'igh collar, stretched out lyke."

"Very high?"

"H'ats ryght. Lyke the kynd youse and the doctor 'as on," he said, pointing to the high starched collar that Holmes was wearing. "But unusua'wy 'eigher, lyke 'e 'ad a wery long neck."

Holmes mused over this point for several seconds before speaking again.

"There was nothing else?"

"Oh, one t'ing more. 'E was smokin', da bloke was. A lydy's fag."

"A cigarette?"

"Aye, 'hat's ryght."

"And you say this encounter took place at the end of Dorset Street where it joins with Commercial Street?"

"Aye, 'hat's ryght."

"Just one street away from Hanbury, where the murder occurred," mused Holmes half to himself.

With this Wiggins reached into the folds of his coat and extracted something from an inner pocket, a small scrap of rolled newspaper twisted at the ends. Placing the makeshift little parcel onto the side table at Holmes's elbow, he pulled it carefully apart with grimy fingers. Inside were several flattened cigarette butts, obviously picked up off the street.

"I went over dere to where 'e said," explained Higgins. "Me 'n me myte, Burt. An' we rummages 'round a bit an' found 'em in da stweet. I t'ought ya myght lyke to 'ave 'em."

Holmes clapped his hands delightedly and rose from his chair, laughing. "Wiggins, you are a treasure, an absolute treasure! If I had not already invented you, I would have to do so at once. You do me proud!"

Wiggins smiled with pleasure, blushing to his roots.

Holmes reached for his large magnifying glass and bent low over the cigarette ends, poking at them with a pencil. He arose within seconds, one of the butts held delicately between thumb and forefinger, a fierce gleam in his eye.

"Wiggins, m' boy, you have accomplished in but a few hours what all of Scotland Yard has failed to do all day. You are deserving of nothing less than a knighthood!"

"Aw, go'awn," said Wiggins, a crooked grin on his homely face. He pulled at his ear and shuffled from one foot to the other. Then something occurred to him and he frowned, and he looked at Holmes with grave suspicion.

"'Ere! Do 'at mean I don' get me shillin', then?"

Holmes and Watson were in a hansom bound for Scotland Yard within five minutes of Wiggins's departure, somewhat more than a shilling gracing the young street arab's voluminous pocket. The treasured cigarette butt, encased in a glassine envelope, was tucked safely into one of Holmes's.

Holmes, who derived no small amount of personal satisfaction from the boy's display of intelligence and initiative, was unsparing in his praise of the boy, whom he was beginning to look upon as a protégé, of sorts. "I tell you, Watson, he could go far with the right sort of education."

Watson raised an eyebrow. "I should think a bath would do for starters."

Holmes ignored the sarcasm. "There's no doubt in my mind about it. Give a young chap like that some decent schooling and he could make his way in the world."

Watson sniffed. "You're talking rubbish, Holmes: Ineffable twaddle. The poor are poor because they're deserving of nothing better. They could rise above their station if they wished. Indeed, some have done so successfully. But those who choose to live like animals do so only because they are animals. No amount of education is going to change that."

Holmes cast him a sidelong glance and smiled thinly. "You have far too generous a heart to truly believe that, your Tory soul notwithstanding."

"And you, I fear, are beginning to sound like one of those socialist fellows who are always stirring up so much trouble."[24]

Holmes gazed out at the passing scene and shrugged. "Yes, well... even they cannot always be completely wrong."

A light rain was beginning to fall as their hansom entered Piccadilly Circus, where early evening throngs promenaded past brightly lit theaters and shops, the lights reflecting garishly from the now-dampened pavement. When the hansom reached Trafalgar Square a few minutes later, the rain quite suddenly became heavier, causing the crowds there to quicken their pace, while a flock of pigeons erupted for no apparent reason from the base of Nelson's Column, making a single circuit before settling helter-skelter amid the mushrooming of umbrellas that erupted almost as swiftly as the pigeons had taken flight.

Within minutes more the hansom carried them into Whitehall, taking them past darkened government buildings. The streets here, unlike the others they had driven through, were almost devoid of pedestrian traffic, for while most Londoners labored six and a half and seven days a week, government bureaucracy takes its weekends seriously, and except for a crisis of truly catastrophic proportions is to be found in evidence only Monday through Friday, holidays excepted. After rattling past Admiralty Arch, the hansom turned, and they now entered the narrow street, just opposite the Admiralty itself, that was their destination.

The collection of undistinguished low buildings of stone and grime-streaked yellow brick which now lay before them took its name from the street. Here resided the brain stem and central nervous system of the Metropolitan Police force and, of greater interest to Holmes at the moment, the offices of the Criminal Investigation Division. The whole and all of its parts – the street, the buildings, the police force, and the CID – were known both collectively and individually as Scotland Yard, a state of affairs which paradoxically was a source of never-ending confusion to anyone who was not a Londoner – a tribute, it seemed to Holmes, to that people's indomitable tolerance of the absurd.

It was a thought that appealed to that small part of him which was French, and he left the carriage smiling, leaving Watson to wonder why.[25]

They entered the main building through a side entrance to avoid the crowd of journalists milling about in front. The latest murder being the major news story of the day, the presence of the journalists, a loud and raucous lot, was only to be expected, and Holmes, who generally held them and their work in low esteem, wished to avoid an encounter.

"It is the only profession I can think of that wholly consists of men who have missed their calling," said Holmes dryly. "The best of them are assassins and lying malcontents; the worst are *lazy* assassins and lying malcontents. If truth were coin of the realm, they would all be paupers."

It was only minutes after they gave their names to the officer at the desk that a tired and worried-looking Inspector Abberline came to fetch them, escorting them back to the rabbits' warren of cluttered offices, drab and cheerless, that housed the CID.

Once he and Watson had been relieved of their hats and sticks and provided with mugs of tepid tea, Holmes lost no time in getting to the business at hand.

"This, I think, you will find of some interest," Holmes said to Abberline, handing him the small glassine envelope. "It was discovered a short while ago at a location where the Chapman woman may have last been seen alive. It, in all probability, belonged to the man with whom she was seen, the very same man who may have accompanied her to number 29 Hanbury Street."

Abberline took the envelope from Holmes's fingers and, barely glancing at it, laid it on the desktop in front of him. "Thank you," he said simply, his face showing no reaction whatsoever.

Holmes frowned, studying the other man's features before speaking again.

"I must say, Inspector," he said quietly, "that while a man in my profession should never be surprised at anything, I am at the moment surprised by your lack of surprise. Oh, I know it is not a crown jewel that I present to you, but it is an item of some value in the matter currently under investigation, and I would have thought you would have reacted with, shall I say, somewhat greater enthusiasm than you have so far exhibited."

Abberline took a deep breath. "I have to inform you, Mr. Holmes, that our prime suspect is not the man your theory suggests. By that I mean he is not a gentleman, but a common laborer of the district. Sergeant Thicke is out looking for him now, and I hope to have him in custody before the day is out."

Holmes placed a finger over his lips and leaned forward. "You not only surprise me, Inspector. You positively amaze me."

Abberline fidgeted in his chair, and his fingers began a nervous tattoo on the desktop. Holmes observed him silently for a few moments, exchanged glances with Watson, and finally spoke again.

"Would it be presumptuous of me to ask who this suspect is, Inspector?" There was a slight edge to his voice.

Abberline refused to meet his gaze, but instead busied himself with a sheaf of papers in front of him. "Not at all," he replied, his diffident tone suggesting otherwise. "It is a man by the name of John or Jack Pizer, who lives in the district and is believed to have been seen in the vicinity at around the same time the murder occurred."

"And the fact of his being seen in the vicinity – *believed* to have been seen, in your words – that alone makes him the prime suspect? I should think that if he resides there, he quite possibly has legitimate business to be seen there."

Abberline shook his head and looked up, meeting Holmes's gaze finally. It apparently took some courage for him to do so. "He is known in the area as 'Leather Apron.' He habitually wears one, you see. He is a cobbler or boot finisher by trade."

"Leather Apron," mused Holmes, "Leather Apron. How very convenient." The sarcasm in his voice, though gently expressed, was unmistakable, and Abberline visibly blanched.

Holmes continued. "I take it that the similar article of apparel that Inspector Chandler found at the murder scene and correctly deduced could have had nothing to do with the crime is what ties our Mr. Pizer to the event. Or am I only jumping to conclusions?"

Abberline sighed heavily. "Look, Mr. Holmes..." he began, spreading his hands in a gesture of helplessness.

Holmes jumped up from his chair and began pacing in front of Abberline's desk. "Of course, of course, that must be it! How stupid of me for not realizing it sooner! For, after all, there cannot be another soul in all of London who also wears a leather apron: Not another cobbler, or butcher, or slaughterhouse worker, not a collier, or farrier or smithy, or hod carrier, not a surgeon or iron worker, or, or... I fear I am running out of occupations! Help me, someone!" He threw up his arms dramatically as if in entreaty and spun about. Then, leaning over the desk with anger in his eyes, he glared directly into Abberline's face.

"Really, Inspector, this will not do! This will not do at all!"

Abberline looked miserable. Clearly, he could marshal no argument in the face of Holmes's assertions, and made no effort to try. He clasped his hands together on the desk and held them tightly. Holmes stood there, exasperated, looking at him.

"Have you followed up on no other lead, then?" he asked quietly.

Abberline shook his head.

"That fragment of the envelope that was found near the body, bearing a regimental crest – the Sussex Regiment, I believe. Has any progress been made in tracking that down?"

"As far as we can tell," said Abberline, "it had no connection with the murderer. It was the woman's apparently. She probably picked it out of a dustbin somewhere and used it to wrap some tablets in, some medication she picked up at the clinic. We've established she appeared there the previous day complaining of feeling ill."

"Yes," mused Holmes half to himself, "such an obvious clue would have been too easy." He stroked his chin. "Nothing else, then?"

Abberline shook his head again.

"No effort has been made to search the streets for more of these cigarette samples? None of your men have attempted to question cabbies? Nothing has been done to seek out the man whose identity I described to you?"

With each question Abberline shook his head.

Holmes gazed at him silently for a long moment, then turned to retrieve his hat and stick. "Come, Watson. Our business here is done."

Abberline rose from his desk and followed Holmes into the corridor, taking him by the arm as they walked toward the front hall. "Look, Mr. Holmes, I am not at all happy about this situation, that much must be obvious to you," he said very quietly. "But as you no doubt are aware, our department has been under severe pressures of late. Surely you must realize that my hands are tied. I do have my orders, after all."

Holmes nodded. "I assumed as much. I am not unaware of the stresses and recent changes that have been inflicted upon the CID.[26] And I know what orders from a superior mean to a policeman. But what I cannot understand is the intellect of the superior who would give such orders. Upon what intelligence are these directives based? Upon what special knowledge or insight?"

Holmes reached out his hand, and in a small gesture of apology for his harsh words gently adjusted the collar of Abberline's suit coat. "You need not attempt a reply, Inspector," he said with a grim smile. "There can be no adequate response, and I expect none."

They had reached the front hall and were just inside the vestibule at the door when the sound of an arriving carriage caught their attention. The door flew open and in walked a figure that caused their heads to turn.

It was a tall, good-looking man in the dress uniform of an army general – boots, spurs, medal ribbons and all. He had a full, drooping cavalry mustache and wore a monocle in his eye. Upon his head, incongruously, was a tall, old-fashioned stovepipe hat of the sort that police constables wore a generation past. The haughty bearing of the man, along with the uniform, the monocle, and the hat, resulted in a total effect so ludicrous that only a stage setting for one of Mr. Gilbert's operatic farces would have done it justice.

Watson gasped and would have laughed outright had not something in Abberline's demeanor — a look of apprehension, perhaps — brought him up short.

Abberline said deferentially, "Good evening, Sir Charles."

"What's this, what's this?" said the general loudly, peering from face to face. "Oh, it's you, Aberdeen. Carry on, then!"

He made as if to continue on his way, but stopped short and spun around on his heel. "And who are these gentlemen? Who are you, sir? And you? Who are you and what is your business here?"

The questions came in rapid-fire order and were delivered at something approaching parade-ground decibels, apparently his normal speaking voice. "From the Home Office, are you? I knew it! I can spot you bloody Home Office wallahs a mile away! Well, I won't have you snooping around here with your striped trousers and effeminate ways! I won't have it, d'ya hear! Don't be bothering my officers with a lot of damn fool questions! They have better things to do with their time, or should, by gad!"

He spun on his heel again and once more started for the inner corridor, only to halt in mid-stride and return a second time. He pointed an accusing finger at Watson. "You are not Home Office! What do you mean by suggesting that? What are you, journalists? Too damn well turned out to be Fleet Street chaps, I should think! Seedy bunch of fellers, all of them. Who are these people, Aberdeen?"

Abberline, who had stood there stoically though all of this, swallowed hard. "May I introduce to you, Sir Charles, Mr. Sherlock

Holmes and Dr. John Watson. Gentlemen, the Commissioner of Police, Sir Charles Warren."[27]

"Holmes? Holmes?" bellowed Warren, making it sound like an accusation. "I thought you said Home Office!"

Holmes bowed slightly. "Actually, I said nothing at all, Sir Charles. But nonetheless, good evening to you."

"Holmes!" bellowed Warren again, a spark of recognition appearing in his eyes. He lowered his head menacingly, his mustache quivering. "Not that so-called consulting detective feller, are you?"

Holmes smiled politely and bowed again.

Warren's eyes blazed. "Well, I can tell you, sir, you are not wanted here! I have heard of you and your so-called scientific methods, and it is pure humbug, sir, that's what it is — codswallop and humbug! Consulting detective, indeed!"

Warren approached within inches of Holmes and waved a finger under his nose. "It's my aunt Fanny's arse, that's what it is! Now, what do you think of that?"

Holmes, who had little patience with those whom he deemed to have "less alert intelligences than his own" (It was *people* he did not suffer gladly; fools he suffered not at all), considered Warren coldly: "I think, Sir Charles, that you should uncock that finger, unless you intend to use it."

Warren peered at him in confusion. "What! What! What did he say?" He turned to Abberline. "What's he doing here anyway?

Abberline, who had visibly paled, searched his brain desperately for an adequate reply, for his career, he realized, was suddenly in great jeopardy. He had gone to Holmes on his own initiative, without the knowledge or consent of higher authority. He had violated the old adage among civil servants: "That which is not expressly permitted is expressly forbidden." He had committed an unpardonable sin, and what was worse, he had done it stupidly: He not only acted on his own but acted without having anyone to lay the blame on.

Abberline's predicament became clear to Holmes in an instant. He jumped in quickly. "My presence here, Sir Charles, has to do with the Whitechapel business. I have been following developments closely and have some theories about the case that Inspector Abberline reluctantly – though I must say, politely – agreed to listen to."

"Oh, he did, did he?" Warren said. He cast an angry glance in Abberline's direction.

"Yes. But the inspector was not interested in my views, and I realize now that I was wasting his time." Holmes waved an angry Watson to silence, for he had opened his mouth to protest. "So, with your permission, sir," Holmes continued, "Dr. Watson and I will now take our leave."

Warren nodded. "You do that! And let me tell you, sir, that I concur wholeheartedly with my officer! He acted quite correctly, quite correctly indeed. This is no business for amateurs, and certainly no business of yours, and I'll thank you to keep your nose out of it. And one thing more, sir. Should you ever meddle in police business again, I shall have you taken in charge. Taken in charge, sir! Count on it!"

With that he turned away a final time and marched briskly down the corridor, calling over his shoulder, "Good show, Aberdeen! Jolly good show!"

Holmes smiled grimly, only the touch of color in his cheeks and the tightening of his jaw revealing his true feelings; Watson stood there sputtering with rage while Abberline, a very pale and visibly shaken Abberline, cast his eyes heavenward and breathed an audible sigh of relief.

"Come, Watson," said Holmes, "I think a visit to Clarences would do us both a world of good, and then perhaps a soothing steam at Faulkners, if that meets with your approval. What say you, eh?"[28]

Waving Abberline's effusive thanks and apologies aside, Holmes took a protesting Watson by the arm and proceeded out the door.

Thus their ignominious departure from Scotland Yard.

Seven

SUNDAY, SEPTEMBER 9-TUESDAY, SEPTEMBER 18, 1888

"I abhor the dull routine of existence. I crave for mental exaltation."
— The Sign of the Four

The day that followed Sherlock Holmes's visit to Scotland Yard was to be a difficult one for him and an anxious one for Watson. Despite Holmes's outward display of indifference, he was naturally upset by Sir Charles Warren's contemptuous treatment, and Watson knew him well enough to see the signs: He was totally uncommunicative at breakfast and unusually subdued, and he barely touched the food on his plate. It was abundantly obvious he was in one of his melancholy moods, listless, moody, despondent. Certainly, he could hardly be blamed.

After all, hadn't he rendered invaluable assistance to Scotland Yard on several occasions in the past? And hadn't he always enjoyed a cordial if sometimes prickly relationship with the police officials with whom he had come into contact? Never had he been treated so shabbily and so rudely by any of them. Never had he been ordered off the premises of the Yard like a poacher, a common trespasser on someone's land. Or ordered off a case under investigation, for that matter. And rarely had his ego – his so tender ego – been so badly bruised.

The day being Sunday, and a damp, dismally gray one at that, the two of them stayed indoors in front of the fire, content to while away the hours in the homey clutter of their sitting room with the newspapers and their respective books and journals to keep them occupied. More than once Watson cast an anxious glance in Holmes's direction, half expecting at any time to see his arm reach out for the little bottle on the corner of the mantelpiece, for the syringe in its neat morocco case. For in those years Sherlock Holmes's customary solution to inactivity and depression was almost always his "seven percent solution."

But he refrained, much to Watson's relief. Indeed, his mood was such, his manner so lethargic, it was almost as if he hadn't had the energy for even that. To his credit, he did his best to hide his true feelings behind a mask of imperturbability, even from Watson – particularly from Watson – for he knew his friend was upset for his sake. But of course it didn't work. Watson saw through him in a minute. Unlike Holmes, he gave vent to his emotions and was visibly outraged by Warren's behavior.

"The man's an ass, Holmes!" he argued in an effort to cheer up his friend. "You must consider the source!"

Holmes merely nodded and did his best to smile, but it was a thin, rueful smile tinged, understandably, with more than a touch of bitterness. And it was obviously rendered more for Watson's benefit than out of conviction.

"Man despises what he does not comprehend," Watson quoted, but even Goethe's wisdom encountered an unreceptive mind. Holmes's response was an apathetic shrug and another feeble nod.[29]

The subject was dropped, Watson not wishing to belabor the point and Holmes not wishing to discuss it at all.

Watson knew that even more than the insult to Holmes's pride, more than the damage to his self-esteem, it was the sudden lack of activity that put him into his present state of depression. He could withstand almost any deprivation, almost any insult – he could go for days without food and even sleep; but he could not go without mental stimulation. He lived for the sudden trample of footsteps on the stairs, the unexpected knock at the door. He lived for the chase; his sole passion was the game, always the game.

And now? Now, for the moment at least, there was nothing. Now there was an emptiness. There was no mystery to solve, no puzzle to unravel. His life was devoid of challenge and was therefore barren. And he, therefore, was miserable.

"My mind rebels at stagnation," he once said. "Give me problems, give me work, give me the most abstruse cryptogram or the most intricate analysis, and I am in my own proper atmosphere."[30]

So naturally, given Holmes's mood, Watson was more than a little surprised (and greatly relieved) when at day's end the bottle still remained on the shelf and the syringe in its case, and not for the first time did he marvel over the one facet of Holmes's personality that was totally predictable: his unpredictability.

They both retired early that night, after a light supper: It was a day that was best done with quickly.

Fortunately, the days and weeks that followed were to be better ones for the lodgers of 221B Baker Street. Holmes's plea for activity, for work, happily was to receive a quick response. He was to become involved in two of the most important cases of his career (along with one or two less so), was to encounter the notorious Jonathan Small, and do battle with the "hound of hell" at Baskerville Hall; and, with a mixture of amusement, pity, and sadness, was to see Watson fall hopelessly, deeply in love — with a woman whom even Holmes, with all of his expressed disinterest in the fair sex, admitted was "one of the most charming young ladies I have ever met."[31]

During all of this time, Scotland Yard's investigation of the two Whitechapel murders was to run its course — and a short, bumpy course it proved to be.

The newspapers were full of it. They made much of the fact that not only was there no motive but there was no real suspect, and frantic efforts on the part of the police were leading nowhere. For a while the attentions of the police inquiry, as Abberline had revealed, focused on a thirty-three-year-old Polish Jew by the name of John Pizer, the man known in the district as Leather Apron. Early on the morning of Monday the 10th, Pizer was traced to a house in Mulberry Street, where he was duly arrested by Sergeant Thicke and taken in for questioning.

The evidence against him was entirely circumstantial and tenuous at best: The presence of the leather apron in the courtyard behind 29 Hanbury Street; the fact that he had a "reputation" for ill-treating prostitutes; the fact that he was seen wearing a deerstalker hat similar to the one worn by Annie Chapman's killer; and the added fact that Chapman's lodging-house keeper told a Press Association reporter that he had ejected Pizer from the lodging house a few months earlier for attacking, or threatening to attack (he was somewhat vague on the point), one of the female lodgers.

The police were convinced they had their man.

A broadsheet hawked in the streets gave these details:

> At nine o'clock this morning Detective Sergeant William Thicke, H-Division, who has had charge of this case, succeeded in capturing the man known as Leather Apron.

There is no doubt that he is the murderer, for a large number
of long-bladed knives was found in his possession.

Thicke was the man of the hour. Adding to the neatness of his case
was the "evidence" found in Pizer's room in Mulberry Street, described
variously by the press as "long-bladed" knives and "long-handled"
knives. The "large number" turned out to be five. They proved to be
boot-finisher's knives, and the reason they were in Pizer's possession
was soon established: Pizer by trade was a boot finisher.

He was taken to the Leman Street police station, accompanied
voluntarily by the friends with whom he had been lodging. He and they
protested his innocence, insisting he had not been out of the house since
the previous Thursday.

Pizer's arrest had immediate repercussions for the sizable population
of Jewish immigrants living in Whitechapel. Within hours, scores of
unfortunate Jews were harassed and beaten in the streets in a wave
of almost spontaneous anti-Semitism. Commented *The Daily News*:
"There may soon be murders from panic to add to murders from lust
for blood..."

That same afternoon another arrest was made, that of one William
Piggott, who bore a resemblance to Pizer. He was spotted drinking
in a pub in Gravesend, wearing bloodstained clothing and boots and
was found to be carrying a bundle of shirts that were also stained with
blood. When questioned, Piggott proved to be a willing witness, albeit
sometimes incoherent, and sometimes all too willing: He willingly
admitted he had been in Whitechapel the Saturday morning in
question. He willingly admitted he had walked down Brick Lane and
had gotten into an altercation with a prostitute. He willingly admitted
he had struck her. As for the bloodstained clothing, he had no rational
explanation, but seemed willing to admit to any explanation at all. The

problem was that none of the police witnesses (or all-too-cooperative individuals who made claim to being witnesses) could identify Piggott, and after a few hours in cells his speech and behavior became so strange and erratic that a physician was summoned. The physician took one look at him and declared him insane.

For several hours suspicion was focused on yet a third man, a market porter by the name of John Richardson, whose mother rented the ground floor of 29 Hanbury Street as well as the yard in the rear and a workshop off the yard. It was soon determined that it was his leather apron that had been found in the yard. He freely admitted it. He customarily wore it when working in the cellar, he said, and it had been in the yard since Thursday. His mother confirmed it: She had washed it on Thursday and left it on the fence to dry, she said.

Richardson was released. Pizer was released. Piggott was sent to the asylum in Bow. The police had nothing and no one, and the press made much of it.

Hundreds more arrests were to be made – anyone and everyone seemed to be suspect. They were to include Irishmen, Germans, Poles, Jews, stockbrokers, seamen, butchers. They were brought in for the flimsiest of reasons, and often for no reason at all. Said *The Times*: "It seems at times as if every person in the streets were suspicious of everyone else he met, and as if it were a race between them who could first inform against his neighbor." And dozens of people, women as well as men, walked in off the streets inexplicably proclaiming their guilt. But the police were to be frustrated at every turn. Few individuals were held for more than an hour or two. There was not a shred of evidence or a single clue to act upon.

Punch, critical of the police for acting on spurious information, published a cartoon showing a blindfolded police constable being spun around by a group of leering criminals. "Blind Man's Buff" was the caption.

The tenor of the times was such, the fear in the streets so great, that a drunken prankster could empty out a saloon by merely claiming he had the murder knife in his pocket. An Irishman by the name of John Brennan made such a pronouncement and quickly found himself to be in sole possession of the White Hart pub in Camberwell. How many drinks he helped himself to before the police arrived was not recorded.

More than one lynching was narrowly avoided, according to the press reports. A foreigner, who spoke not a word of English, was nearly strung up in the East End for merely looking at a woman. *The Times* reported the near lynching was initiated by "an enormous mob of men and women, shouting and screaming in the most extraordinary manner."

Rumors abounded, the police indiscriminately seemed to chase down every single one of them, and the press, often with ill-disguised glee, reported the results, which were invariably, inevitably, nil. Criticism of the police, by press and public alike, rose to such a level that no attempt was made to hide the fact that officials at Scotland Yard were stymied and close to despair. Acting out of desperation, in an effort to ease the criticism, the police issued a terse "description" of the killer:

> Age 37; height, 5 ft. 7 ins.; rather dark beard and mustache.
> Dress —shirt, dark jacket, dark waistcoat and trousers, black
> scarf, and black felt hat. Spoke with a foreign accent.

It was obvious to Holmes and Watson that the so-called description was manufactured out of whole cloth. High-ranking officials at the Yard thought it would be prudent to try to convince everyone that they knew what they were doing, and since they couldn't admit they didn't even know who they were looking for, they decided to invent someone.

"The foreign accent is a nice touch," commented Holmes dryly.

"Who would believe that anyone but a foreigner would commit such a crime?"

During the week that followed, Holmes in his spare moments continued to peruse the newspapers for the latest "developments" in the case, but merely out of curiosity. In any event, his spare moments proved to be spare indeed. Much of his time that week was taken up with the bizarre affair involving Melas, the linguist, and it was during this case that Watson was first introduced to a man he didn't even know existed, the second most fascinating man he was ever to meet: Holmes's older brother, Mycroft.[32] Little did he know then that within a fortnight he was to meet with him again.

Eight

WEDNESDAY, SEPTEMBER 26, 1888

"He will not even go out of his way to verify his own solutions,
and would rather be considered wrong than take the trouble
to prove himself right."
— *The Greek Interpreter*

"You look tired, Sherlock. Have you been keeping well?" said
Mycroft Holmes phlegmatically. He was seated, ensconced, rather,
in an overstuffed leather armchair, one of a cluster of three by a window
in the Strangers' Room of the Diogenes Club, his heavily lidded eyes
studying his brother's features in much the same way a fat lizard might
study an insect it was about to pounce upon, dispassionately but not
without interest.

Mycroft Holmes, seven years Sherlock's senior, was an extremely
large, heavy man, as corpulent as Sherlock was thin, as ponderous in
his manner and sluggish in his movements as Sherlock was graceful
and quick.

The Diogenes Club was Mycroft Holmes's special domain, he being one of its founders and principal members. It was one of the certainties of life that if he could not be found in his lodgings in Pall Mall or in his offices in Whitehall, then the Diogenes Club was the place to look, especially if the hour was between a quarter to five and twenty to eight. "It is his cycle," Sherlock Holmes once remarked, one from which he rarely deviated.

"And you, dear Doctor. How d'ye do? You seem fit enough. How's that gammy leg of yours, or is it your shoulder? How silly of me not to remember which."[33] Languidly he held out a fat paw to be taken.

"Good of the two of you to come on such short notice, 'pon my word. Do take pews, won't you. Forgive me for not getting up, Doctor, but a man of my configuration finds descending into a chair so much more agreeable than ascending from it."

He turned a long, leisurely gaze upon Watson. "You must be feeling fairly well, Doctor, otherwise you wouldn't have convinced my brother to stroll the entire length of Regent Street prior to coming here. But at least you stopped for refreshment at the Savoy, so I trust neither one of you is overly fatigued."

Watson looked at him in surprise. "However did you know all that, Mr. Holmes?"

"Tut, tut, Doctor Watson, you told me yourself."

"I did?"

Mycroft and Sherlock exchanged knowing smiles. "A mere parlor game, Doctor," said Mycroft. "Surely, you have been around Sherlock long enough to be familiar with it. Don't compel me to explain; it's such a bore, y'know." He cast a languid glance in Sherlock's direction as he spoke, knowing full well he would not appreciate having his powers of observation referred to in such disparaging terms. Sherlock favored him with a wintery, reedy smile.

"But I insist! How could you possibly know we walked all the way?

And down Regent Street in particular? And took tea at the Savoy? Of course you saw us through the window as we arrived, so you knew we did not come by cab, but how could you possibly divine the route we took?"

"I had my nose buried in *The Gazette*, actually, and didn't see you come up," he replied, his tone suggesting boredom with the subject, "but your stick is in part the culprit, Doctor. Sticks can be quite revealing, you know. But it's of little consequence."

Watson looked at him. "My stick? My walking stick?"

Mycroft Holmes chortled, plainly enjoying Watson's bewilderment. "It really is so deucedly simple. There's a touch of red clay adhered to the tip, you see. That could have come only from Oxford Circus at the upper terminus of Regent Street, where the pavement is dug up and that particular hue of clay is common. But your boots are quite clean, newly blackened, I perceive. I must conclude you stopped somewhere en route and had them attended to. That it was the Hotel Savoy is a reasonable enough conclusion, though a slight deviation from your course is required to end up there. In addition to its new Edison lights and all the most modern conveniences, the hotel has a most accommodating staff, including a young lad who does nothing but perambulate through the lobby with a shiny little brass box, cleaning gentlemen's boots. That it was indeed that establishment is further supported by the rose in your lapel, obtainable from precious few places this time of year, the Savoy's flower stall being one of them. And surely no sensible individual would find himself in the vicinity of the Savoy at teatime without partaking of the excellent repast they offer there. There's a small residue of their lovely strawberry preserves on your cravat, by the by; a damp cloth should suffice."[34]

Watson started, craning his neck awkwardly to examine his necktie.

"Must I go on, Doctor? You insist? Very well. That you were in

Regent Street is indisputable. That you arrived there afoot from Baker Street is a reasonable conclusion, the distance being too near to justify the hire of a horse-drawn conveyance, except the weather being mean. And it being uncommonly fine for this time of year, I can conclude only that you undertook to walk the entire length of Regent Street and peruse the shops, stopping midway at Pope and Plantes for your new gloves (terribly attractive!), and popping into Alexander Jones & Company for that parcel of stationery I saw you deposit with the cloakroom attendant as you came in – their wrappings are most distinctive. And knowing that Sherlock's dislike of physical exercise is surpassed only by my own, this long, tiring trek had to have been your idea, Doctor, in the well-meaning though mistaken belief that it would have some therapeutic value. Must I indeed go on?"

Watson shook his head in wonder, and put his hands up in mock surrender. The two brothers laughed. Holmes had told him that Mycroft's powers of observation and deduction surpassed even his own, but Watson had found this assertion difficult to believe, attributing the statement to either uncommon modesty on Holmes's part (unthinkable!) or familial pride. What was it that Holmes had said? *If the art of the detective began and ended in reasoning from an armchair, my brother would be the greatest criminal agent that ever lived...*[35]

Watson studied Mycroft with new interest, his stare an obvious one. Mycroft, aware of it, smiled slightly and rendered Watson a little bow, then clapped his hands together. "Good of the two of you to come on such short notice, 'pon my word. As you can see, nothing has changed here since your last visit. Change is anathema to the Diogenes. It bears my stamp, I fear, for I find change – even the most trivial – so very discomfiting. One of the charms of the Diogenes is that everything about it, down to the size of the leaves on the palms and the wart on the doorkeeper's nose, is precisely the way it was ten years ago and,

God willing, will be precisely the same ten years from now. I sometimes think the Empire would collapse should the day ever come when one of the periodicals was out of place in the rack or, far worse, one of the pictures was moved on the wall, heaven forbid."

Watson looked around him.

The Diogenes Club, tastefully contrived in almost equal parts of mahogany and marble, etched glass, brocade, and Persian carpets, was reputed to be the most unsociable, most "unclubable" club in London. Eccentric even by English standards, its members were forbidden by the club's bylaws from communicating with any other member anywhere on the club's premises, except for the Strangers' Room, where subdued conversation was tolerated though hardly encouraged. Indeed, there had been a story going about some years previously that one new member, a peer of the realm no less, made the mistake or had the effrontery of wishing "good day" to another gentleman on his way into the library. He was ejected on the spot and was forever more forbidden reentry. Another story, regarding a small fire started by a dozing member's cigar, was vehemently denied by the club's manager in a letter to *The Times*. The member was indeed awakened prior to the arrival of the fire brigade, contrary to a slander in *Punch*, but he was awakened verbally, wrote the indignant manager, not with the contents of a wine cooler as had been alleged.[36]

"And what is your club, Doctor? Sherlock, I know, is far too misanthropic to belong to one, even this one – not that any respectable club would have him – but you I perceive as being a more sociable creature."

Watson mumbled the name of his club almost apologetically, it being surely among the least exclusive in London. Mycroft nodded politely.

"Have you ever been to the Beefsteak? It's a pleasant little club, I am told, though I have never been there. The food is supposed to be somewhat better than the norm, and I understand their qualifications for membership are not unreasonable. You've either got to be a peer who has learned to read and write, I am informed, or a journalist who has learned his table manners."

Watson laughed appreciatively. Holmes merely smiled – he had heard it before.

Mycroft examined the ash of his cigar. "I find that you can generally judge a man by his club – his tastes, his politics, his interests and preferences, and so forth. And to a large extent even his character as well. Would you not agree, Sherlock?"

"I place more faith in boots," replied Holmes. "Whether a man is well shod or not tells me more of what I want to know about him than the club he belongs to, especially since so many of our gentry belong to one club or another simply because their fathers did."

Mycroft looked at him cunningly. "That latter point supports my argument nicely, I should think."

Holmes, after a moment's pause, had the grace to concede the issue with a small bow. "And it is a point well taken, dear brother. I should have known better than to contradict you."

Mycroft smiled beatifically. "You are growing wiser with age, I am happy to see."

He turned to Watson. "Will you take sherry?" he asked hospitably. "There's a very nice *palo cortado* in the cellars that I can recommend to you, a step above the usual muck you'll find nowadays. Our wine and spirits committee was fortunate in, ah, shall we say, *acquiring* a quantity a fortnight ago. Bertie would just love to get his hands on a cask for his place – and all but told me so, the hint was that broad – but I'll let him stew a bit before I send some around. He suffers from an overabundance of instant gratification as 'tis, what?[37] May I tempt you, Doctor? Sherlock, the same? Excellent! Bledsoe, three sherries, if you please, and some of those lovely sweet biscuits. That should tide me over nicely till supper, I should think. No, don't bother bringing the decanter, my guests won't be staying that long."

Holmes eyed his older brother with sardonic amusement. "As gracious as ever, I see, Mycroft."

"And you, my dear Sherlock, are as stubborn as ever!" he replied tartly. "What's this about refusing poor Matthews over this Whitechapel business?[38] Surely your quaint little practice does not keep you so occupied that you cannot render your Queen some meager service now and again. Have you joined up with the Liberals against the Tories, is that it? Want to see the Salisbury government fall?" Mycroft Holmes chuckled, the sympathetic movement of his body causing cigar ash to fall down the front of his ample waistcoat. He lethargically brushed at himself with pudgy, well-manicured fingers.

"Of course I know you better than that," he continued. "You care or even know as much about politics as poor Lansdowne over there knows what day of the week it is." He gestured toward a very elderly gentleman asleep in an armchair at the other end of the room. "Thinks Louis Napoleon is still emperor of the French and old Dizzy still the P.M. A bit dotty, you know, though a good enough chap in his day."

Mycroft Holmes waved his hand dismissively, as if to put poor Lansdowne out of mind and mark the end to civilities and small talk. He leaned forward in his chair and peered into his brother's eyes.

"Why have you turned Matthews down? It just won't do, you know."

Sherlock Holmes casually crossed one leg over the other and examined his fingernails.

"Tell me, Mycroft, are you acting in an official capacity or are you merely asking out of curiosity?"

"My dear Sherlock," replied Mycroft loftily, "as you well know, I never act in an official capacity. My official duties preclude me from acting officially. Indeed, my only value to the government, and I flatter myself that I am of some small value on occasion, is that officially I do not act at all. Officially, I have no official status. Officially, I do not even exist."[39]

Watson listened to this exchange between the two brothers with growing fascination and just a little discomfort – discomfort because he felt he was intruding, not only in a conversation of a private nature between brothers, but in a conversation of a privileged, highly sensitive nature as well. But that was his secondary reaction, far outweighed by his first: his fascination with the two men themselves. Without doubt they were two of the most intriguing men he had ever met. In the seven or eight years he had known Sherlock (strange after all this time he still called him Holmes), he never ceased to be intrigued by his habits and eccentricities, his moods, his personality traits and thought processes. He was a maze of contradictions, the most complex individual he ever knew – and the most changeable. He could be cold and calculating one moment, demanding and insufferably arrogant, yet kind and uncommonly thoughtful the next. But always – always without fail – he was the most interesting, the most captivating of men.

And now, sitting across from him, was another from the same mold, different in so many ways, at least outwardly: Mycroft was so much larger and heavier than Sherlock, his body positively gross, his whole bearing suggesting that of a fat, self-indulgent individual whose only concern was creature comfort, whose only interest was in satiating an insatiable appetite. But the image was a false one, in part nurtured by Mycroft himself, as if he had chosen a specific role in life and was playing it, as they say, to the hilt.

On closer examination, Watson saw some marked similarities between the two men that were startling. He remembered his impressions of Mycroft when he met him for the first time only a few weeks earlier when Holmes and he became involved in the affair of the Greek interpreter. He had jotted down those impressions in his journal shortly after that meeting and, word for word, they came back to him now:

Heavily built and massive, there was a suggestion of uncouth physical inertia in the figure, but above this unwieldy frame there was perched a head so masterful in its brow, so alert in its steel-gray, deep-set eyes, so firm in its lips, and so subtle in its play of expression, that after the first glance one forgot the gross body and remembered only the dominant mind.[40]

His eyes were the most compelling feature about him and, aside from his high, intelligent brow, the one facial characteristic he shared with Sherlock. A light, watery gray, those eyes seemed capable of penetrating granite at times, yet they always retained a certain faraway look, a look as unfathomable as the deepest waters. And behind them lurked an intelligence, an innate wisdom, that was deeper still.

As if sensing Watson's gaze was upon him, Mycroft now turned those gray eyes in his direction and fixed him with a stare that made him decidedly uncomfortable.

"Surely you, Doctor, must realize the importance of this matter. Sherlock must be made to see reason. You probably have as much influence upon him as any man – more so than I, I dare say. Can you not make him see how vital it is to become involved in this matter once again? How absolutely essential it is? Can I not enlist your aid? I tell you without exaggeration or fear of contradiction that the country is on the edge of a crisis over this, this series of ridiculously trifling acts of violence in the East End."

He leaned forward in his chair and raised a finger. "Can you imagine? I mean, there is no precedent for it! The whole country in an absolute uproar over the dispatch of a few common prostitutes!" He shook his head in disbelief, his steely eyes never leaving Watson's, making Watson feel as if he himself were to blame.

"I tell you, Doctor," he continued, "the perpetrator of these deeds must be apprehended, and apprehended soon. The government is already embarrassed, and patience is wearing thin. Lord Salisbury is most desirous of an early resolution of this matter, most desirous. You see, the opposition would love to see him embarrassed further. It is causing grave difficulties in Parliament and is deflecting attention from the government's legislative programs. I need not tell you how serious this could turn out to be." Again he shook his massive head from side to side. "How very serious indeed." He pointed a finger at Watson, as if daring him to contradict. "I do not exaggerate, I assure you."

Watson threw a glance at Holmes, who was now deeply burrowed in his chair, his long fingers tented in front of his face in the familiar manner. Watson raised his hands in a gesture of helplessness. "I believe you exaggerate one thing, Mr. Holmes, and that is my influence over your brother. It is in no way as you describe; of that I can assure *you*."

The gray eyes did not waver.

"Really!" Watson protested. "I mean, I didn't even know that the Home Office contacted Holmes – your brother, I mean," he stammered foolishly under that gaze. "I was unaware Sir Henry Matthews had requested his assistance. I mean, he didn't see fit to share that information with me – your brother, that is. And it is not my place to interfere in his affairs, surely. I mean..." His voice trailed off and he suddenly realized he was being put upon, made to feel guilty over something that was totally beyond his control and over which he had no say. "Really!" he said again, this time with indignation.

From out of the depths of his chair Sherlock Holmes laughed, a deep, rumbling sound that caused his shoulders to shake. He leaned over and placed a comforting hand on Watson's arm. "Never mind, old fellow. It is just one of Mycroft's ways, one of his lesser talents: Convincing unwary individuals to take on unpleasant tasks by first instilling within them the guilt of Judas Iscariot. He could make the Queen feel contrite over the jewels in her crown!"

Mycroft's cheeks colored slightly, and he frowned, leaning back in his chair with a perturbed expression. And then, seeing the humor in it, gave way to a chortle.

"Her Majesty, God bless her, would not be amused," he said dryly.

The three of them laughed together, enjoying not only the banter but the moment – Watson in particular, because he was made to feel one with them, allowed to share the company of these two extraordinary men and participate in their conversation. He relaxed in his chair and took an appreciative sip of sherry.

"The fact of the matter is," said Sherlock Holmes, getting back to the business at hand, "I only yesterday heard from Sir Henry, in the late afternoon post, and a very complimentary letter it was too: Very complimentary, very flattering, and quite consoling. He invited me to come around to see him in Whitehall to discuss my theories in the case. I wired him directly and told him what I tell you now: I have taken on another investigation, just yesterday morning, and – Watson will bear me out on this – it is one that promises to be most difficult and will require my presence in Devonshire for an indeterminate period of time. I am committed, you see."

"Sherlock, the matter – whatever it is – could hardly compare in importance to this one. Surely, you must see that!"

Holmes shrugged. "As I say, I am committed to it. And I will not go back on my word, Mycroft."

Mycroft Holmes took on an expression of exasperation. "With that kind of an attitude you wouldn't last long in government, I can tell you! What is this case of yours that is so important? Something I'd be familiar with?"

"It involves the death of Sir Charles Baskerville. You may have read of it at the time."

"Baskerville? The Liberal candidate for mid-Devon? Why, his death was months ago!"

"Nevertheless, dead he remains!" snapped Holmes. "And under very peculiar circumstances. Watson and I lunched with his heir this very afternoon at the Northumberland: Sir Henry Baskerville. And I have every reason to believe that his life, too, is in great jeopardy. So I am afraid, Mycroft, that I cannot toss over the matter as easily as all that. It is all settled, you see: Watson and I are to go down to Dartmoor on Saturday in company with Sir Henry and his friend Dr. Mortimer. And that's where the matter rests!"[41]

Mycroft threw up his hands in disgust.

At that point the waiter appeared silently at Mycroft's side with silver salver in hand, a small square of pasteboard placed precisely in the center.

Mycroft took the card from the tray with a look of annoyance and glanced at it perfunctorily, his expression changing at once. "Ah, it's Randolph, good! Show him in, Bledsoe, won't you? And bring another chair."

The man who entered was at first glance an aging, even enfeebled individual, well below medium height, with sad, protuberant eyes and a heavy, drooping mustache. But as he came closer it was obvious that he was not old, except before his time; in reality, he was not yet forty. And despite his appearance of age, his step was brisk and businesslike and his whole being seemed to be possessed with an unusual nervous energy, his manner pugnacious. His eyes swept the room as he walked toward them, as if he were looking for someone, anyone, of importance, but, spotting no one more important than the individuals he was about to join, lost interest in the place and its occupants and gave it and them no further consideration. He seemed a cold man, severe – a man of proud bearing, excessively so. Impeccably groomed and well tailored, he had the obvious look of a patrician: Of a man to the manner born, of someone who was accustomed to giving orders and having them obeyed instantly, and he carried it off with great assurance.

Mycroft greeted him warmly and with deference. "Randolph! How very good to see you!" he said, his tone leaving no doubt that he meant it. But as before, he made no attempt to rise from his chair, once again merely holding out his hand to be taken, leaving Watson to wonder if he would rise for the Queen should she ever be so bold as to invade the sacred precincts of the Diogenes.

"You know my brother, I think. And this is his friend and amanuensis, Dr. John Watson, whose acquaintance I don't believe you have made. (Now, how would he know that? thought Watson.) Doctor: Lord Randolph Churchill."

Tense, highly strung, the description given of Randolph Churchill as a greyhound about to spring was an apt one. He greeted Holmes with guarded formality and Watson in a manner that was perfunctory to the point of being rude. His grip was strong, as Watson knew it would be when he took the proffered hand. But his eyes never moved in Watson's direction during the ritual. They looked elsewhere, as if the man whose hand he took were far too unimportant to take notice of, let alone acknowledge. Watson disliked him immediately, for however well bred or high his station, he lacked good breeding, and that was obvious.

Of course Watson knew who he was at once. There were few in the country who did not. For up until a very few years ago Lord Randolph Henry Spencer Churchill was a rising star in the Conservative Party.

Chancellor of the Exchequer and Leader of the House of Commons at the age of thirty-seven, he was a brilliant politician whom everyone *knew* would be prime minister someday, and sooner rather than later. Lord Salisbury was forced to name him to the post (despite the fact that he did not like him), believing, as he said, "that he would be more dangerous outside the government than in it."[42]

A rising star? He was a shooting star! His light burned brightly but for an instant. Just a few months after taking up his minister's boxes he surprised the nation and the party by flinging them down. Stubborn and temperamental, he quarreled with the prime minister over budgetary questions and in short order resigned from the cabinet, and his star faded. And though still a member of Parliament, and a prominent one at that, he was no longer Leader of the House or a leader of the party. What influence he still possessed, and it was not inconsiderable, was largely due to his forceful personality. He was a natural-born leader of men in every sense of the word, including the truest, having been born the younger son of a duke. And not just any duke, but the Duke of Marlborough.

That fact alone would have been enough to grant him access to the salons of power, to a prime minister who didn't like him, to a prince with whom he once quarreled but who later again befriended him, to a queen whom he angered on more than one occasion but who still called on him for advice.

In the overall scheme of things, much of what went on in government was prompted by a handful of well-placed individuals who were outside of government. Lord Randolph Henry Spencer Churchill was one of those individuals.

Watson couldn't help but notice that there was a faint nervous tremor in Lord Randolph's hands as he removed a cigarette from its case and held it to his mouth for the waiter to light, coughing as he did so. There were deep shadows beneath his eyes, and a slight nervous tic.

"Well, Mr. Holmes, we meet again," he said. He waved aside the offer of sherry. "Whisky, I think," he said to the waiter. "Laphroaig if you stock it, or Bruichladdich. Any of the Islay malts will do, I'm not particular.

"– And under no less agreeable circumstances," he continued addressing Holmes. "But this time it is not merely a foolish scandal involving a future sovereign and the son of a peer, but a far more serious matter: A matter affecting our English system of governance."[43]

Sherlock Holmes raised his eyebrows.

"Oh, yes," responded Lord Randolph to the unspoken query, "that is precisely how serious I view the matter. There are violent changes in the wind. We have already seen signs of it in France and Italy and Germany and Russia: Revolutionary changes, inspired by those creatures Engels and Marx, I shouldn't wonder."

Lord Randolph stubbed his cigarette out in the ashtray beside him and then stretched out his legs and gazed down at his shoes, as if addressing the mirror image reflected in the highly polished leather. "As we all know, those very same forces are at work here in Britain. The trade unionists and all of that. These people would rend asunder the very fabric of our society, and they will not be content to rest on their laurels should they succeed in their aim of organizing workers in the coal mines and woolen mills and iron works. They will not be content until *Mademoiselle Guillotine* replaces Nelson's Column in Trafalgar Square, until the cry, *aux armes, aux barricades!* is heard in the streets of London. Yes, it could mean *révolution!* right here – not merely the fall of the government, or even a change in parties, but revolution! Terror in the streets, citizens' committees, anarchy, economic chaos: The Paris of 1789, or at least 1870, all over again. But this time right here. *Right here!*" He tapped his leg with two fingers for emphasis.

Lord Randolph's words, though quietly spoken, had a profound chilling effect, the more so because they were delivered in so subdued a manner. Despite his outward restraint, it was obvious that he passionately believed every word that he spoke. And the result was spellbinding. Here was a man whose vocation was to move men with words, and that he did it well was clearly evident. Watson found himself gripping the arms of his chair, and the expression on Holmes's face was one of rapt attention.

Lord Randolph lifted his eyes and focused on Holmes. "Your brother has discussed these matters with you, I have no doubt."

"More or less," replied Holmes quietly.

Lord Randolph reached for another cigarette, lighting it himself this time. "Then you know how potentially serious these Whitechapel crimes are. The revolutionists and anarchists will use them – are already using them – to ferment unrest. We are not sitting on the powder keg as yet, but it is being rolled into the cellars."

Holmes nodded.

"And the fuse will not be a long one, I fear," Mycroft added.

"That's quite true," Lord Randolph responded. "As you know, there is a growing republican movement in Parliament. A most vocal movement. They begrudge every farthing spent on the upkeep of the monarchy; the debate over the Queen's allowances gets longer and more vociferous every year. While this movement is essentially middle class in nature, the unrest in the East End serves to add fuel to their fire. The poorer classes have no representation, of course – they have only their gin bottles to turn to. But they're attracting attention to themselves, and they're starting to gain the sympathy of some well-placed individuals – in the House and even in the Church, God help us." He pursed his lips. "Dangerous times, dangerous times."

Lord Randolph paused and took a sip of whiskey. "These murders in the East End constitute the most volatile fuel of all, I shouldn't wonder." He looked directly at Holmes. "Surely you must see that. Surely you must appreciate the potential dangers." Suddenly his eyes became fierce. "These crimes must be brought to an end, and swiftly."

Holmes's face remained impassive.

Lord Randolph studied him for a moment and then continued. "The police are out of their depth in this matter, that much is apparent to all." He spoke the words in a monotone, as if he were speaking them to himself. "They are ill equipped to conduct the kind of investigation that is required. Their detective branch is totally demoralized and has no effective head since Anderson's departure. Their training is insufficient in any case, their methods outmoded. They are just not up to it."

"No one knows that better than Sherlock," Mycroft said. "I tire of hearing him tell me so."

Lord Randolph turned to Mycroft. "Did you tell him of Lord Salisbury's decision?"

Mycroft frowned and shook his head. "I told him of the prime minister's concern. I did not see fit to disclose a decision made in cabinet that is of a privileged nature."

Churchill nodded and looked down at his shoes again. "I have just come from Windsor," he said quietly, like another man might say he has just come from the barber's, or his wife's favorite greengrocer. "Her Majesty has expressed a deep personal interest in the matter."

He lifted his eyes once again and looked directly at Holmes. Leaning over in his chair, he tapped Holmes gently on the arm. "A deep personal interest," he repeated. "And she mentioned you by name."

Holmes lowered his eyelids and nodded.

"Well then, that's settled," said Lord Randolph, rising. "I must be off." Holmes and Watson rose with him.

"You will have the full cooperation of the Home Office and Scotland

Yard, I have no doubt," Lord Randolph said to Holmes. "The Queen has been onto Salisbury, and Salisbury has been onto Matthews, and Matthews will see to it, never fear. And while your brother is quite correct in not sharing confidential government decisions with you, I believe that I, as someone who is no longer in the government, can tell you that you need not concern yourself too much with our friend Sir Charles Warren. I shouldn't be very much surprised if he were to receive a new appointment sometime soon. Sometime very soon and very far away."

He shook his head and smiled engagingly, the first time he had done so since joining their company. "Ah, Sir Charles, Sir Charles," he said with mock gravity. "His solution to every problem is a cavalry charge. My thirteen-year-old son at Harrow would approve; but then, he doesn't have much sense either. Good day, gentlemen. Don't bother, Mycroft, I'll see myself out."[44]

Mycroft Holmes, of course, had not stirred from his chair or had he given any indication he intended doing so. And even after Holmes and Watson resumed their chairs to join him, upon Churchill's departure, there was no conversation among them for several minutes, each being lost in his own thoughts. It was Mycroft finally who broke the silence.

"Interesting man, Randolph," he mused aloud. "One of the most remarkable men of our times. Could have done great things." He thought for a moment and then said, apropos of nothing: "Married to an American, you know – a great beauty, but unfortunately not terrible clever. I believe it was Lady Asquith who said, 'Had Lady Randolph been like her face, she could have governed the world.' Ha-ha."

Then a frown quickly overcame his face and he shook his head. "But poor Randolph. I fear for his health." He turned to Watson. "You took note of it too, I couldn't help but notice, Doctor."

"It was that obvious? Oh, dear."

"An occupational trait, nothing more – to the physician, everyone is a potential patient. I ascertained from the intensity of your facial expression that you were attempting to render a diagnosis – unconscious on your part, I'm sure."

Watson was no longer surprised at anything Mycroft ascertained. He merely nodded. "He's quite unwell. Impossible to know the cause without a complete examination, of course."

"Oh, no mystery there, I fear," Mycroft replied, placing a fat, well-manicured forefinger beside his nose. But he hurriedly changed the subject, not wanting to betray a confidence or dwell on something unpleasant. "Your glasses are empty. Oh, very well, Bledsoe, bring the decanter. My guests will not be departing so quickly after all."

The discussion that followed dealt mostly with details about the Whitechapel murders, the latest one in particular, and possible lines of inquiry to pursue. Unfortunately, those were pitifully few. Mycroft agreed with Holmes that in all probability not much could be done unless or until the murderer struck again. "This time perhaps we will be better prepared for him," said Holmes.

He and Watson departed a short while later, the Diogenes Club the poorer by two more sherries.

It was dark outside when they emerged on the street. The lamplighter had already been by and the reflection of the streetlights flickered against the white marble of the building's facade.

"You will have to go down to Dartmoor without me on Saturday," Holmes said to Watson as they descended the steps. "I'll follow as soon as I can."[45]

"You plan to take up the Whitechapel matter again at once, then?"

"Oh, I never put it down."

"What!" Watson stopped short and stared at him.

"Of course not. Did you think I'd let that insufferable tin soldier

Warren intimidate me? Chase me off like one of his Boers in South Africa? You must not think very highly of me."

"But... but what was that all about in there, then? Why did you make such a point at first of telling your brother you wouldn't work on the case?"

"I never!"

"What do you mean? I distinctly heard you tell him before Lord Randolph arrived that you were otherwise committed! I remember your words precisely!"

"Then your memory is faulty. I never used the word *otherwise*, merely *committed* – committed to assist Sir Henry Baskerville, which I am. I did not at any time tell him I had removed myself from the Whitechapel business, nor can I help it if he jumped to that conclusion."

"But certainly that is what you led him to believe."

Holmes shrugged and gave Watson a little smile. "Surely I am not responsible for my brother's beliefs."

"Holmes! You're quibbling!"

"Oh, yes," he agreed cheerfully.

Watson stared at him with a mixture of confusion and exasperation. "Would you kindly tell me what this is all about?"

Holmes laughed. "My dear chap, my beloved brother, Mycroft, is not the only member of my family with political acumen, no matter what he may think. The French blood of Richelieu flows in my veins as well as his, and I, too, know a thing or two about the manipulation of government bureaucrats and politicians. It does no good, for example, to tell those in authority they are responsible for a problem that must be rectified; they merely become defensive and do nothing. They must be led to discover it quietly on their own, then they are more likely to take remedial action. Mycroft's assistance was invaluable in that regard, as I knew it would be. He was the one who led them to their 'discovery.'"

"But how could you be so sure they would decide to remove Sir Charles Warren?"

"Oh, I wasn't. Even though that was the logical course of action for them to take, one can never depend on officialdom to do the logical. And I do not so flatter myself that the threat of withdrawing my humble services would have necessarily been enough to sway the balance against him."

"Well, then how did you manage it?"

"Oh, I didn't manage it, I left that to another. The most efficacious way to remove an obstacle in your path is to get someone else to do it for you."

"Mycroft, you mean?"

He shook his head. "Oh, no, not Mycroft. He would never jeopardize his position by becoming actively involved in something like this. He works behind the scenes, never onstage."

"Well, who, then?"

Holmes took Watson's arm and steered him toward the curb. He paused and gazed off into space theatrically. "I shall have to thank Her Majesty, should I ever again have the honor and good fortune of being favored with an audience. Lord Randolph Churchill is not the only one who pays calls to Windsor, Watson."

PART TWO

THE WHITECHAPEL HORRORS

HORRIBLE MURDER OF A
WOMAN NEAR COMMERCIAL ROAD

Another Woman Murdered
and Mutilated in Aldgate

One Victim Identified

Bloodstained Postcard
From "Jack the Ripper"

A Homicidal Maniac
or
Heaven's Scourge for Prostitution

– *The Evening News*,
Monday, October 1, 1888

Nine

SATURDAY, SEPTEMBER 29-MONDAY, OCTOBER 1, 1888

"I am not sure that of all the five hundred cases of capital importance
which I have handled, there is one which cuts so deep."
— *The Hound of the Baskervilles*

"Sir Henry Baskerville and Dr. Mortimer were ready on the appointed
day, and we started as arranged for Devonshire," wrote Dr. Watson
in the account that was to be entitled *The Hound of the Baskervilles*.

And also as arranged, Holmes remained behind in London, charging
Watson with the responsibility of protecting the young baronet from
whatever sinister force it was that took the life of his uncle on the moors
of Devon, instructing the doctor on how best to pursue the investigation
in his place until such time that he himself would be able to arrive on
the scene. Until then Watson was to communicate with him periodically
by mail: The post being swift and dependable, Holmes could count on
receiving his reports in Baker Street by the very next day. "I wish you
simply to report facts to me in the fullest manner possible," was his
parting directive, "and you can leave me to do the theorizing."

Watson, once embarked on this new adventure, keenly felt the weight of his responsibility and quickly put out of mind all thoughts of London and the events in Whitechapel, the tangled affairs of the city receding from his consciousness in almost direct proportion to his physical distance from them. And once surrounded by Devon's bleak and forbidding countryside and absorbed in the sinister goings-on in and around Baskerville Hall, London and all of its bustle, all of its worldiness and self-importance, seemed distant and remote, and all of its problems and all of its concerns became reduced in magnitude.

But not for long.

Two days after his arrival at Baskerville Hall he was to pick up a day-old copy of *The Times* and, in shock and in horror, read the following report:

MORE MURDERS AT THE EAST END

In the early hours of yesterday morning two more horrible murders were committed in the East End of London, the victim in both cases belonging, it is believed, to the same unfortunate class. No doubt seems to be entertained by the police that these terrible crimes were the work of the same fiendish hands which committed the outrages which had already made Whitechapel so painfully notorious.

The scenes of the two murders just brought to light are within a quarter of an hour's walk of each other, the earlier-discovered crime having been committed in a yard in Berner Street, a low thoroughfare out of the Commercial Road, while the second outrage was perpetrated within the city boundary, in Mitre Square, Aldgate.

The account continued on, detailed and starkly vivid, for almost three full columns extending the entire length of the page. Watson read it with growing dismay — dismay and a profound sense of helplessness and frustration, for the events he was reading about had occurred two nights before — indeed, on the night of the very day he had departed from London. And here he was, far from the scene of events, isolated in one of the loneliest, most out-of-the-way spots in England, many hours away by rail. The thought that Holmes might be engaged in feverish activity without him being there by his side to assist him, without even knowing what was going on, was simply intolerable to him.

Furiously, he flung the newspaper down and began pacing the room, only to snatch it up again to reread the account, which, of course, only added to his sense of anxiety and frustration. While he knew full well that being in London would change little, that his assistance to Holmes would be of minimal, perhaps even questionable, value; he also knew from past experience that his being there would in some small way be of comfort to Holmes: A settling influence. After all, his presence was something Holmes had come to depend upon — no matter how unlikely it was he would ever admit it.

"*He was a man of habits,*" Watson was to write elsewhere many years later, "*narrow and concentrated habits, and I had become one of them. I was like the violin, the shag tobacco, the old black pipe... When it was a case of active work and a comrade was needed upon whose nerve he could place some reliance, my role was obvious... I was a whetstone for his mind. I stimulated him. He liked to think aloud in my presence...*"[46]

With all of this going through his mind, Watson of course considered rushing to the village to wire Holmes and inquire whether he should return to London, but he immediately discarded the idea. He knew what Holmes's response would be, that for the moment he was more urgently needed in Devonshire and could best be of assistance if he remained there. It was the correct response of course; there could be no other, as Watson knew in his heart.

Still, the realization gave him little comfort, and he spent the better part of the day roaming the moors exploring the countryside, trying his best to follow Holmes's instructions to familiarize himself with the locals and with the lay of the land, trying his best to concentrate his attentions on the problem that lay before him. But despite his efforts, his thoughts kept wandering back to London, to Whitechapel, and, of course, to his friend in Baker Street.

Though Watson had no way of knowing it, of course, Sherlock Holmes was in Baker Street at that very moment, reading the very same article from *The Times*. His ribs ached, his face was bruised, he was in a black humor, and it is doubtful that even Watson's presence would have helped. To the contrary: Given the circumstances, it was just as well that Holmes was alone. Solitude was what he required now, time to lick his wounds, time to think. Time to systematically review the events of the previous few days and attempt to cull something from them that might be useful, something that might turn failure into success.

It was clear — all too abundantly clear — that he was dealing not only with a madman but with a fiendishly clever, highly resourceful individual who, along with everything else, had the devil's own luck.

All of Holmes's careful planning, all of his painstaking arrangements, had been to no avail. The man had escaped him. It had been a close thing, very close, but obviously not close enough: Failure was failure, whether it be by a whisker or a mile, and Sherlock Holmes was not a man who accepted failure with equanimity.

The Times had it accurately. The account of the night's events was well reported as far as it went, but then the correspondent did not have all the details — fortunately.

In the first-mentioned case the body was found in a gateway, leading to a factory, and although the murder, compared with the other, may be regarded as of an almost ordinary character – the unfortunate woman only having her throat cut – little doubt is felt, from the position of the corpse, that the assassin had intended to mutilate it. He seems, however, to have been interrupted by the arrival of a cart, which drew up close to the spot, and it is believed to be possible that he may have escaped behind the vehicle.

That is not quite the way it happened, but that wasn't the correspondent's fault. That is what he had been told by the police, and that is what Holmes had told them to say, or, rather, suggested they say – in the strongest possible terms.

Holmes let the newspaper fall to the floor and reached for his pipe. It had been a long night, an extraordinary night, one filled with tension and physical strain, though it had started out quietly enough.

He had been standing slouched in a dark corner of a packed public house in Commercial Road with a glass of porter in his hand. Even Watson would have had difficulty recognizing him, dressed as he was in the nondescript clothes of a dock worker, a cloth cap pulled low over his eyes, a cigarette dangling from the corner of his mouth. His disguise was simple but obviously effective; that no one bothered him or even regarded him was ample proof of that. He blended in perfectly with his surroundings, remaining virtually unnoticed among the regular patrons of the crowded, noisy pub: A gruff, coarse, boisterous lot given to quick laughter and sudden anger, both fueled by copious amounts of cheap gin and beer. Yet, as if there were an unwritten code among them, one's privacy, one's anonymity, was scrupulously respected, and he was left undisturbed with hardly a glance thrown his way. He said nothing to anyone and no one said anything to him. But no one within his sight remained unobserved, and no words that were spoken within his hearing remained unheard. This was the fifth pub in Whitechapel he had visited that night, the fifth dark, smoky corner he had appropriated, the fifth glass of porter he had held in hand all but untasted. The hour was late, but he was not tired. Nor had his senses dulled or his attention wandered. He was as acutely aware of everyone who came in and everyone who left, and every detail about them, as he had been many hours earlier when his vigil began.

On four previous occasions in four other pubs he had quietly departed the premises at a cautious distance behind four separate women, following them into the fog-shrouded streets. In one way or another, each of the women had borne a marked similarity to the victims of the killer. They were drabs, prostitutes. They were of the same approximate age, of the same general appearance, and in a vague but obvious way in the same desperate circumstances: They were poorly, shabbily dressed, down on their luck, hungry. They hadn't the price of a three-penny gin or a place to bed down for the night.

Staying in the shadows, he stalked each of them in turn, observing unseen as one after another they sauntered through the narrow streets until coming upon a likely "mark," and after negotiating a price, disappeared arm in arm with him into a darkened alley or behind a closed door. Each of the marks were also of a sameness, dressed in rough clothes of the sort that he himself was now wearing, all of them ostensibly native to the area, or at least at home in it, all of them poor. Holmes thought it unlikely that any single one of them would pose a threat to a woman. The worst any was likely to do was try to run off without paying. None of them, he knew, could be the man he was looking for. All were obviously of the working class, of the lowest social order. Only one smoked, and he a pipe. Two were the worse for drink and could hardly walk, and one, a seaman, had a limp and could walk only with difficulty. Most important – and this Holmes was most particular in observing – none appeared to be left-handed. Quite obviously none was the man he was looking for.

Holmes knew, of course, that the task he had undertaken was an impossible one. There were eighty thousand prostitutes in London by some estimates, and there was no way he could pick out from among them a potential victim, just as there was no way of knowing what night the killer would choose to strike again. It was a shot in the dark, nothing more; a feckless gamble, a challenge of the laws of probability. But it was not the only card he was playing, and he undertook what he knew to be a futile exercise not simply out of desperation (though there was an element of that involved), but as an alternative to waiting and doing nothing. He had met with Abberline, they had decided upon a strategy, their forces had been briefed and suitably deployed. It was not unlike a simple military exercise, which was how Scotland Yard looked upon it.

But to Holmes it was more like the blocking of a stage play: The script had been written, the actors chosen and assigned their roles, the scene was set, the rehearsals were over and done with. Now for him came the hardest part, for as director all he could do was wait in the wings for the curtain to rise, and temperamentally he was unsuited for that role. He far preferred to don a costume and tread the boards himself.

Whom was he looking for? What did the man look like? He would know that when he saw him. He knew he would know, it was an absolute certainty; there was not a doubt in his mind about it.

The outside door opened, the grimy chintz curtains covering the lower part of the front window fluttering in the draft, and in scampered a small molelike creature wrapped in a muffler.

From his vantage in the corner, through the crush of people, Holmes quietly observed the newcomer dart quick, furtive glances around the crowded pub, standing on tiptoe to peer over shoulders through the smoke, craning his neck to see. Spotting Holmes at last, he plunged into the crowd, using his arms in almost a swimming motion to make his way through. He did not look up at Holmes upon arriving at his side; indeed, he pointedly looked everywhere else but – his myopic little eyes darting this way and that, his head moving in quick nervous jerks, the eyes casting suspicious glances at everyone around him.

Holmes nudged him with an elbow. "That's quite enough, Squint," he murmured. "No one has noticed you, but if you keep that up, someone is bound to."

"I come fwom Wiggins, sor," the boy whispered stiffly out of the corner of his mouth. "'E send me to... to *report* – 'ats the word he tell me to use."

"And what is it that you have to report, Squint?"

"Well... nuffink, actually." He looked a little puzzled at this. "All's quiet, Wiggins say to tewll yer."

"All the lads have reported into him, then?"

"Aye, sor. Wiggins tell me to say all p'wesent 'n' corweckt, sor."

"Very good, Squint. Be off with you, then. Tell Wiggins that as planned, I'll be at the Ten Bells in an hour and if he needs to he can find me there."

"Aye, sor. Anythin' else, then?"

"Nothing at all. Just tell him to continue the watch."

"Aye, sor – 'tinue da wotch." With that and another furtive look around, little Squint was gone, enveloped once again by the crowd, the abrupt opening and closing of the street door indicating his departure.

The Irregulars were on the job, of course. Holmes fully expected to achieve better results from them than from members of the official police force, including those who were patrolling the streets in disguise.

The Irregulars not only knew the area well but were virtually invisible in it: As unnoticeable as rags in the corner, as the cobbles in the streets. Disguising policemen as locals, taking them out of uniform and dressing them in the garb of the working class, was all very well and good, and Holmes went along with the plan to do so, but he had limited faith in it. The inhabitants of Whitechapel were far too wily, too streetwise to fool easily. Most of them could recognize a "peeler" from the far end of a dark street and beyond, no matter how well disguised. But the Irregulars? They belonged, no subterfuge was required on their part, no feeble trickery. Their presence would go completely unnoticed, arousing no suspicions, causing no inhibitions. For work like this, they had no equal.

Another half hour passed, and Holmes considered leaving. It did not appear as though he were going to have any more success in this place than he had in any of the others. In any event, it was almost time for him to make his way to the next one on his list, the Ten Bells in Commercial Street.

The front door opened once again and he looked over, stealing a glance at the individual who now entered. He stiffened.

Slowly turning his head away, Holmes lifted the glass to his lips and took a sip of the dark, bitter porter, all the while keeping the newcomer at the very edge of his peripheral vision. The man – for it was indeed a man – was wearing a long, dark coat of some rough material and a deerstalker hat pulled low over his eyes, keeping the upper part of his face in shadow. The lower part, his mouth and chin, was hidden by a woolen muffler. But there was nothing sinister about his overall presence, nothing threatening; if anything he cut a rather ludicrous figure in the long, heavy coat and billed cap. The deerstalker was unusual headgear for the city, of course, being generally worn by a gamekeeper or hunter. But that in itself was not significant: Among the poor, articles of clothing were often acquired from jumble sales and dustbins, the castoffs of the more affluent. As to his occupation, he could have been anything – a coachman or messenger, a teamster, or common day laborer. But he was none of these things, that much was obvious to Holmes.

He continued to observe out of the corner of his eye as the man casually surveyed the barroom from just inside the door, not as if he were looking for someone, just merely looking.

From what Holmes could tell through the dark, smoky haze of the barroom, the fellow was of average height and young, in his late twenties or early thirties at most. He seemed to be clutching a parcel of some sort under his arm, a parcel made up of newspaper, neatly wrapped and tied with string. Holmes still could not see his face. It appeared as though he were going to some lengths to keep it at least partially hidden.

Holmes's hand tightened around his glass.

The man was looking in his direction. Holmes forced himself not to turn away – it would only attract the fellow's notice, not avert it.

Several seconds went by. The man was studying him, he could feel it. He tried to remain relaxed, maintaining what he hoped was a disinterested posture, willing his features to remain blank and expressionless, adopting what to all outward appearances was a fixed stare into space.

Sensing rather than seeing the man's head finally turn in another direction, Holmes now allowed his gaze to focus on him full bore. He still could not make out any distinctive features, for the man had now turned completely away and had his back toward him. He was no workingman, of that Holmes was certain. The fellow carried himself like a soldier, thought Holmes; there was no mistaking the set of those shoulders. But not a common soldier, not one from the ranks, for despite his mode of dress, his bearing was that of a gentleman. And he seemed to wear the overcoat uncomfortably, as would a man unaccustomed to wearing it. It was the kind of coat that could easily be purloined from a servants' hall, or taken from a peg in some cheap café or restaurant. Holmes narrowed his eyes; there was little doubt in his mind: The man did not belong, he did not fit. He was not whom he passed himself off as being.

Suddenly Holmes's view was blocked; he lost sight of the man in the crowd. He moved to one side and craned his neck slightly, but it did no good. He tried edging his way over in the other direction.

Still no good.

He put his glass down and began to sidle toward the front door, making a conscious effort to do so quietly, unobtrusively. It took some doing to maneuver through the packed barroom. Not having little Squint's advantage of being able to crawl and scamper betwixt and between, he had to worm his way through the thicket of elbows and shoulders that blocked his path. And it was made no easier by the need to do it inconspicuously.

He was managing with some success, had gotten more than halfway to the door, when without warning the crowd parted in front of him and he was startled to find himself barely an arm's length away from his quarry. And at that very instant the fellow turned and looked him full in the face.

It all happened so quickly, so very quickly that Holmes was taken completely by surprise. And it resulted in an unfortunate blunder on his part: He spun away, spun right away – an automatic, spontaneous reaction, purely involuntary on his part, which no amount of forethought could have prevented. And in the process of turning, he unintentionally jostled someone's arm – the arm of a man engaged in animated conversation with a neighbor – causing the man's drink to slosh over its glass. And that man, a burly, brutish figure, now turned on him angrily.

"'Ere, 'oo d'ye t'ink yer shovin' inta? Ye wasted me bloody grog!"

Holmes peered into the man's face — he could not help but peer into the man's face seeing that it was thrust so close to his own — a doughy, pallid, deeply pitted face with a blue-veined nose, blackened teeth, a twisted lip, and eyes that glared into his: Beady rat's eyes red-rimmed from drink and narrowed into belligerent slits. It did not seem likely that a simple apology would suffice, Holmes considered.

Reacting quickly, he twisted his own features into an insane, ugly glower and emitted a threatening rumble from the back of his throat, a terrifying animal sound. And in an instant the other man found himself confronted by a most menacing-looking character: A mean, dangerous bloke with a maniacal gleam to his eye. Consummate actor that he was, Holmes looked terribly convincing, for the other man now fairly gaped at him, his face filled with hesitation, indecision — with a glimmer of serious heartfelt doubt and reconsideration, of the possibility of reasonableness even. Holmes gave him no time to reconsider further. He pulled some loose coins from his pocket and flung them on a nearby table. "'Ere!" he growled in his best West India Docks cockney. "Now get out o' me fuckin' wa'ay!"

The coins scattered; several eager hands grabbed for them: Holmes, attention now diverted from him momentarily, did not tarry. Quickly he moved toward the exit and, not stopping to look behind him, slammed out through the door, his face still wearing its hideous snarl, as if daring anyone to block his path or impede his progress. But no one would risk interfering with the tall, sullen dockworker with the hair-trigger temper and the lunatic look, and he made his way into the street without further mishap.

Though he was breathing rapidly when he emerged through the

door, and every instinct screamed at him to break and run, he forced himself to maintain a measured step. Without even glancing over his shoulder, he ambled across the narrow street and proceeded to the opposite corner, disappearing around it with a great sigh of relief.

The night was dark; a light, drizzly fog that had fallen over the city earlier in the evening had turned much heavier, becoming what Londoners had taken to calling, with a mixture of brag and trepidation, a "London particular." Distant streetlights glowed eerily, casting dim sulfurous halos through the mist and doing nothing whatsoever to improve the visibility. The street was empty of both vehicular and pedestrian traffic, and what few sounds there were to be heard seemed distant and muffled. Holmes did not have to distance himself too many steps from the public house before being satisfied that he could no longer be seen by anyone who might have had an interest in his departure. He was certain that no one had followed him.

Crossing over to the other side of the street once again, he cautiously retraced his steps, staying close to the side of the buildings and remaining in deep shadow, the rope-soled shoes that he wore making no sound on the pavement. He stopped when he reached the corner and carefully peered around it. Across the way, on the opposite corner, the diffused glow that came from the pub's large front window and glass-paneled door washed the glistening cobbles ineffectually. From where he stood he could see the doorway quite plainly but as though through a veil, the haze was that thick. He could also see a short distance down the side street to his left, where he knew a rear exit from the pub let out. Pulling the wide collar of his pea jacket up around his ears, he settled down to wait.

His vigil was not a very long one. Hardly ten minutes had passed before something in the side street suddenly attracted his attention. What it was, he did not know. Whether it was a movement, or a muffled sound, or a trick of the fog, he could not be certain. There was a tall wooden gate there; that much he knew from an earlier reconnoiter. It led from a small yard where empty crates and beer kegs were stacked, and which the pub's rear exit emptied into. Though he wasn't sure, it was possible that what he saw or heard was the movement of the gate.

He resisted the temptation to investigate, but remained where he was in deep shadow, hardly daring to breathe, straining both his eyes and his ears in an effort to catch even the slightest sight or sound. There was definitely something there – a shape, a presence, the loom of a figure just slightly darker than the darkness around it. Or was he imagining it? He strained his eyes even harder. No, it was not his imagination. There was indeed something there.

Holmes pressed his back against the side of the building. It was an unnecessary precaution, he knew; he had the advantage of almost total invisibility, for there was no light behind him to outline his silhouette even faintly, and the shadows in which he stood were all but impenetrable. He had the further advantage given him by immobility. As long as he did not move or make a sound, it was most unlikely his presence would be detected. His only concern now was to make certain that this was indeed his quarry.

Suddenly the front door to the pub flew open and a wider swath of light splashed out onto the street. Three figures reeled through the door in a burst of laughter, paused briefly, and then, arm in arm, stumbled their way down the alley, fortunately in the opposite direction from where Holmes remained hidden. It was only a matter of a brief minute or two before they and the sound of their drunken hilarity were swallowed up in the fog and the street once again became quiet, still – ominously still.

Nothing moved.

Holmes remained motionless, outwardly calm but seething with impatience.

Assuming someone was there at all, was this indeed the man? he wondered. Was this the devil he sought? It took every ounce of self-control he possessed to keep from rushing into the street to seek him out.

Of course he knew he mustn't. He knew he had to wait. This man would not be caught by ordinary means. He was far too cunning for that.

Oh, he was insane, there was no doubt about that. But there was a method to his madness that transcended the madness itself, defying all human understanding. He was not just any killer, and he was not just any killer who killed with blood lust. He was clever and quick and highly resourceful; he plotted his every move. He was someone who took pleasure not only in the act itself, but in the planning of it, approaching it as an intellectual exercise, or a military one. It only followed that such an individual would want to – no, need to – flaunt his cleverness, prove to the world how truly ingeniously clever he was.

He had never known a man such as this, had never come into contact with someone who not only killed for the pleasure of it, the utter joy of it, but was driven to share that obscene joy with the world.

The note, postmarked London East Central, had arrived at the offices of the Central News Agency in Fleet Street earlier that week. Appropriately, it was written in red ink:

Dear Boss:

I keep on hearing the police have caught me, but they won't fix me just yet. I have laughed when they look so clever and talk about being on the right track. The joke about Leather Apron gave me real fits.

I am down on whores and I shan't quit ripping them till I do get buckled. Grand work, the last job was. I gave the lady no time to squeal. How can they catch me now? I love my work and want to start again. You will soon hear of me and my funny little games. I saved some of the proper red stuff in a ginger beer bottle over the last job, to write with, but it went thick like glue and I can't use it. Red ink is fit enough, I hope. Ha! Ha!

The next job I do I shall clip the lady's ears off and send them to the police, just for jolly, wouldn't you? Keep this letter back until I do a bit more work, then give it out straight. My knife's so nice and sharp, I want to get to work right away if I get a chance. Good luck,

Yours Truly,

Jack the Ripper[47]

Abberline had notified him within hours of the letter's receipt and, with the coercive powers of the Home Office behind him, of course had ordered that it be temporarily withheld from publication. It was one of hundreds, perhaps thousands[48] of similar pieces of mail that had poured into Scotland Yard and the newspaper offices, most of them all too obvious hoaxes, others less so but, on closer examination, hoaxes nonetheless. But there was something about this one that gave at least some of the police officials pause. And Holmes had to agree. There were certain features it contained that he found compelling. The first and most obvious was that in an attempt to disguise his handwriting, the author had penned the letter with the hand other than the one he normally used. The man was left-handed, there was no doubt in Holmes's mind about that.

Then there was the style of his prose, his conspicuous use of street vernacular, improper grammar, and even certain Americanisms such as *boss, fix me, quit* and *right away*. It was all obviously forced, an effort to mislead. He was no American. His use of the word *shan't* belied that idea, as did the phrase, *I shall clip the lady's ears off.* An American would have said, *I will* cut *the lady's ears off.*

And he was not the semi-illiterate he made himself out to be. If anything, he was a well-read individual, and widely read, no doubt with popular American literature on his bookshelf.

Some of the officials dismissed the letter outright, but Holmes wished to reserve judgment. It had the look and feel of being genuine, the smell of being genuine, and while he couldn't be absolutely certain about it, it struck a responsive chord in some indefinable way. For one thing, the letter displayed a flair for the dramatic, and that fit in nicely with Holmes's mental profile of the man. And the handwriting, though disguised, was to his practiced eye that of a highly erratic, even disturbed individual with intense, even uncontrollable emotions; it was the product of a chaotic mind, quick to anger, quick to take offense. The overemphasized capitals that he used revealed that he was vain and arrogant and loved being the center of attention. But most important, to Holmes's way of thinking, the letter told him that its author was not only clever, but considered himself thus. And, if he was indeed the man they sought, decided Holmes, that could be his undoing.[49]

Jack the Ripper indeed! Most fitting, thought Holmes. And very droll. Somewhat theatrical, but fitting nonetheless.

But was the author of that letter the man he was lying in wait for now? And was that man the killer? These were the questions presently uppermost in his mind. If this was the man, it was obvious he was challenging the police, taunting them, harboring as low an opinion of their skills as Holmes himself did.

Holmes had to admire his audacity. The bait he was dangling was irresistible. He was inviting them to take part in a hunt for the wiliest of all game, and he was offering himself up as the prey. How positively sporting. How sublime.

More time passed, more minutes went by. Still no movement, still no sound. And still Holmes waited.

Then suddenly a shadow appeared as if from nowhere, and a figure materialized in the middle of the street, tendrils of fog clinging to it, ghostlike and unreal. It was as if an apparition had come through a solid wall, and the suddenness of its appearance, even though Holmes was half expecting it, made him almost start in surprise.

But still he did not move. He dared hardly breathe. He remained rigid in his place of concealment and watched as the figure emerged from the fog and walked slowly down the middle of the street.

It was his man.

Holmes exhaled slowly.

Soundlessly, the figure came closer, and closer yet. Finally he reached the corner directly opposite, no more than twenty feet away. He stopped and looked up and down the street – as if looking for someone, or as if wanting to make certain there was no one there to be seen.

After some little while he crossed the intersection diagonally and sauntered into the other street. There he paused once again, this time just opposite the front entrance to the pub. Again he looked in all directions. Then, apparently deciding not to tarry any longer, he began walking. Slowly, hesitatingly. Then he picked up his pace, his step becoming more certain. Now with purposeful stride, his footsteps sharp against the cobbles, he faded once again into the fog. Clearly his manner suggested he had a destination in mind.

Holmes waited a brief interval until well after the shadowy figure had receded into the mists, until the sound of his footsteps began to recede as well. Then Holmes cautiously emerged from his hiding place and began to follow.

It was not a difficult task. If he remained a reasonable distance behind his quarry, if he did not get too close, he felt confident he would not be detected. The fact that he in turn could not see his quarry was for the moment of little concern to him. He was content to place his dependence more on his sense of sound than sight: As long as he could hear the man's footsteps, all would be well. And the footsteps were sharply clear against the wet cobblestones, a steady, systematic gait. The sound of them was strangely comforting, not unlike the ticking of a clock or the rhythmic beating of a heart.

But of course such fanciful notions never occurred to Holmes. He devoted his full attention to the task at hand, allowing no extraneous thoughts to interfere with his concentration. He maintained the steady pace of the man in front of him, staying close to the sides of the buildings and avoiding the dim pools of light emanating from the occasional street lamps he encountered, sometimes crossing from one side of the street to the other in order to do so.

A principal concern was to avoid unseen obstacles. Piles of debris were to be found as a matter of course in the gutters and against the sides of the decaying buildings that lined the street. And every once in a while he passed the huddled, silent forms of derelicts sleeping in stairwells or against the building walls. These he detoured around, and took special pains not to rouse.

The going was not easy. The pavement was slippery underfoot and in places even treacherous, despite his rope-soled shoes. To stumble, to slip, to collide with something unseen might create a noise that would carry far in the fog.[50]

His concentration focused as it was, Holmes soon lost all track of time, and because of the dense fog he was no longer completely certain where he was. He knew the direction in which he was heading had remained reasonably constant, and he knew in a general way what streets lay before him, but the darkness and the fog effectively kept him from defining his precise whereabouts. Obviously his quarry had no such problem. The man seemed to be pursuing his course with total confidence, and his familiarity with the maze of streets and twisting alleys was apparent.

At the moment Holmes hardly cared where he was. His only concern was the sound of the footsteps ahead of him. They had stopped.

Holmes halted in his tracks.

He simply froze in mid-stride, not daring to move. He remained totally motionless for several seconds. Then slowly, ever so slowly, he lowered himself down on his haunches. He waited for several seconds more, listening intently. Then, crablike, he inched his way over to the side of the nearest building. There again he waited, straining his ears for the slightest noise.

In an instant he heard a sound, a sharp, scratching noise, and then another. Then a faint pinprick of light appeared through the fog. The man had struck a lucifer, a match. And though Holmes could not see him do it, he sensed he was lighting a cigarette. The pinprick of light disappeared and the footsteps resumed, and Holmes rose from his crouched position and once again took up the pursuit.

Several more minutes went by, and the pace continued unabated. Then, with no warning at all, the sound of the footsteps suddenly became less distinct and then faded completely. It was as if a tap, a faucet, had been turned. One minute there was sound, the next minute nothing.

Holmes rushed forward, his heart racing. Flinging caution away, he all but broke into a run. Coming to the intersection of two alleys, he abruptly halted, jerking his head this way and that in a desperate effort to catch the slightest noise. For a moment all he could hear was his own heartbeat. He took a deep breath and held it. He strained to hear.

There it was.

His man had merely turned the corner. The sound of his footsteps was receding off to the right, the cadence once again steady and reassuring. Holmes shook his head and breathed deeply and once again took up the pursuit.

The way had become narrower and winding, the route now twisted and turned and he lost all sense of direction in the fog and darkness.

Within a short while a soft yellow glow from up ahead told him that he was approaching a wider street, a major thoroughfare, and he soon found himself at the intersection with it.

The street he now entered was lined on either side with lampposts on every corner, hazy orbs of light receding into the fog in both directions. Though the street lamps resulted in a slight improvement in visibility, it was very slight indeed, and for the moment he had no idea where he was.

But that was a secondary problem.

His primary problem was that the man he was following was nowhere to be seen, and the sound of his footsteps could no longer be heard.

He had lost him.

Ten

SATURDAY, SEPTEMBER 29-SUNDAY SEPTEMBER 30, 1888

"There is nothing more stimulating than a case where
everything goes against you."
— *The Hound of the Baskervilles*

S herlock Holmes was at a total loss. The darkness and fog, the thick
yellow-gray fog — so thick he could feel it against his skin and even
smell it — had not only swallowed up the man he was following, caused
him to disappear completely, but had caused Holmes to become utterly,
hopelessly disoriented.

It was a wasteland all about him, an amorphous, dreamlike
wasteland, the street devoid of life, as if the fog had not so much
enshrouded everything as devoured everything. In every direction
there was emptiness, simply emptiness: No movement, no sound, no
shape or form. There was only the fog, pervasive and all-encompassing.
It was what silence looks like, he thought.

The feeble glow of the gaslights on the street corners did not help
to penetrate the vapors; they merely tinged them a sickly yellow.

Where before the visibility was a scant half dozen paces, now, on this well-lighted main street, it was perhaps twice that – no appreciable improvement at all really, because for all practical purposes he was still all but blind. To take a few steps in one direction or the other was to step into a void, swirling and vacuous. It was to walk off the very face of the Earth.

Straining to see, willing himself to see, he could just make out the dark, looming presence of what appeared to be a church across the way, but it took some concentrated study before he recognized it as St. Mary's. And it was only then that he realized he was standing at an intersection with Aldgate High Street, which he knew led into Whitechapel Road, which had to be the street that receded off into the mists to his left. Well, at least now he was able to get his bearings.

Holmes's knowledge of the streets of London was extensive, and he had gone to special pains earlier in the day to reexamine at length a detailed street map of the Whitechapel district to refresh his memory of it, so he had a vivid picture of the area in his mind.[51] And he was well aware of the options he was now faced with: all too many. The man he was following could have taken any one of several routes before losing himself in the fog. The corner of Aldgate High Street, where Holmes now stood, was not a simple four-way intersection but the confluence of several streets and alleyways, all going off in many directions, a disordered spiderweb of streets that twisted and turned without logic and seemingly without purpose. The streets of Whitechapel dated from medieval times and had not been laid out with any rational thought behind them – they merely happened.

Reviewing his mental image of this maze, Holmes finally made up his mind, deciding on what route to take more out of desperation than conviction. He crossed over to the other side of Aldgate High Street and made toward St. Mary's Church, a brooding, grim presence in the mists. He hurried past the church without a glance, his pace quickening now that he had committed himself to a destination, and turned into Charlotte Street, little more than a narrow passage located just beyond the church, almost missing it in the fog though he knew it was there. Once again he found himself cloaked in darkness. There were no street lamps here, and the only illumination was the murky, evanescent glow from behind him. Mindful that his silhouette would be outlined against even that feeble trace of light, he kept close to the sides of the buildings, clinging to what little protection they might provide should the man he was pursuing be waiting for him up ahead. He could not discount that possibility, the possibility that he, the hunter, had become the hunted, that his quarry might have somehow become aware he was being followed and was now lurking in the shadows waiting for *him* to appear.

With that thought in mind, Holmes became doubly alert for any sound, any movement, any obstruction in his path. But there was nothing to impede his groping progress, and no one lurking about to cause him any alarm.

Before long he spotted a patch of brightness up ahead, a hazy light seemingly suspended in the void. He breathed easier. It was exactly where he expected it to be, and he was drawn to it inexorably, like a moth to a flame. As he got closer, the glow became more distinct and he could make out the veiled outline of the public house he knew would be there, the light coming from a soot-blackened globe suspended over the doorway. From the outside the place looked very much like the one he had departed not so long ago: Decrepit, leaning in upon itself tiredly, the single large window looking out onto the street streaked with grime and rendered all but opaque. Holmes knew without trying that there was little he would be able to see by peering through it.

Just across from the pub's entrance was a convenient doorway set back from the street, and he nestled into it gratefully. It was as good a vantage point as he could hope for, and it provided him with a place of seclusion while he decided on his next move.

The problem that now faced him was a simple one, but if there was a simple solution, it escaped him. He knew that this public house was the closest one from the intersection where he had lost his man. It followed that it was the next obvious place for him to come. But if the man was indeed inside as Holmes prayed he was, it would be foolhardy to enter behind him. Holmes would be spotted the instant he walked through the door. He had not the time nor the ready means to alter his appearance once again, allowing him to adopt yet another persona. He berated himself for not foreseeing this eventuality and preparing for it. It was a rule of life of his that if one was prepared, it – whatever *it* might be – was less likely to happen.

The wisest course of action – perhaps the only one – was to wait for the man to emerge, if he was in there at all. But if Holmes's conclusion was wrong, if the man was not inside but had made for some other more distant destination, then valuable time was being wasted, time that would be better spent even wandering aimlessly through the streets in an effort to stumble upon him once again, no matter how futile that effort might seem. There was a risk involved either way, but in neither way did the risk appear justified.

He stood there for several minutes, trying to make up his mind. Then suddenly the door of the pub opened and the decision was made for him. Out stepped the figure of a slim, pinched-faced ragamuffin, the sight of whom gave joy to his heart.

It was one of Wiggins's band of street arabs, hands burrowed deep in pockets, narrow shoulders hunched against the chill and dampness. Undersized and no doubt undernourished, the boy was wearing a ragged cloth cap several sizes too large that would have dropped over his eyes without fail had his ears not been fortuitously prominent.

Holmes watched as the boy looked up and down the street several times before finally crossing over, glancing over his shoulder all the while as if concerned that he might be followed, unwittingly choosing a path that was taking him right past Holmes's place of concealment.

Holmes, keeping one eye on the front door of the pub, waited until the boy had gone right past him, was actually a few steps beyond but still only an arm's length away, then reached out and grabbed him, in one swift motion pulling him back into the confined space of the doorway and placing a hand over his mouth to prevent an outcry. "Gently now, gently!" he whispered urgently, holding the panicking child tightly. "You know who I am. I won't hurt you."

The boy, craning his neck around to look at him, his eyes huge with fright, ceased his struggles at once, his legs almost buckling under him, he was that relieved. Holmes took his hand away from the child's mouth. "Cor, blimey! Is that you, Mr. 'Olmes?"

Holmes released him, and the boy slumped back against the wall and ran a trembling hand over his mouth. "Cor, oy like to foul meself, oy did." His voice quavered. "Ya gave me one bloody fright, guv!"

"Tell me your name."

"I'm Solly. They calls me Solly the Slip."

"Is he in there, Solly? The man whose description you were given? Did you see him in there?"

"Aye, that oy did, Mr. 'Olmes," came the hoarse reply. "I was jist on me wa'ay to find Wiggins to let 'im know. The bloke walked in boldly as you please, 'e did — not three minutes ago. Oy spotted 'im ryght off. 'E's wearin' a long ulster an' a deerstalker 'at an' a scarf 'at cuvvers 'is face, an' 'e's got long mustachios an' strynge oyes 'at gives ya a chill just to look at 'em." He stopped and took a breath and looked out into the street. "Oy was runnin' off to fetch Wiggins at St. Mary's Station when ya grabs me." His thin shoulders began to shake uncontrollably.

"Gawd, oy t'ought me gyme was h'up, oy did." He started to sob.

Holmes reached over and squeezed his shoulder, then awkwardly put an arm around him. "It's all right, Solly, it's all right," he said softly. "There's a brave lad."

The boy wiped his eyes with the back of his hand and snuffled loudly, manfully, holding back the flow of tears.

Holmes reached into his pocket. "Here, take this," he said brusquely but not unkindly. "A little something extra. You've earned it."

The boy snuffled again and nodded, placing the coin in his own pocket with a quick, almost furtive motion, as if fearful this toff with his strange ways and stranger habits would change his mind and snatch it back again.

Holmes pulled him deeper into the doorway and whispered urgently into his ear: "Now, listen carefully. This is what I want you to do..."

When he was finished, he made the boy repeat the instructions aloud. Then, with a parting pat on the shoulder, he sent him scurrying off on his errand. St. Mary's Station, where Wiggins was posted, was not far off, and even in the fog little Solly the Slip, knowing the area intimately, would be able to get there in practically no time at all.

Once again Holmes settled down to wait, this time feeling somewhat better pleased with himself, but not so pleased that he forgot to give thanks to whatever saint it was that watched over the fortunes of bumbling consulting detectives. He was lucky and he knew it, and luck was not something he normally gave countenance to.

Holmes again lost track of time during this renewed vigil of his. He had no idea how long he had been standing in the doorway — it could have been twenty minutes or an hour, for there was not enough light for him to see his watch by. But at least the fog had dissipated to a great extent while he lingered, a soft breeze having come from nowhere, leaving the street around him still in darkness, to be sure, but no longer in its shroud of almost total invisibility.

He did not know whether this would prove to be a blessing or a curse, for if he could see, he could be seen.

But it was not in his nature to concern himself with matters over which he had no control: He knew it to be a fruitless exercise. He would manage one way or the other, whatever the situation, having absolute confidence in his ability to adapt to changing conditions.

But this constant waiting, this lurking about in the shadows, was exceedingly wearing. It was not the physical discomfort so much – that he could bear. It was the tedium, the forced inactivity that was most difficult: The inability to keep his brain occupied.

Given the circumstances, he could not help but allow his mind to wander, conjuring up thoughts about this man upon whose pleasure he awaited. Was it not monstrous, he thought, that this single individual, this creature, had precipitated the greatest manhunt England had ever known, and had caused a surge of fear unequaled in modern times – not simply fear, but a phenomenon entirely new to his experience: Mass hysteria.

It was as if a medieval plague had broken out anew, or a kind of contagion hitherto unknown to modern science: A strain of universal insanity that seemed to be spreading through the populace like an epidemic of smallpox or influenza. Women everywhere were afraid to walk the streets unescorted. Men took to going about armed; a brisk business was being done in weighted walking sticks. Foreigners, and those who were perceived as such, were set upon for no reason by angry crowds. Jews and Gypsies, always the first to bear the brunt of unreasoning fears and invariably the blame for universal ills, were being denounced and attacked in the streets. While politicians in Parliament decried police inefficiency and government inaction, ministers in their pulpits and orators on Hyde Park Corner bemoaned the erosion of traditional moral values, and the editorial writers of the press vied for the distinction of printing the most hyperbolic hyperbole. The man had become the devil incarnate, a symbol of all that was wrong with society, a metaphor for the immorality, the utter depravity that had permeated English life.

The press had taken to calling the period the "autumn of terror." In this instance Holmes wondered if they were guilty not of exaggeration but understatement. Terror had indeed descended upon the city — descended upon it like the fog, affecting everyone, drawing across class lines, clouding judgment and reason and good English common sense.

Holmes almost felt sorry for the man. An imaginative lawyer, he mused sardonically, could probably come up with reasonable grounds for a slander suit in his behalf. He was being made out to be a sort of generic bogeyman, both the cause of and depository for all that was wrong, sick, evil, and ugly in the world. Events which bore not the slightest resemblance or relationship to his outrages were being attributed to him without discrimination.

Only that morning, while stopping at the neighborhood newsagent's, Holmes had eavesdropped on a conversation between two elderly gentlemen, a conversation that both amused and troubled him greatly. One had asked the other as they picked through the periodicals if he had heard of any new developments in the Whitechapel case.

"Well," the other gentleman replied portentously, "there is the matter of the severed arm."

"Severed arm?"

"Yaas," drawled the other. "Seems that about a fortnight ago a portion of someone's anatomy washed up on the foreshore of the Thames off Pimlico. It was a human arm, severed above the shoulder, armpit still attached."

"My word!"

"Indeed. They rushed it off to Millbank Street, where it was examined by a surgeon with some experience in limbs of one sort or another, and he gave it as his opinion that it was the right arm of a woman, and that it had been in the water for some two or three days. The police were unable to decide if another murder had been committed or if the arm was placed in the water as a sort of prank by some medical student. There was something about this in *The Times* around then – are you quite certain you didn't see it?"

"Mmm, no – missed it, I fear."

"Well, it remains a mystery still. And it gets better! – or worse, actually. It seems that some workmen digging the foundations for the New Scotland Yard headquarters on the Thames Embankment came upon a torso. Just the torso, mind you, nothing else – no arms, legs, or head. Altogether a rather revolting sight, I shouldn't wonder."

"Mmm, good Lord, yes."

"Some police surgeon got wind of it, popped in at the mortuary for a look, and announced: 'I have an arm which will fit that!' And would you believe? They brought the thing around and it was a perfect fit – an absolute perfect fit! Now, there's a pretty puzzle for you."

"The man's a fiend!" said the other gentleman with some heat. "Whoever he is, he's certainly not the product of an English public school, I can tell you."[52]

To Holmes, in recalling the conversation, the real puzzle was how a sizable portion of the city's population – decent and compassionate people all – could go about their daily lives knowing so little about the appalling conditions of the poor in their midst. Though few in the affluent West End of London knew it, bodies (and portions of bodies) washed up from the Thames almost every day, many of them the victims of crime, to be sure, but most merely the victims of poverty. Life was cheap in the East End, and if life was cheap, why should death be held any dearer? Wasn't it far more practical and much less expensive to carry the dead to the river or a convenient building excavation than to the undertaker?

Yet the two elderly gentlemen knew nothing of this and would have been shocked and highly indignant if so informed. It was more comfortable, less disturbing, to believe that every unexplained death in the East End was caused by a maniacal killer on the loose rather than by society's own ignorance, insensitivity, and indifference.[53]

Holmes tensed in the doorway, his reverie suddenly interrupted. Across the way the front door of the pub had opened and someone was emerging into the street. In the light of the gas lamp over the entrance, Holmes could see clearly who it was. He smiled grimly. "Ah, the game," he said to himself softly. "The game."

Once again he took up the pursuit. There was no time to wait for the official police reinforcements he had sent for. He had misgivings about that in any event. Too many heavy-footed policemen in the vicinity – no matter how well disguised or hidden – would be more of a hindrance than a help. Yet, he had felt he was duty-bound to have little Solly inform Abberline of his whereabouts – but not until after Wiggins had been located and the other Irregulars were sent to take up positions in the surrounding streets. Their deployment would serve as insurance, just in case he was to lose the man yet again. But he had no intention of doing so, not this time. This time he would cling to him like – like jelly to toast. This time he would never allow him out of his sight, not for an instant.

But it was not that easy. He found that he had to remain much farther behind him than before. The fog had all but disappeared, and even though the night was still dark and the streets poorly illuminated, it was necessary for him to maintain even greater precautions than he had earlier. He was tiring now. The tension was beginning to take its toll and he knew it. It meant that he must be even more alert, more cautious; a mistake now – a fall, a stumble, a sudden sound – and all might be lost. And he might never have this opportunity again.

The man set off at a steady pace, more rapid than before, as if a sense of urgency had overcome him, as if he were becoming desperate.

Holmes had no trouble keeping up the pace. To the contrary, he had to restrain himself from rushing headlong after the man and getting too close. A careless move at this point could ruin everything, and he knew it, but it still took every bit of self-control that he possessed to hold back.

Holmes was the most patient of men when he had to be – an acquired virtue, not one that came naturally to him – but even his patience had its limits, and at this juncture it was rapidly approaching them.

Fortunately, the man he was following reached his destination before his forbearance gave way entirely. His quarry simply turned a corner and was there, and it was as if a stage-setting had been prepared for his coming.

The scene, to Holmes's eye, was perfect, absolutely flawless. It appealed deeply to his sense of the theatrical: A narrow, darkened street, a soft haze, damp cobblestones glistening in the light of a single street lamp. And beneath the vaporous light, leaning casually against the lamppost as if posed, the figure of a woman silhouetted dramatically against a backdrop of dilapidated buildings, amorphous pallid shapes in the haze.

Then suddenly, as if a gauze curtain had been raised or a switch thrown, the haze dissipated and the square was bathed in bright moonlight. The transformation was startling. It was almost too perfect, a touch too melodramatic for Holmes's fastidious tastes, as if contrived by a second-rate designer of scenic settings, unimaginative in the extreme.

The man slowly approached the woman. The woman reached up and preened her hair suggestively. The man lighted a cigarette, a wisp of smoke curling up toward the gas lamp. Eye contact was made, silent words exchanged. Moves were performed as if part of a ritual pantomime. It was like some fantastic tableau, a living, breathing portrait.

Holmes waited in the wings and watched.

Eleven

SUNDAY, SEPTEMBER 30, 1888

"From the position in which the body was found, it is believed that the moment the murderer had got his victim in the dark shadow near the entrance to the court he threw her to the ground and with one gash severed her throat from ear to ear."
– *The Times*, October 1, 1888

Time and all motion seemed to come to almost a standstill, as if somehow retarded or restrained by some inexplicable preternatural force. It was like being part of a dream in which every move is made with unnatural lumbering slowness, every gesture separate and distinct from every other, painfully exaggerated, ponderously heavy, all so very unreal.

But it was not a dream and it was not unreal: It was stark reality and all the more terrifying because of it.

Holmes watched from his place of concealment as the man he had been following took the woman's arm and coaxed her around the corner into a courtyard off the street, just out of view. He waited a few seconds, then followed cautiously behind.

A gateway marked the entrance to the courtyard, and he paused across from it momentarily to make certain his presence had remained undetected, then hurried to the other side of the street. Keeping to the shadows, he inched his way forward until finally reaching a point where he could go no farther without running the risk of being seen. He was reluctant to leave the shadows until the last possible moment.

In any case, the courtyard was in total darkness and it was impossible to see into it. He found that he was clenching his jaw so tightly that his teeth hurt, and his knees were trembling with suppressed excitement.

Suddenly there was a sound that caused him to stiffen. It was a choked-off scream – not so much a scream as a muffled, gurgling protest. It was a sound that made his blood run cold.

He started to run. He hurtled through the gateway and into the courtyard and came up short, his heart pounding against his ribs. It was darker than black: The darkness was utterly impenetrable. He stood still as could be, trying to quiet his breathing, straining to catch the merest sound.

He started. There was something there, he was certain: There was movement and a faint, barely perceptible scraping or scuffling sound perhaps. Yes, there was definitely movement. And there was the specter of a shape looming darker than the darkness around it.

He was on the verge of calling out, had even opened his mouth to do so, when a sudden noise from close behind him caused him to whirl around in surprise.

He heard the sharp sounds of hooves on the pavement, and a horse neighed from somewhere close by. From out of the darkness there was a yell, a high-pitched, guttural yell. Then something hurtled past him from the other direction and he was shoved aside with such stunning force that the breath was knocked from his body. He caught just a glimpse of a heavily cloaked figure charging past. Was that the glint of knife blade, or had he simply imagined it?

He had no time to dwell on the question. Several things happened at once: It was as if a floodgate had burst open. There was a confusion of sounds, a muffled clamor of dissimilar noises: Hurried footsteps, hoofbeats, the neighing of a horse, the creak of wagon timbers, the scrape of ironclad wheels against the cobbles.

There was a startling flash of light. There was an outcry. There was a frenzied movement of shapes, of rushing currents. There was a horror-stricken face that suddenly appeared from nowhere and just as quickly disappeared. There was a garble of voices: Many angry, frightened, excited voices. There were shouts, more flashes of light, reeling forms. Then there were other faces, faces all around him, disembodied faces, bearded faces, all with wild eyes and open mouths and all emitting horrible, unintelligible animal sounds. There was jostling, a surge of pushing and shoving. There was the smell of sweat, of unwashed bodies, a smell of fear. There was a glancing blow, and something stung his ear. There was an arm around his throat. There was a blow to his shoulder, another to his ribs. Something was dragging him down. He was being pulled in several directions at once and pummeled. His legs give out from under him, and he was forced to the pavement, a heavy weight on his chest. His face was ground into the muck of the street. He felt a blow to his kidney; he felt a kick to his ribs. His breath was being crushed out of him. He found himself struggling desperately, now in a panic, flailing and kicking out. He was being pinioned, smothered; his strength was giving out. He was desperate for air. A single breath. A single suck of sustenance.

A sudden sharp blow to the side of his head brought curious relief: A flash of brightness, an explosion of light that seemed to burst in his brain, and he felt himself sliding, slipping, easing away. Then there was darkness, a darkness of a sort — a grayish, deep-violet darkness with streaks of vivid yellow and orange and bright green flashing through it, and the shouts, the noise, the tumult, the frenzied whirlpool of confusion receded off into the distance. And as he slipped further and further away, as the flashes of color began to fade and diminish in intensity, his last conscious thought was how peaceful it was, how very, very calm and peaceful and mercifully quiet.

His first conscious thought, his first awareness of being, was not one of pain — the pain would come later — not one of confusion or disorientation, but one of annoyance, extreme irritation. Then he became aware that he was being roughly handled, pushed, and shoved about. A bright light shone into his eyes. It was unbearable. He tried turning away from it, but he could not, and no matter how tightly he clenched his eyelids, he could not shut it out. The searing, invasive brightness seemed to penetrate his brain.

Then came the pain. His head was bursting with it. His shoulder burned with it. There was pain in his ribs and in his side. One of his legs ached badly. His whole body felt sore — sore and twisted, bruised and battered. He felt as if he had been pounded and pummeled by some fiendish apparatus that had swallowed him, ingested him, and disgorged him.

To ease the pain required movement, but when he tried it he discovered that it only caused more pain. There was so much of it, and from so many sources, that he decided he was better off unconscious and found himself trying to regain it. But in the end curiosity won him over: He was curious to find out what brought on the pain.

It was this curiosity that made him finally force his eyes to open, made him strain to see. But it was futile. The light was like fire, like sharp, burning needles in his brain. It shone directly in his eyes, causing stabs of exquisite pain. Even a raised arm to ward it off did no good. To the contrary, the movement only made him more aware of the other agonies, so he made no protest when the arm fell again, which it seemed to do of its own accord. It was probably this act and the resulting sharp shock of agony that it caused him that brought about full consciousness finally. But it was no godsend.

He became aware once again of faces in front of him and of voices around him, of pungent odors, of stale sweat and urine. Not his own, he fervently hoped. The closest face, once his mind cleared sufficiently for him to distinguish it, was that of homely, steel-eyed officialdom. Beneath the peak of a policeman's helmet there was a most impressive bulbous nose involved, and Holmes in his joy would have reached out and kissed it had he not feared that the probable consequences of such an act would have been the infliction of further pain.

"'Ere!" said a voice of authority. "Bring the blighter to 'is feet." And he felt himself being lifted upright by several rough and all-too-willing hands. The maneuver caused such ache to his head that he almost lost consciousness again. A wave of dizziness left him wobbling: His legs were not his to command, and he was grateful for the support on either side of him. Not as grateful, perhaps, as he would have been had they allowed him to lower himself once again to a prone position.

"You've got some h'explainin' to do, mate," said the voice of authority. "What's your name, then? That'll do for a start!"

Holmes tried shaking his head to clear the dizziness, but that was a major mistake.

"Give me a moment, won't you?" he heard a voice say, and then realized with a start of recognition that it was his own, the sound of it was that strange to his ears.

"C'mon, who are ya?" said another voice, angry and menacing in tone. "Who the hell are ya?"

Holmes tried to take his head in his hands, but his arms were being held in a viselike grip. He shut his eyes and winced.

"All in due time, my good man," he said with some difficulty. "First you will have to allow me to ascertain what I am, or if I am indeed."

"Huh!" exclaimed another voice in the Greek chorus. "Sounds like a proper toff, 'e does."

"I'll 'andle this," said the voice of authority. "Now, back off, the lot of ya, and let me ax the questions."

The light suddenly flashed in Holmes's eyes once again, and he flinched from it.

"Awright now, who are ya?"

"Constable, if you will just lower your bull's-eye so it is out of my eyes, I will be more than willing to identify myself. But first you must send for Detective Inspector Abberline, who will vouch for me, I am sure. And for God's sake, fetch someone to attend to that poor woman!"

At that there was another outcry of angry voices, and a babble of unintelligible tongues, which Holmes couldn't begin to understand. A fist was waved in his face.

"Poor woman, is h'it? Poor woman? A lot ye'd know about that, ya murderin' fiend!"

"Stan' back! Stan' back! H'all o' ya, now. Get back or I'll take the lot o' ya in charge!"

It suddenly occurred to Holmes in his semi-stupor that he was in no small amount of danger: All that stood between him and a lynch mob was this single, unarmed minion of the law.

The human brain works in mysterious ways and on many different levels at once, even (or perhaps especially) when under the severest of pressures, and Holmes, despite his pain, despite the realization of the danger he was in, was able to view his situation with detachment, with something approaching total equanimity. It was a mental process which, considering the circumstances, struck him as being unusual in the extreme: On one level he was marveling over the fact that he was still alive; on another he was examining the very real possibility that it might not be for long; and on still another he couldn't help but contemplate the irony of it all, should he, rather than the man he was pursuing, end up at the end of a hangman's noose. It was a circumstance not without one or two distinct points of interest, he decided – a situation which, though disconcerting, was surely also somewhat... droll.

Then, with sublime irrelevance, another thought suggested itself to him: Poor old Watson, he mused, will be positively beside himself.

But then came deliverance. He was saved, if not in the nick of time, surely within not more than two or three nicks. Rescue came in the form of reinforcements of the Metropolitan constabulary. Within seconds the courtyard was swarming with helmeted men in blue, bull's-eye lanterns flashing and truncheons at the ready. Within minutes he was not so much escorted as carried to a waiting horse-drawn conveyance, shoved inside with two burly constables for company, and carted off into the night, his world pitching and swaying around him.

His most vivid, most lasting memory of the events of that night was to be the eerie scene half viewed through the bars of the small rear window of the police wagon, a neatly framed visual image, grotesque and phantasmagorical, that could have been a depiction of Dante's vision of the nether regions, a painting by Hieronymus Bosch: Flashing lanterns on the cobbles of the street and on the brick walls that lined it, the light like stabs in the darkness; an excited, disorganized milling about of frightened humanity; and the faces, angry faces, pale, terrified faces, receding off into a black void, leaving in his mind a lasting, indelible imprint.

A gentle but capable hand dabbed persistently at his forehead with a cloth sopped in something cold and stinging that made him wince at every touch and caused his eyes to tear. A large overly stuffed bosom in a starched white apron stood stiffly at his elbow, basin in hand, the face above it round, well-fed, and uncompromisingly plain, its features permanently fixed in an expression of stern disapproval. Individuals who engage in street brawls, the expression clearly said, deserve what they get.

The hospital examining room was very bright and very white and smelled strongly, overpoweringly, of carbolic and whatever else hospitals always smell of. Holmes only hoped that it wasn't what was being applied to his face.

"Mmm," the doctor stated authoritatively – a diagnosis, in Holmes's opinion, which was calculatingly vague enough to cover any possibility ranging from total recovery to expiration at any moment. It did little to instill greater confidence on his part in the acumen and sagacity of the medical profession.

However, that was not to be the young practitioner's last word on the subject. A good diagnostician, after all, must take a stand – right, wrong, or otherwise. "Purely superficial," he murmured. The words were spoken half to himself, as if he were not quite certain he was prepared to share that conclusion with the rest of the world as of yet. But, in for a penny, in for a pound, he apparently decided. "Yaas, mostly mild abrasions," he stated, his tone now filled with growing confidence. "Nothing at all to concern ourselves about."

"How very reassuring," said Holmes dryly.

"I am a trifle troubled about the ribs, however." He poked a finger at the region in question and Holmes winced. "Ah, feeling a touch of tenderness, are we?"

"Yes," said Holmes hoarsely.

"Are we experiencing any sharp pain there? Any sharp stabs of pain, as it were?

"No," said Holmes.

"Any difficulty with our breathing?"

"None," said Holmes.

"Are we quite sure about that? I fear a rib or two may have suffered — there are some rather nasty supracostal bruises. We don't want a punctured lung now, do we?"

Holmes lifted his eyes and gazed at the young man coldly. "If it is to be our lot to share the same anatomy, Doctor, I can assure you that I for one do not."

The young practitioner, steeped in the seriousness of his calling, was somewhat taken aback. He peered owlishly at him over thin wire spectacles for a brief moment and then said, "Hmm, yes, quite."

He completed his ministrations quickly and, Holmes couldn't help but notice, with a measurable reduction in gentleness. "No bandages, I think, Sister," he said curtly, wiping his hands on a towel. "These facial abrasions should heal nicely in the open air, but I wouldn't advise shaving for a day or two."

This last remark Holmes assumed was directed toward him, though a surreptitious glance at Sister's upper lip caused him to hesitate before responding: "I for one shall certainly take your advice, Doctor, and I thank you for your solicitude."

Sergeant Thicke, his brow furrowed with concern, was waiting for Holmes outside the examining room when he emerged. Filled with solicitude, the policeman gently helped Holmes to ease into his jacket and would have taken him by the arm to assist him down the corridor had not a glower from Holmes warned him off. Yet his desire to be accommodating remained undampened.

"Why don't we pop in 'ere and 'ave a nice 'ot cuppa, Mr. 'Olmes. Ye look as though ye could use it."

"If I look anything the way I feel, I could use a cauldron of it."

They retired to a small staff lounge, where Holmes lowered his frame gingerly into a chair while Thicke busied himself in the corner with the tea things.

The tea, once delivered, was hot, bitter-strong, and very sweet, and had a faint aroma of disinfectant. Nonetheless, Holmes sipped it appreciatively, savoring every mouthful, though it stung the insides of his cheeks.

"Ye feelin' better now, are ye, Mr. 'Olmes?"

"My entire physical being feels like one huge sore thumb, if the truth be known, but thanks to the quick arrival of your people, I shall survive, I fear.

"Yer 'ead feelin' better too, then?" He was being most solicitous, a note of genuine sympathy in his tone, and Holmes shot him a questioning glance, one mixed with surprise and some amusement.

"They gave me a headache powder of some sort, and I am indeed feeling better, thank you."

Thicke nodded. "Ye 'ad a close 'un now, din'cha? Inspector H'Abberline would 'ave been most upset should anything 'ave had 'appened to ye. As we would 'ave all," he was quick to add.

"Very kind," said Holmes between sips.

Thicke shrugged. "Well, we would 'ave all been in a pretty kettle of fish if ye was — if anythin' did 'appen to ye. God, I dread to think what Fleet Street would 'ave made o' that!"

Holmes had to smile. Any personal concerns for his safety on the part of Scotland Yard, some of them no doubt genuine, would have certainly yielded precedence to professional concerns: The police would have been pilloried in the press if anything had happened to him — and that was no conceit of his; it was fact. They would have been raked over the coals, without question.

Thicke put his mug of tea down very carefully, as though afraid the slightest noise would be disturbing to Holmes. He leaned over and without even a by-your-leave made an elaborate examination of Holmes's face (to Holmes's consternation), clucking sympathetically.

"I don't believe the damage will permanently mar my beauty, Sergeant," Holmes said in a tone of icy forbearance. "You needn't carry on so."

Thicke had the good grace to look embarrassed. "Now, the inspector made it a point to instruct me to make certain that ye get home all right, and told me to say that ye should get a good night's sleep. Or what's left of the night," he added ruefully, glancing up at the clock on the wall. "And he said that he'll see ye on the morrow and go over matters with ye then. In the meantime, he says ye shouldn't concern yerself. Just get a good rest, is all."

Holmes shook his head. "No, I'm fine. As soon as I finish my tea, and perhaps have a second cup, we'll be off. I want to get back to... what street was it?"

"Berner Street. But that's out o' the question, Mr. 'Olmes. The inspector was most h'explicit in telling me to see ye home."

Holmes became annoyed. "Nonsense. Let us speak no more about it."

"Well, I dunno." Thicke shook his head. "I dunno at t'all."

Holmes ignored him. "Now, tell me everything, Thicke. Leave nothing out."

Thicke looked at him and frowned. "I'm not sure what I can tell ye that ye don't know already. It was yerself that was there, not me. But from what we can make out, the Ripper – that's what everyone in the department's callin' him now – the Ripper. 'E was interrupted by the appearance of a 'orse 'n' cart driven by a traveler in costume jewelry." Thicke reached into a pocket and pulled out his notebook. "One Louis Diemschutz, is 'is name, would ye believe. H'it was just about one A.M. when 'e with his nag and his costermonger's barrow turned into the court just off Berner Street, right where ye was. 'E lives in the court, ye see, and is the steward of a sort of local political club there, the International Working Men's Educational Club, h'it's called – mostly Jews and other foreigners: A pack of socialists and troublemakers all of 'em, if ye ask me. 'E was comin' back from a sellin' trip, 'e was, this Diemschutz."

Thicke paused for a sip of tea from the mug. "Well, 'e leads 'is 'orse into the court, and the 'orse 'e shies, ye see – rears right up. Now, this Diemschutz thinks that some rubbish must be in the road, so 'e reaches down and feels around to clear h'it, and that's when 'e discovers the body.

"Now, as near as we can figure it, 'e comin' into the lane with the 'orse and all, and 'im makin' a racket, 'e scares the Ripper away just as 'e's doin' the job on the lady – we've got 'er name now too: Elizabeth Stride, a 'ore just like the others. An' the bawstard bolts, ye see. Never does get a chance to do anythin' but slice 'er throat."

Thicke paused. "That's when ye musta come runnin' up, Mr. 'Olmes, just at that very second."

Holmes nodded.

"Well, this bloke Diemschutz raises the alarm and the club empties out – they was 'aving a late meeting of some sort: Probably conspiring the overthrow o' the Crown for all we knows, the filthy vermin – and they sees ye runnin' up and figures ye for the killer. That's the way we figures h'it, unless ye can tells us different."

Holmes shook his head. "No, that's about right. I hadn't the faintest idea of what descended upon me, but it makes sense. The funny thing is, I didn't hear this fellow, what's his name Dim – something? I didn't hear him come up at all. Obviously, I wouldn't necessarily have seen him, it being so dark. But I should have heard him, unless..."

Thicke cocked an eyebrow.

Holmes looked thoughtful for a moment, then shook his head. "No. Events happened so quickly, it's difficult to reconstruct them. I suppose that in the flurry of excitement, I just never heard him approach. He must have come into the street from the opposite direction."

Thicke stood up and placed his cup carefully on a side table. "That must have been h'it, then. 'E did say 'e was comin' from the direction of the railway, and ye was at the other end, wasn't ye?"

"Yes," Holmes said distractedly. He massaged the back of his neck. The events of Berner Street were so jumbled in his mind that it all seemed like a dimly remembered dream, or something that happened ages ago. He found it disturbing that he had so little recall of what had transpired.

The opening of the door interrupted his thoughts. The grim face of a helmeted police constable appeared in the doorway. Upon spotting Thicke, he came all the way in. "Been lookin' for ye, S'arn't," he announced. "Inspector H'Abberline sent me. There's been another murder."

Thicke's tea mug crashed to the floor. "Whaaat!"

"This one's in the City, in Mitre Square," said the constable. 'E did a ryght proper job o' work this tyme: She's slit from gullet to gizzard, an' 'e copped an ear as well!"

"'E did wot?"

"'E cut off her bloody ear!"

Holmes shot to his feet, all pain forgotten. "I think I shall forgo the pleasure of another cup of tea, after all," he said.

Thicke bolted for the door. "I think ye'd be better off gettin' some sleep, is what I think, Mr. 'Olmes," he said over his shoulder as he hurried down the corridor.

"Sleep!" Holmes spat out irritably, struggling to keep up with him. "I'll sleep tomorrow, Sergeant, or the next day or never – or the day after that. Let us hurry, I pray you."

Twelve

SUNDAY, SEPTEMBER 30, 1888

"The murder in the City was committed in circumstances which show that the assassin, if not suffering from insanity, appears to be free from any fear of interruption while at his dreadful work."
— *The Times*, Monday, October 1, 1888

The scene at Mitre Square was one of orderly confusion: Uniformed policemen and detectives in civilian clothes were everywhere in evidence. The entire area had been closed off by police barricades, and the carriage secured by Thicke for the brief trip from the hospital had been stopped several times before being allowed to proceed to the location of the second murder.

"Mitre Square is outside of Scotland Yard's jurisdiction," explained Thicke after they passed through another roadblock. "The City Police will be in charge of this one."

Holmes nodded, but made no comment. He had already assumed as much; indeed, was counting on it. It was one of the oddities of London that the Metropolitan Police had responsibility for maintaining law and order in every borough of the city except for that one single square-mile portion on the north bank of the Thames known as *the* City. Its proper name was actually "the City of London," but few people ever referred to it as that, and those mainly foreigners. Saying merely "the City" identified it sufficiently to any native Londoner, or indeed to anyone anywhere in the world who had anything to do with international finance.

Geographically, the City was the core of London; historically, it was its most ancient part, occupying the site of the original Roman town of Londinium. It was where William the Conqueror was to erect his principal castle, now known as the Tower of London. But actually the City's true importance far outweighed the accidental distinctions afforded it by history and geography. In a very real sense it was the center not only of England and the British Isles, but of the Western world – and much of the rest of it as well. It would be scant exaggeration to say that the City, in these, the waning years of the nineteenth century, was the most important square mile on the face of the Earth.

Within its narrow confines were such landmarks and symbols of power as the Bank of England, the Inns of Court, Lloyds of London, the Stock Exchange, and St. Paul's Cathedral: It was the City, not Wellington's regiments or Nelson's 74s, that had made England the world power that she was. And it was those offices the City contained that were the true center of world influence, those of the lawyers, merchants, money changers, bankers, brokers, shipowners, and underwriters who collectively ruled England and the British Empire, regardless of what the politicians just around the river's bend in Westminster might think, or the old lady in Windsor.

It was not so surprising, therefore, that traditionally and historically the City had always maintained a measure of autonomy. Not only did the Metropolitan Police require authorization to enter its precincts, but, technically, so did the sovereign herself. The Queen-Empress may reign, but the pound sterling ruled.

But no such niceties were to be observed by the man who called himself Jack the Ripper. He required no special permission to pass through Temple Bar into the confines of the City.[54] It was convenient for him to do so, so he did. It was an accident of geography or a quirk of sardonic fate that the wealthiest, most powerful square mile in the Empire lay side by side with one of the poorest, most power*less*.

The site of the Ripper's second murder that night was barely ten minutes away from that of his first. Mitre Square was off Aldgate High Street, just north of Tower Hill and within sight of the Tower of London itself.

The body was found in a corner of the square facing Church Passage. It was a confined space, no more than thirty yards square, bordered on two sides by warehouses and the other two by workshops and mostly deserted tenements. During the day the square was a busy place, but after six o'clock it was empty.

The woman was lying on her back, with her left leg extended and her right leg bent. Both arms were stretched out, palms upward. She wore a black cloth jacket with an imitation fur collar and three large metal buttons. Underneath was a worn dress with a pattern of Michaelmas daisies and golden lilies. A black straw bonnet trimmed with velvet and beads was still tied to her head with a ribbon. Holmes studied the woman's face. It had been badly disfigured. There were cuts on her cheeks, her lips, and even her eyelids. There was a large gash from her nose to the side of her right cheek. Her right eye had been smashed in. Part of her right ear had been cut off. Her throat had been cut.

Holmes knelt down on one knee and, by the light of lanterns held by the police officers who surrounded the body, made a hasty examination. Her clothes were in disarray, her dress and petticoats pushed up to above her waist. Holmes idly noted that she was wearing a pair of men's laced shoes, which under any other circumstances would have added a comic note to her appearance.

But there was nothing funny about her now. She had been badly mutilated. There was a horrifying gash running from her breastbone downward, and a revolting mess of viscera spilled out from her abdominal cavity. Entrails were ripped from her body and flung in a heap onto her chest.

Holmes got to his feet slowly, his face set in a grim expression. He was studying the position of the body and did not notice the commanding figure who came up quietly alongside of him.

"Morning, Mr. Sherlock Holmes," said the man in a subdued voice. "It seems our friend has had a busy night of it."

What with the poor light, it took Holmes a second or two to recognize the speaker. "Why, Major, is that you?"

The man nodded. "I knew that eventually this monster would cross my path and venture over into the City, and I thought we'd be ready for him, but..." His voice trailed off and he shook his head in frustration.

Holmes knew him well. He was Major Henry Smith, the Acting Commissioner of the City Police and one of the few police administrators whom he respected greatly. Unlike his counterpart in the Metropolitan Police, Smith was a thorough professional and went about his business in a rational, organized way. What he lacked in scientific training he made up in imagination and energy and in a willingness to keep an open mind and not adhere to rigid, outmoded doctrine. He was a man of cool judgment and keen wit and was highly respected among his own men.[55]

"I'm glad you're here, Holmes. Damn glad. It goes without saying that I would appreciate anything you can do to help us. Your opinions would be most valuable."

"Very kind, I'm sure," mumbled Holmes.

Smith gestured toward the body. "She was still warm when our constable discovered her. He was probably just minutes behind the murderer."

"Your constable was the first to come upon the body, then?"

"Yes. His description of the deceased was most colorful: 'Ripped like a pig in the market,' he said. Come, let us walk. I can't bear to look at this obscenity." Smith took him by the elbow and guided him toward the center of the square. "PC Edward Watkins, Number 881, was the man. A thoroughly reliable fellow; I know him personally. It was during the course of his regular rounds that the body was discovered at one forty-five. He had previously been in the square not fifteen minutes earlier – that's how long it takes him to make his rounds – so we are able to pinpoint the time with some accuracy."

"Less than an hour after the first murder in Berner Street," mused Holmes.

"So I understand," said Smith. "And I am told you were there."

Holmes nodded ruefully. "For all the good that it did."

"Well, don't blame yourself, old man. I am certain you did your best. Just bad luck, is all. There is more than enough of it to go around. We've had our share of it here too. What particularly galls me is that we had the victim in custody earlier in the evening, and if my instructions had been followed, this might not have happened."

"Oh?"

Smith explained: "It is our practice to pick up anyone we find lying about in the streets intoxicated and hold 'em until they become sober, particularly the women – for their own safety, you understand. She was brought into the Bishopsgate station at around eight-thirty last night and placed in cells. Having sobered up, she was released shortly before one o'clock. She was last seen walking in the general direction of Houndsditch and this place." He shook his head. "If we had kept her through the night, she'd still be alive. But it was her bad luck to achieve sobriety too quickly, poor soul."

Smith chewed on his lip, clearly angry. "Moreover, if my standing orders had been obeyed, we might have had this fellow in custody as we speak! All women released from cells during the hours of darkness are supposed to be followed by one of our people. Those have been my orders since these murders began. But for some damn-fool reason, she wasn't! If we had followed her, and then called in men to guard the approaches of the square, we would have caught the man red-handed, damn it!"

Holmes confined his reply to a noncommittal grunt. He had little patience with people who agonized over the "ifs" of life and engaged in self-recriminations over what might have been.

Smith gained control of himself and continued in a quieter tone: "She gave her name as Mary Ann Kelly when she was brought into Bishopsgate, and apparently she lived with a man named Kelly in Spitalfields, at number 6 Fashion Street. But we've since found out she was also known as Eddowes, Catherine Eddowes. These women of the streets change their names with the tides." He stamped his foot in frustration. "And I thought we had such a good scheme to catch this fellow, or at least keep him at bay!"

"Your other preparations were all in order?" Holmes asked.

The major sighed. "I certainly did think so. I put more than a third of our force into plain clothes and had them prowling about every public house, doss-house, workhouse, and hidey-hole we know of. I had them stopping and questioning every man and woman seen together on the streets after midnight. Their instructions were to ignore procedures and do every damn thing a constable, under ordinary circumstances, should not do. I knew there was a possibility that this fellow, this Ripper person, might strike on our ground. And damn, I wanted him. That fool Warren has made a proper muck of things, and I don't mind telling you that I would dearly love to show him up for the blathering idiot that he is. Do you know that he wouldn't even allow his people to enter a pub? Not even in the line of duty? The bloody man is a teetotaller, you see!"

"I have had the rare pleasure of meeting him," said Holmes dryly, "but I did not know he included total abstinence among his virtues."

Smith made a rude noise. "Never did trust a man who doesn't take a drink now and again," he muttered.

He stopped under a gaslight to light a cigar. "You know, I really thought I was ready for him. I really did," he said between puffs. He shook his head ruefully. "I was spending the night at the Cloak Lane station and when they aroused me at two o'clock with the news, I said to myself, 'Laddie, you've got him now!' The area was surrounded within ten minutes, and I was here within twenty! You should have seen us, Holmes! It must have been a sight: I bundled into a hansom with one of my inspectors, fifteen stone if he's an ounce, and three detectives hanging on behind. Got here at breakneck speed, I can tell you, and it's a wonder the damn thing didn't lose a wheel or break a spring in the process. Hate those damn things, anyway: Inventions of the devil, those hansom cabs. Cold in the winter, hot in the summer, and unsafe at any time. I'm always smashing my hat getting in and out, and catching my fingers in the doors. And they roll like a ship-of-the-line in a gale."

Holmes had to smile. "Oh, they have their uses," he said. "I prefer them to walking, in any event. But do tell me what happened next, won't you?"

"Yes, yes, of course, forgive me. Watkins – you know, the constable that discovered the body – Watkins told me he didn't even bother to examine the woman, so sure was he that she was dead. And he knew right off it was the Ripper who did it. I mean, it was obvious to him that it wasn't one of your usual cases of homicide. He ran across to that warehouse over there on the other side of the square, Kearley &

Tonge's, and shouted for the watchman inside. The watchman is a retired policeman, so he knew what to do straightaway. He ran up to Aldgate, blowing his whistle for all he was worth, and encountered two more of my men there, one of whom went to fetch the doctor, the other to give the alarm. Stout fellows, both of them. And then I arrived here shortly thereafter. Found her lying as she is, exactly as you see her. My people know not to touch anything until someone in authority arrives on the scene."

Smith stopped in front of a blanket laid out on the cobbles with a pitiful collection of odds and ends spread out on top of it, two lanterns placed at opposite corners of the blanket serving to illuminate them. "These were her possessions, everything she owned, probably."

Holmes knelt down and studied what was there: Two handkerchiefs, one of a checkered material, the other white with a red border; a matchbox containing cotton, a blunt table knife with a bone handle, a man's cufflink, a few pieces of soap, two short clay pipes, a red cigarette case, a small tin containing tea and sugar, a small comb, a single red mitten, and a broken pair of spectacles.

"Not much to show for a life, is it?" commented Smith quietly.

Holmes pursed his lips. No reply was necessary, nor would any have been adequate.

Smith cleared his throat and looked away. "We made a search of the area, of course, but didn't come up with anything worth mentioning: No footprints – the pavement is hard here, as you can see. No one was about in the immediate vicinity, so we haven't been able to find anyone who might have seen the fellow. No one we questioned heard anything – the watchman in the warehouse didn't. These houses on this side of the square are unoccupied, and of the two over there on the other side, only one is lived in, and that by a policeman, by chance. And he was asleep and didn't hear a thing. I now have men searching the nearby streets and alleys to see what they can come up with. We may find something that will indicate what route he took out of the square. Who knows? We may even yet find someone who saw him." His voice trailed off. He did not sound very hopeful.

Holmes looked at him with admiration. "It certainly sounds as if you have covered everything." He pondered for a moment, stroking his chin thoughtfully. "By the by, did any of your men take notice of any cigarette ends lying about anywhere in the square, by chance?"

Smith looked at him. "Why, they've not been told to look. Is that important, do you think?"

Holmes shrugged. "Oh, just a little pet theory of mine. Indulge me, if you will. If a man or two can be spared, I would be most obliged if they would search the cobbles in and about the square with their bull's-eyes and let us see what they come up with."

"Well, I certainly will, if you think it's consequential."

"In the meantime I think I shall just wander around a bit and see if I can find anything. I shall want to examine the body more thoroughly when it's taken to the mortuary, if you have no objection."

"No, none at all, of course." Smith paused and looked around the square at the busy comings and goings of his subordinates, who were still sifting through the refuse of the square, searching for clues. He shook his head. "It's funny, you know – his choice of this place for one of his murders," he said.

"Oh? How so?"

"Well, according to local lore, another woman was murdered on this very same spot in the early sixteenth century – murdered by a monk from the priory that used to be located here, if you believe the legend."

Holmes raised an eyebrow. "I didn't know that," he said quietly.

Major Smith looked thoughtful for a moment. "I wonder if our friend did."[56]

The sound of running footsteps behind them made them turn. A constable and a large detective-inspector in civilian clothes came rushing up, both breathing heavily. "We found somethin' in Goulston Street, Major," said the inspector, wheezing audibly. "A scrap a' cloth wi' blood on it, still wet. Looks like it could have been torn from 'er clothes!"

Without a word, Smith and Holmes rushed off into the darkness, following the inspector's lead. It was only about a third of a mile to Goulston Street, and they made the distance in under ten minutes. A cluster of lanterns shone with pinpricks of light up ahead as they turned into the street, drawing them to the location. Two constables and a sergeant were waiting for them as they came running up, the sergeant saluting and directing them to a narrow passageway just off the street. Inside, a man in civilian clothes was kneeling on the ground, a constable standing behind him with a lantern.

The large detective accompanying them slumped gratefully against the wall of the passageway, gasping for breath. He gestured weakly. "This 'ere is Police Constable Long of H-Division, sir. 'E's the one who found it. Alfy, lad, tell the actin' commissioner 'ow you came upon it, smartly now."

The man knuckled his forehead. "It was like this, sor: I was making me normal rounds, sor, just like I always do, but what with the morder 'nd all, I was payin' particalar attention to the side streets 'nd dark places — the h'alleyways 'nd passages 'nd that — 'nd I come across this bit of rag, sor, right here where it still rests, as you can see for your ownself, sor. 'Nd I shines me bull's-eye on h'it, 'nd I sees the blood, 'nd then I runs to the Leman Street station 'nd makes me report, sor, 'nd then I comes back 'ere. 'Nd that's the whole of h'it, sor. The time was two fifty-five h'exactly. I've got h'it all 'ere in me book, correct 'nd proper."

Holmes had been listening with only half an ear as he examined the rag of cloth lying crumpled on the ground. It was indeed still damp, soaked with something that surely looked like blood. He carefully separated the material with a pencil and spread it out flat. It appeared that it had been used to wipe off an object such as the blade of a knife. He glanced over his shoulder and addressed the large inspector. "You say this fabric was cut from the woman's clothes?"

"Right you are, sir. From the apron she was wearing."

"She wore no apron!"

"Well, sir, not exactly. It was wrapped around her neck when we found her, apparently to staunch the flow of blood from her throat. We removed it to examine the wound, and there was a scrap cut out of it, which puzzled us. There's no doubt that this is it."

Holmes rose to his feet with an effort and looked at Major Smith but didn't say anything. Smith looked away. "I am afraid someone forgot to mention that to you, Holmes."

"Is there anything else that anyone may have forgotten to mention to me?" he asked caustically, his voice reflecting only a hint of his displeasure.

Constable Long cleared his throat. "Well, there is somethin' else, sor, but I dinna forget. I jest was never given the h'opportunity."

All eyes turned to the constable.

Without a word he shone the beam of his lantern onto the wall of the passageway – at a spot just above where the scrap of cloth was lying. The light danced eerily on the lathing for a moment, then steadied. Something was scrawled on the wall in chalk, plain to the eye now that it was illuminated:

The Juwes are The men That will not be Blamed for nothing

Smith was the first to react. He turned on the constable excitedly. "When did you first notice this?"

"Why, jest after I found the bit o' cloth, sor. I searched the entire passageway 'nd the staircase h'it leads to, jest over there. I was looking for bloodstains, or whatever," he explained.

"How do you know it wasn't there before?" asked Holmes.

"Because h'it t'weren't, sor."

"How do you know that?" chimed in Smith.

"Because I looked, sor. I examined this passage 'nd the staircase, 'nd checked the doors to all the flats up above not more than thirty minutes before, sor. H'its all in me book, sor."

Holmes laughed and shook his head in wonderment. He turned serious again quickly. "The time was two fifty-five, you say?"

"Yes, sor. H'exactly. I checked me pocket wotch."

Holmes mused aloud. "And we have placed the time of the woman's murder at between one-thirty and one forty-five."

"That's quite right," Smith agreed.

Holmes pondered for a minute. "So our friend Jack took at least forty-five minutes to well over an hour to reach this spot from Mitre Square. Even longer, perhaps."

"That would appear to be the case."

Holmes deliberated.

"What's your point?" Smith asked, a little puzzled.

"Only that it took us a mere ten minutes."

"So?"

"So, Jack did not come directly here, but went someplace else first. The question is where, and why?"

"Ah," said Smith, comprehending at last. He thought about it briefly then turned abruptly. "Halse!" he bellowed. "Where's Halse?"

"Right here, sir," said a detective in civilian clothes right behind him.

"Oh. Halse, go find Mr. McWilliam.[57] He's still in Mitre Square, I believe. Tell him I want the whole area searched and searched again.

Tell him what we've found here, and tell him we believe the Ripper made at least one other stop first. Tell him to look for bloodstained rags. Tell him to look for... oh, I don't know, anything at all."

"Cigarette ends!" said Holmes. "Look for cigarette ends with a thin gold band!"

Smith and the others looked at him questioningly. Then Smith turned to his subordinate. "Do it, Halse! Cigarette ends with a thin gold band! Go, man, go!"

He was gone.

Smith turned to another one of his detectives. "Hunt, I want a photographic plate made of this." He pointed to the scrawled message on the wall. "Go find someone to do it, quickly as you can."

"Yes, sir," said the man. "But, sir..."

"Well, what is it?"

"I just wanted to point out, sir, that we are out of our jurisdiction. This street is outside of the City's borders and falls under Scotland Yard."

"Oh, damn!" Smith's features registered first annoyance and then indecision. It was a delicate problem, but it took him only a moment to make up his mind. He pounded fist into hand. "To hell with it! Do as I say! Find a photographer without delay! We'll worry about the consequences later."

Then he turned away to give instructions to others in attendance, and if he harbored any second thoughts regarding the wisdom of his decision, he did not show it. Clearly, paying homage to the niceties of interdepartmental protocol were not uppermost in his mind at the moment.

Holmes, standing quietly to the side, said nothing, but his estimation of Major Henry Smith, already high, rose a notch or two higher.

But more pressing matters awaited his attention. He got down on his hands and knees and, with the aid of a lantern, began a methodical examination of the ground in the passageway. Finding nothing of consequence, though he painstakingly searched the ground inch by inch for a good twenty minutes, he turned his attentions once again to the chalked message scrawled on the wall.

He was deeply engrossed in this activity with pocket lens and lantern, when a cry from the street caught his attention and he hurried out through the passageway to investigate. On the curb he found Major Smith in earnest conversation with a constable who had apparently just come running up, for his chest was still heaving. Holmes heard the words "Dorset Street" mentioned as he approached.

Smith caught sight of him. "Holmes! C'mon! Dorset Street!" Without another word of explanation he dashed off, and Holmes had no other choice but to follow, along with a mixed crowd of uniformed police constables and plainclothes detectives.

They ran the length of Goulston Street past Wentworth and past White's Row, the clatter of their heels loud against the cobbles, the lanterns carried by the uniformed force bobbing crazily up and down and appearing like so many fireflies gone berserk. They ran into Crispin Street, where they turned the corner into Dorset, one of the most notorious streets in all of Whitechapel. There, another cluster of fireflies awaited them, and it took but a moment to discover why. Set back from the street a bare six yards and illuminated by the light of a street lamp was a public sink, one of many that dotted the area. The bloodstained water that was in it had not had sufficient time to gurgle completely down the drain, and the half-smoked cigarette on the ground nearby, picked out in the beam of a constable's lantern, was still smoldering.

The entire area was searched, of course, and searched again, but nothing more was found. Policemen knocked on every door and questioned every inhabitant, but no one heard anything, no one saw anything. Their elusive prey had once again vanished completely. From all indications, they had been only minutes, perhaps seconds behind him, but it might as well have been hours or days. The trail was cold, and there was nothing more to be gained by continuing efforts to pick it up again.

Holmes, accompanied by a grim-faced Smith, departed the scene in a thoughtful mood. Hardly a word was exchanged between them. They made their way to the City mortuary in Golden Lane near St. Luke's. There, in a starkly bare white-tiled room, they found two surgeons by the names of Brown and Sequeira, who were in the process of washing up, having just completed their post mortem of the woman's body. The odor of a strong disinfectant predominated but failed to overpower the other smells of the place.

Brown, who appeared to them to be a rather cold and passionless man, strictly professional, did most of the talking.

"The cause of death was hemorrhage from the left common carotid artery," he said matter-of-factly over his shoulder, soaping his hands for the third time. "Death was immediate. The mutilations were inflicted after death." He wiped his hands on a towel, donned a pair of wire-rimmed spectacles, and referred to his notes.

"The throat was cut across to the extent of about six or seven inches. The sternocleido mastoid muscle was divided. The cricoid cartilage below the vocal cords was severed through the middle. The large vessels on the left side of the neck were severed to the bone. The internal jugular vein was open to the extent of an inch and a half. All the injuries were caused by some very sharp instrument, like a knife, and pointed."

He paused for a moment and riffled through the pages of his notes. "The walls of the abdomen were laid open from the breast downward. The cut commenced opposite the ensiform cartilage in the center of the body. The incision went upward, not penetrating the skin that was over the sternum; it then divided the ensiform cartilage. Clearly, the knife was held so that the point was toward the left side and the handle toward the right. There was damage to the liver, several cuts – I won't bore you with further technical details unless you insist."

He removed his spectacles and rubbed his eyes. "In sum, there is evidence of several incisions going in various directions. There was a stab to the groin. There was another wounding the peritoneum. The abdominal wall was badly lacerated in several places. And so forth and so on. In layman's terms, she was totally mangled. The man who did it had a high old time of it, I would say." He nodded. "A high old time." He looked from Holmes to Smith and back again without a trace of expression on his face, only a tightening of the lines around his mouth and a slight tic at the corner of his left eye betraying any hint of emotion.

Smith cleared his throat. "I think we have the idea, Doctor, thank you. Tell me, have you reached any conclusions regarding the size and shape of the knife?"

"Only that it was sharp and pointed and at least six inches long."

"Would you say that the person wielding the knife exhibited any medical skills?"

"Not particularly. Only with respect to the positioning of the organs and the way of removing them: obviously, he knows a little something regarding human anatomy. The way in which the kidney was cut out showed that it was done by an individual who knew what he was about, but there is no indication of any special surgical skills. Very much to the contrary."

Holmes looked up sharply. He had heard only the first part of the reply. "Organs were removed?" he asked.

"Oh, yes. Did I not mention that?" His outward manner was irritatingly casual. "The left kidney, the uterus, portions of both the large and small intestines. But the removal of the intestines must have been obvious to you, mustn't it? They were drawn out to a large extent, pulled out forcibly, and placed over the right shoulder. A section was quite detached and then placed between the left arm and the body."

"Placed?" asked Smith. "You mean put there by design?"

"It would seem so, yes."

"The other organs: The kidney and the uterus?" asked Holmes. "What of them?"

"Oh, they're gone."

"Gone? You mean, missing?"

"Quite."

There was silence in the room for a long moment.

Smith slowly shook his head in disbelief. Finally he asked: "Is there anything else you can tell us that might be useful, Doctor?"

"No, I don't believe so," he replied dryly. "Of course, you noted that the lobe of her right ear was cut obliquely through – why, I cannot imagine. That's the lot of it."

Smith turned to the other surgeon, who had remained silent throughout the interview, his eyes cast downward. "Is there anything you would like to add, Dr. Sequeira?"

The man raised his head and looked at him. He was very pale, obviously shaken. There was a momentary flash of anger in his eyes. "One thing only," he said, clenching his jaw. "When you finally apprehend this creature, I would very much like to be there for the hanging."

Without a further word he rushed from the room.

Dr. Brown stood there for a moment, staring at the floor. Then he returned to the sink and washed his hands again.

It was almost six o'clock when Holmes and Smith left the mortuary and returned by carriage to Mitre Square. A weak sun had risen, casting a thin, joyless half-light over the square. It was a gray and depressing scene. Policemen stood about singly and in small groups, some conversing quietly but most maintaining a weary silence, their faces lined with fatigue. Detective Halse was waiting for them as they drove up. He greeted them nervously, obviously agitated about something.

"What now?" inquired Smith.

The policeman hesitated in his reply, as if having difficulty in finding the words. He looked aged, his eyes in the growing light were watery and rimmed with red. Holmes noticed that his hands were shaking. "The message on the wall, sir – in Goulston Street?"

"Yes, yes. What about it?"

Halse took a deep breath. "It's been erased, sir."

Smith looked at him in disbelief. For a moment he could not speak. "Erased?"

Halse avoided his gaze. He raised his hands in a helpless gesture. "Sir, I did what I could, and Superintendent Arnold of the Metropolitan force was there and he argued against it also, but Sir Charles insisted, and there was nothing any of us could do."

"Sir Charles?" interjected Holmes sharply.

"Yes, sir. Sir Charles Warren. He ordered that it be rubbed out."

"Before the photographs were taken?" demanded Smith.

"Yes, sir. He said he was afraid the reference to Jews might inflame the populace – those were his words, sir – 'inflame the populace,' and lead to further anti-Jewish riots. We did our best to convince him to wait, or to just erase the one offending word, but he wouldn't hear of it, sir. He just wouldn't."

Smith stared at him for a moment and then his shoulders slumped. "Oh, my dear sweet Jesus," he said.

Sherlock Holmes merely gazed up at the sky. "How very extraordinary," he said dispassionately.

* * *

It was well past the breakfast hour when Holmes finally made his way back to Baker Street. The search of the area surrounding the murder scene had been fruitless. The examination of the body at the mortuary revealed nothing of any great consequence. The case was really no further along than it had been two murders ago. Holmes was bone tired and dispirited, and if it were not for the fact that Mrs. Hudson hovered over him, fussing and scolding like a nanny, he never would have partaken of even what little he did of the meal she had so thoughtfully provided, late in the morning as it was. It was almost noon when he finally fell into bed, his body aching, his emotions drained, and he slept the day away, sleeping the sleep of the exhausted, a deep, dreamless sleep that only a few hours earlier he had forsworn – a sleep which in the words of the poet was a divine oblivion of his sufferings.

Thirteen

❦

Tuesday, October 2, 1888

"Now we have the Sherlock Holmes test, and there will
no longer be any difficulty."
– *A Study in Scarlet*

The fingerprint under Holmes's magnifying glass was large and well defined, the loops and whorls sharply distinct from one another with very little of the smudging one would expect to find in a print accidentally applied in the normal course of events. No, this one was purposely imprinted upon the small rectangular piece of pasteboard being scrutinized by Holmes, an ordinary postcard received at the Central News Agency only the day before and promptly turned over to Scotland Yard.

It was apparent that the fingerprint was that of a thumb – a left thumb, Holmes decided. It was imprinted in red. The message above it was brief and was also in red, but of a different hue than that of the fingerprint:

I was not codding, dear old Boss, when I gave you the tip. You'll hear about Saucy Jacky's work tomorrow. Double event this time.

*Number one squealed a bit. Couldn't finish straight off. Had no
time to get ears for police. Thanks for keeping last letter back till
I got to work again.*
Jack the Ripper

The postmark bore the legend "London E. 1 Oct 88," the date
indicating it was mailed on either Sunday the thirtieth or early Monday
the first.

Holmes focused the lens on the thumbprint once again, peering
intently at the magnified image for several minutes, his gray eyes taking
on a fierce, almost hypnotic cast, so intense was his concentration.

"You are familiar with Bertillon's method, Inspector?" asked Holmes
idly, his nose just inches away from the pasteboard he was studying.

Abberline, who was standing at Holmes's shoulder, stroked his chin.
"Well, yes, of course, but much of it is untried, isn't it? Though I hear
the *Sureté* has recently adopted his system, I really don't know how
much credence to place upon it."

"I quite agree with you, though I tend to believe he is definitely on to
something. His work in anthropometry shows great promise, I think. Of
course, much more remains to be done before I shall be willing to fully
accept all of his dictums. The idea that individuals can be identified by
measuring the human body in terms of skeletal dimensions, proportions,
and ratios raises tantalizing possibilities. Criminal identification would
be greatly assisted if his theories prove to be valid."

Holmes lapsed into silence again as he concentrated on the swirling
pattern of the print beneath his lens. After a moment or two, without
looking up, he resumed the colloquy:

"It is with Monsieur Bertillon's theory regarding finger- and palmprints
that I have the greatest problem. I find the notion that no one individual's
digital imprintations are the same as those of any other somewhat fanciful.

It defies logic, does it not, that the pattern on the surface of any given finger or palm must differ markedly from that of every other? That each and every fingerprint is distinctive, none exactly the same?" Holmes shook his head. "The concept is staggering. Tally the countless multitudes which have trod these boards since time out of mind, multiply by ten, and you have the infinite variety of patterns required to make each human digit unique. I cannot help but dwell upon the absurdity of such a premise. Are each of us so exceptional that Nature has gone to such infinite lengths to set us apart? Is our Creator that punctilious, that painstaking in his craft?"

Abberline shrugged. "A question better directed to a theologian than a policeman, Mr. Holmes."

Holmes flashed a quick smile. "Or Mr. Darwin," he said.

He studied the fingerprint for several minutes more. "But how does one prove it?" he said after another lengthy silence. "How does one establish verification without scrutinizing the hands and fingers of every human being on the face of the Earth, living and dead and as yet unborn? Or at least a sizable sample?"

Abberline laughed. "Clearly an impossible task," he agreed. "Yet, they say that no one snowflake is exactly the same as any other either."

Holmes looked up in some surprise. "Do they? Do they indeed? I had not heard that." He thought about it for a moment and then returned to the deliberation of the object beneath his magnifying glass. "And now that I have, I shall do my best to forget it. Cluttering the mind with useless bits of information, no matter how astonishing or quaint, can serve no useful purpose."

Abberline looked down at him, bemused. What an amazingly contradictory character was Mr. Sherlock Holmes. For a man with such a restless, inquiring mind, his range of interests was so surprisingly narrow: He was such a font of knowledge in some areas, and so incredibly ignorant in others. Abberline could not believe he had not known of the distinctive character of snowflakes, a simple fact to be found in the mind of the most simpleminded of schoolboys. He would have been no more surprised had Holmes expressed ignorance of the Earth being round, or of the fact that it traveled around the sun.

Abberline turned the discussion back to the subject at hand. "Yet, the Bertillonists claim that no duplication of a fingerprint has ever been found."

"Yes," said Holmes distractedly, "that is what they claim, and I have no reason to disbelieve them, but still, the idea that the human hand, or any part of it, cannot be replicated in nature is so profoundly implausible that I must insist upon further proof. I find it illogical to assume that because no replications have been encountered in the past, they cannot or will not be encountered in the future. Still, one must not close one's mind to new ideas, no matter how improbable, must one?" Holmes grunted, put down his magnifying glass, and massaged the bridge of his nose with thumb and forefinger.[58]

"As far as this postcard is concerned, it is genuine, in my opinion," he said. "There can be no doubt: The handwriting is the same as in that of the earlier communication that I examined." Holmes could not resist adding: "Of course, thanks to your intrepid chief, we shall never know if it is also the same as that of the writing on the wall in Goulston Street, though I believe it is."

"I tend to think so too," Abberline replied, "though I make no claims to being an expert in handwriting analysis. But handwriting aside, it must be genuine, mustn't it? The postcard was mailed before any of the newspaper accounts reached the streets, so obviously the author of this has to be the killer. Otherwise he wouldn't have known about the two most recent murders when he posted this card, let alone any of the details surrounding them – unless he were a journalist himself, as some of our people seem to think."

"Oh, I considered that possibility," replied Holmes dryly, "and I don't doubt that one or two of our more ambitious, less reputable scribblers would not hesitate to stoop to such depths if they thought it would gain them readership, but I think it rather unlikely in this case. You yourself told me that certain details were withheld from the press, so I believe we can rule out the possibility of an unscrupulous journalist – unless you have a spy in your midst, or one of your own people is being bribed for information, that is."

Abberline stiffened. "I can assure you, Mr. Holmes, that none of my lads would permit themselves to be compromised, nor would any of them ever consider –"

Holmes held up his hand and said quickly, "I don't doubt it, dear fellow. Not for one moment. While I don't give your detective division high marks for imagination or method, I have never found reason to question the integrity of its individual members. In any event, the press in general have shown remarkable restraint in not publishing either one of these communications as of yet, and I should think that if some journalist had fabricated this as a means of embellishing his own reports, he would have been most eager to get it into print. Besides, no journalist could have known about the attempt to cut off one of the ears of the first victim, could he?"

"No, that's unlikely. We revealed that to no one. And no journalist was permitted close enough to view the remains."

"I thought not. And they have not had access to the mortuary, I presume."

"No. My men have seen to that. It's been ordered sealed off until after the inquest."

Holmes nodded his approval. "As I am certain Major Smith has done in the City. But getting back to this (he flourished the postcard), the handwriting is that of a very disturbed, even violent individual, the product of a mind fully capable of murder, if I am any judge. All of the signs are there, unmistakably. And whilst I have among my acquaintances one or two journalists who are quite capable of character assassination, I do not seriously think it likely any would indulge in the actual kind." His mouth lifted in another one of his quick, quirky smiles and just as quickly resumed its customary contours. "No, I do believe this Saucy Jack is the fellow he says he is. My pound to your penny, he's our man."[59]

Abberline pulled at his chin. "Well, if you are right, that is at least something concrete. There is so much theorizing going on, so much irresponsible speculation, even on the part of respected scientists and medical experts, that it is difficult to know what to believe. Why, just yesterday I read somewhere that someone who claims to be an authority on the workings and dysfunctions of the human mind has theorized that the fellow is perhaps a religious fanatic, mentally crippled by his fanaticism, who has forsaken normal relations with women – spurning their favors, and taking up celibacy and that sort of thing – and in an excess of piety and fervor has assumed the role of some sort of avenging angel whose mission is to rid the world of all of those he considers to be wanton and libidinous and so forth."

Holmes responded abstractedly. "Hmm. If so, I should say he has bitten off far more than he can possibly eschew."

"What?" Abberline cast him an odd look. "Oh, yes, quite."

Holmes took up the postcard again and puzzled over it. He rose to his feet abruptly, a gleam in his eye. "Indulge me," he said.

Going directly to the cluttered deal table in the corner, he began busying himself with test tubes and chemicals. Abberline, filled with curiosity, followed behind. He stood looking over Holmes's shoulder as the latter carefully measured out a small quantity of a colorless liquid into one of the test tubes. "Merely distilled water," Holmes murmured in way of explanation.

Abberline stood there, mystified.

"A little test of my own devising," Holmes explained further. "It is very simple, actually. Elegantly simple, if I may say so, and quite infallible. The old guaiacum test was very clumsy and uncertain, you see. And so is the microscopic examination of corpuscles, which is useless if the sample is more than a few hours old."

"Mr. Holmes," said Abberline, wearing a most puzzled frown, "perhaps you would be good enough to tell me just what it is you are doing."

"In a moment, dear chap, in just one moment." He was bent over the table almost double, the postcard once again mere inches from his nose. He had cleared space for it on the table with a sweep of his hand. Now, with a penknife, he began scraping gently at the corner of the fingerprint on the card. "You did say this was submitted to the photographic process, did you not?"

"Yes, we had it exposed to three separate photographic plates and have excellent copies," replied Abberline, "but I don't see what..."

"Good, good. I should not like to think that I was defacing the original without there being suitable facsimiles, though I shan't require more than the smallest of samples. You see how I leave the major part of the fingerprint unscathed?"

"Yes, but I still don't see —"

"Oh, but you shall, dear fellow. And you shall see with the naked eye, I promise you. Teichman's test as well as Bryk's both required the use of a microscope and, as I mentioned, were very limited in what they could accomplish, but the beauty of this experiment is that no microscope is required and the desired result is much quicker to attain. Most important, the specimen need not be a fresh one. Even samples that are weeks and months old may thus be submitted to examination with gratifyingly predictable results. And for all I know, years old as well, though lamentably, I have had no occasion to put it to the test."

Abberline's impatience was growing. "Mr. Holmes, could you not tell me what it is you are doing?"

"Directly, Inspector, directly. Pass me that bottle, won't you? No, no, the other one – the sodium tungstate. Ah, thank you, there's a good fellow." He removed a small quantity of white crystals from the bottle with the blade of his penknife and tapped them into the test tube.

"Originally I used sodium hydroxide as the reducing agent," he rambled on, "but I find the sodium tungstate more effective. Now for the catalyst. If you will be so good as to hand me the acetic acid in that large vessel over there. Excellent! Thank you. Now, as you see, I combine the two and mix them thoroughly, add the mixture to the sample thusly, agitate vigorously, and – *voilà!* There you have it!"

"Have what, for pity's sake?" Abberline peered at the liquid in the test tube, which had turned a dull brownish color.

"Blood, Inspector, human blood! The sample tests positive!" Holmes's eyes were gleaming triumphantly.

"You mean to say that the fingerprint on the postcard was made in blood?"

"That is precisely what I mean to say. I suspected as much, but this little test of mine confirms it. The chemistry involved is a simple oxidation-reduction reaction in which the valance number of the iron in the hemoglobin is increased from two to three and therefore precipitates out of the solution. But I need not bore you with the details. The point is, it is human blood without question!"

Abberline's face went blank. Clearly he had not the faintest idea of how Holmes had arrived at his conclusion.

"Blood?" he said again.

Holmes rose from the stool and returned to his chair by the fireplace, wiping his hands with a handkerchief. "Human blood," he corrected the inspector. "Our friend Jack probably used his victim's blood, but more sophisticated tests will be required to prove that assumption. Lamentably, I have no way of determining the actual blood type with the meager resources at my command, you understand."

"No, of course not," said Abberline, clearly not understanding at all.[60]

Holmes returned the handkerchief to his sleeve and eased himself into a more comfortable position in his chair. His ribs still pained him abominably. "That settles the question once and for all, I should think," he said. "It is all the more likely that he is our man, this Saucy Jack."

Abberline considered this new information. "But knowing that doesn't help us very much, does it?" he said ruefully.

Holmes stared up at the ceiling. "Well... one never knows. Every little bit of information gathered is of use, no matter that its significance is not immediately apparent to us. Every puzzle is made up of several pieces, each having its place and all required to make up the whole – even if the placement of any one particular piece at any given moment remains obscure. At the very least, we know a little something more about the man with whom we are dealing. And that could prove to be of incalculable assistance in tracking him down."

"Oh? I fail to see that we know all that much, or how it can be of any assistance whatsoever."

"Well, take the postcard, for one thing, and the previous note as well. One may deduce something of very great significance from those – particularly the postcard."

Abberline went back to the deal table to retrieve the object in question and peered at it with an expression of fierce determination. After a moment he shook his head in bewilderment. "I don't see that it tells us anything," he said disgustedly.

"Ah, dear fellow, you must read between the lines," said Holmes. "For one thing, it tells us, I think, that this fellow desires to be caught."

Abberline looked at him as if he had gone mad.

Holmes gave the policeman a quick sidelong glance and smiled happily at his reaction: Watson could have served him no better. He continued in the same vein: "Yes, I do believe he wants us to catch him, is even desperate for us to do so."

"You can't be serious!"

"Oh, but I am, my dear chap, I am. The man is quite mad, you see. He is not in control of his own actions. He is unaware of it, of course, but he wants someone to stop him from what he is doing." Holmes frowned and shook his head. "No, that's not quite correct. He does indeed want to be found out, and he wants to be identified: He doesn't necessarily want to be stopped. He's enjoying himself far too much for that, deriving a great deal of personal satisfaction not only from the killings themselves, but from the stir his actions are causing. Obviously, he's quite proud of himself. Quite proud indeed."

"Proud of himself? Why it's pure blood lust! You said so yourself! How could anyone be proud of these vicious, cowardly acts – even a madman?"

Holmes explained his reasoning: "It's clear to me now that blood lust is not the only reason he is committing these atrocities. Nor is he simply a religious fanatic or 'down on whores,' as he phrased it himself in that first missive of his, though all of that surely may be part of it.

"No, I believe he is doing it as a means of attracting attention to himself. He wants to be noticed, you see. He wants to be admired or feared, I don't think he cares which: To his twisted mind it is probably one and the same thing. If he cannot achieve the consideration he desires by acceptable behavior, then he will resort to other means.

Holmes leaned back in his chair and tented his fingers in front of him, gazing up at the ceiling. His voice took on a different tone, as it always did when he thought aloud, formulating a theory in his mind as he spoke.

"He is like a little boy who is being naughty so someone will pay attention to him," he said half to himself. "His father perhaps, or his chums, or the older boys whose acceptance he seeks. No doubt he is incapable of achieving notice in any other way. He is probably a failure at everything he has tried, and has been scorned as a result. He has no one to admire him, no one to look up to him, no one to render him the slightest degree of respect. He is not capable of being best at something, or good at anything. His schoolmates think him useless, his teachers consider him a dullard, and little girls consider him clumsy and feckless. And his father is ashamed of him, probably – or at the very least ignores him or favors another of his progeny." Holmes shrugged. "So he resorts to mischief. He murders helpless women."

Abberline shook his head vehemently. "Really, Mr. Holmes! I can't accept that. Aren't you going just a bit too far? I mean, all boys are somewhat mischievous at a certain age – even I was to a certain extent – but very few of them grow up to become callous, fiendish murderers!"

"I grant you that."

"A normal person doesn't resort to killing because he was no good at climbing trees as a lad or because his mates made him the butt of jokes in the third term, for God's sake!"

"Yes, I grant you that too. But we are not dealing with a normal person, are we?"

"Well, no. Of course not. But still, I think you're going too far. I mean, I subscribe to most of your theories pertaining to the scientific method and all of that, but this? This is sheer, sheer... I don't know what!"

Holmes cocked an eyebrow. "Nonsense?"

Abberline had the good grace to look embarrassed. "Well, you said it, not I. Though I don't mean to be insulting, of course."

Holmes smiled wryly, rose from his chair, and walked to the bow window to gaze down at the street, holding his left side as he did so.

"Our problem is that we have an absence of data, Inspector. Given our predicament, we must abandon the analytic or scientific approach and resort to other means, synthetic means if needs be – to even what might appear to be a fanciful explanation." He raised a cautionary finger. "As long as it fits with known events." He turned from the window and looked at Abberline. "What was it that Shakespeare said? 'Imagination bodies forth the form of things unknown?'"

He reached for a pipe. "I grant you this approach may appear to be inconsistent with my often-expressed axiom that it is a capital mistake to theorize before having all the facts, but then, it is also a capital mistake to be rigid in one's thinking merely for the sake of consistency." Holmes smiled, and added: "I believe it was the American Ralph Waldo Emerson who said, 'Consistency is the hobgoblin of a small mind.' They do say useful things on occasion, Americans."

Abberline picked up the postcard from the side table, where he had placed it and studied it for a moment. He shook his head and put the card down again. "Well, even if you are right, I don't see that this is getting us anywhere further along."

"Oh, I don't know. 'Know thine enemy,' and all of that. I think it always helps to place yourself in the other fellow's shoes, try to figure out what makes his mind work, what he'll do next."

"Yes, but we don't know that, do we? That's just it! We don't know what he'll do next."

"Oh, no mystery there, I think. He'll kill again, and keep on killing until he's stopped – or until he's achieved the attention he seeks."

"Yes, yes. But how do we prevent him from killing again? That's the question. We had the area saturated with men, yet he managed to evade us and commit murder twice. Then he managed to evade us again and vanish into thin air! And talk about attention! He's getting all the attention in the world right now. He couldn't possibly ask for more."

"Yes, just so. But is he getting it from those who matter most? Matter most to him, I mean. Is he getting it from those whose attention he seeks? Obviously not."

"Well, a man who has committed murder just doesn't walk up to one's chums at a dinner party and say, 'Guess what I did last night!'"

Holmes laughed. "No, but I suspect he does derive considerable pleasure by fantasizing about what those chums would think and how very shocked they would be if only they did know: A vicarious thrill of sorts."

Abberline took a turn about the room. "All of this falls into the realm of speculation," he snapped. "We cannot know what is in his mind or what drives him to do murder, nor do I think it would necessarily help us if we did. In any case, I believe he's a lone wolf without friends, holed up in a garret someplace and avoiding society altogether."

"Oh, no," replied Holmes. "That is quite impossible. My analysis of his handwriting indicates just the opposite. He is a very social animal. He is a man who cannot abide solitude, who abhors – even fears – being alone. What we are dealing with, I think, is a man who lives two lives, a Jekyll and Hyde existence, if you will forgive a somewhat melodramatic metaphor – it is the one that readily springs to mind. He has two distinct personas, one of them craving social intercourse, human companionship, the acceptance of his peers; the other... well, you know of the other."

Abberline made a face. "All too well." He plopped himself down in a chair. "Good Lord, I can't believe we're having this conversation."

Holmes laughed again. "Oh, I don't know. I'm rather enjoying it." He turned serious again and pulled at his chin thoughtfully. "Let us assume for the moment that my hypothesis is correct, that we are dealing with a deranged individual who seeks both attention from society and wishes to wreak revenge upon it. How do we draw him out?

How do we flush him from the trees? We must appeal to his vanity, I think. We must acknowledge him to be a very, very clever little chap indeed – the cleverest of all. We must render him the homage he seeks." He paused, frowning. "Or do we do the opposite?"

Abberline sighed heavily.

Holmes put his pipe down and began pacing the room, hands clasped behind him, chin on chest.

Abberline watched him pace with growing impatience. "Well, I for one am willing to give him first prize at the fair if it'll help, but I don't see where this is getting us, I really don't. Even if all of what you say is true – and to be brutally frank, Mr. Holmes, I'm not certain I believe a word of it – what do we do about it? Induce the Queen to include him in the new year's honor's list or something?"

Holmes stopped his pacing and looked up sharply. Then he shook his head. "No, I don't think that would do at all," he said in all seriousness.

Abberline looked heavenward and rolled his eyes.

"Perhaps," said Holmes half to himself, "perhaps we should write to him."

"What?"

"Yes, that's what we should do. Write to him."

Abberline looked at him with jaw agape.

Holmes went over to his desk and reached for pen and paper. "After all, he's written to us, hasn't he? The least we could do is favor him with the courtesy of a reply."

"Good Lord," said Abberline half aloud, "I do believe he's serious!"

Fourteen

FRIDAY, OCTOBER 5-SATURDAY, OCTOBER 6, 1888

"What a chorus of groans, cries, and bleatings! What a rag-bag of singular happenings! But surely the most valuable hunting-ground that ever was given to a student of the unusual!"
— *The Adventure of the Red Circle*

Holmes completed the last mournful bars of the Paganini, lingering lovingly on the final notes, drawing them out just a little longer possibly than the composer had intended. He had been reasonably successful that evening in coaxing from the Stradivarius much of what the instrument was capable of producing in the way of tone – that clear, rich, exquisite quality that was the signature of the Cremona master, a quality unsurpassed by anyone anywhere, before or since.

Of course, Holmes characteristically was not completely satisfied with the result; he was seldom completely satisfied with anything he was able to accomplish on the violin. Or in life, for that matter.

Gently, he wiped the instrument with a soft cloth, admiring the wood's graceful curves and the warm glow of its patina. It was his most cherished possession, this object – his one great extravagance. It was one of only 540 of its kind known to exist in all the world. Simply to hold it in his hands, to caress it, gave him pleasure. To play it, to cause it to make music, was an experience that transported him to the very altar of heaven.

Anyone who thought they knew Sherlock Holmes and had never seen him with his violin had never seen the passionate side of Sherlock Holmes. They had never beheld the dreamy look, the soft, gentle smile, the ethereal otherworldly Holmes; not the distant austere figure of piercing logic and decisive mien, but someone else entirely. Was not this the man who declared, "Whatever is emotional is opposed to that true, cold reason which I place above all things?"[61]

It was this that transformed him, this gracefully formed contrivance of old polished woods and wire, painstakingly shaped and cunningly assembled, which inexplicably produced sounds known to make hardened men weep, sounds only the gods should be privileged to hear. Curiously, it was an acquisition over which he still suffered occasional pangs of guilt. Occasional, *minor* pangs.[62]

Carefully he replaced the violin in its case, making a mental note to change the D string, which stubbornly refused to permit itself to be tuned to that point precisely above middle C, where he felt it should be. Little matter that it would be the fourth time in as many weeks that the string had been changed. And little matter that the sound he was seeking was probably unobtainable. For to Holmes's ear, even a Stradivarius, this masterpiece of man's ingenuity and craftsmanship – *even* a Stradivarius was not perfect.

Holmes went over to the fireplace and poked halfheartedly at the ember in the grate, deciding because of the lateness of the hour not to bother adding more coal. He had already turned the gas lamps down in preparation for bed, so the only light in the room came from the fireplace. What little flame there was cast languid, undulating shadows on the wall and ceiling, a relaxing effect, an effect to fit his mood.

Holmes decided on a last small glass of brandy before retiring, a few sips only. He went to the sideboard to pour it and then returned to the fireplace, glass in hand, easing himself into his favorite chair to gaze at the dying embers.

Unnoticed at his feet in the darkness of the room was the scattering of newspapers all around him, his sole reading matter for that day and for several previous days as well. He had been scanning the agony columns of the daily newspapers for the better part of the week, without result.

The agony columns, those long rows of personals to be found in almost every major London daily, had long been Holmes's favorite reading matter, in addition to the crime news, of course. This "rag-bag of singular happenings," as he referred to them, was to him a barometer of sorts, a pulse beat, a microcosm: A daily ledger of all that was wrong, lost, misapplied, or misappropriated in the normal course of human events in the metropolis. In these columns could be found a daily dosage of man's folly and despair, inch after column inch of dashed hopes, dismantled dreams, and unkept promises, a compendium of bizarre requests, impossible demands, and improbable claims: Truly "a chorus of groans, cries, and bleatings," as Holmes once characterized them. There was anger and bitterness and pitiable expressions of remorse; pathos in heavy measure to be sure – the outpourings of anguished and desperate souls, demanding, pleading, admonishing, forgiving, or simply reaching out pathetically for the simple touch of another.

But for Holmes the agony columns were more than founts of mindless diversion or the objects of curiosity. For in addition to the mundane, the columns contained mystery. And, most important, they provided intelligence – intelligence that had proven useful to him countless times in the past, furnishing leads and supplying answers and even, on occasion, guiding him to individuals he sought.

It had been the longest of long shots from the start, of course, this idea of his to write to this creature who called himself Jack the Ripper. He never had any real confidence the man would respond or even see the advertisement that had been placed in the city's dailies. It had been a whim, an impulsive act, a half-silly notion half born out of desperation (and, of course, out of his weakness for the dramatic gesture).

And even if the Ripper had seen the advertisement, it was possible that Holmes took the wrong approach in his drafting of the wording of it, and succeeded only in driving him further away rather than enticing him to come closer. Perhaps he should not have challenged the man, but instead have appealed to his vanity, or offered him comfort, compassion even. He had counted on the Ripper reacting in anger to his message, had counted on touching a raw nerve, but the cursed man had not reacted at all. The problem was that Holmes had no way of determining what was the correct course to follow, no way of knowing how the man would respond. The machinations of the human brain were so unpredictable, so difficult to fathom – particularly the brain of a man so twisted – that Holmes was groping in the dark.

Someday medical science might find a way to penetrate the secrets of the human brain. Someday it might be possible to diagnose and even treat mental dysfunctions as physical illness was assessed and treated. But for the time being that portion of the anatomy which more than any other separated humankind from the lower forms remained the most mysterious, the least penetrable, the least understood. How curious it was, how ironic, he decided, that the human brain seemed capable of understanding almost everything but itself.

Holmes applied a wax vesta to the tobacco in his pipe and drew in deeply, sending thick clouds of smoke into the air. Then he leaned back in his chair and reviewed the events of the last few days.

While the police of both Scotland Yard and the City force were noisily and with great bluster and bustle going about their investigations of the two most recent murders, Holmes was quietly making his own inquiries. He had spent days prowling Whitechapel and Spitalfields, making contact with various informants whom he had nurtured over the years: Individuals of dubious character and occupation who, for a few shillings or an occasional crisp one-pound note, kept their ears to the ground and passed on to Holmes anything that at any given time could be of interest to him. They proved to be of little use on this occasion: All they were able to provide were false leads, fantastic theories, and unsubstantiated rumors. No one knew anything; everyone was afraid.

Holmes also paid visits to several of the workhouses in the East End, those cold, bare establishments that doled out meager sustenance and a few coins a day to those homeless and destitute who were able enough and willing enough to work for it. The expression "cold as charity" was surely coined by someone who had partaken of the bounty of one of these institutions. Indifferently run by individuals whose mean-spirited, hard-eyed Christianity was compensated meagerly enough with borough funds, these places specialized in watery soup and mealy bread and, on days when the cook was in his cups or in a particularly uncreative mood, an epicurean delight called skilly – a mush made of Indian corn and hot water. A few of the more benevolent workhouses even provided thin slivers of a harsh soap, noted for its ability to redden the skin and make the eyes tear when applied. Most recipients of this largess found it more desirable to go dirty.

One place Holmes visited was in the process of parceling out its main (and only) meal of the day: Ungenerous portions ladled from a large blackened kettle, the contents of which could best be described as indescribable – chunks of sopping bread, bits and pieces of fat and salt pork, gristle and bone simmering in a rancid gruel. It was the leavings of a local hospital charity ward, one of the resident workers explained — the leavings from the mouths of the sick and diseased, scraped from their plates and heaped together in buckets to be carted to the workhouse kitchens and reheated. The meal was eaten from metal plates without benefit of utensils, there being none available, while rats boldly scurried about underfoot, an occasional well-placed kick keeping them from getting too familiar. The stench of the place was positively stultifying: A sickly sour smell intermixed with the aroma of unwashed bodies and the ever-present reek of cheap gin. The totality of it caused Holmes to almost gag upon entry and made him thankful for the gulps of rank, stagnant air that greeted him outside the door upon departure. The East End, after all, was outcast London, "an evil plexus of slums that hide human creeping things," as one observer put it.[63] And surely human creeping things deserved no better.

Not for the first time did Holmes reflect upon the plight of these people, and on his own conflicting emotions concerning them: A mixture of pity and repulsion, of compassion and disdain. He felt sorry for these people, yet he despised them. He despised them for what they had allowed themselves to become. Even he recognized it as a reaction that was unreasonable, but after all was he not a product of his age and of the society which nurtured him, a society which equated poverty and ignorance with moral imperfection? If a man is born poor in this land of plenty, it is God's will; if he dies poor, sir, well then, it is his own damn fault.

It was this philosophy, this heartfelt conviction on the part of respectable Victorian England, that made it possible for the slums of Whitechapel and places like it to exist. It was an attitude that did not tolerate, took no pity on, took no notice of anything that was not clean, decent, proper, or "British."

For years even the established Church ignored these nether regions, turning a blind eye to those deprived and (in the eyes of the godly) depraved subhuman multitudes who lived literally within the shadow of St. Paul's towering dome. No matter, the cathedral's doors remained steadfastly closed to them. God's grace was not for those who did not dress the part.

Not every churchman with whom Holmes came into contact was indifferent to the poor of the East End, of course. There were several who lived and worked selflessly among them in quarters little more opulent, amid conditions little less appalling. The Barnetts of Toynbee Hall came to mind.

Toynbee Hall was a settlement house for university students who worked among the poor, founded by the Reverend Samuel Barnett and his wife, and located in the very heart of Whitechapel. It was directly behind this institution that the murder of Martha Tabram had taken place the previous August.

Mrs. Barnett was a tiny, spirited woman of indeterminate age, brimming over with energy and the milk of human kindness. She was like a little bird that never seemed to alight for more than a few seconds at a time, but flitted about from this place to that, happily engaged in a dozen or more tasks at once, her state of perpetual motion accompanied by an endless stream of chattering and chirping: sentence after run-on sentence of bright, disjointed, unrelated observations, assertions and assessments, one following the other without benefit of pause, breath, period, or comma. Throughout there was a heavy sprinkling of two favorite phrases, a reflection no doubt of her outlook on life: Things were either "very nice" or "not very nice." There was nothing better, nothing worse, and there was no in-between.

She greeted Holmes at the entrance with a small child in her arms.

"Isn't it very nice of you to come?" she said in a cheery voice, adding in the same breath without a change of tone or inflection: "It is *not* very nice to insert your finger into your nose, my deah."

Holmes, taken aback, arched an eyebrow.

"It is not very nice a'tall!"

"I quite agree, madam, I assure you," responded Holmes with great dignity. Then a movement of Mrs. Barnett's skirt caught his eye and understanding came to him at last. "Ah," he said. "*There* is the offending party!"

The object of Mrs. Barnett's reproach was a second little child, partially hidden behind the folds of her voluminous skirt and apron, its presence previously unnoticed because of the dimness of the vestibule.

With no by-your-leave or warning, Mrs. Barnett thrust the child she was carrying into Holmes's arms and swooped down to attend to the other. Holmes, clearly startled, stood there speechless, holding the infant stiffly and with arms outstretched, as if it were an object of unknown provenance and dubious purpose.

"Now, isn't that better?" Mrs. Barnett cooed, straightening. "Do come in, won't you? We don't stand on ceremony here – mind the step – I am very much afraid you will find us in our usual state of dither – my goodness, here it is almost noon and the third post has not yet arrived, I thought you were it, in point of fact; delivery services have been falling off dreadfully, have you not found that to be the case? But I know my husband will be quite pleased to see you, quite pleased indeed – you are somewhat taller than I expected, aren't you?"

Holmes, who could think of no suitable response to any of her observations, and would have been hard pressed to fit a word in edgewise in any event, confined himself to agreeable nods and followed dutifully behind as she conducted him into the recesses of the hall and up a flight of stairs, chattering gaily all the while. In that she had not yet gotten around to retrieving the child from his arms, he had no other recourse but to maintain possession of it, hoping profoundly that it did nothing sudden or untoward.

"Most of our young student workers are out on the streets at this hour, making their visits to our poor unfortunates," she explained, "so you chose an opportune time to call. These are two of our latest arrivals, the dears," she noted, indicating the children, "left on our doorstep, so to speak, by young mothers – hardly more than children themselves – who cannot care for them, poor creatures. We are so fortunate that God has chosen us for their keeping. So very fortunate indeed. I only wish there was more we could do. There are so many in need, so very many. But yet we manage nicely. With God's help we manage very nicely indeed.[64]

"Here we are, then," she announced, having arrived at the top of the stairs. She stopped before a closed door, tapped twice, and entered.

A frowning Reverend Canon Samuel Barnett was seated behind a cluttered desk, a pair of rimless spectacles perched on his forehead, his nose buried perilously deep into the pages of a large volume of religious tracts. An even larger Bible lay open across his knees, and sheets of foolscap, most of them crumpled, lay littering the desktop and the floor around his chair.

"Samuel dear, this is Mr. Sherlock Holmes come to visit. Isn't that very nice of him indeed? Do come in, won't you, Mr. Holmes. Canon Barnett always welcomes diversions when he has a sermon to prepare. He has such terrible difficulties with them, poor dear. And I can't for the life of me realize why. Ordinarily he is so very, very clever with words."

The Reverend Barnett laid the Bible aside and rose from his desk to pump Holmes's hand with obvious pleasure, an act that necessitated some furious manipulation of the infant on Holmes's part. "How good of you, sir!" beamed the reverend, pumping away. "How very good of you to come, and welcome you are! Your reputation is not unknown to us here, Mr. Holmes. It has preceded you, sir, even into these dark corners. I am an avid devotee of yours, I must confess. The accounts of your exploits are among my favorite bedtime reading, along with the Gospels, of course – see what good company you are in! But my word, sir, whatever do you intend doing with that babe? It appears to be decidedly out of kilter."

Mrs. Barnett, suddenly awakening to the fact that Holmes was still in possession, though just barely, of the now furiously wiggling infant, leapt to his assistance with a little cry of alarm. "However can you forgive me! I had quite forgotten!"

Holmes awkwardly but gratefully divested himself of the child and managed to smile politely. "I am afraid you will find it is, ah, somewhat damp, ma'am."

"Oh, dear. I shall attend to it at once," she said, enfolding the child in her arms once again. "You will excuse me, I am sure. Whatever must you think of us?"

Reverend Barnett was all smiles. "Yes, yes, of course, m'dear. And a nice cup of tea for our guest, if someone below can see to it. Thank you so very much, Henrietta dear," he called after the departing figure.

"Mr. Holmes, sir, take a chair, take a chair, please! No ceremony here, none at all. Do make yourself comfortable – and never mind the clutter, I pray you. It is our natural state here, I fear. Clutter, clutter everywhere, clutter and confusion." He laughed. "I no longer apologize for it, you see. I merely fall back upon my Nathaniel Ward!"

Holmes looked at him blankly. "Do you indeed?"

Reverend Barnett took a deep breath and struck a pose, left hand over heart and right index finger stabbing the air: "'If the whole conclave of Hell,'" he quoted with mock seriousness, "'can so compolitize exadverse and diametrical contraditions as to compolitize such a multimonstrous maufrey of heteroclites and quicquidlibets quietly, I trust I may say with all humble reverence they can do more than the Senate of Heaven.' Hah!" he exclaimed. "I believe I have gotten it right, but I am never quite sure. Are you familiar with Ward, sir? Not C of E, of course, but a good man nonetheless. Please correct me if I quoted him wrong!"

Holmes raised his hands helplessly and laughed. "A lack in my education, I am certain, but I fear the gentleman's existence has escaped my notice."

"Yes? Well, never mind, never mind. I am sure you did not come here to discuss the eccentric writings of seventeenth-century clerics with me, though I confess to you quite shamelessly that I am considered somewhat of an authority." He sat down in his chair and leaned back, the expression on his kindly face becoming quizzical. It was obvious he was overcome with curiosity. "But what does bring you, Mr. Holmes? What kind wind favors us with your presence? No, no, don't tell me! Allow me to make use of *my* deductive powers!" He leaned forward and lowered his voice to a conspiratorial whisper that under other circumstances would have been comical. "It must be the dreadful murders, mustn't it?"

"Indeed it must, sir."

"Ah, yes, I thought so. How very sad, how very sad." He shook his head. "The official police have been here on several occasions, of course. We gave them all the cooperation we could, though little enough it was. So many questions, so many questions. And so few answers. There's the pity of it, you see. There just don't seem to be any answers, only questions. But how I ramble on! Forgive me, Mr. Holmes, please do. Of course I shall answer any questions you care to put to me, and answer them to the very best of my ability, of course I shall. The good Lord knows I would like to be of help, and in any way I can."

But there was nothing he could add to the scant knowledge Holmes already had, nor could Mrs. Barnett when she returned five minutes later with the tea. She was saddened by the murders, of course – deeply saddened – but hardly shocked. Nothing that occurred in the East

End could shock her anymore. Holmes sensed that behind that flighty exterior was a sensible, down-to-earth woman, highly intelligent and unusually resourceful, and fully capable of not only understanding the realities of life in the East End, but of dealing with them. His assessment of her was quickly verified.

"When we first came here fifteen years ago to take over St. Jude's," she said, "the bishop told Samuel that it was the worst parish in the district. But even he didn't know how really bad it was! It is a human sewer, you see. There are nine hundred thousand souls in the East End, eighty thousand of them in Whitechapel. Of these, eleven thousand are unemployed and homeless, living the lives of savages, degrading whatever they touch, incapable of helping themselves or even allowing themselves to be helped. The worst part of it, of course, is the children. They are so ill used – abused in the most unimaginable ways."

Reverend Barnett nodded in agreement. "Yes, but there is improvement, there is improvement. We must not forget that. The passage of the Criminal Law Amendment three years ago has helped immeasurably. The age of consent for females is now sixteen, you know, and that at least has put quite a dent into what was a flourishing trade in child prostitutes. Why, up until then it was possible to purchase a twelve-year-old lass for twenty pounds. Purchase one outright. And whilst I harbor no illusions that that sort of thing does not still go on – yes, with young boys as well as girls – at least we now have laws to oppose it, where before we had nothing."

Mrs. Barnett caught sight of a strained expression on Holmes's face. She smiled grimly. "Does the subject shock you, Mr. Holmes? Or does it shock you that I, a woman, should engage in a discussion of it?" She held up her hand. "You need not answer. I fear I've made you feel uncomfortable. Well, I do not apologize for it. While I know it is not something to be discussed in polite society, and decidedly not by a woman, that, you see, is part of the problem. It is not discussed, therefore it is not dealt with. Sometimes I think we English are so very proper that we would rather have our house burn down than disturb public tranquility by shouting 'Fire.' You will forgive a woman's temerity I hope, but shocking though it may be, the matter must be brought out into the open. The rate of syphilis among our children is alarmingly high: One fifth of the children we administer to suffer from inherited venereal disease. And sexual abuse is rampant. Living conditions are so terribly crowded, you see, with as many as six or eight to a single room. Sometimes there is but a single bed, and sometimes the room is shared by two separate families. The incidence of child rape and of incest among father and daughter and brother and sister is deplorable: They simply know no better and see nothing wrong with it."

Holmes was truly dumbfounded by Mrs. Barnett's words. Decent women did not discuss such things, certainly not the wife of a clergyman, and certainly not in mixed company. Such words as *rape* and *incest* and even *sex* were just not used. And though he above all individuals recognized the hypocrisy of Victorian morality, such recognition did not lessen his sense of shock or embarrassment at hearing the words spoken.

Reverend Barnett suffered from no such inhibitions. The subject, and his wife's open discussion of it, was obviously something he was used to. He nodded in agreement with what she had said. "It is the drink that is to blame for much of the degradation, you know."

"Oh, absolutely!" said Mrs. Barnett. "A measure of gin costs a mere three halfpennies. It only encourages our people to drink themselves into insensibility. It breeds violence and cruelty, and causes a breakdown in family life. I have always maintained that if we were to make the cost of gin more dear, it would go a lot further than any act of Parliament in solving the problems we are faced with here."

The canon patted her hand. "You are quite right, of course, m'dear, but there is progress, that you cannot deny. Our task is not a hopeless one, far from it. Our young students work wonders! What a fine group of young men! They are out among the poor every day, giving counsel and aid and helping to spread the gospel. Every day I see progress made, every day!"

It was with difficulty that Holmes managed to steer the discussion back to the murders.

"Your students have taken to patrolling the streets at night since these atrocities have begun, I have been told."

"Quite so. As their warden, I deemed it part of their mission here to join in the hunt for the killer. I will be quite honest with you, Mr. Holmes: Even if our lads are not successful in helping to apprehend the man, the very fact they are able to show they are interested in what happens to these poor, unfortunate women is of assistance to us in our work. It brings us closer to the residents, you see."

"I do indeed. But it is quite possible they can be of material help. I have several questions to put to you regarding where they have gone and what they have seen."

Reverend Barnett, true to his word, answered all the questions put to him, but was able to shed little light on the murders. "I know little more than what I read in the newspapers, I fear. I have my own theories, of course, but of what use they will be to you I cannot imagine."

It took little encouragement on the part of Holmes for Canon Barnett to expound at some length.

"He is not of the district, of that I am certain. Death is no stranger here, to be sure, and cruel, violent death is an everyday occurrence, but not this kind, no – not this satanic, ritualistic sort of thing! It is an outsider, Mr. Holmes, an individual who knows our streets well, who is no stranger to our precincts, but surely not one of our own. What makes me so certain is simply this: None of our people would have the ingenuity, or the energy."

Holmes nodded. It was an astute observation.

Canon Barnett paused and smiled slyly. "As to how this fellow makes his escape? Ah, well, I have my theories there too. I have used your method, Mr. Holmes, in reaching my conclusions, you see. I have ruled out the impossible and have settled upon the merely improbable. If he has managed to avoid the police patrols in the streets, it must mean that he is not using the streets! There you have it, plain and simple! Look elsewhere, sir! Look elsewhere!"

Holmes rewarded the clergyman with a bow of approval from his chair. "You have missed your calling, reverend sir! That is certainly a most ingenious line of reasoning, and I vow I shall pursue it with all my heart."

Both the Barnetts accompanied him downstairs to the front door, but he was unable to make his departure before one parting story from the canon. "You are familiar with Dr. Barnardo and his homes for children, of course? His good works are renowned throughout the district, especially those works performed on behalf of the orphaned and maimed. He took tea with us the other day and he told me this tale:

"He makes it a practice to call regularly at some of the worst of the lodging houses in the district for the purpose of chatting up the female residents known to him, his aim being both to reassure them and commiserate with them and to give them what little comfort he can. The killer's victims, as you know, are all unfortunate creatures from the meanest of these doss-houses, all sisters under the skin, so to speak. They are terrified, of course — absolutely terrified. Dr. Barnardo encountered one such woman just the other day who told him that she knew one of the earlier victims, poor soul — I forget which one it was. And she said to him bitterly and tearfully that it was her belief that the authorities had no interest in catching the killer, no interest at all. 'They just don't care,' she said. 'They don't care about him and they don't care about the likes of us.' Oh, how she ranted on and on, Dr. Barnardo told me. 'We're all up to no good and no one cares what becomes of us,' she railed.

"The pathetic thing of it is, Mr. Holmes, the saddest thing, is that the woman to whom Dr. Barnardo was speaking was Elizabeth Stride, one of the two women who was murdered the other night."

Canon Barnett looked down at the floor. "Dr. Barnardo didn't realize it at the time, of course. He knew her only as Long Liz, the name by which she was known to everyone hereabouts. It wasn't until after he visited the mortuary and viewed the remains that he realized it was the very same woman he had spoken to a few days earlier, the very same woman who expressed such bitterness and sadness and such fear."

His eyes moistened. "Something must be done," said the reverend softly, "something must be done." He gripped Holmes by the arm and gazed earnestly into his eyes. "And I know that you are just the chap to do it."[65]

Holmes awoke with a start at the sound of a footfall upon the stair. The ashes in the grate were cold, and the first wan light of dawn began to materialize at the window. He had fallen asleep in his chair and had remained there the entire night, the snifter of brandy untouched at his elbow. Stiffly he rose from his chair and went to the door. It was Abberline, his clothes rumpled, his eyes rimmed with red, his face drawn and haggard.

"I saw the glow of your lamp through the window as I drove by," he explained, "so I assumed you were already up and about. I hope you don't mind a caller at this uncivilized hour."

Holmes stifled a yawn. "Like you, Inspector, I never did make it to my bed last night. Come in, come in. Mrs. Hudson shall no doubt have a good hot pot of coffee before us very shortly. What news do you bring?"

"News? Oh, no news, I fear. We've been chasing shadows, wills-o'-the-wisp. Just the ordinary routine sort of thing with nothing to show for it. Another sleepless night, is all."

Holmes grunted noncommittally as he busied himself turning up the table lamps.

"You've seen the new description given out by the City Police, I presume," asked Abberline.

"Yes, in the *Gazette*. It bears a vague similarity to that of the man I saw in Mitre Square, insofar as his height and approximate age and costume are concerned. But it differs in some of the other particulars. The red handkerchief around his neck is a bit fanciful, I think, though I was never really close enough to him to see all that much, and the suggestion that he had the overall appearance of a sailor is utter rubbish. Since when does a man of the sea wear a deerstalker hat and a cutaway coat? How they ever reached that conclusion is beyond me."

"I understand it was based on the observations of a passerby who claimed to have seen our friend with the Eddowes woman in the square – just minutes before the murder took place. The man had the gait and bearing of a seaman, he said."

"And this passerby, he could tell that the neckerchief the suspect may or may not have been wearing was red? In the darkness of the night? What enviable eyesight this passerby must have. He would put a cat to shame!"

"Well, he claims the moon was very bright – almost as light as day."

Holmes made a face. "I would not be surprised if he claimed the murderer had horns and tail and cloven feet! Do me this, will you: Go out on the next brightly moonlit night and hang some colored bunting from a line and stand off twenty yards or so – make it five yards, if you wish. I defy you to distinguish what colors they are! What unmitigated rubbish!"

Abberline shrugged. He was too weary to argue. Holmes, on the other hand, was now wide awake and was just getting into stride.

"I am being foolish perhaps," said he, "but I find it difficult to subscribe to the theory that in the absence of concrete fact, it is not only permissible but desirable to fabricate one. How convenient, how very efficacious! Grasp at a straw if you must, but at least have the good sense to grasp at a real straw!"

Abberline shrugged again. "At least it's the City force to blame this time, not the Yard."

Holmes snorted. "I am certain the Yard shall make up for it, given time," he replied, his voice heavy with sarcasm. He got up from his chair and took a turn about the room. "Wherever is Mrs. Hudson with the coffee?" he muttered irritably. "I'll tell you how it is, Abberline," he continued. "We now have three separate descriptions of the killer being circulated. One indicates he was dressed in something like blue serge with a deerstalker cap, another indicates he wore a black diagonal coat with a hard felt hat and collar and tie, and the third indicates he wore a loose-fitting pepper-and-salt tweed jacket with a gray cloth cap and red neckerchief tied in a sailor's knot. All in one night! This man is a wonder! I shouldn't be surprised if he turned up in a clown suit next — ah, there she is."

Mrs. Hudson's unmistakable tread was heard upon the stair at last, and Holmes moved swiftly to the door to open it for her.

"Morning, Mrs. H. Thank you so very much. Allow me to take it from here. You need not trouble yourself further."

She handed the tray over without a word and threw an ugly glance at the early morning visitor before turning on her heel to descend the stairs.

Holmes nudged the door shut with his foot and carried the tray of coffee service to the table. "Sugar? Milk?"

"No, I take it neat, thanks."

"There's some toast here if you wish."

"Thank you, no."

Holmes poured the coffee and handed Abberline his cup. "Aside from this sudden plethora of eyewitness descriptions, what else is new that you can tell me?"

Abberline took a sip of coffee and darted a glance at Holmes before replying. "You have heard about the dogs, of course."

"Dogs? What dogs?"

"The commissioner, Sir Charles?"

"Yes, I know his name," snapped Holmes. "What's this about dogs?"

"He wants to bring in sleuth hounds."

"Sleuth hounds?"

"You know, bloodhounds."

"To do what? Piddle on the cobbles?"

Abberline smiled despite himself. "He has got it in his head that bloodhounds will be able to sniff him out."

Holmes clapped his hands. "Sniff him out? Oh, jolly good!"

"He's given instructions that if or when there is another murder, the dogs are to be brought in before the body is removed so they can be put on the scent. A breeder over near Scarborough has been contacted and has agreed to provide two of his animals. The commissioner has arranged to hold a trial in Hyde Park within the next few days."

"Truly?"

Abberline placed a hand over his heart. "Truly."

Holmes said nothing. Thoughtfully he took another sip of coffee, then put the cup down and walked over to the bow window to gaze down at the street. After a minute or so he turned. "Hyde Park, you say?"

Abberline nodded.

"Bloodhounds in Hyde Park?" Holmes's thin lips curved upward in a puckish smile. "What a vision that conjures up, what a perfectly marvelous show it should be." He turned wistful for a moment. "Pity I shall miss it, but Watson's letters from Baskerville Hall are becoming most insistent. I am afraid I have a long-overdue appointment with another dog, this one on the moors of Devon. More coffee, dear chap?"

Fifteen

SUNDAY, OCTOBER 21-TUESDAY,
OCTOBER 23, 1888

*"I thought at first you had done something clever, but I see
that there was nothing in it, after all."*
— The Red-Headed League

John H. Watson, M.D., gazed out of the rain-spattered window of the first-class rail car compartment, the monotonous, curiously soothing clackety-clack of the wheels against the track combining with the dreary weather to lull him into a state of lassitude, of semi-sleep. The bleak autumnal countryside of rural England, neat and picture perfect despite the weather and the season of the year, had given way to the industrial outskirts of London, soot blackened and grimy gray. The tall chimneys of the factories and foundries that flickered past his window vied with one another in sending aloft dark plumes of greasy smoke that rose to merge with the low-lying clouds, laying a pall over the still-distant city and over his spirits as well.

Still, he was glad to be getting back to London. The affairs at Baskerville Hall in Devonshire had been successfully concluded, but it had been a close thing and a harrowing experience, and he and Holmes were both tired and mentally drained. The homey atmosphere of Baker Street, coupled with Mrs. Hudson's cooking and her other comforting ministrations, would do them both the world of good. Rural life was not always so settling to the nerves after all, he reflected. Not when murder was involved; not when a vicious hound roamed loose on the moors. He would spend tomorrow compiling notes about the case, he decided, in preparation for the day when he would sit down and write the story in its entirety. What to call it, was the question. *The Hound of Baskerville Hall? The Beast of the Baskervilles* perhaps? Yes, that had a nice ring to it.

The rain was coming down harder now, the gray, overcast skies seemed to settle lower over the dreary scene outside his window. It was a somber, depressing Sunday afternoon, one in which the fire of their sitting room and a hot toddy would be doubly welcome.

Across from him, Sherlock Holmes, donned in his familiar traveling costume of Inverness and deerstalker cap, coils of pungent smoke rising from his briar and curling about him, observed his friend from beneath hooded eyes. Good old Watson, he thought. What a pillar of strength he was; what a solid, dependable ally. Holmes could not imagine how he would have gotten along without him these past few harrowing weeks: He had served as his eyes and ears and more. That he, Holmes, was able to bring the Baskerville matter to a successful conclusion was due in no small measure to Watson's selfless contributions.

The affair had been doubly difficult for Holmes. He was not accustomed to having two cases on his mind at once. That intricate mechanism that was his brain worked best when concentrating on one problem and one problem only, and for that reason it had always been a strict rule of his never to take on more than one case at a time. This was one of the few occasions when he had been forced to break that rule. But now that the Baskerville business was behind him, he would be able to devote his full attentions to the matter that awaited him in London.

Holmes reached over and tapped the ashes out of his pipe. "You are quite right, dear fellow," he said nonchalantly. "We shall be arriving at Paddington somewhat later than expected and, yes, we shall in all probability face difficulty in obtaining the services of a porter and possibly a cab as well."

Watson, startled out of his reverie, looked across at Holmes in astonishment. "What's this, Holmes! Have you now taken to reading my mind?"

Holmes chuckled softly. "My dear fellow, after all these years, I should be a dullard indeed if I could not at least follow your train of thought on occasion —"

"My train of thought?"

"— which is so transparently obvious: Like following a trail of bread crumbs left scattered behind you in the woods."

"Bread crumbs?" retorted Watson. "Whatever are you talking about? I have done nothing of the kind, and I must say, Holmes, I consider your — your trickery, or whatever it is, most uncivil. It is nothing less than, than an invasion of my privacy. The very idea!"

Holmes, chuckling, leaned over and patted him on the knee. "There is no trickery involved, merely simple inference. It is you yourself who told me."

"I? I told you nothing. Whatever do you mean?"

"Watson, what am I to think when I observe you looking out of the window, studying our surroundings for the longest while, craning your neck this way and that in an obvious effort to determine where we are? You then reach over to consult the train schedule lying on the seat beside you and pull out your watch, shaking your head in a disheartened manner. Then you glance out the window again and look up at the sky and shake your head again. Your gaze then travels to the luggage rack above my head. You frown and rub your shoulder, the one in which you were wounded in Afghanistan, and shake your head yet again. What am I to make of all of this, if not the obvious? You ascertain that the train is running late, behind schedule. It is a rainy Sunday afternoon, rapidly approaching evening, a time when porters at Paddington are in short supply, which means you will be forced to carry your own luggage. That doleful glance at your bulging grip above me and the massaging of your injured limb tells me that you are not looking forward to that laborious indignity. Nor do I blame you. But really, dear fellow, you must learn to pack fewer things; I could have traveled round the world with less."

Holmes inverted his pipe and blew the moisture out of the bowl. "And by the by," he said with mock hauteur, "I do not especially appreciate being accused of trickery."

Watson looked at him sheepishly. "You always make it sound so simple once you explain it."

Holmes smiled indulgently. "Yaass, well, even the most abstract problem is simple once it is explained. Such as the one we have left behind us in Devon. However, my mind now dwells on the one that faces us in London. That, I fear, will not be so simple."

Watson's eyes narrowed. It had been a fortnight since the subject had even come up in conversation between them, so engrossed had they been in the affairs of Baskerville Hall. While it would be incorrect to say that he had not given any thought to the matter during all that time, it was not something that had loomed high in his consciousness either. London and all its cares had seemed so remote.

"At least there haven't been any more murders since," he said. "The fellow seems to have gone to ground. And if the papers are to be believed, the police don't seem to have made any progress in tracking him down."

Holmes smiled. "Nor did I expect them to." He added ruefully: "But then, neither have I."

Watson knew Holmes would not appreciate the consoling words he had in mind to utter, so he left them unspoken. "Any new thoughts?" he asked instead.

"New thoughts?" Holmes replied self-disparagingly. He shook his head in a gesture of hopelessness. "No, none at all." He gazed out the window silently for a moment. "Only I continue to harbor nagging fears that there is something right under my nose that I have neglected, some obvious little tidbit of information that has escaped my notice."

"Something to do with the cigarette ends that were found, do you think?"

Holmes dismissed that suggestion with an impatient wave of his hand. "No, not that. I have gone as far as I can for the moment in pursuit of answers there, and the possibilities that have suggested themselves as a result are totally impossible. No, there is something else. What it could be eludes me. I have no idea, no idea at all. When it finally does occur to me, I shall kick myself for it, of that I am certain. Well... it will come, it will come."

He lowered his gaze and looked off into space for a moment. "In all likelihood," he added quietly.

The train rumbled into Paddington Station not long after. To their mutual surprise and Watson's relief, they had no difficulties in finding a porter after all, and their wait at the cab stand was happily a brief one. They were back in their rooms in Baker Street within the hour, seated before a cheerful fire in their accustomed places, sharing a hot pot of Mrs. Hudson's tea, which Watson insisted upon lacing liberally with rum.

"Of all of the countless nostrums that have proven to be totally worthless in preventing or curing a cold," he proclaimed, "I find strong spirits to be utterly essential."

Alerted by wire of their coming, Mrs. Hudson had prepared an early supper that did her proud, and to which they in turn rendered swift, unmerciful justice – not to mention what penalties they imposed upon a perfectly respectable bottle of Médoc. They retired to their beds early that cold, wet night, their stomachs too full for prudence or comfort, but their feelings of well-being complete.

When Watson awoke the next morning, he found that Holmes was already gone – "Gone with barely a gulp of coffee," Mrs. Hudson reported disapprovingly. "'E took 'is egg, slipped it between two slices of toast, 'nd popped it into the pocket of his ulster. 'E was off before I could say 'boo,'" she said. "Now, really!"

Watson, having his own long-neglected affairs to attend to, gave little thought to Holmes's whereabouts for the remainder of the day. He spent the morning going through his mail and settling overdue accounts, while a good part of the afternoon was, as planned, devoted to compiling his notes of the Baskerville affair. He knew his memory could be faulty at times, so he was eager to jot down the particulars of the case while they were still fresh in his mind. Holmes was always after him for being cavalier with petty details, particularly in regard to dates and times, chiding him for playing fast and loose with reality and making him, Holmes, appear to be, as he put it, the most ingenious lawbreaker of all time: "If some of your accounts of my little problems are to be believed, Watson, I am not only capable of working minor miracles in the field of criminal detection, but have the capability of being in two places at one time, surely a violation of one of the most basic laws of nature. Is it possible I am more resourceful than even I imagined?"

Of course Holmes did not take into account the fact that he, Watson, was often required by his editor to purposely change not only names and places, but even dates and times and circumstances to avoid the possibility of irksome libel suits. A writer could get away with almost anything as long as he used discretion in resorting to the truth.[66]

His notes completed by midafternoon, Watson had more than enough time to make himself presentable for the evening, which was to be devoted to Miss Morstan. That, of course, had been uppermost on Watson's mind throughout the day. It had been several weeks since he had seen her last, and he was as excited as a schoolboy at the prospect. A visit to his barber was required, and his best cutaway coat and striped trousers, suffering from the effects of being stuffed into a suitcase, were sorely in need of a sponging and pressing. Mrs. Hudson's little slavey, who was clever with a flatiron if with little else, would see to that.

It was after midnight when Watson returned to 221B, the delights of the evening with dearest Mary fairly radiating from his eyes. Dinner at the Monico in Piccadilly was a decided success, and the show at the nearby Pavilion Music Hall most enjoyable, though Watson would be hard pressed to recall what he ate or saw if requested to do so. There was a spring to his step that had not been there for some time, and a rakish tilt to his topper that was decidedly out of character. Holmes still had not returned, which was probably just as well for Watson's sake. It saved him from a caustic comment or two regarding the deleterious effects of love on an otherwise sensible middle-aged English gentleman. He went to bed without giving Holmes's continued absence a second thought. After all, it was not an unusual occurrence: Holmes was often gone for days at a time when he was hot on the scent. He would no doubt appear at breakfast.

But he did not.

Watson was beginning to get anxious. A good deal of mail had arrived for Holmes during his absence, and several heavy stacks of newspapers, delivered by the newsagent the day before, stood by the door near the coat rack awaiting his perusal. Apparently he had arranged with the newsagent to collect them for him on a daily basis, so that he could get caught up on the criminal news and agony columns upon his return from Devon. Their unaccustomed presence and bulk stood as a constant reminder to Watson that Holmes had still not appeared, and as the morning wore on and turned to afternoon, his anxiety increased. He had just about made up his mind to go around to Scotland Yard to seek out Abberline in the hope that he would have some knowledge of Holmes's whereabouts, when the jangle of the front door's bellpull brought him up short. The heavy tread upon the stairs some moments later told him that it was not Holmes, who would have used his latchkey, in any case. Still, in his anxiety he rushed to the door. A large man in macintosh and derby appeared on the landing, a small parcel tucked beneath his arm. He was a policeman unmistakably.

"You must be Dr. Watson. M' name is Halse, City Police. I got here as soon as I could."

Watson, now totally alarmed and fearing the worst, turned pale. "Good Lord, man, what's amiss? Is it Holmes?"

The policeman looked at him in surprise. "Why, I don't know what you mean, sir. We received a telegram this morning from Mr. Holmes, if that's what you mean. I was directed to meet him at this address. Is he not here, then?"

Before Watson could reply, the downstairs bell sounded again. Watson flung back the door and peered down the steep staircase as Mrs. Hudson, muttering to herself, emerged from her front room to answer it. It was Sergeant Thicke whose stocky figure appeared framed in the doorway this time. Watson did not wait for him to make his way up the stairs, but called down to him: "What's the news, Sergeant? Have you heard anything of Holmes?"

Thicke, too, reacted in some surprise. "Wot? 'E's not 'ere, then?

Inspector H'Abberline received a telegram from 'im not an 'our ago, h'askin' one of us ta meet 'im 'ere."

"He's been gone for days!" replied Watson excitedly. "I was on the verge of coming round to you people in the hope you would know of his whereabouts."

"Waal, that's a funny one, I should say," said Thicke, arriving at the top of the stairs. "Hullo, Halse, you 'ere too?"

The two police officers greeted each other with gruff cordiality, obviously having known each other for some time despite their belonging to different departments. They then turned back to Watson. "Gone for days, ye say?" said Thicke. "The wire we received was posted just this morning."

"Ours too," Halse joined in. "I expect he'll turn up shortly. He wouldn't of asked us to be here otherwise."

The slamming of the downstairs door caused their heads to turn in unison. "There. What did I tell you. I expect that's him now."

Once again Watson rushed to the door leading to the stair landing, but before he even reached it he knew from the familiar sound of the footfall upon the stairs that it was indeed Holmes. He wrenched the door open.

"Holmes! Where the devil have you been?"

Tired and disheveled, his gaunt, pale cheeks sorely in need of a razor, Sherlock Holmes reached the landing and shot Watson an amused glance. "Do straighten your cravat, Watson," he said, cocking an eyebrow. "Whatever would Miss Morstan think?"

Watson, angry at being made anxious but relieved that his friend was safe and well, had no choice but to stand there silently fuming as Holmes greeted their visitors.

"I trust I haven't taken either one of you away from pressing duties," said Holmes to the two police detectives as he removed his hat and ulster, "but unless I miss my guess, it will be well worth your while."

Then he spied Halse's parcel sitting on the table, and his eyes lit up. Without further explanation he made directly for it.

"These are her possessions, then? All of them?"

"All of 'em," replied Halse. "They was stored in the central property room and I checked the contents against the inventory we made the morning she was done in."

Holmes tore open the parcel and began sorting through the objects that spilled out, spreading them on the table as he did so. Watson, curious, walked over and peered around his shoulder.

"Whatever is all this rubbish?" he asked.

It did indeed look like rubbish, an odd assortment of miscellany that could have been the dregs of any street corner dustbin: A few soiled handkerchiefs, a matchbox, an old table knife, some slivers of grimy soap, a comb, a mitten, a pair of broken spectacles...

Halse was the one who replied: "The worldly possessions of the late Catherine Eddowes, Doctor – the woman what was murdered in Mitre Square early on the morning of September thirtieth. Though why you would want to rummage through this lot again, Mr. Holmes, is beyond me. There's nothing here of no interest, and that's a fact."

Holmes ignored him, continuing his inspection of the parcel's contents with an intensity that was riveting to those who watched. He found what he was looking for after a few seconds and, his eyes shining with brightness, picked it out from among the other things and held it up to the light.

It was a man's sleeve link, a common, ordinary cufflink. And it appeared to be a cheap one at that, made of some base metal that was coated with rust.

There was silence in the room for a moment. The two policemen exchanged glances. Thicke was the first to speak. "I'm not quite sure I understand, Mr. Holmes."

Holmes smiled enigmatically, continuing to examine the object in his hand. He took it over to the window and submitted it to close scrutiny with his pocket lens.

"You will recall our conversation on the train a few days ago, Watson, when I made reference to something that was nagging at my brain? I knew there was a detail I had overlooked. Well, this was it."

The others joined him by the window.

Halse was the first to comprehend. "You think it was the murderer's?"

Holmes shot him a glance. "It would be a mistake to jump to conclusions, but one must ask what a man's sleeve link was doing in the possession of a woman. I confess it is a question that should have occurred to me when I first examined the woman's property shortly after her murder, and can ascribe my lapse only to either fatigue or gross stupidity. I was guilty of that which I habitually am fond of accusing you, Watson: Seeing without observing. Should I be so arrogant as to ever do so again, please remind me of this occasion."

Watson smiled knowingly but said nothing.

Halse, frowning, shook his head. "I think you're on a wrong track, Mr. Holmes. Let me remind you that it is not uncommon to find all manner of odd things on these women. They're like magpies. They pick things up in their wanderings and stash them away, guarding them like the crown jewels. You'll find them with the most useless, worthless items. Why, I even found one with a set of someone else's false teeth in her pocket, would you believe?"

Thicke, who had left their company and had seated himself comfortably in Holmes's chair by the fireplace, laughed disparagingly. "Wrong track? He's on the wrong railroad! Looky, Mr. Holmes, not only is Halse ryght in what 'e sez 'bout these lydies collecting anythin' and everythin',' but 'e forgot to mention this particalar lydy woz even wearin' a pair o' man's boots, if I recall correct."

Halse nodded. "That's quite right. I did forget."

"I didn't," Holmes said quietly, unfazed by the arguments marshaled by the two policemen. He calmly continued examining the object in his fingers as if he hadn't heard a word they spoke. "Do you happen to recall where on her person this was found, Halse?"

"No, I don't. In one of the pockets of her apron as may be, or in her purse."

"But you don't know precisely."

"No," he admitted.

"Could it have been in the folds of her dress, or on the ground beside her?"

Halse spread his hands and shrugged. "I honestly don't know, Mr. Holmes. I suppose it could have been."

Holmes persisted. "Who would know? Who was it who gathered up these things and searched the body?"

Halse pulled at an earlobe and tried to think. "I don't know that either, really. It might have been Hunt. Inspector McWilliam would remember. I'll have to check with him."

"Do so, if you please. It could be most significant."

Halse shrugged again. "I will do so if you like, but I must tell you, Mr. Holmes, that I believe we're wasting our time." He pointed with his chin at the sleeve link in Holmes's fingers. "Just look at how rusty and dirty that thing is. It probably hasn't been worn in ages. No man would stick that in a shirt cuff."

Holmes looked at him, his gray eyes devoid of expression. "It is indeed dirty, Mr. Halse, but that is not rust. That is dried blood."

Thicke started up from his chair. They all gathered in around Holmes to peer more closely at the object in his fingers.

"Come," Holmes said, leading them over to the deal table in the corner, where he reached for a bottle of alcohol and a piece of cloth.

After a few moments of rubbing, he placed the object down on the table. It was no longer something made of a base metal that had turned brown with corrosion. It was an object of gold and bright blue enamel.

"Good Lord," breathed Halse. "I never would have believed it."

Watson and Thicke merely stood there in wonder.

Holmes picked it up and turned it over in his fingers. The design in the center was a familiar one.

Thicke peered over his shoulder. "Why, it looks like one of those symbols of the old French regime, a watchamacallit?"

"A fleur-de-lis."

"Ryght!"

"I think you will have to agree, gentlemen," said Holmes, "that it is highly unlikely one such as Catherine Eddowes would have carried around a bauble such as this very long. She would have quickly paid a visit to the pawnbroker. The proceeds from its sale would have kept her in gin for a very long time indeed."

The lack of response made it quite clear that neither Thicke nor Halse could disagree with his logic.

Holmes took up his lens once again and bent low over the table.

"Ahhh," he said delightedly after a few seconds. "The goldsmith's hallmark is plainly visible on the back."

He focused the magnifying glass in and out. "It is not a British stamp, that is for certain," he murmured half to himself.

He waved his free hand at Watson and waggled a finger in the general direction of the shelf where he kept his source books. Watson caught his meaning and went to fetch the appropriate volume, handing it to him wordlessly.

Holmes bent over the book and began riffling through its pages until he found what he was looking for and compared it with the hallmark under his lens. He straightened and looked at the others with a grin of triumph.

"It's Kock," he said. "I knew it!"

"I beg your pardon?" said Halse.

"R. & L. Kock, jewelers, Frankfurt am Main. I think you will find them in the Kaiserstrasse within walking distance of the Eschenheimer Turm, if my memory serves me well."

"German?"

"Very."

"Ye know this shop well, do ye then?" asked Thicke.

"Mostly by reputation," replied Holmes, "though I have had occasion to stroll by it once or twice during my travels. It is an exclusive, highly reputable firm, well known on the Continent for dealing in the very best quality of gems and jewelry, the equivalent of our own Lambert's or J. W. Benson or Marx & Company. It does a brisk trade in military decorations and chivalric orders as well. That's where you may pick up your Iron Cross, Thicke, when the Kaiser finally gets around to awarding it to you. Or would you prefer the Order of Teutonic Knights? In any event, as you might imagine, its clientele includes the very *crème* of European society, including" – Holmes paused for effect – "including members of several royal families." He paused again. "Among them our own."

This statement was greeted with a silence that hung heavy in the air. Watson and the two policemen simply stood there looking at one another wordlessly until the spell was broken finally by Thicke, who emitted a long burst of air from his lungs and said simply: *"Jee-ee-sus!"*

Watson's disbelief was more articulately expressed, though only barely: "Are you suggesting, Holmes, that – well, what exactly is it that you are suggesting?"

Holmes lighted a cigarette. His reply and manner were maddeningly tranquil. "I suggest nothing, nothing whatsoever. I merely state a fact."

He studied their expressions for a moment. "See here now, it would be wrong, even dangerous, to make any inferences from this. The worst thing we could do is jump to conclusions that are based on only partial data. We must proceed orderly and cautiously, one step at a time. As I am fond of saying, gentlemen, it is a capital mistake to fall into the tempting trap of theorizing without having all the facts at hand. The object is not to make the foot fit the shoe, but the other way around."

Thicke apparently heard nothing of what Holmes had said. "We are on slippery footin' 'ere, gents – dangerous, slippery footin.' And I don't like h'it one single bit, and that's no lie!"

Halse, at least, had the good sense to take Holmes's caution at face value. "You are right, of course, Mr. Holmes. I think the first thing we should do is establish where the object was found, if possible. I shall attend to that at once. The second thing –"

"The second thing, Mr. Halse, I shall attend to," Holmes said, interrupting. "A quick cablegram to Frankfurt is in order, I believe, and I should think an inquiry from me is more likely to result in a quicker response than one from the official police. Your department would have to go through Scotland Yard, the Yard through the Home Office, the Home Office through the Foreign Office and so on, ad nauseum."

Halse agreed. "Quite right. We have our procedures, as you know, and woe unto us if they are not followed. You, on the other hand –"

"I, on the other hand," interrupted Holmes again, this time with an engaging smile, "I do not have to concern myself about going through your labyrinthian official channels, a realization that gives joy to my heart and comfort to my soul. With any luck at all, we should have a reply from Kock's in a day or two at the most."

Thicke was scowling. "Waal, I dunno. H'its 'ighly improper, if ye aks me."

Holmes patted him reassuringly on the shoulder. "Not to worry, Sergeant. If there is an inquiry, I shall be the miscreant, not you."

Thicke grudgingly consented. But then another thought occurred to him. He did not like being left out of things, and it came to him there was a danger of that happening. He would never be forgiven by his superiors if the Yard was not kept in the forefront of the investigation. "Wot am I to do in the meantime, then?" he asked, his scowl returning.

Holmes took him by the arm and escorted him toward the door. "Why, you, Sergeant, have the most enviable task of all," he said in great seriousness. "You are to start looking for a man with one gold and blue-enameled sleeve link!"

For the longest moment Thicke did not realize that Holmes was joking, for his eyes opened wide with disbelief. It was not until the others laughed at his confusion that the realization sank in, and he smiled in his embarrassment.

"Ye had me goin' there fer a minute, ye did," he admitted manfully. "I'll tell ye, this case takes so many twists and turns, and ye, Mr. 'Olmes, 'as so many queer notions, that I sometimes don't know wot to think. Nothin' should surprise me no more, and that's the truth. Why, ye know they 'ad us bring in photograph h'experts to take pictures of our victim's eyes before they buried 'er. No lie! Someone came up with the idea that a photograph might capture the last thing the woman was lookin' at and give us a picture of what the Ripper really looks lyke."

Watson and Halse clearly did not believe Thicke, and thought that it was he who was joking now, but Holmes did not join in their derision.

"No, no, I have heard of that theory," he said. "There is a body of scientific opinion that believes the final image seen by the deceased is retained on the eye's retina after death and can be magnified and reproduced on a photographic plate. There was even an American physician by the name of Pollock in the city of Chicago some years ago who conducted a series of experiments with a microscope and claimed to have captured retinal impressions from the eyes of cadavers.

And others have tried it as well, from what I have heard. It has one shortcoming, however: It is sheer balderdash, something of which we seem to be in no short supply nowadays."

"Ain't that the truth, though?" said Thicke as he departed with Halse close upon his heels, leaving Holmes to draft his cablegram and leaving Watson a moment of blessed quiet to ponder the imponderables of the case, which also seemed to be in no short supply.

Sixteen

❦

SATURDAY, OCTOBER 27, 1888

"He loathed every form of society with his whole Bohemian soul."
– *A Scandal in Bohemia*

"Come, Watson," said Sherlock Holmes. "I shall show you a side of London you have never seen and know nothing about. It will broaden your horizons and amaze you, that I promise."

It was a Saturday evening and Watson was at loose ends in any event, Mary Morstan being absent from the city, visiting a sick friend in Bath, and he having nothing more absorbing to occupy his time than a newly arrived copy of *Lancet* and a recently published biography (yes, yet another) of Lord Nelson. Intrigued by Holmes's invitation, he accepted readily with anticipation. Holmes was the most unsociable of men, a misanthrope to the very core; he had few close friends, exhibited a disinclination to acquire new ones, and seldom went anywhere except upon matters of a professional nature. For him to suggest an evening out was such a rare event that this in itself piqued Watson's curiosity. That the invitation held the promise of the unfamiliar and even the exotic made it all the more appealing.

It may have been that because Holmes had spent the past eighteen hours in bed recovering from his nonstop exertions of the previous several days he simply needed to get out of doors, but Watson did not think so. Holmes was too wrapped up in this case to be interested in idle amusements at the moment. Watson suspected there was more to it than that.

"Where are we off to, then?" he asked Holmes once the two of them, resplendent in evening dress, were seated in a phaeton a short while later. But Holmes was not very forthcoming. Indeed, he was being positively mysterious, not even giving the cabby the full address of their destination, only the name of the street, one with which Watson was not familiar.

"Oh, you will see," Holmes replied, refusing to say anything more.

Watson did not press him. Holmes enjoyed creating little mysteries when he had none to solve and was in a pawky, playful mood, and Watson knew that any effort to draw him out would not only be unavailing but would simply play into Holmes's hands and give him the opportunity to heighten the mystery. He would have his little games, would Sherlock Holmes.

When they arrived at their destination not long after, Watson was surprised to find that it was a rather quiet, nondescript street in Chelsea, one of upper-middle-class single-family homes, affluent but modestly so, unexceptional in the extreme – a street like hundreds of others to be found in London with nothing whatsoever to distinguish it or set it apart.

"What is this?" asked Watson as he paid the fare. "Is this your idea of a night on the town?"

But Holmes would reveal nothing. He merely smiled enigmatically. "Come," was all that he said, taking him by the arm and steering him down the street.

"Really, Holmes. You try my patience sometimes. Surely you can tell me where we are going. Broaden my horizons indeed! I shan't move another step until you stop this childish nonsense and at least a give me a clue."

Holmes chuckled as he gently coaxed him along. "A clue, is it? Well, let me think, let me think. We are going," he said finally, "to the most fashionable address in London. Is that clue enough?"

"What nonsense. Marlborough House is the most fashionable address in London," Watson responded with some irritation, "and I do not recall being invited by the Prince of Wales to attend him there. And besides, we are most definitely in the wrong part of town."

Holmes chuckled again. In the meantime he had managed to steer Watson around a corner into another, smaller street – a mews, really – one that was even more ordinary and quieter than the first.

"I will tell you only that things are not always what they seem, and that behind the closed doors of unpretentious, bourgeois edifices can sometimes be found a Pandora's box of surprises. Ah, here we are, I think."

Watson took in his surroundings with a glance. "Fashionable address indeed!" he muttered. "Place looks like it was a stable, if you ask me."

Before them stood an ordinary green-painted door, set into the facade of a narrow, two-story brick building that indeed looked as if it could have been a coach house at one time, except that where the wide stable doors once stood was now an expanse of brick obviously newer than that of the rest of the small structure. The windows on the upper story were dark, or at least heavily draped, and the place looked totally unoccupied. Had it not been for a low buzz of voices and laughter that wafted through the door as they approached it, Watson would have sworn the building was empty.

That impression was further dispelled when the door was opened in response to Holmes rapping upon it with the knob of his stick. Out poured a flood of light and a torrent of excited chatter and raucous laughter. They not so much entered the place as were sucked into it, as if the opening of the door had created a pressure vacuum, drawing them in with a sudden rush of air that left Watson dazed and all but breathless.

In sharp contrast to the quiet street, the house they now entered (for it was indeed someone's private house), was noisy in the extreme. They were ushered into a crowded vestibule by a bewigged and powdered Negro boy servant in gorgeous livery of plum velvet, who took their sticks and outer garments – with some difficulty because of the crush – but made no effort to take their names, which Watson considered most peculiar. Glancing around him, Watson made a quick visual survey of the other guests. All of them were men curiously; there was not a woman to be seen. All of them were extremely well dressed, some even foppishly so, and all of them were engaged in furious, animated, nonstop conversation – so deeply engaged that not one had turned to take note of the newcomers to their midst, as if afraid that even a brief pause in what they were saying would result in a lost opportunity. The wonder of it all was that no one seemed to be listening, only talking: everyone at once, and everyone loudly, passionately, and unceasingly.

Through the vestibule was a room paneled in a rich dark wood, a heavy crystal chandelier suspended from the ceiling. It, too, was crowded from one wall to the other with lavishly dressed young men, and some not so young, their chatter and laughter causing a din that was unholy. Through this chamber was yet another, much larger room, opulently decorated in brocade and red velvet, as heavily crowded, if not more so, than the room they had just passed through. The house was considerably larger, or at least deeper, than Watson had suspected, and if it gave the appearance of a coach house from the outside, on the inside it had the appearance of something out of the Arabian Nights.

Watson had to almost shout to make himself heard. "What is this place, Holmes? Some sort of a private club?"

Holmes shot him a sidelong glance. "One may call it that," he said unrevealingly.

"Who are all these people?"

"These, my dear fellow, are the molders of fashion and taste, and this place, as you so gauchely refer to it, is the very center of Aestheticism."

"Of what?" Because of the noise all around them, Watson did not hear the word.

"Aestheticism, old chap. *Nincompoopiana* is a word others have used to describe it," replied Holmes with a slight smile. "It rather fits, don't you think?"

A waiter slipped artfully through the crush with a tray in hand and paused briefly to allow them to help themselves to tall tulip-shaped glasses of champagne. Watson sipped at his while guardedly surveying the room from beneath lowered brows.

"They are all fops," he announced out of the corner of his mouth. "Fops and exquisites and I don't know what!"

"That is very true and most perceptive of you," replied Holmes in a low voice, "though I might suggest it would be prudent not to share your discovery with any of them. They might take umbrage at your characterizing them in that manner. But then again, perhaps not."

Watson let his gaze travel around the room. There was really no other way to characterize them, for they looked like caricatures out of *Punch* or *Vanity Fair*. Their evening dress, though obviously expensively made, was not the product of any conventional tailor. Their waistcoats were of velvet, and their coats were severely cut with wide satin lapels, and were set off with shocking flashes of color worn in the form of cravats and breastpocket handkerchiefs: Scarlet and bright green and blue and violet, and even some hues that Watson could put no name to. Some were wearing coats made of velvet or watered silk, and one or two were in satin knee breeches. The hair on most of the men in the room had been allowed to grow long, excessively long; they were not so much barbered as, well, coiffed, it seemed to Watson, who sniffed disdainfully once having reached that conclusion. And their conversation was accompanied by elaborate gestures, grand gestures: Waves of the hands and little flicks of the wrists and supercilious tosses of their heads, as if each one of them was vying to outdo his neighbor in outlandish statement and elaborate show.

A loud burst of laughter caught his attention, and he turned toward the source of it, a small crowd surrounding a young man seated regally on top of a grand piano in a corner of the room, one leg crossed over the other. He was a striking individual, one who would have attracted attention in any room: Dark, dreamy eyes, a heavy chin and full sensuous mouth, the whole of it framed by luxuriant waves of dark hair that reached his shoulders. He was even more flamboyantly dressed, if possible, than those who surrounded him, and had a long onyx cigarette holder in his hand, which he wielded rather than held, using it alternately as a wand, a baton, and a scepter.

"That," said Sherlock Holmes, "is the reason for this gathering: Mr. Oscar Wilde."

"Oh?" replied Watson disinterestedly. Then: "Oh!"

"You have heard of him, I presume."

Watson was now peering intently at the dandified figure across the room, staring unabashedly. "Of course I have heard of him! I do read some of the more stylish magazines on occasion, though I can't say they hold much interest for me. So that's him, eh?"

The foremost proponent of "beauty for beauty's sake," Wilde in a few short years had managed to take fashionable London by storm, causing a revolution in the world of *beaux arts* and *belles lettres* with his novel ideas, eccentric dress, and outrageous utterances and behavior.

"Only Beauty Brings Salvation" was his ethic. In the beginning was the Word, and the Word was Wilde's.[67]

They edged their way closer into the growing crowd surrounding the notorious young man, who was dressed in a velvet coat edged with braid, knee breeches, black silk stockings, and a large, flowing cravat of emerald green. He was gesturing languidly with his cigarette holder as he spoke, obviously holding his audience enthralled.

"A really well-made buttonhole," he was saying dramatically to those who surrounded him, "is the only link between Art and Nature. For what is Nature? Nature is no great mother who has borne us. She is our creation. It is in our brain that she quickens to life."

The crowd of young men around him seemed to think this was both profound and witty, for they greeted the statement with oohs and aahs, as if a pearl of great wisdom had been cast among them. One young dandy sitting cross-legged on the floor at Wilde's feet shook his head of golden curls with mock disdain and responded loudly in an exaggerated Oxford accent: "You are quoting yourself again, Oscar dear!"

The crowd laughed gaily.

Wilde considered the young man with a condescending look, but one that did not lack good humor. "Who, I ask you, has a better right, Dicky dear?"

The burst of laughter that greeted this remark was even louder than the one before.

Someone else called out: "What was it James Whistler said of one of your quotations, Oscar? 'A poor thing, but for once one of his own?'"

More laughter.

"Yes," someone else cried. "That's when he accused you of having no more sense of a painting than of the fit of a coat. He said that you had the courage of the opinions of others."

"Yaas," replied Wilde with a small smile, "and I retorted that 'With our James, vulgarity begins at home and should be allowed to stay there.' But I was much kinder to him than he was to me. I publicly praised him as being one of the very greatest masters of painting, adding, 'In this opinion Mr. Whistler himself entirely concurs.'"

The laughter that greeted this remark was unrestrained.

"Good Lord," remarked Watson under his breath. He turned to make some comment to Holmes, but Holmes was not there. He had simply vanished.

Watson wandered around the crowded room, champagne glass in hand, threading his way through the clusters of animated, intense, bored-looking young men in a vain effort to find him. He made a complete circuit of the room twice without having any luck, and then found himself in an outer hallway containing a staircase to the upper floor. The hallway was lined with some sort of rich flocked wall-covering and hung with several paintings in the new impressionistic style, which he did not find to his taste. Carefully, he picked his way up the flight of stairs, doing his best to avoid stepping on the young men seated upon them, to the upper floor, where more people were milling about. A corridor with closed doors on either side led toward the rear of the house. Taking the chance that Holmes would be found behind one of the doors, Watson tapped on the first that he came to and stuck his head in. It turned out to be a lavishly furnished bedroom, dimly lit and apparently empty. A large, canopied bed, heavy draperies surrounding it, occupied the center of the room. A gas lamp with a shade of leaded Tiffany glass was the only source of illumination.

Watson started to withdraw when the sound of muffled laughter from the bed brought him up short. In the dim light of the room he had not noticed the two figures lying entwined on the coverlet.

"Well, just don't stand there, lovey," said a mincing voice. "Either leave the way you came or join us, why don't you?"

Watson could not have been more shocked. Turning beet-red, he made a hasty retreat, slamming the door shut and bolting for the stairs. All he wanted now was to leave this place as quickly as possible, furious that he had ever allowed himself to be brought here. And why did Holmes want to come to begin with?

Hastily, he tripped his way down the stairs, badly shaken, muttering under his breath, and rudely pushing his way through the throngs without a word of apology. Once again on the lower level, he began his search anew, making a circuit of all the rooms. Still no Holmes.

Now, beside himself with anger, Watson had all but made up his mind to depart alone, leaving Holmes to his own devices, when he finally spotted him across the room, engaged in deep conversation with a tall, thin, narrow-shouldered young man in a full red beard, dressed incongruously, considering the setting, in a simple country suit of Irish tweed.

"Ah, there you are, old fellow," Holmes greeted him cheerily. "I was wondering where you had gone off to. Come meet Mr. Shaw."

"Holmes! Where the devil have you been? I've been looking all over for you! Why did you leave me like that? Good Lord, man, how could you bring me to a place like this?"

The bearded man laughed, but not unkindly. "It does take some getting used to, doesn't it?" he said. "But as these soirees go, this is a relatively tame one. I don't partake of many myself, but they do allow one to get caught up on the latest goings-on. For a journalist such as myself, that is essential." He stuck out his hand. "G. B. Shaw is the name."

"Mr. Shaw," explained Holmes, "writes music and drama reviews for the *Pall Mall Gazette* and the *Saturday Review*. You have heard me sing his praises on more than one occasion, though to be perfectly honest, I am not always in total agreement with his opinions. He and I were just getting caught up in a subject you know is dear to my heart, cockney dialects."

Watson, angry as he was, could never permit himself to be discourteous or uncivil. Besides, it was obvious this fellow was not one of "them." He had an engaging way about him, a gay twinkle in his eye, as if amused by the world and all who were in it, and he looked as out of place at the moment as Watson felt. Watson gathered control of his indignation and shook the young man's proffered hand politely.

"Holmes is an ardent admirer of your reviews," he said, "and I hear him speak your name often, Mr. Shaw. As to unusual dialects, you have come to the right place. These people seem to speak a language all their own, an outrageous parody of the Queen's English that seems to originate somewhere in the dark regions of the nasal passages, avoiding the vocal cords altogether. And how they do roll their r's and draw out their a's!"

Shaw laughed in delight. "Indeed, indeed. It is a travesty of the language, is it not? Our more exclusive public boarding schools are to blame, I am sure of it. They catch them young and inflict upon them a certain unnatural mode of speech, which their benighted headmasters have decided is the hallmark of a well-bred English gentleman. As a result, the aristocracy simply mangle the language, and of course the middle classes, ever ready to ape their betters, are quick to follow suit. The English, it would seem, delight in doing their language grievous injury. They have no respect for it, you see, and will not teach their children to speak it properly." He laughed again. "It has gotten so that it is quite impossible for an Englishman to open his mouth without making everyone else in the world despise him."

The subject was apparently a favorite of Mr. Shaw's, for he went on in the same vein for some time. His observations, though biting, were quite humorous, and Watson found himself, along with Holmes, enjoying the conversation immensely.

After a while Shaw turned to Holmes. "But tell me, if you don't mind me asking, why are you here? This does not seem to be the kind of place one would normally find Mr. Sherlock Holmes, unless upon a case. I should think you would be hot upon the track of this Jack the Ripper fellow, who has all of London in a positive frenzy."

Watson stiffened. Holmes, on the other hand, displayed no change in his outward demeanor, but merely shrugged and smiled politely.

"A task for the official police, surely," he said.

Shaw looked at him keenly. "They don't appear to be doing a very good job of it. I should think they could use your expertise."

Holmes measured his words with care. The man was a member of the press after all, and they were always on the scent of something.

"Under the circumstances," said Holmes, "I doubt if much more could be done than is being done. Your average individual has no concept of how difficult it is to find someone who does not wish to be found, especially in a great metropolis such as our own."

"And you have not been consulted at all?"

Holmes lit a cigarette. "I have been out of the city, actually. Only just returned a few days ago. Somewhat out of touch with things, really."

Shaw studied him shrewdly for a moment. He had been a journalist long enough to know when someone was being evasive, appearing to answer a question without answering it at all. He took a different tack.

"Tell me, Mr. Holmes, since everyone else in London seems to have a theory of who this fellow is, what is yours?"

Holmes shot him a sidelong glance and laughed. "As Watson here will tell you, Mr. Shaw, I have an absolute aversion to theorizing. It is so much more efficacious to apply oneself to the facts of the matter than to indulge in speculation. Having no facts, I have no opinion."

It was Shaw's turn to laugh. "Then you are the only person in London who doesn't. It is impossible to go anywhere without hearing a baker's dozen in quick order. The prevailing one of the day is that the fellow is a Jewish ritual slaughterer, a *sochet*, I believe they are called in their language."

Watson look horrified. "Whatever is a ritual slaughterer?" he asked.

Holmes turned to him and explained: "The Jewish religion requires that cattle be slaughtered in a certain prescribed way by an individual especially selected and trained for that purpose. It has something to do with their dietary laws, I understand: The animal must be dispatched quickly and humanely, and from what I gather, that calls for some experience." Turning back to Shaw, Holmes said: "That's as good a guess as any, I suppose. Such a person would have the means – a sharp knife and an aptitude for using it – and a knowledge of anatomy of a kind. And it is true there is a large ghetto of Jewish immigrants in the area where the murders have occurred, along with several of their slaughterhouses. Yes, I like that theory. The Ripper could very well be a Jew."

Shaw perked his ears up.

"Of course," continued Holmes blithely, "he could also be an Irish slaughterer of horses or a Polish slaughterer of pigs. An abundance of both can be found in the district as well. And the anatomy of pigs and horses has as much in common with the anatomy of a human as does that of beef cattle or sheep, which is to say nothing whatsoever." He shrugged. "So much for theorizing."

Shaw chuckled, a little abashed. "I see your point, Mr. Holmes, and it is a point well taken. The man could be anyone at all. Or not even a man, but a woman dressed as a man – that is another theory I have heard."

There was an amused gleam in Holmes's eyes. "Oh, I like that one! It would certainly explain how the killer has been able to get past the police undetected. But then, presumably, so could a man dressed as a woman – or two men dressed as a horse, or a little man dressed as a titmouse. The possibilities are limitless, you see – as limitless as the human imagination. I'll tell you how it is, Mr. Shaw: I shall put my trust in facts, thank you, and leave wild speculation to those who are more imaginative than myself."

Shaw smilingly raised both hands in a gesture of surrender. "I can see that I am out of my depth. I best confine myself to music and the theater, where at least I don't have to justify my opinions."

He looked around the room. "You know, there is one good thing to come out of all of this. Less than a year ago the West End crowd, these good people included, were literally clamoring for the blood of the people – hounding Sir Charles Warren to thrash and muzzle the scum who dared complain that they were starving, behaving, in short, as the propertied class always does behave when the workers throw it into a frenzy of terror by venturing to show their teeth. I speak, of course, of the Trafalgar Square riots. Whilst we conventional Social Democrats – yes, Doctor, I am indeed one of those dangerous radical fellows, I am sorry if it shocks you – whilst we were wasting our time on education, agitation, and organization, this independent genius known as Jack the Ripper has come along and taken the matter well in hand. He has done more in a fortnight to call attention to the plight of the poor than we have been able to accomplish in years!"

He took out his watch. "My goodness, I had not realized the hour. But tell me, before I go, Mr. Holmes, were you being quite serious when you told me you could differentiate from among the district dialects of London? Surely you were jesting'"

Holmes smiled. "I have it in mind to write a monograph on the subject someday: It has long been an interest of mine. As the Yorkshireman speaks in a dialect as distinct in its character and makeup from, say, a native of Dover or the Midlands, natives of London speak in dialects that can differ sharply from one neighborhood to the next. Why, I know a professor of phonetics who, I promise you, can listen to the calls of the flower girls in Covent Garden and be able to determine with an uncanny degree of accuracy what districts they come from. He can tell you not only the districts, but in some cases even the very streets in which they live, for the dialects are often subtly different from one street to the next, you see."

Shaw looked at him with interest and stroked his beard. "You amaze me, Mr. Holmes! Can this chap truly do that?"

"With an uncanny degree of accuracy," repeated Holmes. "You will find that the dialect spoken in Lisson Grove, for example, is quite different from that of Earl's Court or Hoxton or Selsey. I flatter myself that I can often place an individual within a few miles of his or her place of origin, sometimes within a few streets, but my ability to do so pales in comparison to his."

"How simply wonderful!" said Shaw, his red beard bobbing with pleasure. "If ever you do complete your monograph, you must send it around to me. I am quite intrigued by what you say." He held out his hand to be shaken. "This has been a most entertaining and instructive little chat. But now you must excuse me, I really should be off. The hour grows late and I have a deadline to meet." He favored Holmes with a parting wink. "Covent Garden, eh? Well, I will be sure to engage the flower girls in conversation when next I go there."[68]

Holmes and Watson departed shortly after, much to Watson's relief. Not only was he decidedly uncomfortable in the company of these fops, these effete dandies with their studied mannerisms and peculiar values (not to mention the, er, sexual proclivities of at least some of them), but he was highly curious to learn from Holmes his reason for wanting to visit this place to begin with. Obviously he did not come on a lark, he had an ulterior motive, and Watson was most eager to discover what it was.

They had retrieved their hats and cloaks and were exiting through the door when the clatter of a coach drawing up at the end of the mews caught their attention. It was a shiny black brougham drawn by a magnificent, glistening pair, leather harnesses liberally appointed with silver trappings. A small, discreet crest was emblazoned on the coach's door, but it could not be made out in the dim light.

Three men in evening dress alighted from the conveyance as Watson and Holmes walked toward it, two of them showing obvious deference to the third, a slight young man of below average height who emerged last from the carriage, a dark, open cloak thrown carelessly over his shoulders. He took in his surroundings with a bored, supercilious air.

The two other men looked to be at least a few years older, and there was something about one of them that suggested he would have been more at ease in uniform, for his bearing was unmistakably military, while the third man bore the careless slouch of a civilian, one hand in trouser pocket, the other casually holding a cigarette.

Their faces became momentarily distinguishable as they passed beneath the streetlight, and Holmes in that fleeting instant studied them intently. The oddest thing, the single most noticeable thing, it seemed to Watson as the trio came closer, had to do with the younger man's appearance, but it took a moment before he realized what it was: The winged collar of his shirt seemed to be cut unnaturally high, almost ridiculously so, the better presumably to hide an unusually long, thin neck, though in reality it served only to call attention to it. Watson caught a glimpse of his face as he walked past. There was something else about him, something familiar, but Watson just could not put his finger on it. He had a small upturned mustache and a vacuous look about him: Large, languid, heavily lidded eyes that moved neither left nor right and seemed focused on nothing, as if everything worth seeing in the world had already been seen and further observation was superfluous. He led his companions past Holmes and Watson without appearing to notice them at all.

Holmes stepped to one side and tipped his hat deferentially, and Watson suddenly gasped in recognition. He, too, stepped aside but was not quick enough to reach for his hat. He merely gaped in astonishment as Holmes bowed his head slightly and said, "Good evening, Your Royal Highness."

Without a nod or upward glance the young man entered the house, his two companions following closely behind. One of them, the civilian, paused momentarily to glance back at Holmes, taking a last puff from his cigarette and casually letting it fall to the ground before proceeding. The green door closed quickly behind him.

"That young man!" exclaimed Watson breathlessly. "Good Lord, wasn't that – ?"

"Indeed it was," replied Holmes, a thoughtful, even troubled look upon his face.

Seventeen

❦

SATURDAY, OCTOBER 27-SUNDAY, OCTOBER 28, 1888

"It is an old maxim of mine that when you have excluded the impossible, whatever remains, however improbable, must be the truth."
— *The Adventure of the Beryl Coronet*

His Royal Highness Prince Albert Victor, known to friends and public alike as Prince Eddy, was a grand-child of Queen Victoria's, one of the many who, by virtue of numerous carefully arranged marriages over the years, was to be found in virtually every major royal Protestant family on the European continent (and some that were not so major, and even one or two that were not so Protestant). Not for nothing was the Queen-Empress known as "the grandmother of Europe."

But Albert Victor held a special place among her grandchildren. He was the eldest son of her eldest son, Albert Edward, the Prince of Wales, and as such was Heir Presumptive to the throne of England.

Watson had been utterly shocked to witness His Highness enter the establishment that he and Holmes had just departed. For an heir to the throne to be seen in the company of such individuals as were present in that house ("fops and pederasts and godknowswhat," in Watson's words) was most unseemly and highly disturbing. Ever the proper Englishman, Watson adhered to a rigid code of what was right and what was wrong, and the higher one's station in life, the higher the standard to which that individual was held. The prince's presence among individuals of questionable morality, to say the least, deeply offended Watson's sense of propriety. Holmes, on the other hand, seemed neither shocked nor surprised, but he was troubled, that much was evident. He remained steadfastly silent during the ride back to Baker Street, the gleam of the streetlights flashing upon his saturnine features revealing a look of concern: Chin in hand, thin lips compressed, eyes staring off into space. Watson knew better than to break into his deliberations. Even though there were several questions he was burning to ask, he showed great self-restraint and remained silent also. But once back in their rooms in front of the fire, snifters of brandy close at hand, Watson could contain himself no longer.

"What do you suppose he was doing there?"

Holmes did not even look up. "I have not the foggiest notion."

"Not a guess?"

"You know I never guess."

"I cannot believe it! The prince, of all people."

"Your eyes did not deceive you, unless mine did so as well."

"I just cannot credit it!"

"You have already made that point abundantly obvious. Further repetition is not required."

"Do you think he is on intimate terms with any of those people? Friends with them, I mean?"

"That point, too, is obvious, or at least can be safely assumed. His Highness has somewhat of a reputation for unsavory associations."

"I had not heard that," said Watson in a shocked tone.

"The palace has not seen fit to announce it."

Watson bridled a little at Holmes's sarcasm, but understood the meaning behind it. The press treated the Royals, as they were collectively called, with the softest of kid gloves, and rarely was anything ever printed about them without the prior approval of those court functionaries whose job it was to manage such affairs. Even the Prince of Wales's notorious peccadillos, well known throughout Europe and the subject of endless gossip, were treated gingerly by the minions of Fleet Street. Scandals involving the lusty, fun-loving heir – and his name had been connected with several – saw print only on the rare occasions when they reached open court. And even then, where he was concerned the published accounts were subdued, cautious, and most respectful. Of his young sons Eddy and George, nothing untoward had ever been printed. Neither had ever had a hint of scandal attached to their names, and Watson was taken aback at Holmes's disclosure.

"You know that as a fact? About Prince Eddy's associations, I mean."

"It is not widely known. The gossip has been restrained, but even his royal father is said to have despaired of him, and that is saying some."

"Good Lord, I cannot credit it!"

"So you have said."

"I just cannot credit it."

Holmes sighed. "Watson, my dear, dear chap, you can be most trying at times."

"I? I can be trying? Really, Holmes, that is most absurd of you. It was not I who dragged *you* off to some – some den of iniquity populated by spoiled, rich sodomites with their preposterous talk and ridiculous mannerisms. It is not I who – who –"

Holmes held up his hand. "Point well taken. I pray you, do not belabor it."

"Why did we go there anyway? Surely you must have had some object in mind."

Holmes nodded. "Sleeve links," he replied.

"I beg your pardon?"

"I went to take note of their sleeve links." He waved a hand airily and added, half under his breath: "Among other things."

"Great Scot!" Watson stared at him in disbelief. "Do you mean you think one of them — one of *them* — might be the Ripper?"

"I don't know, but there is evidence that suggests just such a possibility. Circumstantial evidence, to be sure, but too strong to ignore, far too strong to prevent me from drawing certain inferences. If you were wondering where I was those few days I was gone, I spent a good part of my time in front of a particular house on a particular street in Whitechapel, observing the comings and goings at all hours of an interesting assortment of gentlemen, some known to me by sight, others not. They had one thing in common, these gentlemen: They were decidedly out of place. Every single one of them was a member of the upper classes, and one must wonder what business they had in the slums, in what is without question one of the worst streets in London and one of the most opprobrious addresses."

Holmes warmed his glass with his hands and took a sip of brandy before continuing. "On three separate occasions I followed individuals from that address in Whitechapel to the one at which we were reluctant, not to mention uninvited, guests this evening. Each of those individuals, I observed, was wearing sleeve links of gold and blue enamel."

Watson's eyes went wide. "Three of them!"

"For all I know, there may have been a dozen or more. There weren't that many whose shirt cuffs were clearly visible to me, but of those who were, a total of five wore sleeve links that appeared to be the same. And, as I said, three of them led me to the address in Chelsea."

"And their sleeve links were identical?"

Holmes gave him an exasperated look. "Of course, I did not approach the gentlemen in question and ask to examine their fastenings, but insofar as I could tell from a reasonable distance, they appeared identical."

Watson bit his lower lip and shook his head from side to side, bewildered. "What do you make of it, Holmes? Some sort of club or society, do you think?"

"That would not be an unreasonable inference, but I do not have enough data upon which to draw a definite conclusion. We must await a reply to the wire I sent off to Kock's."

Watson pondered over the matter for a while longer. "This house that you mentioned, what kind of an establishment is it? Whitechapel is hardly where one might expect to find a proper gentlemen's club."

Holmes smiled sardonically. "The street, as I said, has the reputation for being one of the lowest, most notorious in all of London. It most definitely is not where one would locate a respectable club. No, this establishment is apparently a fellowship of another kind. It is a house of prostitution."

"Oh."

"A house of male prostitution."

Watson's features twisted in revulsion. "Oh, good Lord!"

"It is frequented by certain otherwise respectable members of the upper strata of society who undoubtedly harbor, shall we say, unnatural cravings. That sort of thing is not unknown, as you of all people, a physician, should be well aware."

"Yes, but still..." Watson's voice trailed off, his expression one of extreme distaste.

"But still, it is no less repugnant, I totally agree. You know very well my thoughts on the matter, as I know yours, so we need not dwell upon it. But we cannot ignore the fact that the practice is widespread, perhaps more so in our society than anyone has imagined."

Watson thought about the import of Holmes's statement and scowled. "It is so very... so very un-British!" he said finally, unable to come up with a term that could better describe his feelings. "One expects that sort of thing from an Arab or Turk, but an Englishman!"

Holmes considered him with a look of sardonic amusement. "From what I have heard, it has been a practice on the lower decks of the Royal Navy from time immemorial, and even the implementation of the death penalty has been unable to put a stop to it. Sea stories being your favorite reading matter, surely you would know that."

Watson frowned. "It is hardly something one would expect to find broached in the pages of a Clark Russell saga or *Mister Midshipman Easy.*"

"Is the subject totally ignored by the authors who grind out that stuff? If so, they ignore reality. More than one jolly jack tar has been discovered in a shipmate's hammock, and it cannot come as a shock to you."

"No, it doesn't. But those are men of the lowest order, not gentlemen of the type you observed."

Holmes raised an eyebrow. "My dear Watson, you cannot be unaware of what goes on behind the cloistered gates of some of our very best public boarding schools. I seem to recall a rather torrid scandal not too long ago involving several young lads, including the son of a viscount, at one of the more fashionable schools. The housemaster was implicated, I believe."

"Yes, but that sort of thing is an aberration. Are you suggesting it is rampant?"

Holmes shrugged. "When I observe two peers of the realm and a judge of the court of assizes, among others, frequenting a known house of ill repute specializing in young boys, what else am I to think?"

"Good Lord!"

Holmes's eyes danced mischievously. "They were lords, to be sure, but good? There would be more than one vacancy in the Upper House should their escapades ever be made public."

Watson looked decidedly uncomfortable. "Surely this is not a fit subject for conversation, Holmes, and hardly one for jest. I find it most disagreeable."

"Under the circumstances, it is not a subject that can be ignored. And there is humor of a sort in it, after all. One of the peers in question was an ardent, one might even say vociferous, supporter of the public morals bill that was debated so hotly a year or so ago. Lucky for him I harbor no propensity for blackmail." Holmes rose from his chair and stretched. "Well, me for bed. We shall see what tomorrow brings."

Tomorrow brought the eagerly awaited cable from Frankfurt. To Watson's intense annoyance, it sat unopened on the breakfast table, waiting for Holmes to finish his last morsel of toast and final sip of coffee. Watson knew that Holmes was doing it purposely to taunt him.

Finally, with an amused glance in Watson's direction, Holmes took up the flimsy envelope and with studied nonchalance slit the flap with his bread knife. It took only an instant for him to absorb the contents. He knit his brow and wordlessly passed the cable to Watson, who all but snatched it from his hand.

"The prince? They were made for the prince?" Watson stared at the brief printed message, reading it several times over before finally looking up to observe Holmes's reaction.

"You will recall Thicke's observation that the design on the sleeve link looked to him like a fleur-de-lis. In actuality it is the three-feathered heraldic symbol of Wales – more precisely, the Prince of Wales and those of his immediate family. The two devices are not wholly dissimilar."

Holmes rose from his chair and took a cigarette from the silver box on the side table. "It would seem," he continued, "that Prince Albert Victor of Wales had a large quantity of these particular sleeve links made to his special order for the purpose of handing them around as gifts to favored friends both here in England and abroad. No doubt he had stopped by Kock's while passing through Frankfurt during one or more visits to one or more of his German relatives."

Watson nodded. As was well known, the British royal family had many close relations among the royal families of the various German states (by one count, there were twenty-two separate dynasties, including, of course, the Hohenzollerns of Prussia, whose new young king, Wilhelm II, was another one of Queen Victoria's grandsons). The English and German royals were so intertwined by generations of intermarriage that there was an almost constant flow of visits back and forth, the Germans being as much in evidence at Windsor, Sandringham, and Osborne as their English cousins were in the castles and hunting lodges of Brandenburg, Bavaria, and the Schwarzwald.

Holmes was leaning back in his chair, gazing up at the ceiling, smoke curling from his cigarette. "As you no doubt know, it is common practice for members of the royal family to distribute little personal gifts from time to time, the value of which varies according to the recipient and the occasion. A royal grandson or nephew may be handed a knighthood, a favored servant a tortoiseshell hairbrush, a personal friend or acquaintance something in between. It would seem that our Prince Eddy presents certain members of his circle with sleeve links of blue enamel and gold."

Watson digested this information. "So it could be almost anyone. The prince could have handed out many pairs of these sleeve links over a period of time."

Holmes nodded his agreement. "It could be dozens."

"Then it doesn't get us very far along, does it?"

"No, not in itself. But then, there is the little matter of the cigarette."

Watson looked up sharply.

"You will recall that after the Hanbury Street murder, when I discovered that first cigarette in the passageway leading to the yard where the victim was found, I visited several tobacconists and was soon able to ascertain its place of manufacture."

Watson reached for his pipe and began to fill it. "It was Grover's, as I remember."

"Yes. Grover's recognized it as one of their own right off. They didn't even have to consult their records. The blend of tobacco and the cigarette paper were so distinctive, it was identified immediately. This particular cigarette is made for one client and one client only."

Holmes got up from his chair and began to pace the room. "At the time I declined to share with you the identity of that client. And when you touched on the question again whilst we were on the train returning from Devon the other day, I dismissed the matter out of hand."

Watson nodded wordlessly.

"I did so not out of a lack of trust in you, or in your discretion, old friend, but out of a lack of trust in my own findings."

Holmes stopped pacing and turned to look at him. "I learned at Grover's that the tobacco in question was blended exclusively for a member of the royal household, namely young Prince Eddy."

Watson gasped.

Holmes raised a hand to forestall Watson's reaction. "Yes, yes, I know: Unthinkable. Totally unthinkable. That he or anyone close to him be involved in this sordid business is simply beyond belief, not even worthy of consideration, so I refused to credit it. The evidence of the cigarette, after all, was merely circumstantial. It could have been there by sheer happenstance, and to place too much importance upon it without corroborating evidence would be foolhardy.

"Then came the night of the double murder, and once again that very same brand of cigarette was found. Coincidence it was not, that much was apparent. But still I resisted accepting the obvious. There had to be some other explanation to account for its presence, some rational explanation that, for the moment, remained hidden to me. You know my ways: To jump to a conclusion is, twelve times out of ten, to jump to a false conclusion."

Holmes resumed his pacing, hands clasped behind him, chin on chest.

"I continued to seek another answer, any one of a number of which readily presented themselves: It could have been a servant who had access to the cigarettes – it is not unknown, after all, for domestics to filch from their masters' larder on occasion. Or it is possible that a supply of these particular cigarettes came into some other hands before even reaching the prince, unlikely as that may be, for Grover's, of course, would take special pains to prevent that from happening. Even so, parcels do go awry, shipments do fall off the backs of delivery wagons, things do get lost in the mails." Holmes formed a fist. "There just had to be another explanation, and I racked my brain to find one, for I continued to believe that the single explanation that persisted had to be erroneous. Had to be! Someone else had to have access to those cigarettes, either at one of the royal residences – a valet, a footman, a maid (yes, I even considered the possibility it was a woman) – or at Grover's, their place of origin. Or, failing those, at some point in between."

Holmes paused and massaged the back of his neck. "I was able to quickly satisfy myself that it was not Grover's. Their records are most meticulous, and the few employees who have anything to do with the actual blending of the tobaccos or the packing of the tins, or who even have access to the areas where these tasks are performed, have been associated with the firm for several years at least and are well trusted. Grover's is able to account for every single tin. The tobacco, once blended, is kept under lock and key, as is the supply of special cigarette paper. Only a certain set quantity of the cigarettes are rolled at any one time – just enough to meet the prince's regular needs. And that supply is immediately shipped off to him by one secure means or another on a biweekly basis. None of it is kept on hand, and there is no indication of any single shipment going awry."

Holmes shook his head. "It is definitely not Grover's."

Watson spread his hands. "The palace, then? One of the royal servants?"

Holmes shrugged. "Possible, of course, but unlikely. The servants at each of the royal residences are carefully selected, as you might imagine, their backgrounds thoroughly checked. Most of them are employees of long standing, many of them children of retired employees, members of families that have served the royal family for generations. Their loyalty is unquestioned, their honesty above reproach. Besides, none would risk it. They have reached the very height of their profession. To be dismissed from royal service would be ruinous, for they would never be able to obtain another situation in any household of prominence and would most certainly be ostracized by their fellows. The English domestic servant belongs to a proud, noble class with a code as rigid as any of his betters, standards of behavior that are far higher, and a nature that is no less unforgiving. No, for the moment I think we can rule that out as a possibility."

Watson stared at him. "You suspect someone close to the prince, don't you? A companion or a friend: A member of his entourage?"

Holmes did not reply directly. "As I said, in going over the possibilities, the obvious inference was unthinkable. There had to be some other explanation; that was my only thought. The cable from Kock's regarding the sleeve link of course makes that less likely."

Holmes returned to his chair and tented his hands in front of him, lost in thought.

"To be sure," he said after a brief while, "the sleeve link, too, is circumstantial. In and of itself its presence among the effects of Catherine Eddowes in Mitre Square is certainly of extreme interest but hardly conclusive. The object could have been something she picked up off the street, despite my passionate rejection of that possibility at the time."

Holmes continued. "But when you have the presence of two pieces of circumstantial evidence, one would have to be ingenuous indeed not to raise an eyebrow. Is it a mere coincidence that this particular sleeve link happened to be found on her person? It is possible. Is it a mere coincidence that a particular and exclusive brand of cigarette happened to be found near the scene of her murder? I suppose that, too, is possible, but it does stretch credulity to the breaking point. And what are we to think of these two coincidences combined, one on top of the other?"

His eyes sparkled. "It may be mere coincidence should your knife appear at my throat the very instant that you ask if I have the time, but I hope you won't think ill of me if I wonder perhaps whether you don't have designs on my watch." Holmes shook his head from side to side. "No, Watson, one would have to be more than simply ingenuous; one would have to be non compos mentis."

He reached for the coffeepot and poured himself a cup, his tone becoming reflective once again. "While surely we do not have the truth of the matter as of yet — not by any means — what we do have can no longer be denied."

Watson looked at him in disbelief. "Holmes, this cannot be connected to the palace. It is impossible!"

Instead of replying directly, Holmes reached into the breast pocket of his frock coat and took out his wallet, extracting something from its folds, a small white object in a glassine envelope.

"I picked this up from the street last night. It was dropped on the pavement by one of the prince's companions," he said casually.

Holmes placed the object onto the tablecloth in front of his plate, and Watson leaned over to see what it was. His eyes went wide and he gasped. It was a half-smoked cigarette with a thin band of gold near its tip.

"Impossible!" he repeated, this time in a whisper.

Holmes shook his head and looked down at his hands, the skin stretched taut over his sunken cheeks. When he looked up again his gray eyes were deeply troubled. "No, not impossible," he said quietly. "Improbable, but not impossible."

PART THREE

WHITECHAPEL

ANOTHER CRIME BY THE
MURDERER MANIAC

More Revolting Than Ever

This Demoniacal Deed Done in a House

A WOMAN Is Found in a House
on Dorset Street with Her Body Mutilated in a
Manner That Passes Description

The Star: Special Edition
Friday, November 9, 1888

Eighteen

THURSDAY, NOVEMBER 1, 1888

"Circumstantial evidence is occasionally very convincing, as when you find a trout in the milk, to quote Thoreau's example."
— *The Adventure of the Noble Bachelor*

The parcel arrived in the forenoon post and was brought up with their elevenses, their late morning tea. It was certainly innocent-looking enough: a small pasteboard box wrapped in plain brown paper and tied with string, with nothing at all on the outside to indicate that it contained a portion of a human organ. At the moment, the object in question was resting in the saucer which Holmes had hurriedly removed from beneath his teacup especially to accommodate it, and Watson was subjecting it to a close examination.

Holmes waited patiently until he finished. "Well?"

Watson sat back in his chair and pulled at his chin, considering for a moment. He, like Holmes, had been badly shaken when the parcel had been opened and its contents spilled out, but his professional training had quickly come to the fore. "It is the remains of a kidney," he said in a businesslike tone. "A left kidney. It has been preserved in spirits, it has about an inch of renal artery still attached, and it would seem to be from an adult human. Whether it be male or female, I cannot tell."

"But it is a human organ, of that you're certain?"

Watson nodded. "Quite certain."

He was not offended by the question. Holmes in no way meant to impugn his knowledge of human anatomy, and Watson knew it, but certain organs of certain animals, such as sheep and pigs, could bear a striking superficial likeness to corresponding human organs, and more than one unwary lecturer in pathology had been taken in by practical jokesters among his medical students.

"If this organ belonged to an animal," Watson replied wryly, "it was an exceedingly heavy drinker. This is what is called a 'ginny kidney.' Its former owner punished the bottle steadily. It also appears to be in an advanced state of Bright's disease, a form of nephritis. If we had the liver to go with it, I should not be at all surprised to detect signs of cirrhosis."

Holmes grunted. "And I should not be at all surprised to find that it belonged, until quite recently, to a Mistress Catherine Eddowes and is one of the organs removed from her body by the Ripper. The final autopsy showed that she, too, suffered from Bright's disease, did it not? But of course we shall have to send it around to Openshaw, the police pathologist, and have it matched up to be certain."[69]

Holmes picked up his lens and walked to the window, the better to examine the note that accompanied the parcel.

It was written in black ink on a sheet of cheap plain white paper, devoid of any distinguishing watermarks.

I write You a letter in black ink Mr. Detecktif Sherlock Holmes
as I have no more of the right stuf The Scotland Yd lads cant

catch me You think You r so clevr You catch me if You can.
Bloody Jack

There were no dramatic thumbprints in blood this time, no fingerprints of any kind. Yet Holmes was certain the handwriting on this note was the same as the earlier one he had examined.

He put down the piece of paper and picked up the parcel's wrappings. Here, too, he was unable to detect anything that was not readily apparent to him upon his first examination. The postmark was dated the previous day and was from a post office in the West End of London. Holmes's name and address were crudely printed in a nondescript handwriting and there were no detectable fingerprints or distinguishing marks of any other kind.

"Well, at least he responded to my advertisement," he said dryly, adding as an afterthought, "though a letter alone would have sufficed."

The rattle of a carriage pulling up in the street below caused him to glance out the window. The channel storm that had buffeted London throughout the night had all but flagged itself into exhaustion, giving way to a cold but cleansing rain that flushed the gutters and caused the pavement to glisten. A neat black hansom had just halted at the curb in front of their door, its side windows and highly polished woodwork beaded with the rain. The horse in the traces was not the ill-kempt hack one would ordinarily expect to find harnessed to a hired conveyance, but an unusually handsome animal, perky and well groomed, the leather and metal of its trappings bright and well cared for. As Holmes watched, the hansom's half doors were thrown back and an umbrella popped open, shielding the occupant from view as he stepped out onto the street.

"We have a visitor, it would seem."

Watson glanced up. "Oh?"

"A person of consequence, without question, for the carriage is privately owned. That it is a hansom rather than a landau or brougham suggests he is either an uncommonly modest individual not overly concerned with symbols of status, or an eccentric of such sufficient eminence that he doesn't have to be concerned."

"Oh, for heaven's sake, Holmes, do tell me who it is!" Watson demanded.

"Unfortunately, his identity is hidden beneath an umbrella, but if I were to hazard a guess, we are to be graced with the august presence of either the Archbishop of Canterbury or Lord Randolph Spencer Churchill."

Watson hurriedly draped a cloth over the dish containing the kidney and pushed it to one side, and then bent to straighten up the disarray left over from their late morning tea.

"You hadn't mentioned you were expecting Lord Randolph, Holmes!" he remonstrated, somewhat put out at not being forewarned.

"For good reason," replied Holmes, nudging an untidy stack of periodicals out of sight with his foot. "I wasn't expecting him."

Watson looked up. "How do you know it is him, then?"

Holmes turned toward the door at the sound of the downstairs bell and smiled sweetly. "Because it could not possibly be the Archbishop of Canterbury."

It was only a matter of minutes before Lord Randolph (for it was indeed he) was seated in the visitor's chair in front of the fire, a cigarette in one hand and, despite the early hour, a glass of whisky in the other.

He looked haggard and ill: There was an unhealthy gray tinge to his skin and dark bags under his eyes; his hands shook noticeably.

He had entered the premises with hardly a word of greeting, his melancholy countenance bringing as much cheer to the room as the gray November skies outside the window. Now he sat lethargically in his chair, all but motionless, only his sad, protruding eyes showing any sign of vitality. They had a strange, disturbing intensity about them – and, behind it all, a faint glint that could best be described as amused tolerance. Ignoring his hosts entirely, he looked around him with considerable interest, an interest that verged on outright rudeness. Accustomed as he was to the tasteful trappings of the upper classes, the eclectic middle-class clutter of the room in which he now found himself was somewhat of a novelty. He took note of the various decorative objects around him and seemed particularly diverted by the presence of Watson's favorite, the print of General "Chinese" Gordon, the hero of Khartoum, hanging on the wall by the window. It was apparent from his expression that he found the total effect to be terribly... well, bourgeois, for his lips were drawn up into a curl of fastidious distaste.

Holmes, seated with his hands tented in front of him, observed his guest in silence, a thin smile on his lips.

Lord Randolph paused in his visual inspection to take a cautious sip of the whisky, his high, noble brow rising in slight surprise at the discovery that it was eminently potable.

"Teacher's," said Holmes.

"Pardon?" said Lord Randolph.

"You were wondering about the whisky. It's blended by William Teacher & Sons, Glasgow."

"Oh, yes, I see."

There was a long, awkward lull. Churchill took another sip from his glass, and Holmes continued to observe him. Watson shifted uneasily in his chair. It creaked with unnatural loudness.

Churchill allowed his gaze to travel from the jackknife sticking out of the mantelpiece to the wall above, where it was impossible not to notice the patriotic sentiment expressed by the series of bullet holes in the plaster. Either a deplorable lack of curiosity on his part or, as was more likely the case, an overabundance of good breeding, kept him from inquiring as to the reason for its existence or the occasion that prompted it.[70]

Finally his gaze came to rest upon Holmes, and he subjected him to a brief but unmistakably patronizing scrutiny before finally speaking.

"Now then. What do you have to report to me?"

Holmes did not have to meet Churchill's gaze. His own had never left it.

"To you, my lord? Nothing."

A slight furrow developed between Churchill's eyes. "I beg your pardon?"

"No, it is I who beg yours. I seem to be woefully uninformed. It has not been brought to my attention that I was obligated to report to you."

Churchill's eyes took on a noticeable hardness, and there was an edge to his voice when he replied. He was not accustomed to being denied, and most definitely was not accustomed to being met with defiance. "I should have thought, sir, that would have been implicit."

"Oh?" Holmes replied. He folded his arms across his chest and smiled slightly.

Churchill's brows knitted together just a little, an expression of mild surprise at Holmes's effrontery. He dragged deeply on his cigarette and purposefully crushed it out in the ashtray at his side.

"I am not at all certain it is your place to question me, my dear sir," he said in a slightly bored tone, emitting a stream of smoke through his nostrils. "Or my bona fides."

Holmes did not reply but continued to gaze at Churchill unblinkingly, the little smile playing on his lips.

A flash of anger appeared in Churchill's eyes. "Now, see here, fellow –"

Holmes rose abruptly to his feet. Deliberately he turned his back on the peer and went to the window. Churchill, coldly furious, could only sit there, the color rising in his cheeks.

He had made a misjudgment, and he knew it. He had misread his man. In his arrogance he had appraised him wrongly, a rare lapse on his part, experienced politician and excellent judge of human nature that he was. Middle class this chap may be, but he, Churchill, should have realized that he could not treat him as he would some City merchant or mid-level government official. The damn fellow gave himself airs, deeming himself to be a step above all of that, would you believe? And, to be fair, who could say that he was wrong?

Churchill cleared his throat. "I am here, Mr. Holmes," he said in a tone that if not apologetic was at least a good deal less condescending (he could not be expected to actually *apologize*) – "I am here to render what assistance I can to Her Majesty, and I must say that your manner is –"

"If my manner offends you, Lord Randolph –" The quick flash in Holmes's eyes, though almost imperceptible, was as unmistakable as a storm warning.

Churchill raised a hand. "No, no, dear fellow. You misunderstand my meaning completely. I was merely going to say that your manner is somewhat puzzling. I would hope that we can get on together and avoid any, uh – any misunderstandings."

"That, m'lord, would be up to you. I know of no misunderstanding on my part, but allow me to acquaint you with one that appears to exist on yours. I am a private agent in this matter, m'lord. I am in the employ of no one – not Her Majesty, not the government, and not Scotland Yard. I answer to no one except as I please, and unless I am very much mistaken, m'lord, I am under no obligation to answer to you – may I freshen your drink?"

He favored Churchill with one of his quick, disarming smiles.

Churchill looked up at him, his normally protruding eyes positively bulging with astonishment. It was unlikely that anyone had ever spoken to him in such a manner, and for a moment he seemed to be at a loss as to how to respond. But only for a moment. To his credit he quickly recovered his poise and responded to Holmes's smile with one of his own, though one that was unquestionably strained. Without a word he bowed slightly from his seated position and lifted his glass for it to be taken. It was as much of a surrender as any descendant of the great Marlborough could be expected to make.

Watson exhaled audibly.

"The fact of the matter is, Lord Randolph," said Holmes, busying himself at the tantalus, "there is little of any substance to report. Painfully little, I am sorry to say."

He returned with Churchill's drink and resumed his seat. "All I can tell you is that the investigation continues, and while progress is not what I should have wished, there are one or two leads that hold some little promise. Beyond that..." He allowed his voice to trail off and favored Churchill with an apologetic smile. With the change in Churchill's manner, his, too, had altered considerably. The atmosphere in the room became far more relaxed.

Churchill brushed a nonexistent speck of dust from his trouser knee and crossed one leg over the other.

"No progress is being made anywhere, it would seem," he said. "The official police, of course, have gotten nowhere. Quite literally, they haven't a clue: Just a list of suspects that seems to change with the tide. I don't know where they get their ideas, but many of them are quite novel – inventive, even. And no one seems to be immune from suspicion. Why, I heard just the other day that someone at the Yard undertook an investigation of the actor Richard Mansfield, who, as you no doubt know, is appearing in *Dr. Jekyll and Mr. Hyde* at the Lyceum. Evidently it was felt that anyone who could assume such an effective disguise and was capable of working himself into such a murderous frenzy onstage was probably capable of committing murder offstage as well. He's not the only one. Why, even Mr. Gladstone has been named in certain circles, would you believe?" He smiled faintly. "Given his nocturnal pursuits, I would not be surprised in the least if it did indeed turn out to be him. Nor would I be surprised to learn that it was Her Majesty who was the first to suggest that it was he."

Holmes smiled and Watson laughed delightedly, taken by the absurdity of the idea.[71]

Churchill took another sip of his drink and turned serious. "I should think that by now, with four murders attributed to this fellow – at least four of which we are certain – someone would have been able to have developed some sort of theory as to his methods and haunts and modus operandi and that sort of thing, and, by doing so, figured out a way to anticipate what he will do next."

Holmes nodded politely but said nothing.

"For example," Churchill continued, "I should think that it might be possible to detect certain similarities and patterns in his actions that could assist in his being tracked down and apprehended. This, of course, is more in your line of work than mine, but – well, one wonders at the absence of useful suppositions."

Holmes smiled. "From what I read in the papers, Lord Randolph, there is no shortage of suppositions. As for their usefulness, that is another question. And this business fairly abounds in patterns and similarities. For example: All of the murders have thus far occurred between the hours of midnight and five A.M. on either the first weekend of the month or the last, and all within the space of a few square acres. All of the victims were drabs of the lowest order, all were alcoholics, all were killed with a sharp blade with a stroke to the throat, and all were, to some extent or another, eviscerated in the foulest manner possible."[72]

Holmes paused. "What do these similarities tell us about the murderer? They tell us that he is as much a creature of habit as he is of bad habits, and that is all they tell us. As to whether this knowledge will lead to his capture, I cannot say."

Churchill looked down at his hands. "It has been, what? – almost a month since the fellow last struck. Do you think it possible that he is gone to ground, that he has departed from our midst and we have seen the last of him?"

"As to that, I can give you a more definitive answer."

He went over to the table and picked up the dish that Watson had covered so hastily with a cloth, carrying it back to where Churchill was seated. "You may be interested in seeing this. It arrived within the hour. I do trust you are not overly squeamish," he said, whipping away the cloth.

Churchill gazed at the dish's contents and wrinkled his nose.

"Whatever is it?"

Holmes had the decency to take the dish away and recover it before replying.

"We have reason to believe that at one time it was a personal possession of one Catherine Eddowes, also known as Kate Kelly, also known as Kate Conway."

It took a moment for Churchill to absorb Holmes's meaning, and even when the realization came to him, his reaction seemed amazingly controlled. "Is this some sort of joke?" he asked benignly, the expression on his face having turned to one of mild distaste.

Holmes shook his head. "As Watson will no doubt confirm, my sense of humor does on occasion tend toward the unconventional, but never, I hope, toward the grotesque. If you look closely, sir, you will observe that I am not laughing."

Churchill dabbed his lips with a handkerchief. "However did you come by this... object? Is it indeed from the killer?"

"We believe so, yes."

"And he sent it through the post, you say? What a curious thing to do. Now, why would he send it to you, do you think?"

"That is an interesting question, is it not?"

"You have no thoughts on the matter?"

"None."

"Was there no note of explanation accompanying it?"

"None at all."

Watson, surprised at Holmes's reply, could not help but notice that Churchill also looked surprised.

"None at all?" he repeated.

"None," Holmes said again, casting a warning sidelong glance in Watson's direction.

"How very curious indeed," said Churchill, his expression one of puzzlement.

Holmes studied his face with interest. "Quite."

Churchill pondered for a little while. "Well, what is it you intend doing next? Or is that, too, of a confidential nature?"

Holmes gave a fair imitation of a Gaelic shrug. "I have one or two leads to follow that may or may not prove to be fruitful. Beyond that..." He shrugged again.

Churchill rose to his feet. "Well, at least we know the damn fellow has not left London. That is something."

Holmes stared at him.

Watson went to help him with his hat and coat.

"By the by," said Churchill, "I have it on good authority that Sir Charles Warren will be submitting his resignation shortly and that it shall be regrettably though promptly accepted by a grateful sovereign."

Holmes raised an eyebrow.

Churchill shrugged. "Of course, he doesn't know it yet, but he soon shall. I had hoped and expected he'd be gone before this, but as you know, the wheels of government turn slowly. And he does have a good deal of backing in certain quarters – don't ask me why – so they had to find a new spot for him – someplace where he couldn't do any harm but without it looking like a step down. You know the drill, I'm sure. The question now, of course, is who will we get in his place. I'm pushing for Monro, and I believe the Home Secretary is also."[73]

Watson handed Churchill his hat. "You almost have to feel sorry for the poor devil," Watson offered. "Given the fact that he was totally in over his head, he probably did the best he could."

Churchill grunted, and to Watson's surprise patted him on the arm. "You remind me of the chap who felt guilty toward his mistress because he made love to his wife. One can't help but wonder if his feelings, while admirable, were not a trifle misplaced."

Churchill pulled on his gloves and paused at the door, turning one last time to Holmes. "Is there nothing, then, that I may take back to Balmoral to share with the Queen? As you might imagine, she is most disturbed by these murders and has taken a keen personal interest in the investigations. She has been hounding Lord Salisbury and poor Matthews on practically a daily basis. Is there nothing of a positive nature that I may take to her?"[74]

Holmes thought for a moment. "You may tell her that my inquiries are continuing, that I am presently employed in following leads which I believe to be of a promising nature, and that I expect to be able to report further progress very shortly. You may tell her I am... hopeful."

Churchill looked at him. "Hopeful?" He sniffed. "May I tell her nothing more than that? Just hopeful?"

Holmes again reflected for a moment, then smiled enigmatically. "You may tell her that I am *very* hopeful."

Churchill gave him a long, cold look – one that would cause most men to quail – and then departed without another word.

Watson closed the door softly behind him. He did not speak until the sound of Churchill's footsteps had receded down the stairs and Watson was certain he was well out of hearing. "He is quite ill, you know," he said, turning to Holmes. "He may even be fatally ill."

Holmes did not seem surprised. "And have you diagnosed the nature of his illness, Doctor?"

"Impossible to say without an examination. It could be any one of a number of things."

"Would it surprise you to learn that he has syphilis?"

Watson shook his head. "It would not shock me. Your brother hinted at it when we first met with him at the Diogenes in September, didn't he? And there are many of the obvious signs. No, I would not be surprised at all. Indeed, I suspected it, of course, but one doesn't like to make a diagnosis without having all the facts."

Holmes nodded. "The nature of his illness is known to very few, for the obvious reasons, of course. From what I gather, it was detected by specialists some time ago. Apparently he contracted the disease while still in his youth, but it remained dormant for many years and it is only recently that it has become evident. That is quite common with this particular disease, is it not?"

"Quite common indeed. This is not my field, but as you might expect, I was called upon to treat several cases when I was with the army, so I know a little about it. Generally, if allowed to run its course, there are four stages to syphilis, and unless the disease is caught very early in the first stage, it invariably runs its course."

"So I understand. Tell me, what are the effects of the disease in its final stage?"

"Quite horrible, really. Paresis, to begin with: A partial form of paralysis. The brain and spinal cord begin to decay, leading to general bodily dysfunctions manifested in such outward signs as facial tremors, slurred speech, impaired vision, general malaise, moodiness, depression, headaches, and the like. Sometimes even violent rages." Watson shook his head. "It is not at all pleasant. Of course, I have no way of knowing how far along Lord Randolph's case is, but from the outer signs, if what you tell me is correct, it is possible that it is well advanced. Of the four stages, I suspect that he has already reached at least the third, and maybe even the beginnings of the final stage. There is little that can be done for him at this point. The accepted course of treatment, frankly, is of limited value: doses of mercury, potassium iodide, digitalis – that's the usual medication. Bed rest is normally prescribed, and the patient is cautioned to avoid spirits and tobacco which, as you have no doubt noted, our patient indulges in heavily. It is all quite useless, really. Quite useless. There will be spells of normalcy, leading one to believe that the disease is in remission, but in fact it is irremediable. There is no cure, and that is the sad fact of the matter. Once the disease has reached the quaternary stage, there is an inexorable invasion of the nervous system, and there you have it."

Holmes, who had been listening thoughtfully, nodded his head. "And ultimately?"

"Ultimately there is a softening of the brain and insanity. If one is fortunate, death will come quickly." He thought for a moment. "But it seldom does."

Holmes put a match to his pipe and within minutes was enshrouded in a thick noxious cloud of tobacco smoke, deep in his chair and deep in thought. Watson, recognizing the symptoms, left him alone to his deliberations, expecting the rest of the day to pass before Holmes bestirred himself once more.

He was wrong. Hardly ten minutes had gone by before Holmes, knocking the ashes from his pipe, interrupted Watson's thoughts.

"You took note of it too."

"What's that?"

"Lord Randolph's bewilderment when I told him that no message accompanied that unspeakable thing on the table over there. He seemed for the moment to be not merely surprised, but... confused. He even questioned me about it, though of course he tried to affect an offhand manner."

"Well, I must say that I was confused also. Why did you want to deceive him on that point?"

Holmes waved a hand airily. "Oh, a whim, nothing more." He stared off into space.

"I was also rather surprised," Watson mused aloud, "at his *lack* of surprise when you showed him the kidney and told him what it was. You noted that too, of course."

"Of course."

"His reaction was... well, I don't know."

"Almost no reaction at all?"

"Yes, exactly! It was almost as if he actually expected you to have it, as ridiculous as that sounds. Oh, he made a face and all, but it certainly was not what one might expect. I mean, with most laymen, when you show them a bit of this or that from a cadaver, they bolt for the loo. But not this chap, not him. An odd fish, what?"

"Perhaps odder than we think," Holmes replied, chin in hand. "Like the fish in the milk."

"Eh? Why do you say that?"

Holmes waved off the question. "There are two other points that surely you did not fail to notice."

"Oh?" Watson thought for a moment. "I can't say that I know what you're referring to."

Holmes cast him a look. "I refer, of course, to Lord Randolph's reference. The one he made to our dish of kidney over there. You will recall that he noted that it had arrived by post."

"So?"

"How could he know that? I made no mention at all as to how it was delivered. The parcel could have just as easily come by messenger."

Watson raised an eyebrow. "That is odd, isn't it?"

"Most certainly odd. Moreover, on parting, he said something to the effect that we at least know that the killer is still in London. What did he base that knowledge on? He never saw the parcel's outer wrappings, so he could not have known it was stamped with a London postmark. I certainly never gave any hint as to where it came from, or even indicated that I knew."

Watson's face took on an expression of bewilderment. "That's very true. You never did."

"But putting aside Lord Randolph for the moment, there is an even larger question," said Holmes. "One that I find most intriguing of all." He pointed with his chin in the general direction of the table where the kidney sat in its saucer. "Why did the killer send that to me?"

Watson sniffed. "Why, to shock you, I suppose. Or to taunt you."

Holmes shook his head impatiently. "You miss my meaning. Why to *me?* Why was *I* chosen for the signal honor?"

Watson looked at him blankly, forcing Holmes to explain.

"How did the killer know that I am involved in the investigation at all? There cannot be more than eight or ten individuals who are privy to that knowledge."

"Good Lord!" Watson's expression turned to shock. "I don't understand."

Holmes cupped his chin in hand. "Hmm. Nor do I."

Watson got up from his chair and went to the window, his brow furrowed with thought. He turned finally. "What can it mean, do you think?" he asked.

Holmes did not respond right away, but continued looking off into space, chin still in hand. Finally he looked up with a humorless, tight-lipped smile and a strange, almost demonic glint in his eye. "I think that not only is there a fish in the milk, but it is laughing."

Nineteen

Q♪

FRIDAY, NOVEMBER 2, 1888

"'It is both or none,' said Holmes. 'You may say before this gentleman
anything which you may say to me.'"
– *A Scandal in Bohemia*

M r. Mycroft Holmes, without conscious thought, tapped the ash
from his cigar into the silver dish beside his right hand, not having
to move his arm or even open his eyes to do so, the ashtray having been
positioned that precisely by the club waiter, who now stood quiet vigil
in the background, his choice of position being equally precise, just out
of hearing but well within sight so as not to miss that slight crook of an
upraised finger that meant his services were once again required. As the
waiter had learned from long experience, position was everything.

Obviously Mr. Holmes was not napping in his chair as any casual
observer might assume; he was engaged in deep thought. Mr. Holmes
always closed his eyes when he had a difficult matter to consider. It
enabled him to better focus his powers of concentration, which were
formidable under any circumstances.

Across from him, Watson and Sherlock Holmes sat waiting patiently.

The hushed precincts of the Diogenes Club seemed even quieter to Watson's ear on this occasion, the sanctity of the place undisturbed by the slightest sound – not a footfall, the ticking of a clock, the whisper of a drapery, or (God forbid!) the murmur of a human voice. He found the atmosphere of the private room in which they were seated to be positively intimidating. As a result, he sat stiffly in his chair, hardly daring to breathe, feeling like nothing so much as a little boy in church, afraid that the smallest movement on his part or the merest sound would be an unpardonable transgression.

The room, located on one of the upper floors of the Diogenes well away from those most heavily frequented by the club's members, was only occasionally used, having ostensibly been set aside as a boardroom for the club's officers. Since they rarely met, having few matters of business to attend to and little else they ever wished to discuss, it was reserved almost exclusively for the use of Mycroft Holmes on those occasions when he required a quiet, out-of-the-way place for an engagement of a confidential nature.

As Watson had noted, it was a room hardly designed for comfort – mental or physical. Its furnishings and decor were foreign and of another era: Velvets, brocades, and heavy tapestries, an ornate ceiling and varied-colored marbles – different, by accident or design, from that of all the other rooms in the club, the sort of chamber one might expect to find in a Florentine palace, the sanctum sanctorum of some Medici prince or renaissance cardinal (a *gray* eminence without question).

It was a setting in which it was possible to conduct oneself only with great dignity and to speak only in hushed tones (if at all), and then only of weighty matters, affairs of consequence, subjects of great seriousness, certainly nothing that smacked of frivolity or the mundane. And it was a room without question that required obeisance from the visitor toward the host.

Several minutes had passed since Sherlock Holmes had completed his report, and now he sat silently opposite his brother, observing with wry amusement his every facial expression, his every twitch and fidget, as if by doing so he were able to read his every thought – a distinct possibility, thought Watson, who was quietly observing Holmes as Holmes was observing Mycroft.

Mycroft looked up finally, his cold gray eyes meeting those of his brother's. "This business concerning Lord Randolph, while most intriguing, is hardly pertinent. There is a reasonable explanation for all of it, I am sure, but I would not waste one iota of time in seeking it out were I you. It would serve only to distract from the matter at hand. Now, as to this bit of offal you received in the post – a kidney, I believe you said it was" – he allowed himself a look of mild distaste – "you are certain it is not from some prankster?"

Holmes nodded. "Yes, Openshaw at London Hospital has virtually confirmed it. But Watson and I never had any real doubt about it being the genuine article. Everything about it points to its authenticity, and everything about the accompanying note, as well."

Mycroft chewed on his upper lip. "Quite a macabre sense of humor, this chap, what? But then, I would expect nothing less from him. Most of all, I am impressed by his resourcefulness. He would indeed seem to have a friend in high places who keeps him well informed, as you have suggested. And that in itself tells us something, doesn't it?"

"Well," replied Holmes, "it confirms my belief that the 'bloke' is a 'toff,' as they say – if ever there was any doubt." He flashed a quick smile.

Mycroft sniffed, but nodded his agreement. "Beyond that, it tells us that he is probably not an absolute raving maniac, as some would have us believe. Not one who drools or goes without washing, in any event," he added.

"Precisely," said Holmes.

Watson's brows knitted together. "How do you arrive at that?"

Mycroft waved his hand, dismissing the question impatiently. Holmes responded: "The man must appear to his informant, whoever it may be, to be outwardly sane, or at least reasonably so, otherwise the informant – presumably a responsible individual who is unaware of his friend's activities – would not be sharing privileged and confidential information with him. That stands to reason. So we must conclude that aside from a predilection for carving up prostitutes and sending portions of their anatomy through the Royal Mails, he is otherwise quite normal – in appearance and outward demeanor, that is."

"Ah, yes, of course," murmured Watson. "Obvious, quite obvious."

"So he is a man who is able to function in society," Mycroft added. "He probably lives a perfectly ordinary life."

"Two lives, I should think," said Holmes.

"Like a Jekyll and Hyde character, you mean?" Watson asked.

Holmes made a face. "Depend on you to dramatize, Watson. Let's not get carried away with ourselves. I don't think for one moment that our friend is bedeviled by perverted science or the phases of the moon. The facts of the case are remarkable enough without requiring any embroidery."

Mycroft shifted his bulk in the chair. "As to the rest of it, Sherlock – your conclusions concerning Prince Eddy and friends – you are quite correct. I can find no flaw whatsoever in your reasoning."

"How gratifying," replied Holmes dryly.

Mycroft saw fit to ignore the hint of sarcasm in his voice; younger siblings must on occasion be humored. "I cannot say that I am totally surprised by your disclosure. The young man has long been a source of concern not only to his royal father and mother, but to Her Majesty as well. He simply has no character. If the truth be known, he has no brains. He can hardly read, d'ya know. He was the despair of his tutors. The palace put him into the Royal Navy and shipped him off to sea, but that was no good: They quickly determined he'd never pass the lieutenant's examinations – couldn't even learn to tie a knot, let alone learn the ropes, literally as well as figuratively. So then they stuck him in the army, in a cavalry regiment where they figured he'd do the least harm. He can sit on a horse at least, and wears the uniform well – he's a regular tailor's dummy, he is. Has his father's charm, I'll say that for him. I've met him on more than a few occasions, and when he wants to, he can charm the coin right out of your pocket. But empty-headed! All he ever cares about is every possible form of amusement and dissipation. Fortunately he was born of royal blood; he'd never be able to support himself otherwise." Mycroft shook his head. "And this is the man who would be king, God save us."

Watson was shocked by both Mycroft's disclosure and his blunt-spoken speech, and his face transparently showed it.

Mycroft tossed a sardonic glance in his direction. "Don't be upset, Doctor. He won't be the first wastrel to reign over England, nor, for that matter, the first imbecile. We have had our share of both through history, as has every royal house on the Continent."

Watson said nothing.

"The damnedest thing is, he's a wizard at cards, a first-class whist player. I can't understand that." He shook his huge head. "I'm a student of the game and pride myself in knowing a thing or two about it, and can tell you it requires intense concentration and no small degree of intelligence. He's got the attention span of a seven-year-old and the intelligence of a gnat."

Holmes picked his head up at this. "Interesting," he mused.

"Yes, isn't it? It never ceases to amaze me."

"I take it you are not exaggerating – about either his prowess with cards or his lack of intelligence."

Mycroft shook his head. "The boy is a total simpleton, I tell you. Yet he seems to have an amazing facility for memorizing the deck and keeping track of the play. I have never seen anything like it!"

Holmes wracked his brain. "I have heard of this sort of phenomenon before."

"Perhaps you are thinking," suggested Watson, "of that case I called to your attention some time ago from one of my medical journals? The severely retarded individual who displayed a genius for numbers?"

"Yes, that's it! An idiot, brain-damaged from birth, wasn't he? He could recite complicated series of numbers backward and forward, having heard them just once?"

"That's right. He couldn't learn to tie his bootlaces even, but he had a phenomenal memory when it came to dates and numbers – even complex mathematical formulae. There have been other cases of a similar nature, like the chap who could play intricate scores on the piano having heard them just once – Chopin and Liszt and that sort of thing – and without ever having a lesson or learning to read a note. He, too, was feebleminded. Idiot savants, they're called, I believe."

Mycroft drew on his cigar and examined the ash. "I don't know if you could fit His Royal Highness into the category of idiot in a medical sense," he said dryly, "but he comes damn close. Certainly in many respects he is indeed feeble-minded. That you happened upon him at this particular house in Chelsea last night comes as no surprise to me, of course. He is often to be found in the company of that crowd. Indeed, I think you will also find that he frequents the house of male prostitution in Cleveland Street that you took under surveillance, Sherlock. Oh, yes, Doctor, our Prince Eddy enjoys sex in all of its available forms."

He pursed his lips, a mannerism so much like his brother's. "They have tried to keep it from Her Majesty, of course – the worst of it anyway. But sooner or later she finds out everything, has an uncanny ability to do so. Damned if I know how she does it."[75] Mycroft turned to his brother. "You realize, naturally, what will happen if any of this gets out?"

Holmes nodded. "Of course there is no definite proof that it is one of the prince's friends who is the killer," he said quietly. "The evidence is wholly circumstantial."

Mycroft favored him with a look of pained forbearance. "Can there be any doubt? How much proof do you need?"

"What there is would never hold up in the courts."

"Don't be naive, Sherlock. It doesn't have to, as you well know," Mycroft snapped irritably. "The scandal will be intolerable in any case." He sniffed. "The courts indeed! Should any of this get out, the prince's character and sexual proclivities will be revealed for what they are, as will his gross stupidity and unfitness. It will rock the throne, make no mistake. It will call into question the institution of the monarchy itself, and the wisdom of perpetuating it. At the very least, the Salisbury government will never survive. Given today's political climate, this whole filthy business could result in a political and social crisis of cataclysmic proportions, causing a violent and permanent change in our society. It will be the beginning of the end to Britain's ruling class, make no mistake."

Holmes cocked an eyebrow, but Mycroft, anticipating him, raised a hand to forestall his comment.

"I need not be reminded that our ruling class is hardly above reproach, but the fact remains there is nothing to replace it. The alternative is chaos. The lower classes are not trained for the job. They have neither the education nor the background. For countless generations they have been taught to submit, and that is all they know: Absolute obedience to God, the Queen, and their betters, whoever they may be. There are those who would welcome an end to our system, those who feel that the monarchy has become an anachronism, an expensive bit of frippery. I don't happen to agree. I believe the monarchy is indispensable to the preservation of the Empire, and that its survival and well-being is the only guarantee we have to national tranquility."

He puffed out his cheeks. "I do not mind admitting to you that I fear the mob. They are ignorant, they are uneducated, they are not fit to govern themselves, let alone a great empire. I would no more willingly turn over the country to the masses than I would to the Thugees of India or the Fuzzy-Wuzzies in darkest Africa. It is the monarchy that keeps this great beast at bay, that brings equilibrium and order to our society. And that is why the monarchy must be preserved, why the system must be protected."

Holmes was as loyal to the Crown and as patriotic an Englishman as any, but he had few illusions about what Mycroft called "the system." Whatever else it might be, it was a hardly a system that favored everyone equally. The House of Commons, it had often been pointed out, was made up of a handful of rich men elected by a handful of other rich men, while those who sat in the House of Lords were elected by nobody.

He considered his brother with a thin smile. "I heard it said just the other day, Mycroft, that the only truly democratic house in England was the public house, where everyone has an equal voice and you can at least get a drink, which is better than anything provided by either of the other two."

Mycroft scowled. "It was doubtlessly an American who said it," he snapped. "And in the process complained about there being no ice in the drink, I shouldn't wonder." He waved an accusatory finger. "It is all very well and good to be critical of the system, Sherlock, but it has worked for us these many years and has worked quite nicely, thank you. It has made us into the most powerful nation in history, might I remind you."

"I cannot help but wonder why, sometimes," Holmes replied, his voice heavy with sarcasm, "when you stop to consider that the members of our ruling class pass most of their time passing the port."[76]

Mycroft raised his hand again and frowned. "Enough, I beg of you. We are not here to mend the imperfections of our social fabric. Let us return to the subject at hand. We must agree on a course of action."

"What do you suggest?" asked Holmes.

"What can I? I have to go to the Prime Minister with it, of course. And in all probability to the Prince of Wales – that's not something I look forward to, I can tell you. Bertie invariably gets his wind up anytime the subject of his firstborn is mentioned. He can't stand the boy."

"You don't intend taking it to the Home Secretary, Sir Henry Matthews?"

Mycroft waved the idea away. "Henry is not the right man for this. He is a good enough fellow in his way, but his ideas tend to enter the room with a polite cough. Besides, I think it best to go directly to the P.M. The fewer involved, the better it will be. Not a hint of this must get out. We must avoid public disclosure at all costs. And if necessary we will have to derail the official police investigation – lest by accident, despite all of their bumbling, they get onto the right track."

Holmes cocked his head to one side and looked at Mycroft through narrowed eyes. Watson recognized the danger signal.

Mycroft, not intimidated in the least, returned his brother's look. "We are playing for very large stakes here, Sherlock. Need I remind you of that? This is no time to take a petit bourgeois moral stand."

"Mycroft, the murders must be stopped! Without a scandal if possible, but one way or another, they must be stopped!"

"Of course they must! Don't I know that? But at the same time, steps must be taken to insure that none of this is connected to the royal family. That is paramount."

Holmes snapped, "That may not be possible."

Mycroft glared at him. "It is paramount!" he repeated with emphasis. "The throne must be disassociated from all of this!"

Holmes leaned forward, his lean jaw firm, his eyes hard. "Paramount it may be, but it still may not be possible!"

Watson looked from Holmes to Mycroft. In an instant the atmosphere of the room had become highly charged. The two brothers had locked eyes and were glaring furiously at each other, and Watson found himself anxiously gripping the arms of his chair. Holmes looked like a cat about to spring, and Mycroft's face had reddened alarmingly, his eyes, like his brother's, narrowed into dangerous slits.

It was Watson who inadvertently eased the tension. He cleared his throat, nervously and quite unintentionally, but to good effect. It was as if a switch had been thrown.

Mycroft threw an embarrassed quick glance in Watson's direction and, looking chastened, forced himself to regain his composure. Holmes promptly followed his brother's example.

A brief interval of awkward silence was broken finally by Mycroft.

"You must leave this to me, Sherlock," he said in a very low voice but in a tone that left no doubt that it was a command, not a request. "This is a government matter now, an affair of state. You have no voice in it."

Holmes dropped his eyes and sat back. He considered the point. After a moment or two he looked up into his brother's face and studied it carefully, as if seeking a clue. "Just what is it that you have in mind?" he asked at last.

Mycroft shot a glance in Watson's direction. "Doctor, I must ask your forgiveness, but would you be good enough to leave us for just a little while?"

Watson, already on the edge of his seat, leapt to his feet almost gratefully. The turn the conversation had taken had made him extremely uncomfortable, and he was glad for the opportunity to be excused from it, busying himself at a table on the other side of the room, where several large, leather-bound volumes lay scattered about, doing his best to pay no attention to the continuing discussion behind him. After a while, though, his curiosity got the better of him; sheepishly, he found himself actually straining to hear.

"I don't like it!" he heard Holmes say at one point, with Mycroft replying in some heat: "That is of little consequence!"

The low murmur of voices continued for several minutes more, during which time it was impossible to make out any words distinctly. Then another sharp exclamation from Holmes: "I won't have anything to do with this, Mycroft!"

Several more minutes went by. Clearly, Mycroft was using all of his not-inconsiderable persuasive powers to win his younger brother over to his point of view, but was having no easy time of it. Sherlock Holmes could be a very stubborn man, as Watson well knew, especially when he believed himself to be right, which was almost always.

At long last the discussion came to an end and Mycroft summoned him back.

"You must forgive me," he said when Watson had taken his chair once again. "But I think you understand the gravity of the situation and what is at stake here. Given the identity of the personage involved, every precaution must be taken, and the less shared with the fewest number, the better it will be."

Watson nodded.

"We are no longer dealing with the simple matter of the murder of a few unfortunates. You do see that, don't you? As preposterous as it may seem, we are now confronting an affair that could have repercussions of a catastrophic nature. I believe Sherlock understands this now, and it is important that you understand it as well. Whether you like it or not, by accident or design, you are in the thick of it. It is vital that you appreciate what is at stake. I am sure that I do not have to spell it out for you, but the wrong move now – a misjudgment, a simple miscalculation, a misplaced confidence, or a word dropped within the hearing of the wrong ear – could prove to be disastrous. If we are to avoid utter calamity, we must put petty moral scruples aside and act with total resolve. We must consider the totality. I put it to you that nothing as pedestrian as a few gruesome back-alley murders must be permitted to change the course of history. It is just too preposterous to contemplate."

He leaned forward in his chair and looked directly into Watson's eyes. "I count on you, Doctor, to keep whatever you know, and whatever you think you know, to yourself."

"Of course," Watson mumbled.

"I am aware that Sherlock has absolute faith in your discretion, and I shall depend upon it. I am sure I shall not be disappointed."

His gray eyes were cold and piercing, and Watson had difficulty in meeting them. There was no question that a threat was implied in Mycroft's tone. While it made Watson angry, most of all it made him uncomfortable, for it suddenly dawned on him that Mycroft Holmes was not a man to make idle threats.

Mycroft unlocked his gaze and leaned back in his chair. "This is a most difficult situation, fearfully difficult. It is far and away the most delicate matter that has ever come to my attention in all my years in public service. It must be handled with great care and finesse. I do not look forward to laying it before the P.M. Lord Salisbury's health is not as robust as it should be. This is bound to affect him badly." He lumbered to his feet, grunting with the effort.

"Belcher!" he called to the waiter. "Have a four-wheeler summoned at once!"

Holmes and Watson trailed behind him in the general direction of the door.

"The next few hours will be most trying, I fear. Most trying indeed." He glanced back at them. "Well, c'mon, you two! Don't hang back. You're coming with me!"

They entered the small, unpretentious Georgian building without being stopped or delayed for a moment by the constable on duty in front of the entrance. He merely took a sidelong glance in Mycroft's direction and saluted, allowing the three of them to pass through the door without question. Mycroft Holmes, it would seem, was not an infrequent visitor to number 10 Downing Street.

Watson did his best to acquit himself in a manner that suggested that he, too, was no stranger to the bastions of power, but he feared he carried it off with something less than total aplomb, for he badly fumbled his hat and stick in the process of handing them over to the porter inside the vestibule.

The anteroom on the second floor, to which they were ushered without delay, had several chairs in it, but even Mycroft Holmes, who never stood when he could sit, declined to take one. Instead, the three of them remained standing by the tall window overlooking the Horse Guards Parade, waiting to be summoned by the principal private secretary, who informed Mycroft (not without some display of pique) that he would endeavor to fit him in between two appointments.

Watson stole a glance at his two companions as they waited. Though they both wore brooding expressions, only natural considering the circumstances, neither appeared particularly ill at ease, which to Watson was quite unnatural, considering their surroundings. He, on the other hand, was highly nervous, never having dreamed when he awoke that morning that he would be standing where he was before day's end. Indeed, in his wildest dreams he had never imagined he would ever be standing where he was.

The wait was a brief one. The great Lord Salisbury was, for a peer of the realm, and a wealthy and powerful one at that, a very simple man who cared nothing for pomp, so the summons when it came was made without ceremony: A door merely opened, a young man in frockcoat appeared, and with a simple gesture they were directed into the Prime Minister's presence. Watson straightened his cravat and threw a nervous glance at Holmes, who seemed totally unaffected by the importance of the moment, for his face was as composed as that of a Red Indian.

Lord Salisbury was an impressive figure, someone who would quietly dominate any room: A large, stout, balding man with a thick, unruly gray beard that all but covered his chest – a tired old man, he looked to be (though he was only in his late fifties), whose rounded shoulders no longer carried the weight of Empire without difficulty, for there were heavy dark shadows under his eyes and a weariness upon his face that made it evident that the burden had become all but unbearable. He did not rise as they entered, but he did glance up from the sheaf of papers in his hand. It was impossible not to be immediately taken with him, no matter what one's political persuasions. He had a face that bred confidence and trust, a massive brow, and wise, intelligent eyes; the face of a man without vanity, without guile who, given a choice, would far prefer to be among his books, studying the classics, than caught up in the hurly-burly of party politics and the intrigues of international affairs. But he had no choice; he was born to the role. It was his duty to serve the Queen, just as two of his ancestors had served previous monarchs as first ministers three hundred years before, as it was the Queen's duty to reign over the Empire. It was a duty that came with his name and titles. Lord Salisbury, it had been said, was one of those few who had inherited all of the privileges of being an aristocrat without losing any of the responsibilities.[77]

"Well, Mycroft, and what delights do you bring me today?" he said in a gruff, not unkindly voice. "I had not expected to see you until our usual Monday meeting."

"Good day, m'lord. You must forgive my unannounced call."

"I must assume it is a matter of some importance for it to intrude upon your normal routine."

The prime minister's gaze moved wordlessly from Mycroft Holmes to Watson and then to Sherlock Holmes, his bushy eyebrows lifting noticeably upon recognizing the latter, which said much for Holmes's rising celebrity, for Lord Salisbury was notorious for his inability to remember names or faces.

Mycroft made the introductions, and the three of them were gestured into the chairs arranged in front of the prime minister's table.

It took only five minutes for Mycroft to explain the purpose of the visit and to lay the matter out entirely. Accustomed to briefing men of power on the most complicated of issues, his presentation of the facts was short and to the point, admirably concise yet complete. Clearly he was endowed with a vivid memory: His recitation was flawless. That his delivery was dispassionate, devoid of any form of emotion, served only to make what he was saying all the more incredible. And all the more horrifying. To Watson's ear, listening to someone else relate the facts of the matter for the first time, the whole business sounded so very fantastic that he would not have been surprised had the prime minister summoned his secretary to have the three of them ejected into the street.

But the prime minister listened without interrupting, motionless in his chair, only his eyes betraying that he was listening at all, for they widened dramatically as the import of Mycroft's news was revealed, and his breathing became alarmingly heavy. By the time Mycroft had finished, the old man seemed to have shrunken in size; his jaw hung slack and his hands trembled noticeably. He looked at the three of them with horror upon his face, unable even to speak. For a second or two Watson feared that his professional services might be required, for the man appeared to be in a state of shock.

But when he did finally speak, his voice was surprisingly firm: "I have grave difficulty in believing any of this, gentlemen, as I am sure you will understand. Indeed, if it hadn't come from you, Mycroft, I wouldn't have believed a word of it. You will forgive me, but I require a moment or two to absorb all of this. Are you saying to me that one of Prince Albert Victor's close associates may in some way or another be involved in the Whitechapel murders? That is what you are saying, is it not?"

"Yes, m'lord," replied Mycroft. "I fear so."

"And you are saying that His Highness, or at least one of his friends, may in some way be *personally* implicated?"

"The evidence strongly suggests that possibility, m'lord."

"Good God, it cannot be!" He stared at Mycroft in disbelief.

Mycroft looked down at his hands and said nothing.

The prime minister turned to Sherlock Holmes. "You are certain of your facts? You are absolutely certain there can be no mistake?"

Holmes, without a word, rose from his chair, leaned over the prime minister's desk, and deposited three small glassine envelopes in front of him.

Lord Salisbury looked down at the envelopes and then up again at Holmes, questioningly.

"In one is the sleeve link, my lord, with the three feathers of Wales upon it. In the other, a sample of the cigarette found at the scene of the Hanbury Street murder. The third contains the cigarette end I observed one of His Highness's companions discard in the street last night."

The prime minister made no move to examine the contents of the envelopes. "And you are certain the young man you saw was with Prince Albert Victor?"

Instead of replying, Holmes gestured to Watson. Watson cleared his throat. "Yes, my lord. There is no question about it. I had occasion to observe His Highness at Epsom Downs last racing season, though from a distance, of course. But I have a pair of excellent binoculars, and was able to study his face, and those of the others in the royal enclosure, most carefully. There is not a doubt in my mind that it was he."

"And the identity of this young man?"

Holmes shrugged. "That should not be difficult to ascertain, but as yet I have made no effort to do so. It is someone who quite obviously is often in the prince's company, so we may assume he is an intimate of his."

Lord Salisbury looked down at his desk for several minutes and stroked his beard, deep in thought. When he raised his head at last, he did so with a heavy sigh.

There was a light tap at the door, and the prime minister's young secretary stuck his head in. "My Lord, His Grace, the Duke of —"

"Oh, do go away, Stillwell! Bugger His Grace!"

The secretary looked positively shocked. Lord Salisbury was known to be a very religious, highly moral individual who never, *never* — even when under the greatest stress — used intemperate language.

The door closed quickly.

Wearily, the prime minister directed his gaze to Mycroft once again. "All this comes upon me too suddenly, I fear. I am in somewhat of a quandary. We must act immediately, of course: Prompt measures must be taken. The matter is far too explosive to consider it at our leisure. First, I must ask you, how many are there who are aware of all of this?"

Mycroft replied: "Only those of us who are in this room, m'lord."

Lord Salisbury looked at Holmes and Watson. "No more, you are certain?"

"Absolutely, m'lord."

The old man nodded. "Then it must remain so. No one else is to be brought into it without my knowledge and express approval. No one."

"Yes, m'lord. That point is already understood by both my brother and Dr. Watson."

To Watson's discomfort, the prime minister then directed his gaze at him. "Ah, yes, Dr. Watson." The question in his eyes was unstated but unmistakable.

Sherlock Holmes responded to it: "The doctor has been intimately involved in this investigation from the very start, Lord Salisbury. His services are invaluable to me. He is a man of unquestionable integrity and has my absolute trust."

The prime minister turned his great shaggy head toward Holmes and studied him briefly. Holmes met his gaze unflinchingly.

Mycroft cleared his throat. "Prime Minister, the reason Dr. Watson is here is because his involvement, whether, er, desirable or not, is a fait accompli. I thought it best — and you will forgive me, Doctor, for being direct — I thought it best that he be included in our little circle as the surest way of insuring his silence."

There was an awkward moment in which no one said anything. Then Holmes spoke once again. "As I say, he has my complete trust. If that is not good enough..."

Lord Salisbury closed his eyes and raised his hand. "Then he shall have mine also. And that shall be an end to the matter."

He turned in his chair and gazed out the window for a few moments.

"I need not tell you, gentlemen," he said finally, his back still toward them, "that I do not intend to spend my final days in office and on Earth presiding over the dissolution of the British Empire." He turned to face them, his tired eyes boring into them. He smiled gently.

"Now that we have settled on that," he said dryly, "we have only to decide on the simple matter of how best to go about preserving the Empire. Mycroft, what course of action do you recommend? I can always count on your clear thinking in a crisis."

Mycroft did not hesitate. "First, m'lord, the young man in question must be identified and, ah, neutralized. And His Highness must be taken in hand."

The prime minister looked at him. "How? Send him away, you mean?"

"For the moment, a lengthy overseas tour would serve nicely. I have no doubt the Foreign Office can arrange one in quick order. India, perhaps – or Australia. But of course he must be closely watched at all times. Someone whom we can take into our confidence, at least to a certain degree, must be in constant attendance upon him. That person must be carefully selected."

Lord Salisbury nodded and considered the matter. Then he looked up sharply and studied Mycroft through rheumy eyes. "What do you mean, 'for the moment'?" he asked, the tone of his question suggesting that he was not going to like the answer.

Mycroft did not falter in his reply. "A more lasting solution, m'lord, will have to be considered at some point. It is an absolute necessity. There is no alternative in my view."

Lord Salisbury continued to stare at him.

Mycroft held his ground. "There is no alternative whatsoever."

"I need not remind you," said the prime minister, his voice weary beyond belief, "that you speak of the Heir Presumptive to the throne of England."

Considering the import of his words, Mycroft seemed amazingly calm and self-possessed. His reply was almost offhand. "M'lord, I have considered every possible solution. You must believe me when I say there is no alternative. Absolutely none whatsoever."

The implications of Mycroft's statement hung heavily in the air. A shiver went down Watson's spine. He looked at Holmes. Holmes's face was like stone.

Twenty

SATURDAY, NOVEMBER 3, 1888

"The circumstances are of great delicacy, and every precaution has to be taken to quench what might grow to be an immense scandal and seriously compromise one of the reigning families of Europe."
— A Scandal in Bohemia

"His Royal Highness will see you now," said the equerry from the other side of the room, his manner a good deal more lordly, more pompous, than was either necessary, desirable, or justifiable. He was a self-important young man, tall and straight and good-looking in a blank sort of way, impeccably groomed and with the unmistakable stamp of "good family" in his bearing. His pronouncement, being one that he was called upon to make many times during the course of a given day, had been refined through diligent practice to what he considered the absolute peak of perfection, and that he was abundantly pleased with the result, as well as with himself, was abundantly obvious.

That Mycroft Holmes was not pleased with *him* was also obvious. "Insufferable little twit," he snapped, making certain his voice was loud enough for the young man to hear across the room.

But if he had, he would never permit it to be apparent. It was his lot to endure, to suffer in silence. His role as a junior aide-de-camp to the Prince of Wales required a certain thickness of hide and at least a nodding acquaintance with the principles of stoicism, for his master could be most trying at times, displaying as he did both a propensity for regal testiness and a predilection for practical jokes.

If Mycroft Holmes was aware of the young man's unenviable position in life, he was not in a particularly caring mood. It was nighttime, well past the dinner hour, and he had not as yet dined. Mycroft Holmes was not the sort of man who could miss a meal and look upon it with equanimity. He did not like to miss his meals. He did not like it at all.

Aside from feeling decidedly peckish, he was looking forward to this engagement with the Prince of Wales with positive dread. No one in his right mind would relish confronting HRH with disagreeable news, let alone disagreeable news regarding one of his progeny, especially when it concerned his firstborn, who was very much of a disappointment to the prince, an embarrassment and a sore point. Added to it was the fact that Mycroft Holmes was genuinely fond of the prince and considered him a friend, and he, basically a kindly man beneath it all, did not savor the prospect of telling a friend that his son and heir was a degenerate and... possibly worse.

Under the circumstances, it was only natural that he be in a foul temper, and his brother, recognizing the danger signals earlier on, had plotted a course to steer well clear of him. Watson, following Holmes's lead, had wisely tacked in succession.

It had not been easy, for the three of them had been in close company for the better part of the day. Following their meeting with the prime minister, Mycroft had sent an urgent message to Marlborough House, requesting an immediate audience with the prince. They then returned to the Diogenes Club to await a reply and plot out a course of action. The reply was not received until very late in the day. It came from Knollys, the prince's personal private secretary, and was delivered by hand. His Royal Highness, said the note in flawless copperplate handwriting, because of the press of official engagements, regrettably found it quite impossible to meet Mr. Mycroft Holmes's request for an audience that day, but would be pleased to grant him a few moments of time at three-fifteen o'clock on October the eleventh instant.

A scrawled note at the bottom, in Knollys's handwriting, added:

Mycroft –
  Suggest you try to catch HRH at his club around midnight.
  He's bound to pull himself away by then. Usually manages to.
    K.

Accordingly, the three of them, parting briefly to dress in evening clothes, appeared at the appointed hour in front of the doors to the Marlborough Club in Pall Mall, just across from the prince's official residence, Marlborough House, from which the club took its name.

The Marlborough was unquestionably the most exclusive gentlemen's club in London – the most exclusive, the most lavish, the most extravagantly furnished. No expense was spared to equip it with every conceivable luxury and convenience, and to do so in the most opulent manner possible. To be made a member of the Marlborough was to be accepted in the very highest strata of male society, a sign of recognition that in its way was akin to being awarded a knighthood or a peerage. It was no accident that only those who were well known to the Prince of Wales and were in his good standing were invited to put their names up for membership. After all, the club was founded by the prince and it was he who decided who was acceptable.[78]

Mycroft, while not a member (few commoners were), was well known to the doorman, so he and his two companions were shown directly to the Strangers' Room while his card was conveyed upstairs. Within five minutes the imperious young equerry appeared to ask their business, and just as quickly disappeared, not to return for another half hour.

Now the young man was subjecting the three of them to a quick but thorough scrutiny, and was making no effort to be discreet about it. It fell to him to assure that there was nothing in their attire that would offend His Highness, for the prince was most particular in matters of dress, changed his own several times a day, and had very definite ideas of what was proper to wear in his presence. It was not unknown for him to publicly take to task anyone who had the cheek to appear dressed in a manner inappropriate to the time of day or occasion. While the young man did not exactly resort to examining their fingernails, he did cluck over the bit of dandruff on Mycroft's shoulder, but after a flickering glance into the latter's eyes wisely thought better of calling for a valet to attend to the matter.

These preliminaries concluded, the equerry conducted them up a sweeping marble staircase to the second level and, beneath glittering chandeliers, down a long red-carpeted hallway, its walls hung with oils depicting English hunting scenes. Everything was bright and shining and highly polished – the woods, the brass, the silver, the marble, the crystal – creating an atmosphere of comfort, of tasteful though unabashed opulence that was unmistakably masculine in flavor.

From the hallway they were conducted into a dimly lit billiard room smelling of rich leather, fine brandy, polished wood, and good tobacco. It was like no other billiard room Watson had ever seen (and he, being partial to the game, had been in many in his day). It was a large rectangular-shaped room, its walls wainscoted in paneled walnut, covered above with a tartan fabric, predominantly dark green in color.

Green leather banquettes lined two sides of the room, the leather obviously dyed to contrast perfectly with the color of the material on the walls. The banquettes were situated well back from the magnificent table that was the room's centerpiece and which occupied its space with great dignity and unmistakable authority.

The room sat in hushed splendor when they entered, there being no one else present, and it took a moment or two to become accustomed to the dim light, for only the surface of the table was brightly illuminated. If the facility was used often or at all, it was not apparent; everything in it looked perfectly new. But in actuality it was a popular room with the members and was occupied frequently during the course of an average day. The secret of its pristine appearance was that it received, like the other rooms in the club, a thorough going-over after each and every use, and any signs of wear or stain or age were quickly attended to. The effect was to create the illusion that the room and its contents were prepared solely and especially for whatever party of individuals happened to next walk through the door, and that once they were gone, the room and everything in it would be gone also.

The equerry, having done his duty, departed without a further word, closing the door soundlessly behind him.

"Insufferable," muttered Mycroft Holmes, scowling.

His younger brother considered him with one of his looks of wry amusement. Watson considered him not at all, having not heard him. He was totally captivated by the billiard table, lost in awe of its magnificence.

Although feeling that he shouldn't, he could not resist placing a hand on the table to lightly caress its cushioned banks. The covering of green felt was in flawless condition, not a sign of wear in evidence, not a blemish or speck of dust. The highly polished wood of the table was a rich, warm walnut, the same hue as the paneled wainscoting of the room.

Watson leaned over to read the small bronze plaque affixed to the side of the table.

Presented to HRH the Prince of Wales on the occasion of
his fortieth birthday Messrs. Thurston & Co., Ltd.
Of Leicester Square

Of course the table would have come from Thurston's: They were the premier manufacturers of billiard tables in all of England, and therefore the world. Deftly inlaid with mother-of-pearl and ivory, its workmanship was flawless, the grain of the wood without peer. It was, simply, a thing of beauty, a work of art equal to the finest piece of furniture that Watson had ever seen. He ran his hand over the highly polished surface. He could not even begin to estimate its cost, but guessed that it would amount to many times his annual pension. Indeed, it was probably a sum that would feed a working-class family for several years.

Watson crouched down and lined up an imaginary shot. The cue ball, thoughtfully, had already been spotted on its mark, placed in position for the opening shot. All that was required was the blow to send it on its way.

At the other end of the table, precisely aligned on the green felt surface, was a perfect inverted pyramid of red balls, standing like a formation of soldiers on the field of battle, dumbly awaiting the violent blow that would destroy its perfection and cause it to burst apart with sudden fury.

Several minutes went by. The three of them waited quietly. Not a word passed among them.

Holmes wandered over to a rack of cue sticks along the wall and examined it disinterestedly. Mycroft merely stood and fumed. He did not like to be kept waiting in any event, but on this occasion was particularly eager to get it over with.

Several more minutes went by.

Suddenly and without warning a pair of double doors on the other side of the room flew open and, heralded only by a sharp intake of breath by Watson, in strode the Prince of Wales.

"Ah, Mycroft, old chap," he boomed. "How very good to see you!" He strode around the billiard table, his hand extended.

The prince was an extremely large man of truly Falstaffian proportions – not tall, merely large. Indeed, Watson was surprised to find that he was well below average height, five foot six or seven at most, but his girth made him seem almost massive. And he looked considerably older than his forty-seven years, more like a man who was in his sixties. He had a large head, protruding, heavily lidded eyes, a long and rather full nose, and a neatly trimmed beard, pepper and salt in color. The admirable cut of his evening clothes made his swelling girth majestic and that, along with his booming voice, gave him a most imposing presence. It would not take much of an imagination to picture him dressed in the costume of an earlier age, bearing an uncanny resemblance to his distant ancestor, King Henry VIII.

Mycroft stepped forward, took the prince's hand, and bowed. "Good evening, Bertie. Forgive me for taking you away from the tables."

"It is just as vell that you had," laughed the prince. "I was losing abominably. It is not my night for baccarat." Then, catching sight of Watson and Holmes in the subdued light: "Who's this you have vis you? Have these gentlemen been presented to me?"

"Yes, I believe so, though perhaps not formally. My brother I think you will remember, but you may not recall his friend. May I name Dr. John Watson to Your Royal Highness?"

Watson bowed deeply, Holmes less so.

The man who would someday be King of England came forward. He ignored Watson for the moment and concentrated his gaze on Holmes, considering him with a distinctly cold look.

"So, Mr. Sherlock Holmes, we meet again," said the prince, his tone suggesting that the memory of their previous meeting was something less than pleasurable to him. It was not quite a withering glare that he bestowed upon Holmes, but it came close.

Holmes returned the prince's gaze without flinching. He waited an interminable moment before saying with icy correctness: "Your Royal Highness is kind to remember me."

There was another awkward interval of silence during which Holmes and the prince continued to stare at each other, the prince with a fixity that any other man would have found terrifying, Holmes with a total lack of expression that under the circumstances could be considered only impertinent.

Mycroft coughed delicately and, casting his brother an urgent glance of warning, stepped in quickly to save the moment.

"Good of you to see us on such short notice, sir. Good of you, indeed."

The prince finally looked away from Holmes and turned his gaze on Watson, changing his manner abruptly.

"Doctor, did I hear Mycroft refer to you as? A medical chentleman, are you?"

His voice, strange to note, had a guttural quality to it, a slight but obvious Germanic accent, and he seemed to have particular trouble pronouncing his r's.[79]

"Yes, Your Royal Highness, though I am presently retired from active practice, I fear."

"I see," said the Prince. Then, harumphing: "There are those who vould say that I, too, am retired from active practice, so you needn't apologize on my account." He harumphed again, then threw back his head and laughed – an explosive, boisterous, jolly laugh that was highly infectious, the quality of the humor notwithstanding.

Mycroft and Watson joined in, of course, for when a prince of the royal blood is disposed to deliver of himself a merriment, a joke – especially a self-deprecating joke, even a feeble one (*most* especially a feeble one), it is only natural and polite, and certainly politic, to laugh along with him. Somehow, strangely, a joke seems that much more amusing coming from royalty, or from anyone in authority, for that matter.

Holmes did not laugh. His features remained devoid of expression.

The prince considered him under lowered brow for a moment, then purposely turned his broad back to him and walked to the billiard table, where he picked up a ball at random from out of the perfect pyramid and idly began tossing it in his hand.

"Vell, what is it, Mycroft? Somesing tedious, I warrant, from your brother's sour countenance."

Mycroft cleared his throat. "Something most delicate, Bertie. And I fear quite painful."

"Oh!" The prince stiffened and gave him a look. "Really tedious, then. You come from Her Majesty, do you?"

All of a sudden he had become apprehensive. His accent had thickened noticeably, as it always did when he became upset.

Mycroft smiled weakly. "No, it is not that, Bertie."

The prince sighed gratefully.

It was no secret that His Royal Highness did not get along with the Queen, and it was barely a secret that he was positively terrified of her. It was strange to see any man who was past middle age afraid of his mother, let alone such a commanding figure as the Prince of Wales. But then, the Queen was not any mother. She was strict, domineering, and demanding and held her family to the highest standards of conduct; and in her eyes her eldest son fell far short of the mark. She disapproved of him in no uncertain terms, being highly critical of his intemperate habits, his hedonistic, pleasure-seeking ways, and even his choice of friends. And she let no opportunity go by without telling him so.

That Mycroft did not bear ill tidings from the Queen was such a relief to the prince that whatever ill tidings he did bear could only pale in comparison. Accordingly, the royal mood brightened considerably.

"Vell, this calls for a trink, if anysing does. Brandy, everyone? Doctor, I take it you are not vun of those tiresome practitioners who adfocates abstinence?"

"Heavens no, Your Highness! Indeed, I often prescribe spirits for a variety of ailments – in moderation, of course."

"Do you now? Do you indeed? I must consider you for the post of my Physician in Ordinary. The fellow I have now sinks I imbibe too much, damn him." As if in reflex, he pulled his cigar case from an inner pocket.

"Sinks I smoke too many Havanas too. But a fellow's got to have some vices, don't he?" He favored Watson with a broad wink, and Watson, flattered beyond words, flushed with pleasure.

He could be forgiven. The prince had the knack of putting people at their ease and could be most charming when he set his mind to it. Indeed, some of his critics claimed he made a career of it. "He can charm the birds from out of the trees and the ladies from out of their knickers," someone once said of him with only slight exaggeration and the merest hint of envy. That he also had remarkable success in calming the wrath of husbands he had victimized said much for the versatility of his talent, and, if anything, added to his stature.

To his critics, and there were many, this much-vaunted charm of his was one of his few saving graces, for he was not the most clever of men or the most knowledgeable or the hardest working. He had little talent for diplomacy or patience with the tiresome details of governance; he rarely read a book, knew little about world affairs, less about scientific matters, had a short attention span, and could be most intolerant, cruelly insensitive and highly irascible, especially when someone had the effrontery to subject him to anything that was the least bit boring. Early in life he discovered that charm could cover a multitude of sins, and if artfully applied could bend others to his will. Since it was something that came naturally to him anyway, it was a talent he was able to cultivate with such success that he deemed it unnecessary to make any serious effort in any other direction. And besides, what he could not accomplish with charm, he found he could generally accomplish by bullying. He was equally good at that.

At a summons on the bellpull, brandy and glasses were brought in without delay, not by one of the club's servants, oddly enough, though they were conspicuous in great numbers throughout the club, but by a tall, cadaverously thin gentleman referred to by the prince, with obvious fondness, as Xtopher.

Mycroft, well-acquainted with the gentleman, made the introductions. He was the Honorable Christopher Sykes, known in the prince's close circle of friends as the Great Xtopher. A rather humorless man from the look of him, and somewhat dull-witted in both appearance and manner, he seemed a strange choice to be on such close terms with the ebullient, fun-loving prince. But it was obvious he enjoyed the royal favor and, equally as obvious, that he was as devoted as a puppy. He catered to the prince hand and foot, performing the most menial tasks for him, anticipating his every wish. Rarely was he seen far from his side, despite the fact that he was sometimes used badly by his royal friend, and was often the butt of his practical jokes. More than one glass of port had been poured down his neck over the years, the contents of more than one ice bucket deposited in his lap.

Perhaps this was why the prince insisted upon keeping him in close attendance: The Great Xtopher was good for a laugh. He was the perfect fool and could always be depended upon to take it in good grace. No matter how great the indignity or cruel the treatment, he invariably responded (to the glee of those present) with a long-suffering, "As Your Royal Highness pleases." And he was always there for the next time.[80]

Dull-witted appearance notwithstanding, he was perceptive enough to realize that Mycroft Holmes's presence – along with that of his well-known brother, the consulting detective – must be of a confidential nature and of some importance, so after pouring the brandy and handing the glasses all around, he made his excuses and discreetly withdrew, neatly sparing himself the awkwardness of being dismissed by the prince and thoughtfully sparing the prince of the awkward necessity of having to do so.

The door closed softly and once again the room became silent.

The prince took a sip of his brandy, observing Mycroft and Holmes over the rim of the snifter. He did not like the looks on their faces, and never one to readily undertake distasteful business when there was the possibility of putting it off, he didn't give Mycroft an opportunity to explain the purpose of the visit.

"Come!" he said with sudden jollity. "Ve shall shoot a game of billiards. Who vill play vis me? Not you, Mycroft – you are a terrible player! In your hand a cue stick is a dangerous veapon. Doctor, how about you? You have the commendable look of a man vis a misspent youth. You know the game, do you?"

Watson looked very pleased to have been singled out. "I am not totally unfamiliar with it, Your Highness," he admitted modestly.

"Ah-ha! I don't like the sound of dat. I shall take care to be on my guard. And let me varn you, sir, that mine vas a misspent youth also, so you had best be on *your* guard. Come, choose your cue stick and name your vager."

Watson looked flustered for a moment, then smiled and bowed.

"Allow me to defer to Your Highness," he said politely but not wisely.

Mycroft winced, knowing what was to come.

"Very vell," the prince said. "Let us make it interesting: Is ten pounds comfortable for you?"

Watson blanched. His army pension, his sole source of income, totaled a munificent eleven shillings sixpence a day. Ten pounds equaled more than two weeks' earnings. To him it was a princely sum indeed, no pun intended. He swallowed hard. "As Your Royal Highness pleases," he said with a casualness he did not feel.

It was just as well that he could not see the expression on Holmes's face, which was hidden by shadow. It would have neither inspired confidence in his judgment nor done anything to improve his game.

Both men removed their coats and, in shirt-sleeves, went about the ritual of choosing their cue sticks and chalking them, like two duelists preparing for combat.

The table was set up for snooker pool, the most popular of the various billiard games. It was played with fifteen red balls (those placed in the inverted pyramid) and one each of pink, brown, black, green, yellow, and blue, those of the latter colors being spotted in designated locations around the table. In a classic demonstration of noblesse oblige, the prince waved aside the ritual drawing of lots to decide the order of play and generously invited Watson to make the first stroke, giving himself the advantage, of course, since there was virtually no chance at all of scoring with the opening shot.

But he hadn't counted on Watson's skill at the game. The best strategy in such a situation was to play for safety, and that was what Watson chose to do, aiming at the outside of the inverted pyramid of red balls, at the very last ball in the farthest row. Despite his nervousness, he hit it bang on target with just the right degree of force, the ball barely being nudged from its place. But the cue ball, amazingly, did just what the book says it will do when it is aimed precisely and at just the right velocity. It deflected off the target ball at exactly the right angle, struck the back cushion, careened off the side cushion, and, with stately grace, rolled slowly, slowly back toward Watson to return over the balk line, where it finally came to a halt – right behind the brown ball on the center spot.

It was a classic shot.

The prince contemplated the placement of the balls with a scowl, slowly shaking his head from side to side. "Snookered, by gad!" said the heir to the throne, glancing across the table at Watson with admiration. "You've played this game before," he accused him.

Watson, to his credit, managed the affair with total aplomb, for no one was more surprised at the beauty of the thing than he. He stood tall and very dignified, his cue stick held in the parade-rest position, looking for all the world like a man who had done nothing out of the ordinary. But the truth of the matter was that in fifteen-odd years of trying, not only had he never made the shot before but had rarely seen anyone else make it so perfectly. Nodding his head politely in the prince's direction, he said with almost excessive dignity: "Your Royal Highness's stroke, I believe."

From out of the darkness came a single word, a sound really, the source of it unmistakably Sherlock Holmes – one must assume that it was involuntary: *"Hah!"*

Watson's opening was so deftly accomplished that the prince was left with an impossible shot. No matter what he did he would suffer a penalty, for the rules required him to strike a red ball before that of any other color, and this he clearly could not do, the brown ball being in his way. But he had no choice but to attempt it anyway, which he unwisely did like a bull in a china shop rather than with finesse, succeeding only in scattering the field to Watson's benefit, leaving him now with a choice of several excellent possibilities.

Watson circled the table and examined the layout of the balls with care, absently chalking his cue all the while. Rather than selecting the easiest, most obvious shot, he chose one that if executed properly would leave the cue ball in the perfect position for yet another. Leaning over the table, he swiftly made it.

Kerplocketa! Into the corner pocket it went.

The next ball and the next were similarly dispatched – quickly, cleanly, and decisively, one after another in rapid succession.

The prince could only stand there and watch, the scowl on his face becoming deeper and deeper.

Finally came a ball that was not so accommodating. Watson attempted a tricky deflection shot that required some backspin, but it did not come off the way he had intended and the ball bounced off the rim of the pocket and stopped nearby, leaving the prince with an easy potshot. He took it effortlessly. However, he had no luck with the next one, and it became Watson's turn again.

The remaining balls on the table were potted in short order, with Watson employing a variety of shots from his repertoire with admirable poise and skill. He had never played better. Almost every stroke that he attempted he made, and the few he did not were managed so well that the prince was left in an untenable position every time – tied up and in a tangle with nothing but impossible shots and forlorn hopes.

He was noticeably angry.

"We vill have another game," he announced curtly when Watson dispatched the final ball with a click and satisfying clunk. "Same stakes."

There was no mistaking the tone in his voice. Clearly, it was not an invitation but a royal command.

But this time Mycroft was determined. "Bertie, you must forgive me," he stepped in, "but our business is of extreme importance."

The prince shot him a look of displeasure, a look that men ignored at their peril. "It vill vait!"

Mycroft stood his ground, apologetically but insistent. "Of the utmost importance, I am afraid."

The prince glared at him for a long moment, then sighed and dropped his stick on the table with a clatter. "Very vell then. You have my total attention."

Mycroft took a deep swallow from his glass and began.

It was a pale, shaken Prince of Wales to whom Watson gently handed a second glass of brandy five minutes later. He sat slumped on the leather banquette, looking nothing like the imposing figure of before. His face was gray and haggard; his eyes were dull in their sockets. He had taken the news badly, and there was little that could be said or done to ease his distress.

Mycroft had done his best to be gentle, using all of the tact he was capable of, but even so, the prince was in a state of shock. He knew that his son associated with some fairly objectionable, even disreputable characters — what young man didn't on occasion? (certainly *he* had when at that age) — but he never dreamed it was a homosexual crowd to which Prince Eddy belonged. And to think that one of them could be involved in this infamous series of murders that was in all the newspapers! It was beyond belief! The very thought that his son and heir was in some way implicated, or could be tied even remotely to someone who was, came as a terrible blow, and it was enough to make him physically ill.

If the news should get out, the consequences would be disastrous, and the prince knew it. The scandal would be unbearable. It would have repercussions that would last for years, well into his own reign when the time finally came for him to ascend to the throne – if it ever did come.

And good God! What would he tell Alix, the boy's mother? She would be inconsolable. And what would the Queen say? How could he ever face her? She would be furious, positively livid, and would blame it all on him, of course – just as she always blamed him for everything!

Maybe this time she will be right. He should have devoted more attention to the boy, kept him on a tighter rein. He should have been more strict, more aware.

The Queen will be unmerciful.

But that was the least of it. He looked up at them in disbelief, the full realization of it striking home. This scandal would cause incalculable damage; it would rock the very foundations of the monarchy. He harbored no false illusions: Given the tenor of the times, this thing could topple the throne. Victoria would be the last of the royal line, and he would never reign. After all these years of waiting, he would never be given his chance. They would all be sent off into exile, the lot of them: Uncles and sisters and cousins and sons, all to live out their lives in genteel poverty in some foreign place, humiliated, despised, and, worst of all, pitied, to join the ranks of other failed royal houses, useless to themselves and to the world, the objects of contempt and universal scorn.

The thought carried the Prince of Wales to the very depths of despair, and for the second time that day Watson feared that his medical services might be required.

But he had forgotten with whom he was dealing. This was a man whose background and training throughout the whole of his life had prepared him for one thing and one thing only: To lead other men, to set them an example. This was not a man to give into despair.

Calling upon some hidden resource, he rallied. He somehow gained control of himself and sat upright, the color returning to his cheeks. Pushing them away, he rose to his feet and began pacing the room, furiously puffing upon a fresh cigar. The three of them could only admire his strength and resilience and recuperative powers.

"We must decide what to do!" he announced in a strong, determined voice, once again the commanding figure. "We must come up with a scheme, we must choose a course of action! None of this must be allowed to compromise the throne, to tear the nation asunder. That is our first concern, and in deciding upon the course we will follow, that must be our first consideration."

He pointed his cigar at the three of them, his bulging eyes burning with intensity. "We vill not allow this to destroy our nation and our Empire! Is that clear?"

Then, to no one in particular and half under his breath: "Damn that boy, vat is wrong with him? Vat in God's name is wrong with him! It is the influence of that damn Stephen, I am sure of it!"

"Sir?"

"Oh, that Stephen fellow – Eddy's tutor at Cambridge. I never should have allowed it! I vas given terrible advice about that damnable man. He is to blame, I just know it!"

Then, a thought suddenly occurring to him, the prince jerked his head around.

"Where is Eddy now? Do you know, Mycroft? In London, is he, with his goddamn Nancy-boys?"

"No, sir. In York, I believe, with his regiment."

The prince's eyes were practically bulging out of their sockets, he was so angry.

"Vell, bring him back – instantly! I vant him here, before me! Now!"

"No!"

The prince spun around in surprise.

Holmes, who had remained quietly in the background until now, startled everyone with his sudden exclamation, the prince most of all, for it was a rare occurrence for anyone to dispute an order of his, or even question one.

The prince glared at him wide-eyed, his mouth open in disbelief.

Holmes's tone was respectful but firm. "That would be a serious mistake, Your Royal Highness, and I must caution you against it."

The prince looked from Holmes to Mycroft, not believing his ears.

Mycroft cleared his throat nervously. "At least hear him out, Bertie," he said, appealing to reason. "I think you will find that he has good and sufficient motives."

The prince glowered at them both, breathing heavily, his bearded chin outthrust. He was not a man who welcomed unsolicited advice at any time, nor was he accustomed to it being offered.

"Please, Bertie. Listen to what he has to say, I beg of you. To make a wrong move, to do anything precipitous, could have tragic results." Mycroft stood in front of him, palms upward. "I beg of you," he repeated.

The prince considered him for a moment, then exhaled. "Very vell," he said. "Go on, I am listening."

Holmes clasped his hands behind his back and, leaning forward like some gaunt bird of prey, his sharp features silhouetted dramatically by the single light over the table behind him, he marshaled his arguments with all the force at his command. He spared the prince nothing, using none of the delicate, tactful language that royalty was accustomed to hearing. The matter was extremely grave, he said. The future of the country was at risk. Now was not the time to give in to anger and play the role of the outraged father, but to think of the greater good. It was the time to act the statesman, to make difficult choices and personal sacrifices. The welfare of the nation must come first. It was, he suggested in no uncertain terms, the time to act like a king.

He was as merciless in his choice of words as he was in his choice of argument, and the color once again had drained from the prince's cheeks. No one had ever dared speak to him that way; no one had ever been that blunt or that bold.

"If we are to save the day, sir," Holmes said, concluding, "if a scandal is to be avoided and if the throne is to be kept secure, the killer must be stopped. He must be identified and taken into custody – and quickly, before he can act again. He must be prevented from committing another murder. To alert him now, to let him know that we are getting close, would be to ruin everything. If he was to learn that Prince Albert Victor has been summoned to your presence and confronted with the facts available to us, then our chance may well be lost. He is very shrewd, this man. If he discovers that we are on his track, there is no predicting what he will do. And if he is as close to the prince as I suspect him to be, he will find out, sir, make no mistake."

Holmes looked earnestly into the eyes of the Prince of Wales.

"We must play him like a fish, Your Highness. We must show him the lure and allow him to take it, and then I shall set the hook and reel him in, sir. I shall pull him in and take him! Depend upon it!"

After Holmes had finished, the prince considered him for the longest while without speaking, his eyes boring through him. Then he took a turn around the room, deep in thought, to come back finally to where Holmes was standing. He looked at him for another long moment before saying anything.

"Vut vill you do? How vill you go about this... this fishing business of yours?" His eyes bored into Holmes.

Holmes shrugged. "For that I shall require your cooperation, sir. I shall need your permission to, ah, delve into your son's private affairs to some extent – his friends, his acquaintances, his servants, his comings and goings.

"Spy on him, you mean!"

Holmes met his gaze directly. "Yes, sir."

Mycroft shifted his bulk nervously.

The prince considered this amazing request, then returned his gaze to Holmes. His face was pale, his features worked with conflicting emotions. When he spoke again, it was in a tired voice, barely audible.

"Very vell. You vill have your vay. It is obvious I have little choice in the matter. I vill give instructions to have you furnished with everything you require. You vill have carte blanche."

He nodded to Mycroft and turned as if to leave, but stopped and looked back at Holmes, his jaw quivering, his eyes once again fierce.

"But I tell you this: If you are wrong, Mr. Sherlock Holmes – if you fail – I shall curse you with my dying breath."

He spun on his heel and quickly left the room.

Twenty-One

MONDAY, NOVEMBER 5, 1888

"This case grows upon me, Watson. There are decidedly some points
of interest in connection with it."
— *The Adventure of the Priory School*

The late afternoon post arrived along with the first tentative thrusts
of a typical autumn gale sweeping up from the Channel. The
cold rain that had been falling sullenly throughout the day had turned
heavier, and fitful gusts began to rattle roof tiles and chimney pots
across the city, definite indications that the night would be one of fierce
winds and freezing, wet discomfort — an evening best spent indoors
in front of the fire with an engrossing book and a glass of something
warming close at hand. The rain began beating steadily against the
windowpanes as Mrs. Hudson climbed the seventeen steps to their
rooms with the mail delivery in hand.[81]

Watson was busy adding coal to the fire, so it was Holmes who
greeted her at the door. He had only recently returned, having been
on the street the better part of the day, and he was glad to be in out

of the rain and into dry clothes.

"It would seem we are in for a nasty one, Mrs. H.," said Holmes cheerfully. It was typical of his perverse nature that the onset of a storm should perk his spirits up.

She glanced toward the window and sniffed. "And the newspaper called for 'bright intervals' today. Shows you how much they know."

"Quite so, quite so."

"You'll be wanting your tea now, then?"

"Anytime it is convenient for you, dear lady," replied Holmes absently, sorting through the post.

"There'll be mutton for yer supper. Yer won't be going out now, will ye?" she asked with a suspicious look, as if daring him to reply in the affirmative.

"No, no. We are in for the night, I believe. It won't be fit for man or beast in any case. Mutton will do very nicely. You will be more generous with the onions this time, won't you? You know how partial I am to roasted onions with your lamb. And we shall have it with a bottle of the Médoc from the cellar, if you would be so kind."

She nodded and departed, and Holmes, still engaged in flipping through the mail, nudged the door closed with his foot. "Sampson's is advertising reduced prices on selected items of haberdashery, I see," he called to Watson. "Did I not hear you say the other day that you were in need of new shirts?"

Watson looked up. "No. Pajama sleeping-suits, actually."

Holmes wrinkled his nose. He did not approve of the newfangled sleepwear, an innovation from India that had become increasingly popular in recent years. Watson, of course, had been introduced to the garment when he served on the subcontinent, and had tried to convince Holmes of its practicality, even presenting him with a pair the previous Christmas. Holmes, creature of habit that he was, would have none of it ("Can't see the logic in removing my shirt and trousers upon retiring, only to replace them with another shirt and another pair of trousers" was his observation). The pajamas resided untouched in the bottom drawer of his dresser along with the frightfully flamboyant necktie Watson had given him the year before.

Holmes continued sorting through the mail.

"Anything there for me?" asked Watson, rising from the fireplace and dusting off his hands.

"Oh, nothing of any great interest by the looks of it," Holmes replied casually. "Only this from Marlborough House."

"Marlborough House!"

Watson dashed over and snatched the letter out of Holmes's hand. Holmes chuckled as Watson excitedly broke the seal and ripped the envelope open.

"It's from Sir Francis Knollys, the Prince of Wales's personal private secretary," Watson said. "Why, there's a five-pound note enclosed!"

Watson held up the crisp new bill to the light and examined it with wonder.

Holmes chuckled again. "Fancy that!"

"The letter says His Royal Highness enjoyed meeting me and apologizes most profusely for neglecting to pay his debt before departing last night following our game. Can you imagine?"

"Five pounds?" remarked Holmes, a sly smile on his lips. "Wasn't the wager for ten?"

"Oh, I am sure His Highness forgot, or Knollys got it wrong. The fiver will do nicely. I think I shall have it framed."

Holmes laughed. "I had heard that HRH has a very selective memory when it comes to paying off his gambling debts, and apparently it is true. When he wins, he invariably remembers the correct amount to the penny. When he loses, he can remember only half the amount. It must be splendid to have a mind like that – and to be able to get away with it."

Watson was paying him no heed, occupied as he was with reading and rereading Knollys's note.

Holmes prattled on: "A peculiarity of the royal education, I shouldn't wonder: When he was learning his sums, he was evidently taught to divide but not to multiply. I'd be curious to know how many of his cronies have had the temerity to correct his arithmetical mistakes down through the years," he mused. "Not many, I would wager."

"What, what?"

"I said, I should be willing to wager that not many of the prince's gambling friends have ever had the courage to insist on full payment of their winnings," repeated Holmes. He added: "I should be willing to wager, but not with the prince – most definitely not with the prince."

Watson had not heard a word he had spoken. "Can you imagine that?" he marveled. "A five-pound note from the Prince of Wales. He actually remembered! With all that he has on his mind, he remembered. Yes, I shall definitely have it mounted and framed. What a wonderful keepsake!"

"Oh, that is one game of snooker I don't think he shall soon forget," said Holmes. "Your play was simply brilliant. I never dreamed your skills at the game were that advanced. And such poise, such savoir faire! You never cease to amaze me, old chap. I never seem to get your limits. You really raked him over the coals, you know."

Watson smiled and blushed and looked very pleased with himself. "Yes, I did, didn't I."

"It was highly impolitic of you, by the by. You do realize that, don't you?"

"Oh? How so?"

"HRH does not like to lose, you know – at anything. Especially when there is money involved. Most who play with him know enough to let him win, or at least not to show him up as keenly as you did last night. If they ever wish to play with him again, that is. So I wouldn't count on ever being invited back to the Marlborough Club, if I were you. That was a capital error in judgment on your part, I am afraid."

"Piffle!"

Holmes shot him a mischievous glance. "Indeed, I am surprised he did not have you frog-marched to the Tower straightaway, or transported to Australia, like they used to do."

"What nonsense!"

Holmes watched him in silent amusement as he continued to examine the note, holding it up to the light and turning it this way and that.

"He must hold his mother in great reverence," remarked Holmes wryly. "I see that he has contrived to have her portrait imprinted upon it. It is she, is it not? Or is it one of his mistresses?"

Watson cast him a look. "It is unworthy of you to be so disrespectful, Holmes."

Holmes snorted loudly, causing Watson to turn his full attention to him.

"Why this great enmity between you and the prince, Holmes? You were positively rude to him last night! And he seemed none too pleased to see you either."

Holmes did not answer at once. A faraway look came into his eyes, and unconsciously he fingered the gold sovereign affixed to his watch chain, a gesture that did not escape Watson's notice.

Finally Holmes spoke. "On the two or three occasions that I have had the dubious honor of meeting His Royal Highness, I have been particularly impressed with the singular degree of shallowness and insensitivity he often displays in his intercourse with others, a selfishness and lack of concern that borders on cruelty. He is a very superficial person, I am afraid, interested mainly in the pursuit of pleasure, and he doesn't seem to very much care if anyone gets hurt in the process – hardly an endearing quality in any individual, let alone in one who shall someday be king."

Watson well remembered Holmes's last encounter with the Prince of Wales, right here in this very room the previous March (though he was not surprised the prince did not remember *him*, given the circumstances of the meeting). He remembered how Holmes had even declined to shake the royal hand when it was offered to him upon the successful conclusion of that affair, that "matter of considerable delicacy" that caused the prince to seek his services incognito. And of course he remembered the woman involved, and how shabbily the prince had treated her. *The* woman, Holmes always referred to her as: Irene Adler.

Irene Adler was one of the few women Holmes had ever admired – perhaps more than admired, if the full truth be known, though Holmes, self-professed misogynist to the core, would be the last person in the world to ever admit it. Yet the telltale signs were there. For one thing, he invariably toyed with the gold sovereign on his watch chain whenever her name came into the conversation, and rarely at other times: It was she who gave Holmes the coin.[82]

It would be best to change the subject, Watson decided.

The ring of the downstairs bellpull saved him from having to do so.

"Now, who could that be in weather such as this? Are you expecting anyone, Holmes?"

Holmes shook his head. "A friend of Mrs. Hudson's come to tea, perhaps." His eyes twinkled. "Or a messenger from Marlborough House with your other five pounds. Though I would not count on it if I were you."

The tread of Mrs. Hudson's footsteps were once again heard upon the stair, and Holmes raised an eyebrow.

"It only goes to prove what I have always said, Watson, about rushing to judgment without having sufficient data. Would you be so good as to get the door?"

Mrs. Hudson, breathing a little heavily from the climb, handed a card to Watson without a word, and he in turn crossed the room and handed it to Holmes.

Holmes glanced at it for a moment, then called out: "Thank you, Mrs. Hudson. Kindly ask Captain Burton-FitzHerbert to join us, and there will be three for tea, if you would be so good."

Holmes handed the card back to Watson.

THE HONORABLE PEREGRINE BURTON-FITZHERBERT, it read, CAPTAIN, COLDSTREAM GUARDS AND AIDE-DE-CAMP TO HRH THE PRINCE OF WALES.

It was immediately apparent to both of them that the young man who entered, though not in uniform, was unmistakably what his card said he was: An officer in the Brigade of Guards. Tall and ramrod-straight, his black bowler set squarely on his head, his blond mustache trimmed with military precision and his regimental tie knotted to perfection, Captain Peregrine Burton-FitzHerbert was as much in uniform wearing civilian clothes as he would have been if he were wearing his bearskin and bemedaled scarlet.

He peered from one to the other of them with the aid of a monocle. "Mr. Sherlock Holmes?"

"At your service, sir," replied Holmes benignly.

"Ah, yes, of course. Burton-FitzHerbert, at *your* service, sir."

"Indeed?"

"I am sent by His Royal Highness to assist you," he said in clipped tones. "I am under instructions, Mr. Holmes, to do your bidding – to be, sir, your liaison, so to speak, with the royal household. And, may I say, sir, that I am honored to make your acquaintance and look forward to serving under you." The man snapped a quick bow of his head and actually clicked his heels, Prussian style.

Holmes seemed taken aback. "Serving under me? Surely not."

"It is His Royal Highness's wish, his explicit instructions, sir, that I place myself under your command – so to speak."

Holmes looked at the tall young guardsman with a mixture of bewilderment and wry amusement.

"Well then, Captain Burton-FitzHerbert, my first order to you – so to speak – is to join Dr. Watson and me for tea, for unless I am sorely mistaken, that is Mrs. Hudson's stately tread that I hear once again upon the stair, and from her having paused on the eighth step, as she usually does, when bearing a heavy burden, I deduce that we are about to be joined by Earl Grey."

It was the captain's turn to look bewildered. "Earl Grey? May I ask why his lordship would be... haw! *Earl Grey!* The blend of tea! Oh, jolly good, sir. Jolly good, indeed!"

Holmes exchanged a secret look of wonder with Watson, and the latter, doing his best to hide his smile, turned to the door to assist Mrs. Hudson with the tray.

Captain Burton-FitzHerbert turned out to be not only an entertaining companion who brought cheer to their rooms on a cold, damp afternoon, but also a fount of knowledge with all sorts of arcane information about the royal family in general and young Prince Albert Victor in particular.

"Collars 'n' Cuffs he's called around Buck House," confided the captain between sips of tea and generous mouthfuls of Mrs. Hudson's buttered scones.

"Buck House?"

"Buckingham Palace, don'tcha know."

"Ah, yes."

Even though the Queen was rarely in residence at Buckingham

Palace – she liked neither it nor London, preferring the quiet bucolic setting of Windsor Castle on the outskirts of the city – the huge, soot-begrimed edifice on the edge of Green Park was now considered the official seat of the monarchy and, as such, its name was used generically when referring to anything having to do with the royal court.[83]

"Why do they call him Collars 'n' Cuffs?" asked Watson.

"It's because of those ridiculously high collars he wears, and his prominent shirt cuffs," Burton-FitzHerbert explained. "One or the other of his royal cousins named him that, and it stuck. I've even heard Tum-Tum refer to him that way on occasion."

Watson's raised his brow. "Tum-Tum?"

"Oh, HRH, the Prince of Wales. I'm afraid that those of us who serve at Buck House have a tendency, sometimes, to be a trifle irreverent."

Watson looked scandalized; Holmes allowed himself a wry smile.

"All in good fun, of course," Burton-FitzHerbert was quick to assure them, dabbing his mustache clean of clotted cream. "And, heaven forbid, never within earshot of any of Their Royal Highnesses."[84]

"I should think not," sniffed Watson.

Once the tea things were pushed aside, Holmes lost no time in bringing the discussion around to more important matters concerning the royal family.

"Prince Albert Victor – or Prince Eddy, if you prefer – he's in York at the present time?"

"I believe so, yes. With his regiment, the Tenth Hussars."

"But he was in London just a few days ago."

"Yes. So I understand."

"Does he spend much time in London?"

Burton-FitzHerbert shrugged. "Certainly he is absent from his regiment more than the average officer. Of course, he is *not* the average officer, is he? He comes and goes pretty much as he pleases – within reason, I should add. Aside from his obligations to his regiment, he is naturally called upon from time to time to perform certain royal duties as well: Ceremonials and official functions of one sort or another; that sort of thing. Much of it, of course, is here in London. And he has a very busy social schedule, as you can imagine. Naturally, he is not subject to the same exigencies of the service as I, for example, would be, but he doesn't take advantage of his position either." He smiled. "Not *too* much, in any case."

"He was here in town Saturday night last," said Holmes, "and was seen in the company of two other gentlemen, one undoubtedly a military man such as yourself – his aide or equerry, I should think – the other a civilian. From what I have been able to gather, the civilian gentleman was a Mr. James K. Stephen."

At the mention of the name, Burton-FitzHerbert curled his lip slightly and Holmes was quick to spot it. He leaned forward in his chair eagerly.

"I see that name is not unknown to you."

"Quite so," responded the other stiffly. He shifted his position and crossed his legs.

Watson cocked his head. "Was he the chap who dropped the cigarette outside the door of that establishment we visited in Chelsea, Holmes?"

"That is correct. I was able to establish his identity without too much difficulty. It seems he is often seen in the company of the young prince."

Burton-FitzHerbert looked from one to the other of them with a quizzical expression.

"We had the briefest of encounters with Mr. Stephen the other night," explained Holmes to the army officer. "He's a particular friend of Prince Albert Victor's, I understand."

"Yes," replied Burton-FitzHerbert with a frown. "A particular friend indeed. He was the prince's tutor at one time, actually, though he is not all that much older. He is supposed to be quite a brilliant fellow, I am told – Cambridge and all of that. One of those classical scholar chaps, his head filled to the brim with Latin and Greek and such. A published poet, too, though not a terribly successful one, from what I've heard."

"I can understand why," responded Holmes dryly. "I had the dubious pleasure of skimming through some of his efforts at the library this afternoon. Dreary stuff indeed. He was the prince's tutor, you say?"

"At one time, yes. More of a companion and general dogsbody, actually. Especially chosen for the job after an exhaustive search, as one might imagine. I mean, you just don't put a future king-emperor into the hands of anyone, do you? As things turned out, he and young Eddy became close chums straight away. *Terribly* close, if you know what I mean. He's had quite an influence on him, not always for the best, if the truth be known." Burton-FitzHerbert tapped the side of his nose meaningfully with a well-manicured forefinger.

Holmes looked at him sharply, his gray eyes keen with interest. "In what way?"

Burton-FitzHerbert seemed reluctant to reply.

Holmes had to prod him gently. "I ask not out of idle curiosity, you understand, Captain, nor out of interest in mindless court gossip."

"Yes. Yes, of course. Well, he has the reputation of being, er – one of *those*, you know."

"Ah, yes, I see."

Burton-FitzHerbert sniffed. "Quite. And he makes no secret about it, you know. Quite shocking, really. His sort would never be tolerated in the Guards, I can tell you. He'd be drummed right out of the service, or sent to Coventry, which almost amounts to the same thing. Heard of a chap serving in the – well, not in my regiment, in any case – who chose to become intimately acquainted with the muzzle of his service revolver rather than face the disgrace of public disclosure. Had no other choice, of course; it was the only decent thing to do. Would have brought disgrace on his regiment otherwise. It was hushed up, of course — for his family's sake as well as the regiment's."

Holmes impatiently drummed his fingers on the arm of his chair. "What else can you tell me about this fellow Stephen? My researches, by necessity, have been somewhat hurried and therefore scanty."

Burton-FitzHerbert thought for a moment. "Well, he's from a good family, of course, the son of Sir James Fitzjames Stephen, you know."

"Ah," said Holmes, *"that* Stephen. A most distinguished name."

The young officer nodded. "But they're a queer lot from what I've heard. It's been whispered that insanity runs in the family — more than whispered, actually. The old man is quite dotty, I understand."[85]

Holmes raised an eyebrow. "That being the case, young Mr. Stephen was a strange choice as a tutor to royalty, I should think — especially if his deviant behavior was as blatant as you suggest."

"Yes, well, one must presume that all of that wasn't known when he was selected, mustn't one? He was recommended to Their Royal Highnesses by the Reverend Dalton, who had been tutor and governor to both Prince Eddy and Prince George when they were together in HMS *Bacchante*.[86] The Princess of Wales was very keen on Mr. Dalton, so she was quick to take his advice, too quick, if you ask me. Someone should have taken a closer look at the chap. Not the best influence on a young, impressionable fellow, particularly one such as Prince Eddy, who does like his pleasures and is not, I'm afraid, all that fussy how he comes by them. He's not too swift up here, you know." He tapped his forehead. "Oh, he is charming enough in his way, but — do promise not to breathe this to a soul, not that it's any state secret — but he's really somewhat, er... somewhat..."

"Retarded?"

Burton-FitzHerbert blanched. "Ahhem. *Your* choice of words, not mine. I should have chosen another."

Watson entered the conversation. "Why bother with a tutor at all, then? I mean, if his mental abilities are that limited, I should think it would be a waste of time."

"Well, as I understand it, they had no choice, did they? I mean, the boy is heir to the throne and all of that, even if he is a hopeless case, so to speak. It's not as if he were of a lesser station and could be shunted off to the country to hunt and party, or a younger son who could be married off to some foreign princess and sent out of the country altogether to be left to his in-laws to deal with. Besides, his father wasn't ready to give up on him. He can't stand the sight of him, of course, but he wasn't about to admit that the fruit of his loins, as they say, was a ninny or a cretin. So he agreed to send him up to Cambridge for a term or two in the hope that he'd benefit from a whiff of some of that rarefied atmosphere. And, on the surface at least, Jimmy Stephen seemed to be the ideal choice to look after the lad. You know — show him about and teach him the drill, so to speak, keep him out of trouble and such. Well, it was like putting the fox in charge of the chickens. Eddy was up there for the better part of two years, I believe, and from what I gather, for all the good it did him, they just might as well have enrolled him in a brothel for the period, or sent him off to study the mating habits of ancient Sodom. Stephen was the worst possible influence on him. Never had any use for university chaps, myself. Give me a Sandhurst man anytime."

He started, realizing he had committed a gaffe, and looked a little sheepish. "Present company excepted, of course."

Watson sniffed.

Holmes smiled and reached into his pocket for his cigarette case and offered it around. "It was after Cambridge that the young prince went into the army, I understand?"

"Yes, that's right. In June of 'eighty-five. They sent him to Aldershot for some initial training, then found him a commission in the Tenth Hussars up in York. Wanted to get him away from Stephen and from that whole crowd of simpering illuminati in Cambridge – and out of London and away from its temptations as well. That's why one of the Guards regiments wasn't chosen, I suppose – because they're all stationed in or around London. And the Tenth Hussars is the Prince of Wales's old regiment, after all – he serves as Colonel-in-Chief – and it has a long and distinguished history behind it, so it is quite socially acceptable, of course: Nothing at all to be ashamed of. But... well, it is not the Guards, is it?"[87]

"So Prince Albert Victor has spent most of his time with his regiment since then? In York, you say?"

"Well, in York or Scotland or Aldershot, depending – the regiment has moved around a bit. But most of his time? I couldn't say that, necessarily. A good part of it, anyway. But he's also spent a good deal of it here in town or at Sandringham, or at Windsor, or at Osborne. It all depends on the time of the year and where the Queen is in residence, and where the Prince and Princess of Wales are staying. Of course, during the Season, he would spend more time in London, as a rule. How much time, I couldn't say, really."

"Is it possible to find out, though? To determine precisely when he's been in town over the past few months or so – since August, say?"

"Yes, I suppose so. The court keeps detailed records of that sort of thing on all the Royals, going back into history, I should think."

Holmes put up a hand. "I don't mean that you should simply refer to the Court Circular, Captain. I don't need you for that. I could as easily refer to back issues of *The Times*. No, what I am asking is whether it is possible to delve deeper than that. The Court Circular wouldn't necessarily list the prince's private activities, would it?"

"No, not as a rule. Generally, only the official activities of the royal family are covered. It might list the occasional weekend house party, but engagements of a truly private nature would not be circulated – for reasons that must be abundantly obvious." He winked broadly. "All those royal mistresses would be put out of work, what?" He turned serious again right away.

"Yes, it will take a little doing, but I think I might be able to come up with something."

"And would it also be possible to learn exactly when the prince has been in the company of Mr. Stephen?"

Burton-FitzHerbert mulled that question over for a moment. "That will be a trifle more difficult, I should imagine."

"Someone must know. An equerry such as yourself, a gentleman-in-waiting, a secretary? Surely, someone of that stripe must keep a journal or a personal diary."

Burton-FitzHerbert gave him a look. "If anyone does, they'd be well advised to keep it damn well hidden, I can tell you – if they value their hides, that is." He snorted. "It will require considerable sniffing about, Mr. Holmes, and I am loath to do anything that would call attention to myself. I was under the impression that this was all to be kept *entre nous*, so to speak."

"It is indeed, but I should think you would be able to make some discreet inquiries among your colleagues at, er, Buck House, and perhaps among a chosen servant or two – carefully chosen, you understand. Naturally, we don't want to excite anyone's curiosity. And we certainly don't want any of this to get back to the young prince, of course."

"Of course," agreed Burton-FitzHerbert, "I quite understand. Well, I shall see what I can do, but it isn't as easy as one might think. There is gossip among the royal staff, of course, that's only to be expected, but rarely anything *serious*. The staff are chosen as much for their discretion and their ability to emulate brass monkeys as they are for their skills at whatever. Besides, a bit of prattle into the wrong ear could be ruinous for them, and they know it. But I shall do what I can, depend on it. Prince Eddy's equerry-in-waiting, Alwyne Greville, is a good chap and a friend of mine. If anybody can tell me, he's the one.

Burton-FitzHerbert departed soon after – bowler placed squarely on head, umbrella wielded adroitly – promising to report back to Holmes within a day or two, leaving Watson with the distinct impression that he was highly taken with the idea of playing the role of detective. It would, after all, be a break in the daily routine for him. High honor though it might be to receive a posting to "Buck House," when all was said and done, royal service got to be pretty dull after a while.

Holmes was in a reflective mood for some little time after the visitor had departed, but he broke his silence by and by and shared his thoughts with Watson. "This fellow Stephen intrigues me," he said from behind a thick haze of pipe smoke.

"So I gather." Watson peered at him over the top of his newspaper. "A strange companion for a royal prince, I should think."

"Rather."

"He sounds thoroughly disagreeable."

"Thoroughly."

Watson studied him for a moment. "Yet, it seems you still have some questions in your mind about him."

Holmes nodded. "A few."

"Do you think Captain Burton-FitzHerbert was exaggerating in his assessment?"

"No, not at all. To the contrary. I've made some inquiries about him on my own – that's what I have been doing the better part of the day, in point of fact – and, I must say, that if Mr. James Kenneth Stephen has any likable traits, he has managed to keep them well hidden from the rest of humanity. Among other things, he has the reputation of being a virulent woman-hater. He doesn't merely dislike them, you understand: He positively *hates* them, and makes no efforts to hide it. His poetry – what little I have been able to find of it in the book stalls and library – reflects this most graphically. It also reflects something else, if I am any judge: He would appear to be a thoroughly degenerate individual whose attitudes and perceptions are of such a disagreeable nature that it would come as no surprise at all to learn that murder and mutilation were numbered among them. Indeed, from what I can gather – and it is an opinion shared by more than a few of the people I have interviewed who know him intimately – from what I gather, he may be quite mad."

Holmes put his pipe down and stretched his long legs out in front of him. "Moreover, he is known to be a frequent visitor to some of the more odious homosexual fleshpots of the city, one or two of them located in Whitechapel, so he is no stranger to the district and no doubt is quite familiar with its geography. He would appear to be a very prominent suspect, indeed."

Watson put his newspaper down. "You don't seem to take much satisfaction in that knowledge, Holmes. Nor do I see you racing for your hat and coat to do something about it."

Holmes did not reply right away, but gazed down at his feet, lost in thought. "What? I'm sorry, old chap. Did you say something?"

"Only that you don't seem to be very much in a hurry to have him taken into custody."

"Who?"

Watson became exasperated. "The Ripper, Holmes – this fellow Stephen!"

"Stephen? Oh, he is not the Ripper. Whatever in the world made you think that he was?"

Twenty-Two

WEDNESDAY, NOVEMBER 7, 1888

"We must begin from a different angle. I rather fancy that
Shinwell Johnson might be a help."
— *The Illustrious Client*

If there were any merit, any scientific basis in fact to the theory that
the use of tobacco somehow stimulated the brain and thus increased
man's capacity to solve difficult problems, Holmes during those few
days should have been able to unravel the mysteries of the universe. He
spent the greater part of his time enveloped in dense, odoriferous clouds
of smoke, seldom moving from his chair and seldom removing the pipe
from his mouth. It was to little avail.

Though several ounces of his favorite black shag had been expended,
and the sitting room's atmosphere made no sweeter in the process, he came
no closer to finding answers to the questions that plagued him. If anything,
the questions multiplied in his mind and became more perplexing.

Watson? He was at a total loss. He did not have the faintest idea of
what to make of recent events. It was beyond him. Holmes's bewildering

statement that James K. Stephen was not the Ripper had set his mind on endless trails of speculation, trails that twisted and tangled and got him nowhere, leading him ever deeper into thickets of confusion. If Stephen was not the Ripper, who, then, was? And if Stephen was not the Ripper, why, then, was Holmes so interested in him?

Holmes, of course, would provide him with no further enlightenment – that was a foregone conclusion. He rarely revealed his thoughts until they were totally clarified in his own mind, until he was satisfied that any ideas that resulted were valid and any judgments that were made were correct. And besides, like the stage conjurer who delights in mystifying his audience by drawing out the suspense, the *artiste* in him required just the right moment to perform his sleight-of-hand, the perfect time to make the dramatic gesture.

Meanwhile, Captain Burton-FitzHerbert, true to his word, made a concerted effort to obtain the information that Holmes had requested, but he was unable to come up with anything very helpful. For the most part, he could confirm only what was already known, that Mr. James K. Stephen was a particular friend of Prince Eddy's and an almost constant companion during the prince's private moments in London, the two appearing to be all but inseparable. Sometimes they were joined by others of a select group in attending the theater and dining at one or another of the city's more fashionable restaurants: the Café Monico, the Criterion (the "Cri," as it was called by habitués), the Café Royal in Regent Street's Quadrant, or Florence's at Rupert and Coventry Streets, the latter two known to be popular with Oscar Wilde's set. Sometimes they were entertained at small dinner parties in private homes. And, reported a stone-faced Captain Burton-FitzHerbert, sometimes they paid a visit to a certain address in Cleveland Street off Tottenham Court Road, that same homosexual establishment which Holmes had placed under personal surveillance.

That the captain was most uncomfortable in divulging this last bit of information was evident. "Atrocious bad form," he muttered – his way of letting it be known that he was not at all happy to be discussing matters that any proper gentleman would consider inappropriate under any circumstances. He was doing so only because he was instructed by the Prince of Wales to cooperate fully with Holmes, and he wanted that made abundantly clear.

Curiously, Holmes displayed little interest in the information the Guards officer had to impart, hardly questioning him at all as to the details. To Watson, who was listening quietly in the background, Holmes seemed more interested in the sources of Burton-FitzHerbert's information than in the information itself. He questioned him closely about the identity of his informants.

His major source, as it turned out, was a none-too-circumspect coachman by the name of Netley who was usually to be found hanging about in the Royal Mews near Buckingham Palace. Netley was not a regular palace coachman, but belonged to a pool of spare drivers who were taken on as needed during particularly busy times, or as substitutes for staff coachmen who were ill. Generally members of this pool drove for lesser palace aides and royal messengers, but now and then, when things got really tight, Netley was assigned to younger members of the royal family or their visiting cousins from the Continent. On more than one occasion, he drove for Prince Eddy, and on more than one of those occasions, Prince Eddy was accompanied by one Mr. James Kenneth Stephen.

The coachman, highly flattered that a Guards officer and royal equerry would grant him anything more than a sniff and a nod, let alone actually initiate a conversation with him, was pleased to share his store of knowledge with Captain Burton-FitzHerbert, a store that was not inconsiderable. What Netley had not amassed through personal observation (and he was a most ardent observer), he learned secondhand from his colleagues who, it seemed, gossiped among themselves incessantly. The prattle in the mews "flowed as freely as feed grain from a split sack," noted Burton-FitzHerbert with a smug little smile, savoring what he considered an uncommonly clever turn of speech. Yes, he said, many a choice tidbit made the rounds of the tack room, along with the saddle soap and metal polish, and in the stalls while the lads attended to their equine charges, and in various palace courtyards while they loitered about waiting for their human ones.

And that basically was it. Aside from the stable gossip, Burton-FitzHerbert was able to provide little else. However, he did give Holmes a short list of recent dates when Prince Eddy had been in London, a list that Holmes glanced at only briefly before placing it into the closest handy depository, a copy of *Burke's Peerage*, which happened to be on the table next to his chair.

But it would seem that Burton-FitzHerbert had failed to come up with the information Holmes was most interested in obtaining, for Watson could not help but notice the look of disappointment on his face after the military man had departed.

"Really, Holmes, I don't know how you expect people to gather intelligence for you when you won't even let them know what they're looking for! There is such a thing as being too secretive."

Holmes favored him with a wintry, thin-lipped smile. "Oh, I don't know. One can never be too circumspect. If I tell our young friend what it is that I am looking for, there is always the danger he will let it slip to someone else, and that would never do. But if he were to come upon it in the natural course of events – even without knowing what it was – it is the kind of thing he almost certainly would report to me without being prompted, and very likely without recognizing the full extent of its importance. And that would be most desirable. I find that a secret is best kept by keeping secret the fact that it is a secret." He reached for a fresh pipe.

Watson considered him for a brief moment. "Came upon what?"

"Hmm?"

"You said that if he were to come upon it, he would tell you even if he didn't know what it was. Exactly what is it that you wish to know?"

Holmes shot him a sidelong glance, but did not reply. He smiled faintly at Watson's expression of annoyance.

"In any event," he said, reaching for the Persian slipper in which he kept his tobacco, "it is of little consequence."

But his manner belied his words, for he once again retired to his chair to brood, long legs outstretched, chin on chest, billows of smoke rising in splendid puffs from his great yellowed meerschaum.

There was much to brood about. To begin with was the fact that the murderer knew that he, Holmes, was involved in the investigation; it was unlikely it was sheer guesswork on the man's part. The only possible answer was that he was close to someone who had reason to know and who willingly (but in all likelihood, unwittingly) shared that information with him, someone who was either with the police, the Home Office, or, less likely, connected to the prime minister or the Prince of Wales – or, least likely of all, connected to Mycroft.

Holmes shook his head silently. No, the latter notion was totally out of the question. Mycroft's secrets were inviolate. He rarely confided in anyone, and then only if there was good and sufficient reason for the individual to know. In that respect, he was not very much different from any other government bureaucrat. He had a positive dread of sharing information on any account, whether it be sensitive or not, for he believed almost devoutly that to know something that somebody else didn't was, to put it crassly, money in the bank.

It had to be some other source – a source that perhaps Lord

Randolph Churchill had access to as well, for he also appeared to have knowledge he should not have. No matter how good his connections and channels of information, there were certain things he could not possibly know and yet did, and Holmes was as much confounded by this as he was by anything.

Little wonder that he had remained the better part of the past few days burrowed deep in his chair, pipe rack and tobacco slipper close at hand. To Watson he seemed depressed and discouraged – understandably so. He was no further along with his investigations than he had been weeks earlier. Indeed, the new disclosures served only to confuse matters further, adding, in his words, "layers of mist to the haze that already enshrouds the fog."

As if in sympathetic response, the room filled with a haze of his own making, and he withdrew behind it gratefully, as if behind a protective curtain that insulated him from the routine annoyances and petty disturbances of life around him.

But not all of Holmes's time in that period was spent in quiet contemplation. It had been anything but a tranquil period at 221B Baker Street. There had been an almost constant procession of visitors – incessant comings and goings and telegrams at all hours of the day and night. It was a period of activity that had all but driven poor Mrs. Hudson to distraction, and, had it not been for the timely addition of Billy to the household several days earlier, all of the bustle and bother would have surely been beyond her endurance.

Billy was young and energetic; a flight of stairs meant nothing to him. He scampered up and down with the ease of a mouse, and even several dozen ascents and descents a day (and there averaged at least that many during that period) failed to sap his energy or diminish his enthusiasm. He was like a puppy's tail that never seemed to tire of wagging, a poor working-class lad with large dark eyes and small prospects, eager to please and do well, puffed with a newfound pride, his neck and hands scrubbed unaccustomedly clean, unruly hair newly clipped and, if not totally subdued, at least reasonably amenable to the blandishments of hairbrush and pomade, the brass buttons of his tunic shined to a fare-thee-well, almost as bright as the glitter in his eye, almost as shiny as the apple glow of his cheek.[88]

Billy was not from the neighborhood but from some poorer district across town, the young son of a local shopkeeper's widowed sister who had gone tubercular and could no longer care for him properly. Boys like him usually ended up in the workhouse or worse, and he knew it. So if during those first few days he seemed annoyingly too willing, too eager to please, too desperate to do the right thing, surely – surely – he could be forgiven.

It was not his labors or long hours but his stiff new shoes that finally slowed him down, raising blisters the size of ha'pennies on the heels of both his feet so that by the time Sunday evening came around he was reduced to a painful hobble, a not-unwelcome predicament insofar as the rest of the household was concerned, because the shoes squeaked horribly, a most irritating noise that no amount of tallow seemed able to dampen.

But neither could the discomfort of mere blisters dampen Billy's enthusiasm. He was almost as proud of his new employment as he was of his page's uniform, which, though secondhand (or was it third?), showed hardly any signs of sag or wear and fit him admirably – this last point, if he only knew, being a far more compelling reason for his selection over the other applicants than any of his other qualifications.

Watson, still not accustomed to the boy's presence, his scurrying about, and his constant popping in and popping out, was in the process of taking a sip of his morning coffee, when Billy's head appeared through the door yet again.

"What now?" Watson asked over the top of his newspaper, irritability creeping into his voice, the tranquility of his morning having been marred by all of the activity.

"Mr. Shinwell Johnson!" piped the boy manfully, his high-pitched voice betraying only aspirations of ever becoming manly.

"Oh, for heaven's sake," muttered Watson, as much in response to the boy's vocal performance as to the significance of his message.

Holmes, in contrast, reacted with surprising pleasure, given his subdued and distracted manner those last few days. "The blithe Shinwell?" he cried. "Show him up, Billy, show him up! How eagerly I've awaited his porcine, plaid-vested presence. And more coffee from the kitchen, lad, and bring another cup!"

Shinwell Johnson, or "Porky Shinwell," as he was more familiarly known in the shadowy precincts of Blackfriars, was a large, coarse, lumpy individual with puffed and bloated features, a rubicund nose, thick, beefy lips perpetually curled in a sly smile, and dark, piggy eyes that were equally crinkled with pleasure and narrowed in cunning. His arrival at the top landing, red-faced and wheezing, was heralded in a marked and most striking manner by an almost combustible reek of brandy, which had ascended the stairs far enough in advance of him to make Billy's announcement of his approach seem altogether superfluous.

The exertions of the climb left him breathless but hardly speechless, for Mr. Shinwell Johnson was a most loquacious man, as chatty as he was stout and as stout as he was shrewd. He carried in his brain and pockets an accumulation of knowledge which if ever divulged could place several dozen (or more) in the dock, including the odd one or two who in the normal course of their day were accustomed to looking down upon it from the bench.

It was Holmes's habit to use Shinwell as his agent in the vast serpentine underworld of London, for he was well known and welcome in the darkest recesses of that world, and, being trusted by its inhabitants as few others were, was able to obtain information where no one else could. Information was his stock in trade, a commodity he dealt in as other men dealt in foodstuffs or cotton goods or ribbons for "m'ladies' hats." His store of knowledge pertaining to the activities of London's criminal class was unequaled, and it was this that endeared him to Holmes. That in the early years of his career he had been known to the police as a dangerous character did little to harm him professionally. To the contrary. To those with whom he customarily did business, the fact that he had two terms in Parkhurst on his sheet was a definite point in his favor. That he had somehow managed to evade a third term, through the intercession of a certain individual who shall remain nameless, only enhanced his reputation further (and, incidentally, was what endeared Holmes to him).[89]

It was a rare occasion when "the blithe Shinwell" graced Baker Street with his "porcine, plaid-vested presence." Holmes used his services sparingly and with discretion so as to limit the possibility of their association ever being revealed to the world at large. Exposure of their dealings would reflect badly not so much on Holmes as on Johnson, whose customary business associates – most unforgiving of indiscretions on the part of any of their number – had a tendency to make their displeasure known in emphatic ways.

Johnson, settled into the room's sturdiest chair with a cup of well-laced coffee close at hand, needed little encouragement to get right down to business. He cocked his massive head to one side and beamed at Holmes affectionately, fingers laced across his ample middle, thumbs twirling in contentment. When he spoke it was with a slight impediment of speech, and not with any single distinguishable regional accent but with a combination of several, as if he had sampled them all and, not being able to make up his mind, had decided to partake of them all.

"Wh'ell, Mawster Sherlock, m'dear," he said. "I 'ave been most h'active in yer be'alf, 'aven't I? – tew'rribly, tew'rribly active." He snorted – something he did loudly and often, to Watson's annoyance, an unmistakable barnyard sound that could make heads turn in the street.

"This bushel o' coke what calls himself Jack the Wipper is becoming a w'right pw'roper nuisance, h'ain't he? – w'right pw'roper, indeed!" He snorted again. "I must tell yer, he's as much a myster'wy to our sources o' h'information in the stw'eets as he is to the clubs n' sticks in Sco'lin' Yard, and that's an actual fact. But that don't come as no surprise to yer now, does h'it? No, o' course not," he chuckled.

Holmes waited patiently, knowing that Shinwell would not be rushed.

"I'll say this much: He's not a local bloke. Me people would find him out quick enough if he was. No, he's not from the East End a'tall, if yer axes me. 'Strewth, I think he's a p'woper fw'lag unfurled, if yer catches me meanin'." He cocked his head to the side and smiled slyly, pausing for Holmes's response.

Playfully, he had salted his comments with the rhyming slang of the cockneys, knowing full well that it would get a reaction from Holmes.[90] Johnson, who was no cockney, spoke it as a matter of course, as he also spoke a smattering of Yiddish and Gaelic, for they were the languages of people with whom he came into daily contact and with whom he had commerce, and being able to communicate with them on *their* terms helped him win their trust. Besides, it amused him.

Holmes regarded him coolly, but not without a faint sparkle in his eye. "If I understand you correctly, Shinwell, your friends don't have any better idea of who the murderer is than the detective division of the Metropolitan Police, but most of them agree he is probably a person of quality. Do I have that right?"

Johnson bobbed his head and laughed, hugging himself delightedly.

"Aye, an' they fink it's an uncommon poor way for 'im to get his jollies, they do. They fink he's *mushuganah* – a crazy bloke what wud be well adwised to confine 'is play to his giggle stick, I shoul'n't wonder."[91]

Holmes cracked a smile at last, which pleased Johnson very much, for he enjoyed making people smile, particularly people he was fond of.

"Now, if you don't mind, Shinwell," said Holmes in the mock tones of a schoolmaster, "may we get on with it?"

Shinwell nodded and turned serious. "In point of h'actual fact, 'ere's the truth of h'it," he said, "this bw'loke is as much an upsetting influence to me fw'riends and h'associates in B'wackfw'riars as 'e is to yer fw'riends in Whitehall. I h'assure you, if h'any o' our people knew who he was, they'd do for 'im, and 'at's no lie. He'd get a good, 'ealthy dose o' his own medicine fer certain. Why, his life wouldn't be worth a dicky diddle. H'it's been most unsettling, this whole bleedin' business. The chaps don't like h'it, you see. It's no good for commerce, is h'it? Why, h'it calls h'attention to fings, don't h'it? Which h'it bw'rings the Sweenies into the distw'rict, an' none o' us wike that. Not even the Sweenies." He smiled puckishly and snorted. "'Strewth, least o' all the Sweenies."[92]

Johnson brought out a small, old-fashioned silver snuffbox.

"A pinch, m'dear?" he said, offering the box to Holmes. "No? You won't mind if I partake? Fank you so veddy much indeed, I'm sure. A nasty 'abit, I know, but a modicum o' snuff can be most h'efficacious, I find."

So saying, he deposited an ample "modicum" of the brownish-white powder into the palm of his hand and proceeded to inhale it with a violent snort. Without pause, he reached into an inside pocket of his bulging frock coat and drew out a thick and untidy wad of papers bundled together and tied with ribbon, looking not unlike a lawyer's brief. Moistening a fat thumb, he began systematically flipping through the bundle, patiently scanning each and every leaf until he found what he was looking for.

"'Alf a mo," he said.

He studied the piece of paper for a moment, holding it almost at arm's length to do so, and snorted once again.

"Now then," he said finally, "about that certain 'ouse at number 19 Cleveland Stw'reet, that which yer particular'wy asked about by way of enquir'wy, as h'it t'were. H'it is an addw'ress which o' course is not unknown to us. H'it has a intw'esting 'istory to h'it and an unusual provenance – a story what will no doubt h'amuse you, but for another time perhaps, as h'it 'as no bearing on the matter afore us and I am sure that you and the good doctor is h'occupied wiv matters of far more h'importance and of a pw'ressing nature, as h'it t'were. Now then, I will tell yer 'ow h'it t'is: The ownership of the estabwlishment in question, namely number 19 Cleveland Stw'reet, is somewhat murky at the moment, which h'it 'aving changed 'ands more than once over the course o' the past sevewal months. Up until midsummer h'it was owned by one Ephraim Tysall, h'esquire, who is of wittle inter'west to us and of no conseqwence to the matter at 'and, I can h'assure yer (snort)."

Holmes nodded, satisfied.

"The new owner of w'record is one Mr. Michael Loughlin, a waiter and barman by twade, and he, too, is of wittle inter'west to us in that if ya bel'wieve that an unemployed barman (snort) what don't have two coins to rub togevver what ain't copper, and whose old dad is a dealer in coal and wegetable gw'reens and is a gent what is not unknown to certain h'associates of our acquaintance (broad wink) – if you bel'wieve he has the sugar 'n' honey to purchase said pw'remises, why then, Master Sherlock, m'dear (snort), I'd wike to talk to yer about buying some shares in the new bw'ridge they be buildin' across the Thames, thank ya nicely, if ya get me meaning, which I'm sure ya does (snort)."[93]

Retying the bundle with its ribbon, he returned it to the pocket from which it came and pulled out another, beginning the same painstaking process all over again, chattering away nonstop all the while as he subjected each piece of paper to a frowning scrutiny, as if seeing it for the first time. It seemed that he carried within his numerous and commodious pockets a unique filing system of sorts, one unquestionably of his own devising. But if there was a method to it – an orderly, organized whole made up of its diverse and independent parts – only Shinwell Johnson held the key, for its formulation seemed well beyond the scope of simple logic or *any* form of human understanding.

Again he found what he was looking for and announced the fact with a snort. "Now then. If ya wike, I can supp'wly ya wiv the name of the tw'rue owner of number 19 Cleveland Stw'reet, though it won't do ya much good to know h'it, an' I can tell ya to the penny how much he clears in 'is weekly wents, though h'it won't be o' much inter'west, and I can supp'wly ya wiv a wist o' the names o' them young buggers employed at the telegw'raph office what makes much more in their off hours at number 19 Cleveland Stw'reet. And I can pweesents yer wiv a wist of the toffs' names what goes there w'regular, though that might take some wittle time and expense because they wike to maintain their h'anonymity, don't they? But I suspecks ya knows as well as I do who they is, anyways (snort)." He favored Holmes with a quick, shrewd glance and chortled.

"As for the particular gent ya inquired about – a 'andsome bloke what tw'ravels in exalted circles o' the 'ighest kind and what is bew'lieved to wisit number 19 Cleveland Stw'reet often an' w'regular? Aye, he is sometimes to be found in the company o' anuvver gent whose face is nev'r seen, because why? Because he takes special pains and keeps h'it well cuvered, now, don't he? But this 'ere gent, ya can't help but notice 'im, can yer? Which he's a gent what has certain distinctive features and peculiarities o' dress, such as wearin' veddy 'igh collars h'attached to 'is shirts. Veddy 'igh collars an' wide cuffs. And his face would be known anywhere, now, wouldn't it? And his name shall remain nameless for reasons what I shall not get into, if yer pl'wease." He glanced at Holmes meaningfully.

"Understood," Holmes responded tersely.

"As I well knew ya would, m'dear. An' since ya also already knows the name an' h'identity o' the first gent, I won't bovver to mention h'it either. His wesidential addw'ress is noted on this here swip o' paper, which I duly places into your possession."

Holmes took the proffered slip.

"As to the dates o' h'is w'isits to number 19 Cleveland Stw'reet during the last fortnight or so, yer will find them noted down on *this* here sw'lip o' paper, which I likewise places into your possession."

Holmes took the second piece of paper, glanced at it, and arched an eyebrow, then stuck it away into the folds of his wallet along with the first.

"Now, don't be putting away your purse jest yet, m'dear. There's a bit more to come."

He resumed thumbing through his wad of scraps until finding the next one he wanted.

"On this here sw'lip o' paper we have a certain addw'ress in Grosvenor Square – Seventy-four Brook Street, to be exact – which has been wisited on three occasions by the wery same gent what is on that first swip. It is an addw'ress what is not only a residence, as ya will find, but (he bobbed his head deferentially in Watson's direction) is a doctor's surgery an' belongs to a certain wery h'important and distinguished member of the medical perfession."

Holmes reached out for the new scrap of paper Johnson handed to him, studying it for a few moments in puzzlement. "Sir William Gull, the royal physician?"

He looked across at Shinwell, who tapped the side of his ample nose meaningfully.

Shinwell obviously felt that the information it contained was of some importance, and Shinwell's instincts were usually good.

Holmes put the slip of paper away along with the others and extracted a five-pound note from his wallet, but Johnson stopped him.

"No, no, m'dear, not this time," he said, holding up his hand. "This one's on me." He smiled roguishly. "I considers h'it me public-spirited duty, don't I? I don't know what any of this 'as to do with the killings of those poor ducks, but if anything I can do will 'elp to catch the fiend what did h'it, why, cor'blimy, dear chap, I'm 'appy enough to do h'it. Indeed I am."

So saying, he bundled up his papers and stuffed them into various pockets, rising to his feet with a grunt.

"As to what all this means, if it means anyfing a-tall, well, I'm sure I don't know, and that's an actual fact. This is more yer line of country, ain't h'it? We'll leave h'it to yer to make heads or tails of h'it, m'dear, ya bein' the best judge an' all."

Collecting his ulster and billycock hat at the door, he turned to look once again at Holmes, who was still seated in his chair, gazing contemplatively into the fireplace. Shinwell's beady little eyes took on a mischievous glint.

"Which 'e does h'it one of two ways, this bloke, if yer was to ax me, Maw'ster Sherlock, m'dear," he said. "Makes 'is excapes, I means."

Holmes looked up.

Shinwell Johnson cocked his head to one side, relishing the moment. "Unless he uses one of those 'ot air ballwoons an' tykes to the sky, I fink he goes undergw'round, 'at's what I fink. He takes to the sewers, in me 'umble opinion – wike the bloody, filthy sewer rat that 'e is. An' that's God's 'strewth."

Clapping his billycock onto his head at a jaunty angle, he gave one last parting snort, as if for good measure. "G'day to ye, m'dears. *Mazel tov*, as they say. Faith 'n' begorra. No h'extra charge."

With that he was gone, the sound of his good-natured chortle following him down the stairs to the lower landing, there to be joined by a shriek of youthful delight, caused no doubt by the sudden discovery that a shiny new tuppenny had been lurking behind Billy's left ear.

Holmes remained unmoving in his chair following Shinwell Johnson's departure, staring moodily into the fire and mentally reviewing the information that had been passed on to him, rolling it over in his mind in a vain effort to find some significance in it, something new, some little shred to go on.

Watson did his best to tiptoe around him. Taking advantage of the quiet moment that had descended upon them, he brought out his letter case to catch up on his correspondence, and for some little while the scratching of his pen was the only sound in the room to compete with the soothing tick-tock, tick-tock of the clock on the mantel.

It was that much more of a shock, therefore, when Holmes, with no warning at all, leapt up from his chair with a cry and made a sudden rush for the door.

Watson's pen went skidding across the page.

"What an unmitigated ass I've been!" exclaimed Holmes, grabbing his coat, stick, and hat and bolting out the door.

He was gone before Watson could recover from his astonishment, leaving in his wake, as evidence of a hurried departure, his dressing gown draped over the stairwell banister where he had flung it and, at the foot of his chair, his meerschaum pipe lying smoldering on the carpet.

EDITOR'S NOTE

There is an unaccountable gap in Watson's narrative at this point: Three pages of his notes are missing. Whether they were accidentally lost or misplaced or were purposely removed, it is impossible to say, but as a result of their loss, there is regrettably no record of Holmes's activities between the afternoon of November 7 and the morning of November 9.

However, we know from other sources – *The Times* and *The Daily Telegraph* in particular – that no major events, save one, occurred during that brief period that had a bearing on matters relating to the ongoing investigation of the Whitechapel murders.

The one exception occurred on Thursday, the eighth of November. Sir Charles Warren, under unrelenting pressures from the press, Buckingham Palace, and Parliament, finally submitted his resignation to the Home Secretary. It was done so quietly that two days passed before the press (or even his own chief aides) became aware of it.

We know from the historical record that during this period police officials in Whitechapel, expecting another murder at any time (for none had occurred in over a month) made what preparations they could to prevent it. They increased routine patrols, assigned detectives in disguise to key locations, and flooded the district with plainclothesmen.

Their precautions were to no avail.

Twenty-Three

Friday, November 9, 1888

> "'Is there any other point to which you would wish
> to draw my attention?'
> "'To the curious incident of the dog in the night-time.'"
> — *Silver Blaze*

A young man, a detective in civilian clothes, separated himself from the others straining to peer into the two windows at the end of the alley. He lurched to one side and vomited.

"For God's sake, don't look!" he warned another officer who came running up. "Whatever you do, don't look!"

Holmes and Watson had just entered the enclosed yard – Miller's Court, it was called – through a narrow, covered passage from the street. Even though it was only early afternoon, there was little light. It had been raining sporadically throughout the day and the sky was dismally gray. They had to force their way through the crush of people who were gathered behind a makeshift police barricade at the entranceway to the court, craning their necks to see. There was the rank smell of poverty about the place, and a redolence of fear.

Holmes elbowed his way to one of the windows and peered over someone's shoulder through filthy glass panes into what was a small, cluttered hovel of a room. When he turned away, his face was deathly pale.

The telegram summoning Holmes to Miller's Court had arrived as he and Watson were sitting down to an early luncheon, the second telegram of the morning to bear momentous tidings. Their shepherd's pie left on the table untouched, the newspaper on the floor where it fell, the pair of them were out on the street within minutes, commandeering a passing growler for the dash across town.

But it was some little while before they were able to make their way to the East End. The streets were packed with jostling throngs and the progress of their four-wheeler was frustrated by unusually heavy traffic. It was Lord Mayor's Day, and soon the Rt. Hon. James Whitehead, wigged and robed and burdened by the heavy weight of his chain of office, would proceed in baroque splendor to his investiture at the Law Courts in the Strand. The crowds lining the route of the procession were already thick, spilling over into the side streets adjoining the route as well. That it was also the Prince of Wales's birthday, his forty-seventh (they could hear the distant boom of the cannon as the royal salute was fired from the battery at the Tower), added to the holiday mood. Street peddlers were everywhere, sprinkled here and there with stilt walkers, musicians, and grotesque clowns with painted faces. The cries of the costermongers and food vendors hawking meat pies and trotters, plum duff and baked potatoes, pickled eels, hot wine, and roasted chestnuts, competed for attention with the chatter of performing monkeys, the banter of pitchmen and pearlies, and the blabber and antics of street performers of every stripe, the noise predominated by the dissonance of one-man bands and hurdy-gurdies.

Over all and pervasive was the ammonia stench of manure and horse urine, for even on a normal day with ordinary traffic the streets of the city were receptacles for hundreds of tons of droppings; more so on a day like this, when the traffic was decidedly heavier. The little street arabs plying the major intersections with brooms were having a good day of it sweeping paths clear for "the quality," it being well worth a penny to the gents to avoid fouling their shoes and to keep "m'lady's" skirts clean.

Several detours were required for the carriage to reach its destination: The area surrounding Guildhall, where the Lord Mayor's banquet was to take place following the investiture, had to be given a wide berth, and it seemed to take ages before the driver of their coach was able to make any progress at all.

But at long last they crossed Bishopsgate into Spitalfields and wended their way up White's Row into Crispin Street to the corner of Dorset, a short, narrow road bordering the vast Spitalfields meat market – so narrow there was barely enough room for two drays to pass, and so notorious that even policemen, residents boasted, feared to walk its brief length unaccompanied.[94]

The entrance to Miller's Court was easily missed: A narrow, arched portal set into a brick wall between two nondescript doorways, one of them belonging to number 26 Dorset Street, behind which the court itself was located. It was reached from the street by a dark, forbidding passageway – a tunnel, really – twenty feet long and barely three feet wide. On the far side, the passage opened into a garbage-strewn yard looked down upon on all sides by the rear windows of low-rising tenements.

Miller's Court was not a place one would normally choose to enter, let alone live in, assuming one had the choice. It had all the charm of an open sewer, and it was a dangerous place besides. Curiously, those who did live there were predominantly women. Most of them were prostitutes, slatternly looking, gin-soaked, and sour-smelling, aged before their time and hard pressed to earn even the small amount required for the rent they paid. They dwelled in a warren of rickety, vermin-infested single-room flats, rented out no-questions-asked for a mere four shillings a week, and overpriced at that. The landlord was named John M'Carthy, and the rooms were known collectively as M'Carthy's Rents.

Holmes, standing in the middle of the court and surveying the dismal scene, turned as he heard his name called. It was Abberline, accompanied by a senior uniformed official introduced as Superintendent Arnold, who clearly was in charge, for within a matter of seconds he sent everyone scurrying: Policemen were hurriedly assigned posts and given their instructions, and the court and the street beyond were soon cleared of those who did not belong.

The two windows that were the focus of so much attention looked into number 13 Miller's Court, a small single room with no amenities, unless you counted the windows themselves, which were situated side by side with one being smaller than the other.

The entrance to number 13 was just around the corner, the first door on the right directly off the passageway. The door led directly into the room, there being no such extravagance as a vestibule or foyer to impede one's way. But the door seemed locked, or something was jamming it, and they had to remove the larger of the two windows to get in. An officer climbed over the sill, found the door bolt fastened, and opened it from the inside.

The horrible, indescribable stench that met them when they entered caused them all to gag. Abberline covered his nose and mouth with a handkerchief before he was able to cross the threshold. Holmes and Watson, just behind him, did the same.

Holmes halted just inside the door to allow his eyes a moment or two to adjust to the gloom. Despite the two windows, the room was dark, for very little light ever penetrated the enclosed courtyard. But the room being only twelve feet square, it did not seem at first glance there would be much to see. The furnishings were sparse: an old iron bedstead, two rickety tables, and a single chair. There was a fireplace opposite the door, in which it was obvious an enormous fire had recently burnt; there was a large quantity of ashes on the hearth, and they were still smoking.

Then, as their eyes became accustomed to the dim light, they began to make out details.

On the bed was sprawled the body of what had been a young woman. She was practically naked and lay on her back. She had been horribly mutilated. Her face, which was turned toward them, was slashed and disfigured. Her long dark hair, badly disarranged, was matted with blood. Her throat had been deeply cut from one side to the other, and her head was almost severed from her body. There was blood everywhere – on the bed, on the floor, on the walls.

Like the others, she had been eviscerated, gutted. The killer had been most meticulous about it and very thorough.

On the table by the bed there were little piles of flesh neatly laid out. The heart and the kidneys were there. And other parts...

Watson could not bear to look. Sick at heart, he turned his gaze away, toward the wall.

Oh, God!

What he saw caused him to cry out involuntarily, and Holmes and Abberline both spun around. Their gazes followed his. Abberline retched and rushed from the room.

Parts of the woman's body hung from picture nails in the wall: The place was festooned with her intestines.

Watson staggered out through the door and into the courtyard, sucking in air, forcing himself not to throw up.

Sergeant Thicke was there, having just arrived on the scene. "It's that bad, then, is it?" he said, looking at Watson's face. He had already read the expression on Abberline's as he had rushed past him.

Watson, his eyes reflecting the horror of it, could only look at him. He could find no words to describe what he saw.

They went back in together, Thicke taking Watson gently by the elbow, as if to lend his support.

There was Holmes, somehow managing to ignore the blood and butchery all about him, making a careful inspection of the floor with the aid of a policeman's lantern.

"Disturb nothing, I beg of you," he importuned, "and do watch where you step."

Independently, they went about the grim business of examining the room and its contents. Thicke, pale but firm of jaw, looked around and began making jottings in his notebook, while Watson undertook a visual inspection of the body. After a few minutes, a silent, visibly shaken Abberline rejoined them and Holmes looked up.

"Who was it who discovered the body and under what circumstances?" he asked without preamble.

Abberline responded in a subdued voice, his manner strained: "It was a man by the name of Boyer, a shop assistant who works for M'Carthy, the lodging-house keeper. He was sent over to try and collect some back rent the woman owed. When he got no response to his knocks, he peered through the window – that one, I think, the small corner window closest to the door, the one with the broken pane. He saw the body and ran to tell M'Carthy. M'Carthy came back with him, took one look through the window, and sent him running off to the Commercial Street station. The time was around a quarter to eleven,

I'm told. Inspector Beck, accompanied by Sergeant Betham, was the first to respond. He immediately telegraphed Divisional Superintendent Arnold and notified me, and I telegraphed you."

"And we were the first to enter? No one went in before us?"

"That's right."

Holmes nodded in satisfaction. What with all the frantic activity in the courtyard, any clues to be found outside the woman's room would have been lost to him; he was glad to find that the interior, at least, had been untouched.

He looked sharply at Abberline. "The body was discovered before noon, you say. Why so long a delay in gaining entry? It is past one-thirty now."

"We were under instructions to wait for the arrival of Sir Charles Warren; it has been a standing order of his since the last murder. But when he did not arrive or respond to our summons, Superintendent Arnold decided not to wait any longer and took it upon himself to order the door forced."

"It is good that he did," responded Holmes dryly. "You should know that the commissioner of police will not be joining us here today, with or without his dogs. Your telegram arrived just after a wire from my brother informing me that Sir Charles has tendered his resignation to the Home Office. I have it on the best of authority that it was accepted."

It was an indication of Abberline's absorption with the matter at hand that he barely reacted to Holmes's amazing news, so long awaited by so many people both inside and outside the department.[95]

Holmes went to the window and gazed at the broken pane thoughtfully for a moment. As Abberline had pointed out, it was the one closest to the front door – just a few feet away and at right angles to it since the door was set in the adjoining wall. Holmes glanced from the window to the door and then back again. "This broken windowpane — it is as you found it?"

"Yes. I was told it has been that way for some time."

Holmes gave a dry little chuckle and then, with a gesture of dismissal directed at the window, turned his attention to the body of the woman.

"So she's been dead for some little while, then?" Holmes said. He looked to Watson for confirmation.

Watson went over to the bed and gingerly picked up the dead woman's wrist and let it fall. There was pronounced stiffness in the limb. Watson shrugged. "Given the indication of rigor mortis, it could be anywhere from six to twelve hours. There's no way to be more precise without a thorough autopsy and an examination of the contents of her stomach and the like. If we can find her stomach," he added ruefully, looking around the room.

"Six to twelve hours," mused Holmes. "That would mean she could have been murdered anytime between midnight and six A.M."

"Something like that," Watson agreed. "Perhaps the police surgeon can be more precise. As you know, pathology is not my line of country."

"Dr. Bagster-Phillips has been sent for and should be along shortly," Abberline offered. "He's had many years experience as a police surgeon and is one of the most knowledgeable men I know in his field. And he's also had the benefit of examining one or two of the other victims."

Thicke spoke up: "A neighbor upstairs in number 20, a Mrs. Elizabeth Praten, told me she thought she 'eard a cry at around three-thirty or four in the mornin', she couldn't be sure. An' by the by, if anybody's h'interested, 'er name's Kelly," he said, pointing with his chin toward the bed. He referred to his notebook. "Mary Jane Kelly, twenty-four or twenty-five years old, a resident 'ere since February or March. She also went by the name of Marie Jeannette Kelly. Fancied herself a Frenchy, she did. Gave herself airs, I suppose, like so many of 'em does. Most everybody around 'ere called 'er Black Mary — 'cause o' 'er long, dark 'air, I suppose."

Holmes looked thoughtful. "It would be helpful if we could find someone else to corroborate the time of that outcry, if there indeed was an outcry. Medical science may fail us on this occasion, I fear, and a witness who heard something may be our only means of pinning down the exact time of death."

Thicke nodded. "I 'ave the lads goin' door to door now. Let me go check an' see if they've come up with anythin'."

Holmes turned back to Watson. "Do tell us what else you can, Watson — though I know from the condition of the body it will not be much."

Watson glanced over to the bed where the woman was still lying. He shook his head.

"It's impossible, Holmes. Simply impossible. He's hacked her to pieces."

Holmes persisted. "The neck wound — does it look to you as if it were inflicted by the same hand that slashed the throat of the Nicholls woman?"

"Good Lord, Holmes, it's impossible to say, the damage is so great. It was probably done by the same hand, but I could not swear to it."

"So you cannot tell where the knife entered the throat — on the left side or the right?"

"Impossible to say."

Abberline, who had been listening to their exchange, interjected: "Do you doubt that it was the same killer, Mr. Holmes?"

"It is fatal to assume, Inspector. It is always best to doubt everything until you have good and sufficient reason not to. These murders have attracted uncommon attention, and it would not be at all surprising should some other demented individual decide to take a leaf from our friend's notebook and attempt to make a name for himself by copying his style."

Watson brooded. "Well, if he's not the same killer, he's done him one better. And if it is the same, he has outdone himself! I have seen what the Pathans in Afghanistan can do with their fiendish blades, and that is horrible enough, but I have never seen anything like this. Never!"

Abberline looked around him and nodded. "It's as if he were in some sort of a frenzy when he did all of this. And it must have taken him no small amount of time, mustn't it?"

"Oh, yes," agreed Watson. "He would have been at his work two hours or more."

Holmes went over to the fireplace and knelt down on one knee. The ashes were still warm to the touch. He poked around for a minute or two.

"Hullo," he said. "What have we here?" He used the tip of his walking stick to pick up what looked to be the remains of an old tea kettle. "Look at that," he said. "The handle and spout have practically melted away. That must have been one hot fire to do that."

Abberline got down on his haunches beside him. "What do you think she was burning in here, I wonder."

"Not she," said Holmes. *"He."*

"The killer started the fire, do you think?"

"He must have. Look here!" He started sifting through the ashes with his fingers, picking out bits and pieces of partially burnt material. "This is from a woman's dress, and here, this, it looks like a piece of a bonnet, doesn't it? Now, why would the woman burn her own clothes? Particularly since, from the looks of things, they may have been the only clothes she had to her name, aside from what she was wearing."

Abberline pondered the question. "Do you think he burned them because they were bloodstained?"

Holmes shot him a pained glance. "Look around you, man! There's enough blood here to fill a washtub. No, I think he wanted light – light to see by, light to enable him to do his hellish work! Her clothes were probably the only fuel he could find. And how merrily they must have burned. But at what risk! I should have thought our friend would have been afraid to attract attention. Flames as high as these could have been seen through the window by anyone happening by in the courtyard. What strikes me is that the man just didn't seem to care whether he was seen at his work or not."

Abberline got to his feet. "Well, that is certainly something we can be asking the neighbors about – whether any of them noted any bright light coming from either of the two windows at any time during the night."

Holmes shrugged. "By all means ask, but I would be surprised if you were to receive a positive response. If anyone saw even a hint of high flames, the fire brigade most assuredly would have been summoned without delay. Fire is to be greatly feared in this section of the city, given the age and ramshackle condition of the buildings here, and the density of the population."

The search of the room continued. Holmes went back to examining the floor of the room, and when he was finished he turned his attention to the fireplace once again, and when he was satisfied nothing more could be found there, he went to the area surrounding the woman's bed and, as best as he was able without disturbing the body, examined the bedclothes. Some time went by before he concluded his investigation, and when he finally did, it was clear from his troubled expression that he was far from satisfied with the result.

By then the police surgeon, Dr. Bagster-Phillips, had arrived and was making his preliminary examination of the body in preparation for its removal to the morgue. Photographers retained by the police were also on the scene, eager to do their work and be gone.

Holmes had just about decided that there was nothing more he could do there, that he was only in the way, when Thicke stuck his head in the door, a note of urgency in his voice. "We've picked up somebody who says he saw 'er late last night," he announced. "An' 'e claims 'e got a good look at the bloke what was with 'er!"

Holmes was out of the room in a flash, Abberline and Watson close on his heels.

The police had set up an informal temporary headquarters in the nearby Ten Bells, a pub located close to the Spitalfields Market on busy Commercial Street.[96] It was here that they found Mr. George Hutchinson, securely in the custody of two burly constables and a sergeant, and well in his cups.

As far as they could make out, Hutchinson, an unemployed night watchman, knew Black Mary well. They were old friends, he claimed, and often had pink gins together here in this very pub, on this very spot, or in Mrs. Ringer's place, The Britannia, at the corner of Dorset and Crispin streets. It was a claim supported by the publican of the Ten Bells, who confirmed that he had seen them together on occasion. Sometimes they even went to the Cambridge Music Hall together, when they could scrape together the price of two four-penny seats in the upper stalls. And, yes, he had seen her the previous night, at around two A.M. He was wandering the streets, he said; he hadn't the sixpence for a bed. As he turned off Whitechapel Road into New Commercial Street, he noticed a man standing on the corner under a street lamp.[97] It was raining lightly. Then he noticed the figure of Mary Kelly coming toward him from the opposite direction, the direction of Dorset Street. Seeing her alone, he thought he was in luck. Maybe he could borrow a little money from her, enough for the price of a night's lodging. It would not be the first time she granted him a small loan. They stopped to chat, but before he had the opportunity to ask, she started pouring out her troubles to him. The rent was past due, she told him, and the lodging-house keeper was getting nasty; and she had had nothing to eat all day — could he lend her a little something? At least enough for a meat pie, or a penny glass of gin? Wordlessly, said George Hutchinson, he pulled out his empty pockets; sadly, he was unable to help. Mary shrugged and moved off toward the man standing under the streetlight.

Hutchinson stayed and watched. He saw the man put out a hand toward Mary as she drew near him. The man put his hand on Mary's shoulder and they chatted for a few minutes and laughed together. Then they began to walk toward him, back toward Dorset Street, the man's arm around Mary's waist. They walked right by him, and, for want of anything better to do, he followed discreetly behind.

He followed them into Dorset Street, right to the entrance to Miller's Court. They disappeared into the court together. After a few minutes, he entered the court himself. He went right up to the door of number 13, Mary's door. He couldn't hear anything, so he rounded the corner to where the windows were. There was no light, and he could hear no sound. He retraced his steps to the entrance, and just stood there, waiting. For what? He didn't know. He had nothing better to do, he had no place to go, so he just waited.

And the time was two A.M.?

Yes, around then. He had heard the bells of Christ Church strike the hour.

How long had he stood there at the entrance to Miller's Court?

Oh, maybe about three-quarters of an hour.

What then?

Well, he got tired of waiting for the man to reappear, so he just wandered off.

Could he describe the man?

Well, he was wearing mole-colored gaiters.

What else?

He was well dressed, too well dressed for that quarter of London, and that was queer.

Describe his clothes.

Well, there were the gaiters, and a long, dark coat trimmed with some kind of fur at the collar and cuffs.

An astrakhan?

If that's what you call it.

And what else?

Well, he had a white collar with a black necktie. He had a heavy gold watch chain and a horseshoe pin in his necktie, and the watch chain had a seal with a red stone, and, oh, yes, he was wearing dark gaiters, did I mention that?

You said they were mole-colored,

Yes, *dark* mole-colored.

Did you see his face?

Yes. He had a mustache which curled up at the ends. He had bushy eyebrows. And he was very pale.

What else?

He had dark eyes. He looked like a foreigner. He had a dark complexion.

He was very pale and he had a dark complexion? You could make out all of this by the light of a gas lamp?

It was a bright night.

You said it was raining lightly.

The corner was brightly lit.

How tall was he?

He looked to be around thirty-five years old.

How *tall?*

Oh. Tall? About five feet six inches tall.

Five feet six inches?

Yes, and thirty-five years old. A foreigner, if you want my opinion.

And he was wearing a pin in his tie?

A horseshoe pin.

And he had a watch chain?

A heavy watch chain with a seal, and the seal had a red stone. And he was wearing a long, dark coat. And, oh, yes, he was carrying some kind of a satchel under his arm, a bag made of shiny cloth, maybe oilcloth.

And he was wearing a silk hat?

I didn't say that.

What kind of hat was he wearing, then?

I don't know. It was a billycock, maybe. That's right, a billycock. And he was wearing a light waistcoat under a dark-colored jacket.

All of which was under a long, dark astrakhan coat?

Yes, that's right, a long, dark coat with a fur collar.

Abberline and Thicke, well versed in the art of questioning felons, took turns in questioning Hutchinson, and relentlessly tried every trick they knew to catch him up in the details. But it was no good. He stuck rigidly to his story, as preposterous as parts of it sounded, despite repeated efforts to break it down.

Holmes listened to the entire performance without comment.

"Worthless!" he said after the man had been taken out. "All quite worthless."

"Waaal," said Thicke, "there's parts o' h'it, at least, what 'ave a ring o' truth."

"And larger parts," scoffed Holmes, "that positively resonate with the dull thud of absurdity."

Poor Hutchinson was taken to the Leman Street station for continued questioning, and Abberline ordered the bar opened so they could avail themselves of some refreshment — a small restorative, as Thicke put it. He managed to down three of them in quick order.

The police surgeon, Dr. Bagster-Phillips,[98] joined them in the interim, and they spent the better part of the next thirty minutes reviewing his findings, which, not surprisingly, were sparse and as yet incomplete. Still, Holmes was impressed with the careful, systematic approach that the medical man took in gathering together the threads of his investigation. He was most thorough in his report, even though it was still a preliminary one.

"Cause of death was the severance of the right carotid artery," he said matter-of-factly, "inflicted while the victim was lying at the right side of her bedstead. In my opinion, the blade was wielded by a left-handed individual."

He swallowed down his whisky in a single gulp and grimaced. "Good Lord, is this dreadful stuff!"

Dabbing at his lips with his handkerchief, he continued. "Perhaps I shall be able to tell you more after I examine her at the Shoreditch mortuary," he said. "I have ordered the body taken there rather than to Montague Street, the facilities being far superior. But I believe I can state with a degree of certainty that death occurred between three-thirty and four A.M."

"That would be at around the time a neighbor said she heard a cry."

"Well, it would seem to fit, I think."[99]

"You have participated in the postmortems of a few of the earlier victims, I believe," said Holmes. "Is it your opinion this murder was carried out by the same hand?"

"Oh, yes. There can be no doubt. None whatsoever. The wounds to the throat by themselves tell the tale. And there is a definite similarity in the abdominal incisions, as well – in their location and the manner in which they were carried out."

"Ah, then, well, that settles it," said Abberline.

Holmes nodded, apparently satisfied. "Is there anything else you wish to call to our attention?" he then asked.

"No, I think not. You have seen the body and the mess that has been made of it. What more could I possibly tell you? Oh. She was with child, if it matters."

He finished his whisky and with a nod was gone.

Abberline studied his notebook thoughtfully for some minutes. "I have only this one remaining question on my list," he said to Holmes finally. "As if the murders were not enough, the damnable fellow now leaves us with this new mystery to unravel."

"Oh?" said Holmes. "And what mystery would that be, Inspector?"

"Why, the means of his exit from the premises. Surely you could not fail to notice that the inner bolt to the door was thrown. I saw you examining both the bolt and the lock on the door, so I know you noticed. It is a pretty little puzzle, is it not, how the killer managed to exit the premises given the fact that one of the windows was nailed shut and the other was too small for a man of average size to fit through?"

Holmes raised an eyebrow. "I fail to see the puzzle in the matter. He walked through the door and then reached through the window – the one with the broken pane of glass – and merely threw the bolt. Surely you noticed that the bolt was in easy reach of the window."

Clearly Abberline had not.

"And if you examine the lock on the door, I think you will find that it has been some time since a key has been inserted into it – several weeks, at least. There is an absence of fresh scratch marks, as one would expect to see on the surface of any lock whose key is invariably inserted in the dark by someone who is often the worse for drink. And there is even a slight tint of new rust in evidence around the keyhole. I expect you will learn upon investigating the matter that our Mistress Kelly misplaced her key and had gotten into the habit of using that conveniently located broken pane to work the inner bolt. Obviously the killer saw her do it and followed her example."[100]

Abberline quietly shut his notebook, noticeably embarrassed. "Yes.

Of course," he mumbled. Then he shook his head, whether in wonder or in self-disgust, it was impossible to know.

"You do have a way of cutting mysteries down to size, Mr. Holmes. How very simple indeed you make it seem."

Holmes assumed an expression of perfect innocence. "Every mystery is simple once it is explained."

"Yes," Abberline said with a heavy sigh. He stood up. "Well, that's it, then. I should think we are finished here, unless you have something else, Mr. Holmes?"

"Well, in actual fact," replied Holmes, who had remained seated, "there is the small matter of the cigarette end with the gold tip."

Abberline was clearly taken aback. He gave Holmes the strangest look.

"Mr. Holmes, there was *no* cigarette end! My men searched everywhere, and none was found."

Holmes looked very pleased with himself. "Precisely the point I wished to make, Inspector. Thank you so much indeed for making it for me."

Twenty-Four

FRIDAY, NOVEMBER 9, 1888

"The tragedy has been so uncommon, so complete, and of such
personal importance to so many people, that we are suffering from
a plethora of surmise, conjecture, and hypothesis."
— *Silver Blaze*

"What I do not understand," said Watson as he and Holmes
stepped out into the rain-slicked street, "is that on the one hand
you seem to agree that this latest outrage was performed by the same
individual who committed the earlier ones, yet on the other hand you
continue to question whether it was indeed the same."

It had been raining off and on for the better part of the day and
had just begun to rain lightly again. A mist was beginning to form,
combining with the coal smoke that lay heavy over the city. Watson
grappled with his umbrella as he fell into step alongside Holmes, who,
taking no notice of the rain, set off down the street at a brisk pace. "I
was merely commenting on the fact," he said crisply, "that if it were the
same killer, it is rather odd that none of his cigarettes had been found

at the scene of the murder or anywhere in the vicinity."

"Well, I don't know..." Watson mused. He gave a little laugh. "I don't suppose it's likely he gave up smoking?"

Holmes made a derisive sound. "The trouble with a habit is that it is a habit. And the use of tobacco, as I have good reason to know, is a habit of the most formidable kind. I don't believe he has stopped smoking any more than he has given up his other pernicious practice which, as we all have reason to know, he has not."

"Perhaps he disposed of them in the fireplace, then," offered Watson.

Holmes nodded. "That would indeed account for the lack of their presence in the room where the murder took place, and is my own presumption. Still..." His voice trailed off, his meaning clear.

Leaving the Ten Bells public house behind them, they headed along a gray and cheerless Commercial Street in the general direction of the Spitalfields Market, which lay just a short distance ahead through the haze. In the early morning hours, when the market was at its busiest, the area was the scene of clangorous activity, but at this time of day it was typically almost empty of traffic, a bleak and dispirited place filled only with the litter and leavings of its commerce.

Watson glanced around him and shivered. "Do you have a destination in mind?" he asked, hunching deeper into his coat. "This is hardly a desirable neighborhood for a constitutional, even if the weather were conducive to it."

The grimy tenements, which closed in upon them from both sides of the street, wore a mean and menacing look, and Watson felt distinctly ill at ease despite the presence now of uniformed constables at every corner.

But if Holmes were in any way affected by the dismal surroundings or the weather, he did not show it. From his outward demeanor, one would have thought he was out walking in Regent's Park on a fine spring day. "I thought we just might get the lay of the land whilst we are here," he replied carelessly. But a keen glimmer in his eye belied his nonchalance. He was on to something; Watson could sense an undercurrent of excitement crackling just beneath the surface of that calm, imperturbable exterior.

Watson peered at the buildings as they walked. Without him realizing it, they had retraced their steps and were once again in Dorset Street, just down from the entrance to Miller's Court where the murder took place. The onset of the rain had effectively cleared the dark, narrow street ahead of them of most of the morbidly curious that had flocked to the scene once word of this latest murder had spread through the district. The last of the idlers had been chased away, the sidewalk hawkers had disappeared with the crowds, and the members of the press had rushed back to their offices to meet their deadlines. Now, except for one or two stragglers, the entire area was in almost the sole possession of a forlorn squad of constables from H-Division who, under their glistening oilskin capes, paced aimlessly up and down, singly and in pairs, stamping their feet against the chill.

Holmes stopped and looked up and down the street. Then, casually, he walked over to an open iron grating set into the pavement near the curb and, bending over, peered down into it. The odor emanating from it was foul, but he took no notice of that; the smell of bad drains was a normal part of London life, and one became accustomed to it. Shaking his head, he straightened and without a word continued toward the corner, about one hundred yards farther on. There he came to another grating in the street. Once again he stopped to peer down. And once again he shook his head and resumed his walk, this time crossing over to the other side of the street, where a cast iron cover of another kind was set into the pavement. This was not an open grating like the others, but a solid oval plate about three feet in diameter.

"Ah," he said delightedly, "this just might be it."

Bending almost double, he pointed with his still-furled umbrella to some raised lettering cast into the center of the plate and surrounded by an ornate design. Watson had no difficulty making out the words, EAST LONDON RAILWAY was what it said.

Holmes ignored the metal plate for the moment, concentrating his attentions on the pavement immediately surrounding it. Lowering himself on his haunches, he examined the paving blocks to one side of the cover with growing excitement. He rose to his full height with his nostrils flaring.

"Here, Watson, give me a hand if you would." So saying, he stooped down and grasped one of two recessed handles set into the edge of the iron cover. "Pray, lift straight up. Try not to scrape the street surface," he instructed. Watson grasped the other handle and together they lifted. Despite its weight, it came up fairly easily, and they managed to shunt it over to one side without major difficulty.

Crouching down, Holmes peered into the hole that was now exposed. A vertical brick-lined shaft was revealed, descending deep into darkness, the diameter of the shaft being just wide enough to accommodate a man. That it was intended to do just that was further suggested by a series of rusted iron rungs set one beneath the other into the brick wall of the shaft. They beckoned no invitation to Watson; instinctively, he took a step backward. One did not require an active imagination to conjure up all sorts of images of what horrid things might be lurking down there. He would no sooner descend into that hole than he would into a pit of vipers.

Holmes, on the other hand, seemed delighted with his discovery. "What have we here?" he said, his eyes flashing.

"What*ever* do we have here?"

A constable, curious to see what they were doing, came strolling up.

"Here, my good man!" said Holmes. "I'll have the loan of that bull's-eye at your belt, if I may."

The constable, who knew a voice of authority when he heard one, handed the lantern over without question.

"You're not going down there, surely!" admonished Watson.

"Oh, no, not I. Not at the moment, at least." Holmes shone the light down the shaft until they could see to the bottom, which was not as far down as Watson had first thought, not more than twelve feet or so. It seemed to lead directly into a tunnel, which went off in two separate directions, following pretty much the same course as the street in which they were standing. Surprisingly, it was quite dry and clean down there – actually, from all appearances, a good deal cleaner than the street above. Watson had expected it to be a flowing sewer, a place where only rats would venture, rats and, on occasion, the filth-covered "toshers," who made a precarious, odoriferous living scavenging underground for lost valuables.

Holmes turned the light away from the bottom of the shaft and shone it onto the rungs of the ladder rising from it – on each of the rungs in turn until he was satisfied he had seen everything there was to see. What that could possibly be was a total mystery to Watson, for to his eye there was nothing down there. But obviously not to Holmes's eye. It flashed with excitement as he straightened.

Thrusting the lantern back into the policeman's hands, Holmes grasped one of the handles of the iron cover and dragged it back into place, this time refusing Watson's help. It took some little effort, but he was able to manage it on his own, and he seemed to achieve great satisfaction in doing so, for he smiled with satisfaction once he had wrestled the heavy cover into its former position. "Come, let us see what we can see farther on," he said, wiping his hands on his handkerchief.

Leaving the constable at the curb standing dumbly confused with arms akimbo, Holmes led the way back to the corner of Commercial Street and once again turned toward the giant Spitalfields Market with its row upon row of empty butcher stalls, devoid of activity at this late hour. As they approached the market, they became aware of a sickening, putrid smell in the air, the unmistakable cloying odor of rotting meat, which became stronger and stronger the closer they got until it became positively pervasive, predominating over the other smells of the area, the smells of human detritus, decay, and poverty, and even over the ever-present acrid stench of manure from the roadway, an odor so familiar to the nostrils throughout the entire city, even in the best of neighborhoods, as to be virtually unnoticeable except on those rare occasions when it was absent altogether.

Once past the market, they found themselves at the corner of a street which to Watson's eye looked vaguely, disturbingly familiar. He looked up to read the street marker affixed to the side of the corner building.

"Why, we are in Hanbury Street!" he said, surprised. "Good Lord, Holmes, isn't that the passage to where one of the earlier murders occurred?" He pointed to a doorway, number 29.

"Indeed it is. That's where the Chapman woman met her death in the early part of September."

"I didn't know how close we were to it. Why, the two murder sites are only a few hundred yards apart!"

"Exactly," said Holmes. "And I think you will find that we are only a few minutes' walk from the other three murder sites. Buck's Row, where the first of the murders occurred, is over to our right. And Mitre Square, where the Eddowes woman met her death, is behind us."

"I hadn't realized they were all so close to one another."

Holmes did not respond. He may not have heard him. He was standing in the gutter, peering down at yet another street grating. Without a word he reached down, grasped one of the recessed handles, and pulled up on it. "No, don't help. I want to be absolutely certain that I can manage it on my own."

He grunted with the effort, but he was able to do it. Lifting the heavy cast iron cover a scant inch or so – just high enough for one edge of it to clear the lip of the recessed iron rim fixed permanently in the pavement – he was then able to drag it to one side, far enough to clear the entrance to the shaft that descended below the level of the street. As before, iron rungs set into the bricks lining the sides of the shaft served as the means of climbing down into it.

"Where do you suppose this goes, Holmes? Does it connect with the other one, perhaps? Is it some sort of underground passage, do you think?"

"That is precisely what it is. And I do not think; I know! They do indeed connect." Holmes straightened and peered first up the street and then down, his sharp, hawklike features appearing to actually lean with anticipation in the direction toward which he was looking.

"Come! Help me with this thing!" Together they manhandled the iron plate back into its position, and Holmes, hot on the scent, took off down the street, Watson hard pressed to keep up with him.

Within a few minutes they found themselves in Bishopsgate, a wide, heavily traveled thoroughfare that served as a boundary separating Spitalfields from the precincts of the City.

The sky had darkened; visibility was dwindling. There would be a choking fog by nightfall for certain: One of those impenetrable, carboniferous "London particulars," caused as much by smoke and soot from the railways and factory chimneys and from coal stoves in every kitchen and parlor in the city as by the heavy, saturated masses of air that drifted in as a matter of course from the sea, the two phenomena – one nature's doing; the other, man's – mixing together to form a noxious yellow-gray-brown sulfurous porridge that would soon descend upon the metropolis, as it did with disconcerting frequency, and simply smother it.

The rain had become heavier, but Holmes continued to ignore it. Watson, who was forced to close his umbrella to keep pace with Holmes, could not help but take notice of it; he was getting soaked. The pair of them, he feared, would soon be sopping wet at this rate. "Holmes! For God's sake, where are we bound?" His leg was beginning to ache and he was already panting with effort.

"Steady on, Watson! Steady on! It's not far, I promise you."

"What's not far?" he gasped.

Holmes pointed triumphantly. "There! There it is! What did I tell you?"

Watson peered through the rain. "Why, it's an underground railroad station," he said incredulously.

"Precisely!"

From the extent of Holmes's excitement, one would have expected it to be the ghostly ramparts of Camelot that was emerging from the mists in front of them. "For God's sake, Holmes. What the devil is this all about? It's merely an entrance to the tubes!"

"It is the Bishopsgate station of the Metropolitan Railway, to be exact," responded Holmes, "and that, dear chap, is how our friend Saucy Jack has managed to depart the area without being detected! It took Shinwell Johnson to put me onto it, for I was too stupid to figure it out on my own. Shinwell Johnson and Canon Barnett of Toynbee Hall, if the full truth be known," he added plaintively. "That befuddled old gentleman who delights in nonsensical quotations and has difficulty remembering that his spectacles are perched on his forehead."

It was over mugs of hot tea and a dish of penny Abernethys in the station's small café that Holmes made his explanations. Abberline, summoned to join them, sat on the other side of the checkered oilcloth-covered table. Spread out between them was a large detailed diagram, a map of sorts, the seal of the Metropolitan Board of Works prominently displayed in the lower right-hand corner. Abberline had brought it with him, as Holmes's hurried message had requested.

"It cannot have escaped your attention," said Holmes to Abberline, "that not only have all of the murders occurred within a few streets of one another, but all of the victims resided within a few streets of one another also. Indeed, there is a suggestion, I understand, that at least two of the women even knew each other. Maybe all of them did, for all we know; but that is conjecture."

Abberline's eyes lit up. He saw the possibilities at once. "It is certainly a line of inquiry we can open at once. It should not be difficult to establish fairly quickly. If they all knew one another, or if even only two or three of them did, they will in all probability have had other acquaintances in common – male acquaintances, without doubt."

"Do conduct your inquiries by all means, Inspector," Holmes replied. "I am certain your findings shall not be without interest. But for the moment I wish to direct your attention to a circumstance even more singular than the proximity of the, er, ladies' domiciles." He tapped the diagram spread out between them.

"Do you see?" said Holmes, tracing his finger along a maze of varied-colored lines. "We are here, where Bishopsgate extends into Shoreditch and is bisected by Bethnal Green Road. This is Commercial Street down here, and just off it is Wheeler Street, here. Observe the intersecting lines? See how they all come together at this point? That is where we are presently sitting – or sitting above, to be more exact. What we are actually looking at is a street map of this area, only it is an underground street map showing the sewers and the various tunnels and passageways that run beneath the pavement. These are tunnels that service the underground railways and carry gas lines and water pipes and telegraph wires from one place to another. See? This is a gas line here, and these are water pipes. And these are the underground tunnels through which they pass."

Abberline spoke: "And these marks here, every other inch or so? They denote access from the street above, you say?"

"Exactly. The Board of Works quaintly refers to them as 'manholes.' They're positioned about one hundred yards apart. They are those round saucerlike metal plates we are beginning to see at almost every intersection nowadays: The things that make such a clatter when carriages drive over them, and in which ladies are forever catching the pointed heels of their ridiculous footwear."

Abberline set his mug down. "And I always thought those openings gave access to the sewers," he mused.

"No, not the ones shown here. Those are marked differently on the diagram, do you see? The metal plates that cover the holes leading down to the underground railway service tunnels are generally marked with the name of the rail system. See here? These belong to the inner circle line of the Metropolitan Railway, and these over here belong to the East London Line, which runs from Aldgate to connect over here with the Metropolitan and District lines. It is marked quite clearly. It is the new portion of the underground, opened just four years ago.[101]

"And these tunnels are all connected, you say?" noted Abberline.

"Connected and interconnected. There is an entire network beneath the streets, a veritable maze of tunnels. The main tunnels are quite wide and surprisingly dry and bright, due to the fact that vertical shafts carrying light and air from the roadways above are situated so close together. Even the branch tunnels are sufficiently large so that a man of normal height can comfortably traverse them without even having to bow his head, and they are astonishingly clean and free of vermin."

"And this is the way you think the Ripper has managed to evade us?" asked Abberline.

"Without question."

Abberline looked dubious. "It strikes me as being – well, improbable, Mr. Holmes, if you will forgive me for saying so."

Holmes eyed him with a cold look. "Would you prefer to believe as others do that he simply vanishes ghostlike into thin air? Or ascends into the sky by the use of some sort of inflatable device, as a scientific chap of my acquaintance has suggested?" He raised his eyes heavenward. "It would seem that the manifestly impossible has a greater appeal to the imagination of most people than the merely improbable." He took out a pencil and marked a series of small circles on the diagram. "At each of those positions you will find a manhole leading to an underground passageway. Please note the locations of them."

At Holmes's bidding, Abberline bent over the diagram and read the locations off: "Hanbury Street... Dorset Street... Berner Street... Goulston Street... Buck's Row – good Lord! Every one of them is a street where the Ripper has struck!"

"Note the tunnel leading from Buck's Row. Where does it go?"

Abberline squinted his eyes and studied the diagram closely. "It runs for, oh, a scant two hundred yards or so toward Whitechapel Road. My God! It goes directly to the Whitechapel station of the underground!"

"Now look at the mark I made near Mitre Square. Where does that tunnel lead?"

Abberline leaned over the diagram again, his eyes inches from it. "To another station of the underground, the Aldgate station."

"Precisely. You will find in each case that the manhole entrances I have marked lead directly to underground stations. In some instances, my marks are quite close to the stations; in others, somewhat farther away. But never at a distance so great as to make it impractical, or even terribly difficult, for a determined man, armed with a map such as this, to reach the stations in short order."

Abberline pulled at his chin. "Well..." The dubious note he sounded was unmistakable.

"Look, you here!" Holmes jammed his forefinger at a spot on the diagram. "See! Mark the position of this manhole – mark it well! It is located at the intersection of Dorset and Crispin Streets, just up from the entrance to Miller's Court. Go back there and examine the paving blocks around it, if you will. You will note fresh scrape marks in the street where the cover was dragged across by a single individual – a left-handed individual, I might add – who desired access to the tunnel below but was unable to lift the cover completely clear of the manhole by himself."

Holmes noted the unspoken question in Abberline's eyes. "Oh, for God's sake, man! The cover was dragged to the *left* of the hole as you face it from the curb! If he were right-handed, the scrape marks on the pavement would have been to the right of the hole!"

"Ah, yes, of course," said Abberline.

Holmes resumed: "Now, should you lift the cover, you will find, on the top two or three rungs of the ladder leading down into the tunnel, fresh traces of a black and particularly viscous sample of muck. Unless I am very much mistaken, those traces will match with samples taken from the interior of Miller's Court."

Abberline blew out his cheeks and he nodded silently, conviction appearing in his eyes at last.

"And," continued Holmes, "if that is not sufficient proof, take particular care when you reach the bottom of the shaft. There you will find, at the foot of the ladder, unless my eyes deceived me in the dim light, the flattened remains of a rather distinctive gold-tipped cigarette."

He could not help but smile slightly at the expression on Watson's face. "You see? Our friend has not given up his pernicious habit, after all," he said caustically.

A long, heavy silence ensued. Abberline was the first to break it.

"The... um... tunnel," he said, peering down at the diagram. "This particular tunnel on the corner of Dorset Street? Where does it lead?"

"Oh, no great mystery there," replied Holmes. "It leads right here, to the underground station beneath our feet."

Abberline nodded knowingly. "That is what I expected you would say." He pulled at his chin again, musing aloud. "But more to the point, where does the trail go from here? That's the real question."

Holmes leaned back in his chair and lowered his gaze, a troubled, faraway look in his eyes. "Unfortunately," he said, sighing deeply, "to tell you the truth of it, there is no great mystery there either."

He looked up. His eyes went from one to the other in turn. They were staring at him expectantly.

He returned their look, his face innocently devoid of expression.

Twenty-Five

SATURDAY, NOVEMBER 10-SUNDAY, NOVEMBER 11, 1888

"It is not too much to say that it is of such weight it may have an
influence upon European history."
— *A Scandal in Bohemia*

"Life," Sherlock Holmes observed on one occasion, "is infinitely
stranger than anything which the mind of man could invent."[102]
As a physician, decided Watson in a moment of quiet contemplation,
as a physician he would heartily agree, but from the perspective of a
writer, life left much to be desired. It had a tendency to disappoint.
Fiction was far more reliable.

Seldom did reality possess the neatness and dependability of
fiction, its precise framework, its orderly structure, its predictable
unpredictability, its carefully composed story line progressing step by
methodical step toward that inevitable, ineluctable climax so essential
to any plot. And that, as he perceived it, was the trouble with life. It
was imperfect.

"The public gets the wrong impressions from your accounts of my little problems, Watson," Holmes once remarked. "You aim for the dramatic effect in your stories, yet in actuality there is little physical excitement to most of my investigations, as well you know. The science of detection depends largely upon one's gray matter. Precious little flash to it, I can tell you. Usually what is involved is unrelieved tedium and dogged, painstaking researches. And, regrettably, there is seldom a smashing outcome, few of the thrills and rousing finales your editors dote upon. Far, far too seldom and far too few," he added wistfully.

He was right, of course. For one thing, life's affairs all too often did not come to a conclusion, satisfactory or otherwise. They simply stopped – abruptly, artlessly, and without a shrug of apology. All too often there was no proper finish, no clear resolution or sense of finality, no ending at all; merely a cessation of activity. All too often there lacked that indispensable element of drama, that sense of wonderment, discovery, and surprise – those essential twists and delightfully serpentine turns leading inescapably to the neat and tidy ending the reader of fiction had come to expect.

Was this, then, how the horror was to end? With no grand climax, no clash of cymbals, no startling discoveries or revelations?

No. There were to be none of these things: No surprises. No dramatic confrontations. No scenes of satisfying retribution. The murders were to simply stop.

Somewhere upon or beneath the mean streets of Spitalfields, in the early morning hours of November 9, 1888, the man known as Jack the Ripper disappeared forever. It was as if he had never existed, or, tiring of the game, merely chose to absent himself and move on to other things, other entertainments.

But of course no one knew it at the time. No one realized then that Mary Jane Kelly was to be the last of his victims, that the persona of Jack the Ripper was no more. Some little time would have to pass before

Londoners gratefully came to that realization and no longer started at every nighttime sound and shadow. But no time at all was required for them to launch and indulge in a wave of baseless, reasonless conjecture unequaled in its inventiveness and unparalleled in its scope. Gone he might be, this Ripper chap, but hardly – *hardly* – forgotten. He had already gained celebrity, achieved renown. Now he was to attain immortality. Now he was to enter the folklore, to acquire legendary status – even before the wreaths of rosemary were to wilt upon his last victim's grave. For poor Mary Jane Kelly was laid to rest with much touching solicitude and at some expense, funds being quickly raised for the purpose from a suddenly generous, most sympathetic public, her leaving of this world having attracted far more attention and far more charity than her brief, sad, tawdry existence in it ever had, and her interment being far grander an occasion than anything she could have known in life or ever dreamt of attaining in afterlife.

Throughout London, speculation was rife, the rumors rampant, the theories wild, varied, numerous, extravagant: All of positively epidemic proportions. Not too much to say that the name *Jack the Ripper* was on virtually every tongue, in every journal, on the lips of every shopkeeper, vendor, lord, and idler, of scullery maid, whore, and bejeweled dowager alike, of even the little children playing in the streets. In row house, tenement, town house, and palace, above stairs and below; in club room, tack room, dining room, and pub, his whereabouts, his fate, his identity, were the subject of conversation over practically every cup of tea, glass of port, or pint of bitters. But Holmes? – Holmes garbed himself in a cloak of stubborn silence, thin-lipped and obdurate, remaining steadfastly mute, refusing not only to express an opinion or share his thoughts, but to even listen to discussion of the matter or suffer casual allusions to it.

Later, in retrospect, Watson, with the insights only the passage of time allows, would wonder privately what Holmes had known then, had known the very day of the Kelly murder and perhaps before, had possibly known all along, or at least very early on. Of course Watson could only speculate; he had nothing whatsoever to go on. But it was a safe bet, was it not? Did not Holmes always know more than he let on?

Yes, of course he knew. He must have. But he chose not to reveal it, or, rather, chose to share his knowledge only with those whom he felt had to know along with him. *Had* to know.

Clearly, Watson did not have to know.

In the coming days, during that tense period when all of London lay in doubt and still very much in fear – still half expecting to awaken the next morning, or surely the one after, to new cries in the streets of "Murder! Horrible Murder! Another Murder in Whitechapel!" – a few carefully chosen individuals would be taken into his confidence, the absolute minimum number of those who had to be in possession of the knowledge. For if a conspiracy is to have any chance of success, it is always best to limit the number of conspirators. In this particular instance, given what was at stake, even two could be one too many.

As Holmes once said on another occasion: "The only safe plotter is he who plots alone."[103]

The coroner's inquest was held three days after Mary Jane Kelly's body was found. Held in unseemly haste, some thought, and far too soon after the murder for all the facts of the case to have been ascertained or be readily available. In a departure from the usual practice, it was held outside the jurisdiction of the district where the death occurred – in Shoreditch as opposed to Whitechapel.[104] The coroner for Shoreditch, a Dr. Roderick McDonald, was known to be sympathetic to the authorities, far more tractable than the man who had presided over the earlier inquests and had been so highly critical of police procedures and the authorities in general. Dr. McDonald proved to be an excellent choice, insofar as officialdom was concerned. His inquest was a hurried, slipshod affair. Witnesses and even members of the jury were hectored and browbeaten by him, and under his direction, evidence was suppressed, information withheld, testimony unheard, obvious questions unasked. The proceedings were brought to a conclusion after less than a day, the verdict arrived at without even bothering to obtain the victim's name for the official record: "Willful murder against some person or persons unknown."

The press was outraged, and a cover-up broadly hinted at. Some newspapers called for an investigation, others for a new inquest altogether. But it was not to be. Mary Jane Kelly was hurriedly lowered into the ground, and the controversy over her inquest put to rest with her.

This, of course, did not mean the business was over. The investigation was to go on. Scotland Yard and the Home Office, under pressure from the newspapers, were forced to reverse a long-standing policy and offer rewards for information, to be added to those already put up by various citizens' groups. And the search for the killer continued. The streets and back alleys were scoured. Dozens of suspects were rounded up, questioned, and released. New theories were advanced and discarded. But of course the investigation went nowhere. It was not supposed to. The police were looking for someone who no longer existed.[105]

In the months to come, other murders were to take place, murders which the press and public, and even some members of the police, quite naturally attributed to the Ripper, for they were similar in several respects to those that came earlier. But as is now known, and as Holmes no doubt then knew, they could not have been the work of the same hand, for Jack the Ripper was no more.

But at the time, as far as the press and a frightened public were concerned, the killer had once again emerged and was at large. There was the outcry to be expected from an aroused citizenry: Demands for more patrols in the streets, for better lighting, for an increased allocation of funds, for modernization of the detective branch, for greater zeal on the part of the government. And from some quarters – a scant few – there was even a call for compassion. Compassion for the poor "unfortunates" who were the targeted victims.

"I can't help but wonder if we are not all 'unfortunates'," Lord Randolph Churchill commented to Holmes and Watson after they had been ushered into his presence in the study of his Mayfair town house. "All unfortunates and all victims," he lamented. Dejectedly, he tossed aside the newspaper he had been perusing, its lead editorial attributing the Whitechapel outrages to "the moral failures of a flagitious and decadent society." The idea seemed to hold some fascination for him. "Are wc to believe that what we are witnessing is some sort of twisted, obscene morality play? Is that what it is?" He shook his head slowly from side to side. "I find the very thought depressing. The Almighty may have a bizarre sense of the theatrical, as has been shown time and time again in the course of man's paltry affairs, but surely he is a better dramatist than all that."

Watson looked at Churchill with some alarm, and not because he was shocked by what others might consider blasphemous thoughts. The man's hands were shaking, almost uncontrollably. His eyes, red-lined and feverish, were deeply shadowed, his complexion unnaturally sallow. He sat huddled in his chair by the fireplace, looking small and sickly.

Watson went to his side instantly. "You are ill, Lord Randolph!"

Churchill waved him away. "It is nothing. It comes and goes. Merely a bad spell, is all."

"You must allow me to examine you!"

"Thank you for your concern, but it is not necessary." He jerked his arm away from Watson, who was trying to take his pulse. "I am under the care of Sir William Gull."

Watson raised an eyebrow at that, though he was hardly surprised. Gull, one of the foremost medical practitioners in the country, was the personal physician to the royal family. He was highly fashionable among the gentry, as was to be expected, but Watson had heard that he himself had lately been ill and was no longer seeing patients.[106]

"He has prescribed for you, then? You have seen him recently?"

Churchill shook his head. "It is nothing, I tell you. Do be seated, Doctor. You can do nothing for me."

There was such resignation in his voice, such a note of melancholy acceptance that it brought Watson up short, causing him to search Churchill's eyes, as if for more information. But there was none forthcoming; the man's jaw was set. Reluctantly Watson backed away; having no other recourse, he took the chair that was indicated. Holmes, who had in the meantime quietly taken up a position by the fireplace, was studying Churchill intently. He, of course, had not missed a thing.

"I am sorry we find you unwell, Lord Randolph," he said softly. There was great kindness in his voice, tenderness even. "I trust you will forgive us for calling at what must be an inopportune time."

Churchill waved aside his apologies feebly. "I take it you are not here on merely a social call. What news do you bring? Do you have fresh leads in the latest killing, is that it?" He leaned forward in his chair expectantly. His sad, tired eyes had enlivened with sudden interest, becoming bright with intensity.

Holmes gave him a hard, shrewd look. His manner, when he spoke again, was brusque, even harsh, in sharp contrast to the considerate tone he used only an instant earlier.

"I shall get directly to the point, Lord Randolph. I should like to know why you have gone to such great lengths to convince me that you are the Whitechapel murderer? It won't do, you know. It won't do at all."

Churchill gave a little cry and slumped back into his chair, throwing his hands up in a gesture of helplessness.

Holmes and Watson were on the earliest train to the old market town of King's Lynn early the following morning, and within a short while they were passing through the bare sepia countryside of Norfolk, the landscape appearing flat and lifeless beneath the low November skies. The train arrived at its destination agreeably close to the time Holmes's *Bradshaw* said it should. The sky had cleared a little by then, and a pallid sun appeared diffidently through the low clouds to greet them as they stepped onto the platform, the brackish scent of the nearby North Sea in their nostrils. It was a wan and cheerless sun, Watson thought, as devoid of welcome as it was of warmth. A waiting trap carried them the final eight miles to Sandringham, arriving in ample time for them to freshen up before luncheon.

The manor house, of orange brick and white stone, was a large, architecturally unpretentious structure in an attractive wooded setting, with a deer park located conveniently nearby. It was designed as a casual weekend and holiday retreat, purely for comfort, and as such had no pretenses about it. There was no need for pomp or ceremony here.

The Prince of Wales, dressed in comfortable tweeds, turned from the large bay window with its view of the Norfolk countryside and forced his gaze to rest on Sherlock Holmes. Watson was also present in the room, as was Sir Francis Knollys, the prince's private secretary, the two of them subdued, even anxious, both exhibiting great concern on their faces. But the prince did not spare them a glance. He had eyes only for Holmes, glaring at him with a look approaching malevolence, the expression on his face clearly communicating the hostility that he felt.

He took the cigar from his mouth; it tasted bitter to him. He moved over to the table, placed it in a silver ashtray, and turned back to the window. Finally, he turned to face Holmes once again and, scowling fiercely, addressed him in guttural tones: "I need not ask whether you are certain of your facts."

Holmes met his gaze. "Regrettably, sir, I am most certain."

"How came you by this information?"

"Much of it has been the result of personal investigation and observation over a period of some time, Your Highness. As to the young prince's unfortunate malady, that was confirmed by Sir William Gull, the royal physician."

"You questioned him! By what right?"

"By the right Your Royal Highness gave me. You will recall, sir, that you gave me carte blanche."

"And Gull told you that the boy – my *son!* – was a syphilitic!"

"Not in so many words, sir. That much was deduced from the symptoms he described. What Sir William told me, in the strictest of confidence, of course, was that His Highness appeared to be suffering from a softening of the brain brought on by an undiagnosed complaint. It was his opinion, sir, and as you know he is a specialist in disorders of the brain, that the young prince, as a result of this ailment, is... forgive me, sir... growing increasingly unbalanced."

"Unbalanced! What means this, this... unbalanced?"

Watson touched Holmes's arm. "By Your Royal Highness's leave, perhaps as a physician I might be permitted to explain."

The prince nodded.

"It is clear from all of the medical evidence that your son contracted a venereal disease sometime in the past, perhaps whilst out of the country visiting abroad, and that the infection has been permitted to go without treatment. As a result, it has run its inevitable course, and has caused... irreparable brain damage. I am so sorry to have to tell you this, sir, but the young prince is very ill and is no longer responsible for his actions."

The prince stood there, popeyed. "Irreparable? You mean there is no cure?"

Watson looked down at his feet. "No, sir. None. The disease at this stage is quite irreversible, I am sorry to have to tell you."

"And it's because the damn boy has got the *clap*!"

Watson flinched. "Apparently he has been afflicted with it for some time, sir."

"Vell, for God's sake, it's only a simple matter of some sulfur and molasses or somesing. Half the army has got it, and probably two-thirds of the Royal Navy. And I vould vager that a goodly portion of the House of goddamn Lords has got it too! You don't have to be a bloody doctor to know how to deal vith that!"

"Unfortunately, sir, it is not as simple as all that. His case, from what I understand, is far advanced. It is too far along to be cured by such means. His brain has been affected, sir. He is no longer in control of his faculties. He is, from what I gather, no longer... mentally capable. Of course, I have not personally examined the young man, so I cannot certify as to all of this, but..." His voice trailed off.

The prince, very pale, was shaking his head disbelievingly. Unconsciously, he unfastened the belt of his Norfolk jacket and undid several of the buttons of his waistcoat. His chest felt constricted, as if a band were being tightened around it. He breathed deeply.

Holmes spoke: "You will recall, sir, that when we first acquainted you with this matter, the possibility was raised by my brother that unusually strong measures – extraordinary measures – might have to be taken to prevent the royal family from being associated with a scandal from which it could not recover."

The prince nodded feebly.

"That it might be necessary, in order to guarantee the security of the throne, to resort to means that under any other circumstances would be... would be unthinkable."

The prince merely stared into space.

Holmes looked down at his feet. The skin was drawn unnaturally tight across his cheekbones. "I have to tell you, sir... I have to tell you that the time has come."

There was a heavy silence in the room. The prince continued to stare off into space, his usual florid features deathly pale, an expression of disbelief on his face, an expression which, as realization came to him, transformed itself into one of extreme anguish and bottomless pain. He shuddered and sighed heavily.

"Ja, well, then," he said quietly, his voice barely audible. He turned back to Holmes. "Vat is to be done?"

Holmes did not hesitate in his reply, but the expression on his face was one of great sympathy and his tone was now gentle and kind. "Clearly, sir, the young man – His Royal Highness – must be confined."

Anger flashed in the prince's eyes. "Confined? *Must* be confined?"

Holmes stood his ground. "It is advisable, sir. For the young man's sake, as much as anything. For his own protection, if for no other reason."

The prince's face reddened alarmingly. He spat out his words between clenched teeth, his accent highly pronounced. "Must I remind you that you speak of your future king! You would confine an heir to the throne?"

Even now he did not fully understand.

Holmes and Knollys exchanged meaningful glances. Then Holmes bowed solemnly. "No more willingly, sir, than I would confine simply your son, if that is all he was to the world." He spread his arms. "If it were in my power to make it otherwise, I would do so. This is the most painful duty I have ever performed, Your Highness, and I curse the day it fell to my lot to perform it. But you must understand that it is not my decision to make, one way or the other." He raised a cautionary finger. "Nor, in all due respect, Your Highness, is it yours."

The prince's eyes widened.

Sir Francis Knollys, who had been sitting quietly, rose to his feet. "By your leave, sir, might I speak?"

Knollys was a tall, handsome man of noble bearing, noted as much for his intelligence and common sense as he was for his extraordinary patience and powers of diplomacy and, most of all, for his unquestioning loyalty to the prince and the royal family. It was well known that the prince valued his judgment above all others and was greatly dependent upon him.

Knollys's even features showed the pain he felt, and it was clear that he spoke reluctantly. "Mr. Holmes is quite correct in every respect. Unhappily, there seems to be no alternative to what he has suggested. I must inform you that the matter has been taken up with the Marquess of Salisbury, who has met with the cabinet in secret emergency session and has the advice and consent of the other ministers. I have been in communication with him this morning, sir. Sadly, he fully concurs with Mr. Holmes's view, as does Mycroft Holmes as well."

"Emergency session? The cabinet?" The prince looked shocked.

"That is correct, sir."[107]

"Good God! Can it be so? It has gone this far?" He turned back to the window, his shoulders bowed. Full awareness of the matter had finally come to him, and the gravity of it all – the gravity and the utter hopelessness of it – had fully struck home. It was a matter of state now, no longer simply a family affair. It was out of his hands. He was powerless. All he could do was acquiesce. He, above all people, knew the weakness of his position, knew that despite his exalted status, with all of his titles and all of his privileges, he was merely an instrument of national policy.

"And you, Francis?" he asked with his back still toward them, his voice sounding strained and muffled. "Is it also your opinion?"

Knollys bowed to the prince's back. He was crestfallen. His heart went out to the man he had served so loyally for so long. He faltered when he spoke, and his tone was hardly above a whisper. "You will forgive me, sir. I say this with the greatest personal pain and sadness, but I do not believe there is any choice. It can be no other way. Above all − first and foremost − we must consider the family's welfare, and the country's."

Knollys, who knew the Prince of Wales better than any man living, his great strengths as well as his weaknesses, his great sense of duty as well as his petty and frivolous ways, knew that it was not necessary to remind him where his responsibilities now lay. But he also knew that as a man, as a father, the prince was being called upon to do the unthinkable and that he desperately needed confirmation from someone whose judgment he valued that the sacrifice was unavoidable, inescapable.

The prince shook his head from side to side. He seemed to have shrunk in size. His shoulders were bowed and his eyes were moist as, once again, he turned away from the window to face them, bearing the look of a man who had been beaten down and utterly defeated. But, that notwithstanding, there was something else: A quiet dignity. "How is the matter to be handled?" he asked weakly.

Holmes said quietly: "It would be best if you were to leave that to me, sir."

The prince thought about it. "He must be... confronted in my presence."

Holmes considered the question, then shook his head. "That, sir, would not be advisable. Not at all advisable."

"Nevertheless, I desire it."

"I must take strong exception, sir."

The prince stamped his foot. "Damn your impudence! I desire it, and that is an end to the matter! And damn you, sir!"

Knollys cleared his throat delicately. The prince's eyes turned immediately toward him. Others might enjoy a closer relationship with the Prince of Wales, others might claim his personal friendship, but as his private secretary and a trusted aide for more than eighteen years, Knollys knew best – better than anyone – how to manage things, how to do away with vexing problems, how to make everything right. His whole manner, his mere presence, was a calming influence upon the prince.

Knollys raised his hand in a simple, quiet gesture – almost as if in benediction. "Your Royal Highness..." he said softly.

The Prince of Wales looked at him imploringly, the tears welling up in his eyes. "Francis," he said. "Please... please."

EDITOR'S NOTE

Yet another gap appears in Watson's chronicle at this point; several additional pages of his notes are inexplicably missing. Precisely how many, it is impossible to tell, for the pages were not always consecutively numbered or even in sequence. As before, one can only speculate as to whether the absence of this material is due to mischance or design, and if the latter, who was responsible for its removal. Surely suspicion is not unwarranted, for the interruption comes at what is unquestionably a crucial juncture in this account of the Whitechapel murders. And, as we know from other Watson chronicles, during part of the period presumably covered by the missing pages, Sherlock Holmes was also missing. He was absent from London for almost three years, absent and believed dead.[108]

Twenty-Six

MONDAY, JANUARY 28, 1895

"Once or twice in my career I feel that I have done more real harm
by my discovery of the criminal than ever he had done by his crime.
I have learned caution by now, and I had rather play tricks with the
law of England than with my own conscience."
— *The Abbey Grange*

The news was in all the papers, of course; detailed accounts were to
be found on the front pages of every journal in the country. The
death four days earlier of Lord Randolph Henry Spencer Churchill,
at the age of forty-six, was front-page news indeed, as was only to be
expected of the man who some considered "the greatest elemental force
in English politics since Cromwell."[109]

Churchill's funeral in Bladon churchyard the previous day, and
the memorial service that followed in Westminster Abbey, were
attended by the highest in the land: By members of the royal family
and representatives of the major noble houses of Britain; by cabinet
ministers, leaders of both Houses of Parliament, and backbenchers of

every political persuasion; by former friends and colleagues and by former enemies from across the aisle as well.

But Sherlock Holmes remained insensible to all of that. The man's political importance and his position in society were of no more than incidental interest to him. His preoccupation with Lord Randolph Churchill was for other reasons entirely, reasons that would never appear in an obituary or future biography.

And so it was that when Watson came upon him, the detective was deep in the folds of one of his characteristic brown studies, downcast and contemplative. The good doctor had, by chance, found himself in the vicinity of Baker Street while making his rounds late that cold, gray, drizzly morning, and with an hour or so to spare between patients decided to stop by his old quarters for an unannounced visit. It had been some little while since Watson had last seen Holmes, their relationship having been reduced to infrequent encounters, and though he was a bit concerned to find him appearing drawn and somewhat haggard, he seemed otherwise well and reasonably fit. Aside from a few deeper lines around the eyes and mouth, Watson could detect no appreciable differences in his friend's outward appearance, joyless countenance notwithstanding. Middle age had chosen to make its initial forays upon Holmes with gentleness and uncommon solicitude, leaving him thus far unscathed and little altered. There was still the same tall, spare frame, the same noble brow and sharp, gaunt visage, the same deceptively languorous manner and antipathetic intensity of gaze and, of course, beneath it all the same keen intellect and restless, probing mind.

Seated moodily in front of the fire in dressing gown and slippers, with one of his commonplace books in his lap and his armchair surrounded by the debris of the morning's clipped and discarded newspapers, Holmes glanced up with a wan, faintly mocking smile of greeting as Watson entered. Wordlessly, he motioned him to the teapot sitting still warm on the dining table.

Watson helped himself to a cup and looked around him. Few changes had been made to the rooms they had shared for so long prior to Watson's marriage some years earlier.[110] All seemed much the same. The old furnishings, the old familiar objects, all appeared to be in their accustomed places. The sitting room was as snug and as warm and as cluttered as it ever was, its homey Bohemian atmosphere permeated with the signal aroma of strong tobacco and pungent chemicals, an ineradicable condition by now, one would think, the not wholly unpleasant odor having long since impregnated the draperies and upholstery and probably even the very plaster of the walls themselves.

There was a permanence to the place and an air of serenity which Watson found both comforting and reassuring. Entering it was like donning a favorite old tweed jacket which, though sagging and worn and hopelessly out of fashion, one would never consider discarding or even altering. It had, after all, taken so long to get it that way.

He sighed. Time, from all outward appearances, seemed to have stood still within these rooms. They had become a fixed point in an otherwise changing world. The twentieth century would soon be upon them, but here, at 221B Baker Street, one was beset by the idea, the irrational conviction, that somehow it would always remain the 1880s.

Holmes waved Watson to his old chair in his usual manner – that air of casual disinterest he adopted when it suited him – but the delighted glimmer in his eye was unmistakable and his spirits perked up markedly at the sight of his friend. "Somehow I knew I would be suffering the pleasure of your company before the day was out," he drawled, simultaneously subjecting Watson to a brief but intensive scrutiny. "And I see that I must congratulate you on your burgeoning medical practice. Business has picked up prettily since last I saw you, I perceive."

Watson shot Holmes a startled, quizzical look, causing him to chuckle.

"Tut, tut. It is obvious," he said, holding up his hand to forestall the question he knew was to follow. "What else am I to think when I spot an almost depleted pad of prescription blanks peering out of your pocket and the day not half gone? – and peering out of the pocket of a handsome new frock coat, I might add. From Shingleton's in New Bond Street, isn't it? Ah, yes, I thought so. Quite becoming."

The expression of pained awareness that came over Watson's face brought another chuckle from Holmes. "Yes, I know, I know," he intoned. "'It is so deucedly simple once explained.'" He gazed upon his friend in a rare display of open affection. "Dear old Watson, you never disappoint me."

Within no time at all the two of them, eminently comfortable in each other's company, were deep in conversation – that familiar, easy communion of old that only intimate friends of long standing can ever know – and once having attended to the mundane essentials of their workaday lives, exchanging mutual assurances as to each other's health and general well-being, their talk inevitably turned to the major news item of the day, and, of course, to those related matters that had so occupied their energies seven years earlier, thoughts of which had unconsciously, though inexorably, drawn Watson back to Baker Street.

It had been some little while since the topic had last come under discussion between them, as if there had been a tacit understanding that it was best left alone, best not even thought about. Watson could not help but recall that the previous occasion had been under remarkably similar circumstances, the death of another highly prominent figure. How vividly he remembered that day, one of those rare days in every lifetime that are so unforgettable: How he drifted awake to the sound of church bells mournfully tolling and the urgent cries of newsboys in the street. The jolt of sudden awareness, the sharp stab of sudden, unknowing fear.

It, too, was a day in January, almost exactly three years before. Even now he could clearly visualize the black-bordered front page of *The Times*, rushed upstairs to him on that cold blustery morning, bearing the news: The death, from pneumonia brought on by influenza, of His Royal Highness, Prince Albert Victor Christian Edward of Wales, Duke of Clarence and Avondale and Heir Presumptive to the throne of England. Prince Eddy was dead. It was indeed a day forever fixed in Watson's memory.[111]

All of Britain had been plunged into mourning, for the slender, doe-eyed young prince, who had celebrated his twenty-eighth birthday less than a week earlier and whose engagement to be married had only recently been announced, was a highly popular figure.[112] People in the streets were genuinely grieved by his untimely death. Was he not, after all, the very embodiment of what a royal heir should be? – dignified, wholesome, regal, and dashing in his hussar's uniform, in every way an ornament to the British nation: A fitting symbol to rally round in times of crisis, a wellspring of pride and majesty in times of tranquility. What a welcome change from the wearisome image of his royal grandmother in her perennial widow's weeds, and his overstuffed, self-indulgent father with his prodigious appetites and unseemly aging-playboy ways. How shocked the nation was by his passing, how deeply, truly saddened.

Watson shook his head at the memory of it. For him, the death of Prince Eddy held a different meaning, of course. Never would he be able to hear the name spoken, never would he be able to visualize that insipid face, those languid, vacant eyes, without experiencing a chill of perfect, unreasoning horror.

He shivered slightly, and then sighed. Numerous pages had turned since that grim, cold day spent in the East End following the murder of Mary Jane Kelly, and much had happened in the intervening six years. He and Holmes had shared so many adventures and had such a multitude of memories to look back upon that he found it daunting just thinking about it.

Watson stole a glance at his friend, sprawled listlessly across from him in his armchair, his dressing gown draped loosely about him, his gray eyes bleak, his manner once again distant and withdrawn.

Of the countless cases in which he and Holmes had been involved over the years they had known each other, many had been difficult and demanding, many profoundly complex, but none – *none* – had ever been so challenging, so bewildering, so frustrating, and so frightening as the Whitechapel affair. And none had ever been so upsetting to Holmes personally.

Holmes chanced to look up at that instant and smiled softly as their eyes met. "I must confess to you that it was the most unpleasant, most burdensome business I have ever been involved in," he said as if reading Watson's very thoughts. He nodded to himself. "Burdensome and painful. Most terribly painful, as you surely realize."

Watson nodded also.

Holmes's thin lips compressed. "It must never get out, you know. Any of it. Even a simple mention of my involvement in any aspect of the case would be unwise. So far my name has been kept out of it, and it is best that it remain so. Should I, or you, for that matter, be in some way connected to the business – even at this late date – it might cause some inquisitive journalist to start sniffing about, digging up bones best left undisturbed. Aside from the national scandal it could precipitate, we have our own reputations – indeed, our own tender necks – to worry about, remember."

Watson, frowning, nodded again. "Of course I realize that. Yet..."

Holmes raised a finger and smiled knowingly. "Yet you cannot help but wish the story could somehow be told."

"That's it, of course. It is terribly frustrating to find oneself sitting atop of what is surely the most compelling mystery of the age and not be able to tell it. I know that's out of the question completely, given the harm disclosure would cause. Still, it is only natural that I regret being unable to reveal the facts of the matter. It would go down as your most famous case if it ever saw the light of day."

Holmes's jaw tightened and his eyes became hard. "It would go down as my most infamous debacle, you mean! And, apart from everything else, would hold me up to personal ridicule, though that hardly matters."

Watson raised his eyebrows. "Ridicule? You? Nonsense."

Startling Watson, Holmes sprang to his feet and began to pace the room, highly agitated. "It would be nothing less than I deserve, after all. The whole affair was shameful — absolutely shameful! Not least of all my participation in it!"

Watson looked at him in surprise. "Shameful to Scotland Yard without doubt — and to the Home Office, too, for that matter — but why to you? Surely you have nothing to condemn yourself for."

Holmes's eyes flashed. "For God's sake, Watson! I assisted in a conspiracy to secretly and unlawfully confine an heir to the throne of the realm! I concealed evidence in a murder! I committed several violations of the Criminal Acts, any one of which would see me in the dock at the Old Bailey and earn me a prolonged holiday at Her Majesty's expense. And you don't even know the worst of it!" He threw up his hands. "Good Lord, you don't even know the *half* of it! Which is probably just as well, for whilst it is a weight I would willingly unload from my conscience, it is not knowledge I should wish anyone else to be burdened with. Certainly not you!"

He took another swift turn around the room, the skirts of his dressing gown billowing about his legs as he paced, chin on chest, hands clasped tightly behind him. Watson looked on in confusion and concern.

"The whole matter was mishandled from the start!" Holmes cried, pivoting around. "And I am to blame! I never should have permitted myself to become involved in the filthy business to begin with! *Never!* Mycroft and his infernal palace intrigues! And – *and* – I should have caught that fiend," he said, banging fist into palm. "I should have gotten him!"

Watson's expression turned to one of astonishment. "Holmes, whatever are you talking about? You did catch him!" He lowered his voice to what amounted to a conspiratorial whisper: "It was the prince!"

Holmes shot him a scornful look. "The prince? You think so?"

Watson was rendered almost speechless. "But... whatever do you mean? What is it you are saying?"

Holmes, a man who rarely revealed his emotions, had become so distraught he could respond only with a savage gesture and a noise of exasperation. Furiously, he made another circuit of the room while Watson sat there in bewilderment. Bewilderment and considerable trepidation, for in all the years he had known Holmes, he had never seen him in such a state.

It took several minutes before the detective was able to calm himself sufficiently to return to his chair, and another moment or two for him to put his thoughts in order. He then undertook to explain:

"The prince had nothing to do with the murders, Watson – nothing whatsoever. The business involving Prince Eddy was altogether separate and apart from the murders. Something else entirely. He had to be attended to because he could no longer be trusted on his own. He was no longer a responsible individual. The weakness of intellect which he was born with, coupled with the syphilis that was attacking his brain, his increasingly bizarre behavior, embarrassing to say the least, his unnatural sexual proclivities, and the danger of it all being publicly revealed: These were the reasons why he had to be, er...

sequestered, as he was. Clearly, in time, had no measures been taken, his true character would have become common knowledge. He would have been revealed for what he was and a scandal of catastrophic proportions would have ensued. All of this was made abundantly obvious when he was caught up in that notorious police raid on the male brothel in Cleveland Street."[113]

Watson's eyes went wide. "He was involved in *that*?"

"Naturally, it was all hushed up. But it was a close thing. It almost got out that he was implicated. One of the more scatological scandal sheets somehow got hold of it, and only a good deal of scurrying about and the personal intervention of Lord Salisbury prevented him from being named. The fine hand of Mycroft could also be detected there, of course. Had it been disclosed, given the climate of the times, the monarchy would have undoubtedly suffered a telling blow. It was clear now – to all concerned – that he was not fit to rule and that steps had to be taken to remove him from the succession."

"Good Lord!"

"And of course there was the other factor, one that was of even more immediate concern: He could not be permitted to father a child, could not be permitted to breed."

Watson's eyes went even wider.

Holmes sighed deeply. Dredging up these memories was clearly painful to him. "The prince, you will recall, had just recently become engaged to be married, an engagement arranged by his mother, the Princess of Wales, with the concurrence and connivance of the Queen. Both of them felt marriage would do him good – a misconception all mothers have in common, it would seem. Neither of them was aware of his incurable disease or of his deviant behavior, of course, that being kept from them to spare their sensibilities."

Holmes's brows came together. He fiddled nervously with his

pipe. "Well, it was quickly decided by... by the powers that be that this marriage had to be prevented at all cost. It was feared in certain quarters that any offspring he would sire would be born not only with his weakness of brain, but with the vile infection he now carried in his blood. Consider the ramifications, Watson! The English royal line is already plagued by hemophilia, as is well known, and there is the fear that through intermarriage that affliction could be spread to other reigning families of Europe, particularly those of Imperial Russia and Germany, which are both tied to our royal family by marriage. To permit a new indisposition to be introduced into the royal bloodline – and one as virulent as a venereal disease – well, it could mean an end to monarchies everywhere, including that of England, of course. *Especially* that of England."

His tone became biting: "Prince Eddy was put away for these reasons and these reasons alone, because it was expedient to do so. Because the future of England's throne depended upon it. Because our entire social structure was in jeopardy. Because if the monarchy was at risk, our ruling class was at risk, along with all of its titles and perquisites and pretensions and wealth. In other words – in other *noble* words – it was all for the good of England and the Empire." Holmes's eyes hardened. "So they tell me."

Watson was clearly taken aback. "And all this time I thought..."

Holmes arched an eyebrow. "That an heir to the throne was guilty of... violent murder?"

Watson nodded mutely.

Holmes sniffed. "Surely it must have occurred to you that that poor, simple-minded creature was not up to the task."

"Well, of course it had," he said hurriedly. "Still..." His voice trailed off.

Holmes threw him a look of wry amusement.

Watson rubbed his jaw to cover his confusion. "But however was it managed? I mean, he was constantly in the public eye, attending official functions and cutting ribbons and so forth – almost right up to the time of his death!"

"Just so."

"He was in custody all that time?"

"Most of it."

"How could it be? This is quite impossible, Holmes."

"Unlikely, yes, but not impossible."

Watson was stunned. Clearly he found it all too difficult to absorb. "But he was seen in public. He was in the newspapers constantly!"

Holmes shrugged. "It was *reported* he was seen in public. That part of it was not all that difficult to arrange."

"Not difficult!" Watson looked at him open-mouthed.

"Surprisingly simple, actually. At first, all that was required was to keep a close watch on him, round the clock – to promenade him about like a lapdog on a tether. A small coterie of hand-picked royal equerries saw to that. But as his condition deteriorated, as his mental state became more erratic and his appearance more sickly, he had to be confined. It then became a matter of informing the public that he was where he wasn't. A schedule of activities was put out by the Palace every day as usual, and everything was made to look as normal as possible. In retrospect, it succeeded quite well, I must say."

"Do you mean to tell me that it was all a tissue of lies?"

Holmes smiled humorlessly. "What I mean to tell you is that brother Mycroft has a rich and creative imagination when it comes to the finer points of dissembling."

"Mycroft arranged it?"

"None other."

"It was all his doing?"

"Waaal... not *quite* all."

"But *The Times, The Daily Mail, The Telegraph*! They all carried accounts of the prince's activities. Almost daily!"

"Just so."

"Mycroft arranged that too?"

"Mycroft, among his other talents, is most adroit at conveying artful prevarications to the press when he finds it... convenient for his purposes. In the national interest, so to speak."

Watson gaped at him.

"The papers can be quite gullible, you know," Holmes continued. "They are well accustomed to printing what the Palace tells them, and without question. No journalist is ever permitted to get too close, after all, so it is either print what they are given, or nothing."

"But for all that time, Holmes! Why, it must have been several months!"

"Well, not *several* months. He was in close confinement for less time than that – only a relatively brief period of time, actually. But even so, Mycroft's ingenuity *was* becoming rather strained near the end. He was growing bored by it all, I shouldn't wonder."

"Close confinement, you say. He was actually incarcerated? A prince of the realm? Good Lord, where?"

Holmes made an impatient gesture. "An isolated royal hunting lodge. Let us just say that it was somewhere out of the way, safe and secure – abroad, on the Continent."

Watson gave him a look. "So that is where you really were all that time."

Holmes said nothing.

Watson, still finding it all difficult to believe, lapsed into thought. After a while he said: "Holmes – do you mean to say that everything the newspapers printed was false, that *none* of it was true?"

"Oh, some of it was, I dare say."

"And Prince Eddy's death? That was false too?"

"Oh, no. He died, all right. I can testify to that."

Watson glanced at him sharply. In making his reply, Holmes's voice had taken on a certain acerbic edge. What was it – sarcasm, scorn, self-contempt? Watson shook his head.

"What I meant was the *cause* of his death. It was reported that he died of pneumonia brought on by influenza. Was that not true?"

Holmes examined his fingernails.

"Holmes?"

Holmes looked away, his eyes expressionless.

"Good Lord!" Watson seemed to shrink in his chair.[114]

Twenty-Seven

Monday, January 28, 1895

"Some facts should be suppressed, or, at least, a sense of
proportion should be observed in treating them."
— The Sign of the Four

"These are the sacrifices one makes for one's country, Watson."
— His Last Bow

It was some little while before they spoke again. The two of them sat
in labored, awkward silence for the longest time – an indeterminate
period, really – avoiding each other's eyes, preoccupied with their own
separate thoughts.

In actuality, Watson found it impossible to think, to focus his
concentration, to make sense of what Holmes had told him – to make
sense of what he had *not* told him, for it was obvious much was missing.
It was such a hopeless muddle in his mind, a jumble of several jigsaw
puzzles stirred up and combined, and he struggled pathetically to fit all
the pieces together.

The silence in the room had become oppressive, intolerable. It was Watson, with a conscious effort, who broke it finally.

"It is the missing pieces that I don't understand," he said, shifting in his chair to face Holmes. "Where do all those clues fit in – the sleeve link you found among Catherine Eddowes's effects and those gold-tipped cigarette ends scattered all about. And where does J. K. Stephen, the prince's friend, tie into all of this? I never really understood why you ruled him out as a suspect when you did."

Holmes's brows came together. "Oh, it could never have been Stephen. I was able to dismiss him from my mind early on. He was simply incapable of murder. Just not the type. He was far too timorous a beastie, far too fainthearted – for all the influence he exercised over the prince. He hated women with a passion, there was no question about that, and he certainly was mentally unstable – indeed, in time he became incurably insane and was institutionalized – but he could never have carried off the murders. And besides, he was out of London on the night of at least one of them – that much Captain Burton-FitzHerbert was able to ascertain during the course of his inquiries at the Palace. Stephen was but a minor player. I was merely using him as a ploy to gather intelligence about the prince's comings and goings, not wishing it to be known that it was *he* I suspected. That would never have done." Holmes shook his head. "No, it was not Stephen. He was insane, but was not capable of taking a life. Except his own, lamentably."[115]

Watson looked at him intently. "But that sleeve link, Holmes. And all those ubiquitous cigarette ends? Where did they fit in?"

Holmes gazed up at the ceiling. He seemed to take an inordinate amount of time to respond. When he did finally, his manner was too matter-of-fact, his words too carefully, too evenly cadenced.

"Don't allow yourself to be drawn into the pit of meaningless minutiae, Watson. Those were inconsequential details, nothing more.

Merely annoying little distractions; most diverting at the time, but of no practical value, of no... consequence, as I said."

Watson's brow rose in surprise.

Holmes's face took on a remote cast, his eyes curiously empty and cold. Yet, he could not repress a slight telltale flutter of his eyelids. "I foolishly permitted myself to become preoccupied with them at the time, but I know better now." He waved his hand deprecatingly. "Meaningless minutiae," he repeated, "totally meaningless." He gazed off into space, lapsing into an uneasy silence.

Watson was incredulous. *Meaningless minutiae? Inconsequential details?* Never before had he heard Holmes refer to tangible clues – vital facts! – in such a manner. Why, his entire investigative method was based on close attention to such details – "founded upon the observation of trifles," as he said time and time again. How fond he was of saying: "It has long been an axiom of mine that the little things are infinitely the most important," and "The gravest issues may depend upon the smallest things." How often in the past had the successful conclusion to a mystery depended upon such... *minutiae*.

Watson opened his mouth to protest, to question him further, to challenge him even, but there was something... something in Holmes's demeanor that told him not to pursue the matter. Something that told him it would not be appreciated by his friend, and would be a useless effort in any event.

Suddenly Watson's eyes widened in realization. He gasped. "It was Lord Randolph Churchill, then, wasn't it?" He pointed an accusatory finger. "By God, despite everything, it *was* him!"

Holmes's shook his head slowly. His eyes were clouded with sadness. "No, it was not Churchill," he said. "He tried to make me believe that it was, and at one point nearly succeeded, but I was able to see through him. It was a close thing though. He damn near had me fooled."

Watson slumped back into his chair. "Holmes, I confess I am totally, hopelessly confused."

Holmes knocked cold ash from his pipe and reached for a box of vestas. "*He* thought it was the prince, don't you see? And he greatly feared the consequences should it ever get out. Rather than permit scandal and dishonor to touch upon the throne, rather than see the government torn apart and perhaps the nation as well, he decided he would bring it all down upon his own head."

Holmes paused to strike a match and apply it to the bowl of his pipe. "He did everything he could to convince me that it was he and not the prince who was to blame. He knew the young man was weak-minded and impressionable and had become the tool and plaything of undesirable elements. He knew of his sexual aberrations and the fact that he was no stranger to the Whitechapel district and frequented certain low establishments with some regularity."

Holmes puffed thoughtfully on his pipe. "He probably also knew of the prince's acute illness. Or guessed at it. After all, he shared the same physician, Sir William Gull. And it no doubt occurred to him that he shared the same horrible, debilitating disease as well. If he did not actually learn it from Gull himself."

Watson made a face. "I can't imagine a man of Sir William's position betraying medical confidences, Holmes. No reputable physician would – particularly where a patient of such prominence was involved."

Holmes dismissed the objection testily, with an impatient wave of his hand. "Well, then Churchill deduced it. It couldn't have been all that difficult for him to do. Gull, after all, was not the prince's regular physician. He was a well-known specialist in mental disorders, specifically those ancillary to syphilis. Good Lord, probably half the aristocracy was being treated by him. It would require no great powers of deduction to conclude that the prince was not seeing him for an ingrown toenail!"

Watson sniffed. Then something occurred to him and his face lit up. "So that's where you bolted off to in such a hurry after Shinwell departed that day! You almost set fire to the place!" He glanced down, noting that the burn in the carpet at the foot of Holmes's chair was still in evidence. After all those years.

Holmes smiled weakly. "You remember that, do you? Yes, I went off to Gull's. I was slow in realizing it, but it came to me at last that he, Gull, was the common denominator in all of this. Quite possibly the key to the entire puzzle. He was not only treating his young royal highness and Churchill, but James Stephen as well. And that was just too much of a coincidence. But unfortunately, my visit gained little. Sir William was ill from the effects of a recent stroke. Other than confirming what I already knew or inferred, he was not able to tell me very much at all. His memory had quite left him – not that he necessarily had much to tell, in any event."

"So you knew Churchill was a patient of Gull's even before he told us that he was?"

Holmes shrugged. "It followed that a man of Churchill's position would go to the foremost specialist in the country, so it was hardly a brilliant deduction on my part." He waved his hand. "But none of that matters. The point I wished to make was that Churchill must have somehow known of the prince's illness and mental infirmity. With his numerous and well-placed contacts in government and at the Palace, he always managed to keep himself well informed, and was privy to all sorts of goings-on. Knowing what he knew, or what in his troubled mental state he thought he knew, he convinced himself that it was Prince Eddy who was committing the murders. And in an effort to forestall a ruinous scandal, with all of its attendant dangers to the nation, he made the conscious decision – incredibly courageous or hopelessly insane, depending on your point of view – that he would rather bring it all down upon himself." Holmes paused to reflect. "I suppose he figured that his days were numbered in any event; that this would be a last, final service he could render to Queen and Country: A *beau geste*, if you will; or a crashing Wagnerian finale – who knows what was going on in his mind? The man was tortured, you know that; his illness had made him unbalanced. And besides, he was ever the lover of high drama. I suppose this appealed to his sense of theater."

Holmes pondered for a long moment, drawing steadily on his pipe, surrounding himself with angry swirls of smoke. "No. That is unfair," he said softly. "I never liked him, but I must give credit where credit is due. The man was a patriot, Watson. Say what you will about him, he was a true patriot! Can you imagine? Having accepted the inevitable, he was actually prepared to take the blame for those horrible crimes, to dishonor his own name and that of his heirs – indeed, that of the entire House of Marlborough – rather than allow the throne of England to be compromised." He hesitated. "Such selflessness is the one aspect of the story that *should* be made known, but, like the others, unfortunately never can."

He looked down at his hands and smiled grimly. "He was so *damn* clever. He thought of everything. And I almost fell for it. He even had the motive, would you believe? And he was cunning enough and subtle enough not to overtly remind me of it, knowing that I was bound to come upon it on my own."

Watson looked up sharply. "Motive? What motive?"

"Oh, that ridiculous business he was involved in years ago as a young man when he and the Prince of Wales had a falling out over some incriminating letters. The prince accused him of attempting to blackmail him and actually challenged him to a duel over the matter, remember? It was years before things were patched up between them."

Watson recalled the matter. "Ah, yes. Lord Randolph was exiled to some post in Ireland, was he not? His career in politics almost ruined?"

"Just so. And the entire Marlborough clan was banished from court for some period of time as well. The whole family was shut out of the Palace, which meant it was snubbed by all of society, and it was quite a while before things were patched up and they were welcomed back. Churchill counted on me remembering the entire sordid business. He also counted on human nature coming to the fore. He and the Prince of Wales actually became quite close again, but he knew that I, in retrospect, like so many others, would question whether his regard for the prince was truly genuine. He guessed that in casting about for a motive, I would reject it as mere pretense and would come to the false conclusion that he, Churchill, still carried a grudge, still smarted at his treatment after all those years, and was vengeful enough or venal enough to even want to take it out on the prince's eldest son. And, by God, that is exactly the conclusion I did come to! He played me like a fine instrument. And he had me fooled completely. He even pretended to have prior knowledge of my having received that parcel from the Ripper – that damnable slice of kidney." Holmes's eyes shone with respect as he recalled the details of Churchill's deception. "How very subtle he was about it!" he said admiringly. "How very cunning indeed!"

Watson's brows came together. "But I don't understand. You said, *pretended* to know. He seemed, at the time, to know very much indeed."

"That's just it – your word, *seemed,* is the key one. The fact of the matter is, he came here on that day not only to fish for information, but, like the canny angler that he was, to spread chum in his wake as well – to leave a scent behind. A false scent, naturally. His whole purpose was to arouse my suspicion. And he succeeded admirably. When he entered these rooms, he of course had no way of knowing I had received that parcel from the Ripper. It was I who told him, if you recall, and he had the presence of mind to not look surprised. Ha!" Holmes shook his head from side to side, his eyes gleaming at the memory. "How well he planted the seed of suspicion in my mind! Yet, he did express surprise a minute or two later when I lied and told him that no note accompanied the parcel, remember?"

Watson nodded in dumb silence.

"My immediate reaction to that was further suspicion. I suspected him of *knowing* that a note had been included. Well, I was wrong. Yes, he was surprised; of course he was surprised! It was a natural reaction on his part, after all. One would *expect* such a singular offering to be accompanied by a communication of some sort." He gave a sardonic laugh. "I mean, it just isn't *done* to send someone a human organ through Her Majesty's mails without even a word of explanation!"

Shaking his head again, he put down his pipe. "I was guilty of misreading his reaction. Of seeing in it what I wanted to see. I, in short, was guilty of one of the crimes I am always accusing you of, my dear Watson. Of jumping to conclusions and of allowing preconceived notions to prejudice my thinking. How often have I said to you, 'There is nothing more deceptive than an obvious fact?' Well, I ignored my own maxim." His tone turned bitter. "And quite rightly, I was made to suffer for it!"

Watson was no longer listening to his friend. He was busy puzzling over another notion. "But, Holmes, I recall at the time that you made a point of mentioning that Lord Randolph also knew the parcel had been delivered by post rather than by messenger. And he even made reference to it being posted from somewhere within London."

"Yes. And there again I read more into it than I should have. He merely jumped to those conclusions, that's all. He simply *assumed* it." Holmes shook his head ruefully and laughed. "Because it is not something I myself would ever do, I allowed the fact that he was a man of such intellect to mislead me into thinking that the workings of his mind were similar to my own. Since I would never assume anything, I assumed he wouldn't either. How is that for brilliance?" He laughed again despite himself, but there was no humor in it, only bitterness and self-mockery. "Think of it, Watson!" He slammed a fist down onto the arm of his chair. "*Imagine* it! I gave him more credit than he was due and simultaneously ascribed knowledge to him that he did not possess. I both underestimated him and overestimated him at one and the same time. Now, *there* is genius for you! There is brilliance beyond measure!"

Watson threw up his hands in confusion. "I must say, I don't know what to make of any of this, Holmes. I'm at a total loss. If the young prince was not the Ripper, and Lord Randolph wasn't either, who in God's name was?"

Holmes looked down, a faraway look in his eyes. For a moment Watson thought he had not heard the question. Finally, in a barely audible tone Holmes said: "Who, indeed?"

Watson stared at him.

Holmes looked up at last, his eyes lifeless. He avoided Watson's gaze. "The world shall never know," he said. "Nor, to my everlasting chagrin, shall I."

"*What?*" Watson gaped at him now in disbelief. He could not possibly have heard him correctly.

Holmes's eyes met his for just an instant and then quickly looked away again.

"Holmes! You don't mean to tell me the killer's identity remains unknown to you!"

Holmes's response was to spread his arms suddenly and dramatically in an exaggerated gesture of helplessness. He let them drop heavily, as if of their own accord, as if he no longer had the simple strength or the power of will to support their weight. "I haven't a clue as to who he is," he said tiredly. "Not a single clue."

Watson was rendered speechless.

Holmes rubbed his eyes, then put his head back and gazed up at the ceiling. "We have, I fear, one of those occurrences which in fiction is so unacceptable but which in life is so terribly commonplace: A crime without a solution." He gave a dispirited shrug and smiled faintly – a pathetic little half-smile intended to convey an attitude of philosophical resignation, but of course it did not succeed in fooling Watson.

Holmes was obviously upset, and Watson bit his lip in concern. In all the years he had known him, he had never seen him like this. Generally the most self-contained of men, reserved and inexpressive to the point of coldheartedness, he was a man to whom a display of the slightest emotion was abhorrent. But now, as Watson observed him, his fingers were actually trembling and a vein throbbed at his temple.

Could it be that failure had so completely unnerved him? After all, it had always been so foreign to him, so completely outside the realm of his experience. If he ever thought of failure at all, he did so only in abstract terms, for it was not something with which he could even easily identify.

Watson did not know what to say. He was no less taken aback. He, also, had become so accustomed to his friend's invariable success – at almost everything he undertook – that even the possibility of his ever failing had ceased to occur to him.[116]

Holmes looked across at him and smiled gently, as if knowing what was in his mind. Then he rose from his chair and went to the fireplace, propping an arm on the mantel to gaze into the fire. When he spoke again, the words came haltingly. "Sometimes, Watson... sometimes we are forced to make choices, to... perform certain deeds that we would not think of performing ordinarily. A job that must be done – not out of personal preference, but in actual opposition to it. Because there is no alternative; because we simply *must*. Not to put too fine a point on it, but out of a sense of duty, perhaps. Out of loyalty to a higher purpose."

He shrugged. "At least, that is what we tell ourselves, what we delude ourselves into thinking. It somehow seems to make it easier, more palatable, but... well..."

He made a feeble motion with his hand. "I have come to the inescapable conclusion, Watson, that self-delusion is essential to our well-being – as essential as a healthy spleen or liver. It allows us to live with ourselves, you see; it enables us to go on, filtering out the poison that is painful truth." He made a derisive sound. "Fortunately, we as a species seem to be endowed with an infinite capacity to disregard that which is evident. It has been our salvation, you see. We would never have come this far otherwise. We would never have survived."

With almost unsettling calm he resumed his seat and tented his fingers before him in the familiar manner, a bleak, brooding look in his eyes.

Watson could only regard him with bewilderment and anxiety. He did not really understand any of it.

Then Holmes, suddenly becoming aware of his friend's discomfort, and realizing he was the cause of it, shook off his mood. Smiling engagingly, he clapped his hands together loudly, a sharp, startling, punctuating sound – a note of finality, Watson thought. Almost gratefully he took it as a cue and rose to make his departure. But Holmes lifted a hand, causing him to pause a moment.

"You do see," said Holmes, "why all of this must remain confidential, do you not? And why I must ask you to avoid the temptation of putting any of it to paper? You do realize that it must never, *never* see the light of day. You do understand that, naturally." His voice had an intense quality to it.

Watson nodded. "Yes, more's the pity. Of course I do. You have my word on it."

Holmes seemed satisfied. After a moment's further reflection, he smiled. "Of course, should the temptation ever become so great that you must reduce your thoughts to writing after all, you will have the decency to withhold it from publication until well after I am gone, will you not? After *all* of those involved are gone. And, might I suggest, until after you are gone as well? Fifty years should be an appropriate interval, I should think. I have no plans to tread the boards longer than that. No great harm shall be done after fifty years."

He reached for his violin, but hesitated. "Best make it one hundred to be sure," he said. "Yes, one hundred should do nicely. No one shall care then. No one shall even be interested."

Nodding his response, Watson struggled into his coat and reached for his hat and stick. He turned at the door and looked at his friend one last time.

"You *do* know!" he whispered fiercely. "You *do* know which one it was, after all, don't you?"

Holmes glanced up at him quizzically. When he spoke, it was in a quiet, even tone. "There are some things it is best *not* to know, old fellow, some things it is best not even to question."

Subdued and reflective, Watson took his leave, and Holmes began a mournful tune on the Stradivarius, the strains of which filled the rooms of 221B Baker Street for the remainder of the afternoon and into the evening. A haunting, melancholy tune it was, strange and surreal, without melody, without beginning or end. A tune that one heedless of the passage of years might imagine hearing beneath the muffled clip-clop and clatter of a ghostly passing hansom cab, should one have occasion to be in the vicinity of Portman Square on a particularly foggy evening and just happen to turn the corner into a gaslit Baker Street of enduring memory.

A Final Word

♁

"We reach. We grasp. And what is left in our hands at the end?
A shadow."
— *Sherlock Holmes, The Retired Colourman*

F ew events in the annals of violent crime, not even the murders of
kings or the assassinations of major political or religious figures
have aroused as much interest over the years as the deaths in London
in the autumn of 1888 of five common prostitutes.

Their killer has captured the imagination as no other ever has,
becoming one of the most written about, most speculated about, most
thoroughly investigated of all time. Even those gentle souls among
us who may not be all that well versed in the subject of murder, or
personally acquainted with individuals who have homicidal tendencies
— those of us who might have to pause a moment or two before being
able to identify any one of a number of other well-known murderers
in history who have been responsible for far more deaths, or for more
important ones, and whose violent acts have had a far greater impact

on the times in which they lived – even we instantly recognize the name Jack the Ripper. Yet as well known as he is, virtually nothing is known about him.

This, in part, explains our continuing morbid fascination with him: The fact that his identity remains a mystery. This, and of course the unspeakable horror of his crimes, for it is a curious phenomenon that the human animal is, at one and the same time, both repelled and attracted by horror.

But there is more to it than that, of course. There is the sheer audacity of the man and his single-mindedness of purpose: His uncanny ability to stalk his victims and do his grisly work – all in the face of the most elaborate efforts to prevent him from doing so, making fools of the authorities in the process, which in itself is enough to gain him a measure of public approbation. Let's face it, there has to be grudging admiration for the man, despite his crimes, despite his obvious insanity, despite the sheer evil and repugnance of his deeds. And, in spite of ourselves.

After all, he got away with it.

Down through the years, literally *hundreds* of books have been written about the Ripper and his crimes, and the magazine and newspaper articles number in the thousands. There are individuals who have spent lifetimes pursuing the mystery, who have immersed themselves in every aspect of it, who have become authorities in the most trivial details of the crimes and the victims of them. Yet little new light has been shed over time, little the "experts" can agree upon. Indeed, as the years go by, the theories seem to become wilder, the list of suspects longer and more fantastic, the controversy ever deeper, the mystery ever more tantalizing. And the known facts more problematic. Even the number of murders actually committed is a subject for debate: Some say five, or eight, some say eleven, a few say as many as fourteen.

All we can ever be reasonably certain of is that a single individual was responsible for the five murders and mutilations committed between August 31 and November 9, 1888 – those of Mary Anne Nicholls, Annie Chapman, Elizabeth Stride, Catherine Eddowes, and Mary Jane Kelly. Beyond that, there is hardly a fact that is not in dispute (including whether the man was indeed a man – more than one "expert" has theorized that he was a she).[117]

What little we know about the killer has been pieced together from the often conflicting descriptions provided by witnesses who saw him (or thought they saw him, or merely said they saw him), and by police officials and medical examiners who made certain inferences – educated guesses, if you will (and some of them *not* so educated) – based on his modus operandi and on the postmortem examinations of his victims.

This is what we know: He had a mustache, he was five feet six or seven, seemed to be left-handed, seemed to have had a familiarization with the Whitechapel district, *may* have had some knowledge of human anatomy, and *may* have been a member of the upper classes. (If he smoked, his cigarettes were *not* custom-made and gold-tipped as far as is known.)

That is *all* we know. Incredible as it may seem, after all the years of research and investigation and all the hundreds of studies, that – and *only* that – is all we really know about him. And even then there is disagreement. Valid arguments can be made and ample "evidence" submitted to refute most of the above.

Some think, because of the killer's apparent knowledge of anatomy, he was a physician or surgeon. Others think that because he was not all *that* skilled with a knife, he could not have possibly had medical training. He could have been a butcher or slaughterer (there were several in the area). He could have been a cork cutter or a shoemaker. He had demonstrated enough skill with a blade to suggest that he at least had had experience as a deer hunter, a theory that lends support to those who believe he was a member of the upper classes. (All "gentlemen" of the period were assumed to know how to "gralloch" – i.e., disembowel – a deer.) And he could have been none of these things.[118]

It has been theorized by armchair psychiatrists that the killer was probably someone who contracted a venereal disease from a prostitute, had become mentally deranged, and committed the crimes out of revenge – to put right the wrongs that were done to him. Or he was a religious nut whose self-appointed mission in life was to rid the world of fallen women and "excoriate the evil from their bodies."

Some years ago, as an exercise, the FBI put together a profile of the Ripper, and as educated guesses go, it is probably as good as we are going to get: He was a white male, single, in his mid or late twenties, of average intelligence, who in all probability lived alone. "He was not accountable to anyone" and could therefore come and go as he pleased at all hours. He lived in the area of the killings and had an intimate knowledge of its geography. He would not have reacted well with people. He would have been a loner. He would have engaged in erratic behavior. He would have preferred nocturnal activities. In all probability, he was of unsanitary personal habits. He hated women and was probably intimidated by them. He most likely had an unhappy childhood, was probably raised by a woman alone, and may have been sexually molested by that woman. He was, the profile concluded, a "predatory animal."

Over the years, several candidates have been put forward – Scotland Yard's computer printout lists 176 individual suspects – but few of them have stood the test of time and none has survived close scrutiny. After all is said and done, after all the research and all the theorizing, we are no closer to an answer now than we were one hundred years ago. Quite simply, we do not know who the killer was.

As to whether anyone ever did know... that is another question.

There is persistent evidence of an official conspiracy of silence – a cover-up at the highest levels – the purpose of which, one must assume, was either to conceal the identity of the killer or, what is more likely, to hide from the public the depth of ineptitude displayed by the police and various government officials involved in the case, from the cabinet ministerial level on down.

Scotland Yard's files on the Whitechapel murders were supposed to have been officially sealed until 1992 (coincidentally, the one hundredth anniversary of the death of Prince Eddy, if anyone cares to read anything into that). Instead, they were opened to the public in 1988, the one hundredth anniversary of the murders. However, there were some who claimed to have had access to those files earlier, and those individuals indicated that much appeared to be missing. A few went so far as to state that the records seemed to have been *deliberately* purged of essential information, of anything that was of any real value and could possibly lead to the identification of the killer. Time after time we were told of lost archives, stolen letters, purloined documents, mysterious disappearances of pertinent material, files that were purposely destroyed or systematically "sanitized" or simply "misplaced." While this state of affairs has surely been overdrawn and overdramatized, some of it just as surely has taken place. Careful searches, for example, have failed to reveal the whereabouts of the original detailed postmortem report of Catherine Eddowes, prepared by Dr. Frederick Gordon Brown, the City Police surgeon. It is not enough to blame it all on "inefficient record keeping" and "crude file indexing" or the "insufficient budgets" of the agencies responsible for securing the files, as has been the case.

Moreover, private notes and diaries belonging to individuals who were retired officials, or who were otherwise personally involved in the investigations of the murders, or had information pertaining to them, have on several recorded occasions "disappeared" – in at least a few cases within days of an individual's death. Dr. Thomas Stowell's files were destroyed within *hours* of his death by his son, who never explained why and refused to discuss the matter at all. Sir Melville Macnaghten's personal files – he headed the CID and had firsthand knowledge of Scotland Yard's entire investigation – simply "vanished" shortly after his death.

So the possibility of a cover-up cannot be dismissed lightly. The question then remains, why bother to go to such pains unless there was something to hide, something the government, or at least certain highly placed officials within the government, did not wish to have revealed? (It is a question of the trout in the milk, to quote Holmes quoting Thoreau.)

There is another source of frustration: Much of the information that has come down to us is not merely incomplete, but incorrect. For example, the so-called "writing on the wall" found in the passage off Goulston Street following the murder of Catherine Eddowes. As has been pointed out by Richard Whittington-Egan (*A Casebook on Jack the Ripper*), at least seven different versions of that message exist (an indication of how difficult it sometimes is to establish even simple facts of the case). And each version is from a "reliable," respected source, one of them being no less a personage than Sir Henry Smith, who actually saw the original message before it was ordered removed.[119]

The point is, one can't help but wonder whether such instances as this (and there are others that can be given as examples) are the result of carelessness and simple lapses in memory, or whether efforts were made to purposely deceive and mislead.

(It is only fair to say, by the way, that as much as Sir Charles Warren's directive to erase the message from the wall is to be deplored, his motives for doing so at least were pure: To prevent the spread of violence against Jewish residents of the district. And in that he succeeded.)

So much has been written about the Whitechapel murders through the years that it is virtually impossible to keep track of it. In 1972 Alexander Kelly put together a well-organized and highly useful bibliography that had to be updated twelve years later because another one-hundred-odd books and articles on the subject had been published in the intervening period. The revised edition, too, soon became outdated. Jack the Ripper had become a cottage industry.

Much of what has been written, at least in recent years, is well researched and scholarly, but a good deal of what has come down to us over time is, in whole or in part, simply nonsense. The one thing that almost every single "expert" has in common with every other is the ability to articulate logical reasons why the newest most-favored suspect could not *possibly* be the Ripper. Where they all fail – every single one of them – is when they offer their own candidate for the distinction. This is where imagination most often comes into play, where supposition comes to the fore, where data becomes selective and credulity is stretched to the breaking point. Where – in the words of Donald Rumbelow, a former London detective and author of one of the best works on the subject (*Jack the Ripper: The Complete Casebook*) – "every fact is capable of being wrenched into the weirdest of interpretations."

And, as we have seen, it does not help very much to go back to "original" sources, to the writings of those who were on the scene and were directly involved. That, very often, serves only to compound the confusion. Still, it is entertaining, if not always entirely instructive, to review the record.

Among those officials who could have known the identity of the killer, or *might* have known, are the following:

Major General Sir Charles Warren, Commissioner of the Metropolitan Police. His grandson, in his biography of Warren (*The*

Life of General Sir Charles Warren by Watkin W. Williams), wrote: "I cannot not recall that my grandfather... ever stated in writing his personal views on the identity of Jack the Ripper. It was a subject about which he very seldom spoke. My impression is that he believed the murderer to be a sex maniac who committed suicide after the Miller's Court murder (of Mary Jane Kelly) – possibly the young doctor whose body was found in the Thames on December 31, 1888."

Sir Robert Anderson, Assistant Commissioner in charge of the CID of the Metropolitan Police, who claimed to have known who the Ripper was. In his biography (*The Lighter Side of My Official Life*), Anderson wrote that the man was a Polish Jew: "I am almost tempted to disclose the identity of the murderer... But no public benefit would result from such a course, and the traditions of my old department would suffer. I will merely add that the only person who ever had a good view of the murderer unhesitatingly identified the suspect the instant he was confronted with him; but he refused to give evidence against him. In saying that he was a Polish Jew, I am merely stating a definitely ascertained fact."

Lieutenant Colonel Sir Henry Smith, Acting Commissioner of the City Police. Arguing in his memoirs that there was no man living who knew as much about the Whitechapel murders as he did, he was equally as definitive in his viewpoint as Anderson was: "I must admit that, though within five minutes of the perpetrator one night, and with a very fair description of him besides, he completely beat me and every police officer in London; and I have no more idea now where he lived than I had twenty years ago."

(It is hard to believe, albeit possible, that Anderson knew something that Smith did not.)

Sir Melville Macnaghten, Assistant Chief Constable of Scotland Yard who headed the CID from 1903 to 1913. He had access to the complete file and claimed (according to two separate reliable sources) that he had documentary proof of the Ripper's identity, but he burnt all of the papers without explaining why. All Macnaghten would disclose in his memoirs was that he believed the man to be a sexual maniac who "committed suicide on or about the 10th of November 1888."

This is a view shared by his successor, Sir Basil Thompson, who wrote (in *The Story of Scotland Yard*): "The feeling of the CID officers at the time was that they [the murders] were the work of an insane Russian doctor and that the man escaped arrest by committing suicide in the Thames at the end of 1888."

But Macnaghten also left behind a packet of private notes in which, according to his daughter (in a letter to the *New Statesman*, November 7, 1959), he named three individuals whom the police strongly suspected at the time. The names are: Kosminski (no first name can be found for him), Michael Ostrog, and M. J. Druitt.

Kosminski was described as "a Polish Jew who lived in the very heart of the district where the murders were committed" who "had a great hatred of women" and had "strong homicidal tendencies." He was sent to a lunatic asylum around March 1889.

Ostrog was described as "a mad Russian doctor and convict... unquestionably a homicidal maniac [who] was said to have been habitually cruel to women, and for a long time was known to have carried about with him surgical knives and other instruments; his antecedents were of the very worst and his whereabouts at the time of the Whitechapel murders could never be satisfactorily accounted for."

Macnaghten wrote that he was "inclined to exonerate" Kosminski and Ostrog. Druitt was another matter.

Druitt he described as "a doctor of about forty-one years of age and of fairly good family, who disappeared at the time of the Miller's Court murder, and whose body was found floating in the Thames on

December 3, i.e., *seven* (my italics) weeks after the said murder. From private information I have little doubt that his own family suspected this man of being the Whitechapel murderer; and it was alleged that he was sexually insane."

(The notes, from which the above was taken, were written in 1894, six years after the Whitechapel murders, and were copied "almost verbatim" from the original by Major Arthur Griffiths, the Inspector of Prisons and author of *Mysteries of Police and Crime*.)

Macnaghten, who was wrong about Druitt's profession – he was a lawyer, not a doctor – and wrong about the dates – Mary Jane Kelly was murdered in Miller's Court during the night of November 8-9, approximately *three* weeks before Druitt's body was recovered from the river, not *seven* – was probably just as wrong about Druitt being the Ripper.

Chief Inspector Frederick G. Abberline, the Scotland Yard officer who (along with Chief Inspector D. S. Swanson) was in charge of the Ripper investigations. Abberline never wrote his memoirs and, as far as is known, left no notes behind, but was said to be one of the first to suggest the possibility of the perpetrator being a woman. But after his death he was quoted by a close colleague as saying that he believed the killer was George Chapman, the infamous "borough poisoner" who was taken into custody in 1902. Chapman, a Pole whose real name was Severin Antoniovich Klosowski (not to be confused with Kosminski), was the candidate of choice on the part of several officials at Scotland Yard, a view confirmed by Superintendent Arthur Neil in his memoirs *Forty Years of Man-Hunting*.

Yet, Chief Inspector Walter Dew, a young detective assigned to Whitechapel at the time of the murders (it was he who was warned in Miller's Court, the site of Mary Kelly's murder: "For God's sake, don't look!" – see page 299), wrote in his reminiscences that there were no real grounds for believing Chapman/Klosowski to be the Ripper. Said Dew: "I was on the spot, actively engaged throughout the whole series of crimes. I ought to know something about it. Yet I have to confess I am as mystified now as I was then by the man's amazing elusiveness."

Another officer who was directly involved in the investigations, Detective Sergeant Benjamin Leeson, wrote in his memoirs, *Lost London*: "I am afraid I cannot throw any light on the 'Ripper's' identity, but one thing I do know, and that is that amongst the police who were concerned in the case there was a general feeling that a certain doctor, known to me, could have thrown quite a lot of light on the subject. This particular doctor was never far away when the crimes were committed."[120]

After that tantalizing offering, Leeson went on to write: "Many stories and theories have been put forward, but, with one exception, I doubt if any of them had the slightest foundation in fact." The exception, he wrote, was Chapman/Klosowski who, he felt, "could" have been the Ripper.

But then, having slightly cracked the door open, he quickly and firmly slammed it shut again: There lacked proof, he said, there were inconsistencies; the evidence, though strongly suggestive, was inconclusive.

In the final analysis there was only one conclusion he could come to: "Nobody knew," he flatly stated, "and nobody ever will know the true story of Jack the Ripper." When all is said and done, he was probably right.

Or, at least half right.

NOTES

1. It may be only a coincidence, but an "accommodating neighbor" by the name of Anstruther was mentioned in Watson's account of *The Boscombe Valley Mystery*. Watson also had a medical practice in Queen Anne Street at the time, just around the corner from Harley.

2. Holmes and Watson had obviously been to see a performance of the popular success of the 1888 season, *Dr. Jekyll and Mr. Hyde*, which opened at the Lyceum Theater in August of that year with the American actor Richard Mansfield in the title roles.

The Lyceum, which was soon to play a brief role in the Holmes adventure known as *The Sign of the Four*, was coincidentally where the play, *Sherlock Holmes*, starring William Gillette, was first performed in September 1902.

3. It had indeed been an active period for Holmes. According to the great Holmesian authority William S. Baring-Gould (*Sherlock Holmes of Baker Street* and *The Annotated Sherlock Holmes*), the private consulting detective was involved in several cases that summer that Watson never got around to writing up, including *The Bishopsgate Jewel Case* and an affair Watson made passing reference to in *The Sign of the Four* as "the case of the most winning woman Holmes ever knew." The only other reference to be found to a Mrs. Cecil Forrester is also in *The Sign of the Four* in which Watson makes casual mention of Mrs. Forrester's "little domestic complication." This is the first inkling we have that it was an "amusing" complication, and sadly we will never know what made it so.

4. Simpson's dining rooms have survived the years and it is still a popular dining spot in The Strand, located just a few steps away from the entrance to the Hotel Savoy and the Savoy Theater.

5. Inspector (later Chief Inspector) Frederick George Abberline joined the Metropolitan Police in 1863, was promoted to sergeant in 1865 and to inspector in 1873. Detective Sergeant William Thicke had been a member of the Metropolitan Police since 1868 and was well known in the streets of London's East End slums as "Johnny Upright."

6. A reference to this curious habit may be found in *The Musgrave Ritual*, in

which Watson, admitting that while he himself was not the tidiest of individuals, commented: "... When I find a man who keeps his cigars in the coal-scuttle, his tobacco in the toe end of a Persian slipper, and his unanswered correspondence transfixed by a jackknife in the very center of his wooden mantelpiece, then I begin to give myself virtuous airs."

7. G. Lestrade (first name unknown) was a twenty-year veteran inspector with Scotland Yard by 1888. He had been involved in several of Holmes's cases through the years, including *The Hound of the Baskervilles, The Sign of the Four,* and *A Study in Scarlet.* While professing disdain for Holmes's methods, he sought his advice time and time again and advanced his career, in part, on the strength of help that Holmes was able to give him. Holmes, in turn, considered him "the pick of a bad lot... quick and energetic, but conventional... lacking in imagination and normally out of his depth." Watson, in *A Study in Scarlet,* called him a "sallow, rat-faced, dark-eyed fellow," the only thing approaching a description that we have of him.

8. Spitalfields had fallen on hard times long before the Whitechapel murders, being already notorious in the reign of George III, a century earlier, and becoming by 1861, in the words of social reformer Henry Mayhew, "one of the most notorious rookeries for infamous characters in the metropolis." Charles Booth, the pioneer sociologist, called the residents of the district "of the lowest class... vicious, semi-criminal." It was a place, he said, "where murder was considered a dramatic incident, and drunkenness as the buffoonery of the stage."

Jack London, who visited in 1902, the year of Edward VII's coronation, was to write in *The People of the Abyss*: "Spitalfields was a welter of rags and filth, of all manner of loathsome skin diseases, open sores, bruises, grossness, indecency, leering monstrosities, and bestial faces." The women of the area, he was told, "would sell themselves for thru'pence or tu'pence or a stale loaf of bread."

9. Much was made of the fact by social reformers of the times that East London, with a population of 2,000,000 – greater than the total populations of most European cities – had no mortuary worthy of the name despite the area's extremely high death rate. The shed behind the workhouse on Old Montague Street was all there was – "a disgraceful hole-and-corner hovel," *The Daily Telegraph* called it.

10. Holmes had been studying analytical chemistry and "morbid anatomy" at St. Bartholomew's Hospital (or "Bart's" as it is affectionately called) when he and Watson first met in January of 1881, as Watson related in *A Study in Scarlet*:

"Dr. Watson, Mr. Sherlock Holmes," said Stamford, introducing us.

"How are you?" Holmes said cordially, gripping my hand with a strength for which I should hardly have given him credit. "You have been in Afghanistan, I perceive."

A bronze plaque commemorating the event may be found on the wall of the hospital's pathological laboratory.

11. This was from *The Star* of August 31. For some inexplicable reason, Watson was reading a two-day-old newspaper. But he is right about some of the facts being wrong: Mary Anne (Polly) Nicholls was removed to the *mortuary*, where her abdominal wounds were discovered, not the hospital. And, strictly speaking, she had not been disemboweled.

12. It is difficult to appreciate just how badly shaken Londoners were by the Nicholls murder. The brutality of the attack was unprecedented, and sex crimes per se were virtually unknown – so foreign to Victorian England that the murder of Polly Nicholls was not even recognized as a sex crime until years later, the term not having yet been created.

Sir Melville Macnaghten, who was to join Scotland Yard the following year as assistant chief constable in charge of the Criminal Investigation Division, was to write: "No one who was living in London that autumn will forget the terror created by these murders. Even now (1915) I can recall the foggy evenings, and hear again the raucous cries of the newspaper boys: '"Another horrible murder, murder, mutilation, Whitechapel!"'"

13. Strangely, there are only two references to the gasogene in the writings edited by Conan Doyle: one in *A Scandal in Bohemia*, the other in *The Mazarin Stone*. Yet this ingenious apparatus, which produced carbonated water, is certainly among the better-known furnishings of 221B Baker Street. The gasogene, or *Gazogene-Briet* as it was properly called, was of French manufacture and consisted of two wire-bound glass globes, one on top of the other, connected by a glass tube. The lower globe contained water, the upper globe the chemicals for producing the carbonation. Michael Harrison (in *The London of Sherlock Holmes*) thinks it was probably purchased by Holmes at Mondollot Fils's London establishment, 13 Little James Street, Bedford Row.

14. Holmes had at least three dressing gowns, or long lounging robes, that have been mentioned from time to time by Watson: one blue, one purple, and one "mouse-colored." His favorite (based on the number of references to it) would appear to be the latter.

15. This "interesting little matter" could only have been *The Manor House Case*, which Watson mentioned briefly in *The Greek Interpreter* but never bothered to write up, apparently feeling it lacked in dramatic interest. Baring-Gould sets the probable date of its occurrence as Monday, September 3, 1888.

16. Holmes must have been referring to Oscar Wilde's condemnation of fox hunters as being "the unspeakable in pursuit of the uneatable." However, he was somewhat premature in that the line had not yet been written. It was taken from Wilde's play *A Woman of No Importance*, which did not have its London premiere until 1893.

17. The London telegraph system was truly a marvel of the age, and Holmes made frequent use of it, even after the telephone came into wide use. Occupying several of the upper floors of the General Post Office Building at St. Martin's le Grand, the telegraph department employed some 3,000 operators in the 1880s, most of them women. Once a message was received over the wires in the central office, it was rushed by underground pneumatic tube to one of a network of district offices scattered throughout the city, and then by foot messenger to the recipient, often being delivered within minutes of being sent.

18. London's police constables had been known colloquially as both "bobbies" and "peelers" for several years, the names taken from Sir Robert (Bobby) Peel (1788-1850) who, after taking charge of what was then a small disorganized department, made it into the world's foremost metropolitan police force.

19. The crest was that of the Sussex Regiment. Some sources give the date of the postmark as 28 August.

20. Holmes could never be accused of false humility, but it would be misleading to leave the impression that he was a braggart. He was simply honest to a fault. "I cannot agree with those who rank modesty among the virtues," he is on record as saying. "To a logician, all things should be seen exactly as they are, and to underestimate oneself is as much a departure from truth as to exaggerate one's own powers." (*The Greek Interpreter*)

In any event, there can be no doubt that he was indeed the world's leading authority on the subject of tobaccos, being the author of the seminal monograph *Upon the Distinctions Between the Ashes of the Various Tobaccos*. (See *The Sign of the Four*.)

21. Of the Baker Street Irregulars, Watson quotes Holmes as remarking (in *A Study*

in Scarlet): "There's more work to be got out of one of those little beggars than out of a dozen of the force. The mere sight of an official-looking person seals men's lips. These youngsters, however, go everywhere and hear everything. They are as sharp as needles."

Holmes employed the Irregulars to good advantage in several cases, including *The Sign of the Four, The Crooked Man,* and *The Disappearance of Lady Frances Carfax.* This description of Wiggins, by the way, is somewhat more detailed than any found in Watson's earlier accounts, although this is not the first time he was referred to by Watson as "unsavory and insignificant." (See *A Study in Scarlet.*)

22. This would have been a park-keeper's wife by the name of Elizabeth Long, who testified at Annie Chapman's inquest that she was on her way to early morning market when she also saw and heard the man who was with Annie. She confirmed the conversation "Dicko" heard, but her description varies somewhat. He was indeed wearing a deerstalker and long coat, she told police, but his accent was that of a foreigner, not of a cultured English gentleman. Since he had his back turned to her as she passed, she did not see his face.

23. One authority, Tom Cullen (*Autumn of Terror*), says that according to some "witnesses" who claimed to have seen him, the man carried a Gladstone bag (what was then known in America as a "carpet bag"). Others claimed he carried a bag of a shiny black oilcloth, or "American cloth" as the Victorians called it. Such bags, says Cullen, were popular novelties in the '80s, but after the murders began, anyone spotted carrying one in the East End "was not only in peril of arrest, but in positive danger of his life."

24. Watson, by alluding to socialists "who are always stirring up so much trouble," may have been thinking about two events that rocked England's complacent upper classes in the mid-1880s: A riot, during the winter of 1886-87, of unemployed dockworkers and laborers who rampaged and looted their way through Piccadilly and Mayfair before being dispersed; and the events of "Bloody Sunday" in November 1887, both widely believed to have been sparked by socialist agitators. "Bloody Sunday" occurred when troops were called out to disband thousands of unemployed workers who were camping out in Trafalgar Square and St. James's Park in protest. Altogether four thousand constables, reinforced by grenadiers and mounted cavalry, were deployed to break up the mob, described by the conservative press as "a foul camp of vagrants" and "the scum of London." A pitched battle ensued, and before the day was over hundreds were injured and more than three hundred arrested.

25. To add to the confusion, when the headquarters of the Metropolitan Police moved to larger quarters on the Victoria Embankment in 1891, the new building became known as *New* Scotland Yard and the old site became *Great* Scotland Yard (originally named because it occupied the site of a palace maintained in medieval times for visiting Kings of Scotland).

It did not end there. Approximately one hundred years later, police headquarters was to be moved yet again, this time to a modern glass office block at Broadway and Victoria Street. It is known as the "new" New Scotland Yard.

26. As a matter of fact, we know now that the CID was then in a badly demoralized state due in part to the forced resignation, that previous August, of its popular and able chief, Assistant Commissioner James Monro. Monro had been replaced by barrister and socialite Sir Robert Anderson, who was physically, and probably professionally, unsuited for his new post. (He immediately left on a month's holiday in Switzerland upon his appointment, thus leaving the detective branch without an effective head during what was to be a highly critical period.)

27. Major General Sir Charles Warren, Royal Engineers, Commissioner of the Metropolitan Police from 1886 to 1888.

Cullen, in *Autumn of Terror*, comments that Queen Victoria "could hardly have been less fortunate in her choice" of commissioner than Warren, "whose chief qualifications for the... post seems to have been his ability to handle the Bantu in Grinqualand West." His previous experience in police work was in dealing with the Boers in South Africa, where he earned a reputation as an efficient but ruthless keeper of the peace.

Watson's portrayal of Warren in this account may appear to be broadly drawn, but it is not. Warren's physical description and demeanor, and his penchant for wearing his general's uniform with an old-fashioned policeman's "chimney pot" hat, matches existent portraits of him. Wrote one contemporary: "He has a massive cavalry mustache in the Prussian style, curling below the edges of his mouth, an exceptional silver-brown growth that is distractingly different in color from the hair on his head, which is jet-black and pomaded into a severe, straight line across his forehead."

Warren habitually wore a monocle, which caused a perpetual frown, and he has been described by another source as "stiff-necked and overly military in bearing." It was "Bloody Sunday" that earned him his knighthood (and the enmity of London's working-class population): He was the one who commanded the troops and police forces that routed the unemployed squatters from Trafalgar Square. "He sat a horse well," wrote Cullen, "but his appointment as police chief was little short of a national disaster."

28. Clarences was a nearby public house popular among off-duty police officers of the detective branch; Faulkner's Hotel (which still exists as the Adelphi) was located in nearby Villiers Street and was a favorite of Holmes and Watson for both its two-shilling table d'hote and its Turkish bath. "Both Holmes and I had a weakness for the Turkish bath," wrote Watson in *The Illustrious Client.* "It was over a smoke in the pleasant lassitude of the drying room that I found him less reticent and more human than anywhere else." (See *The Disappearance of Lady Francis Carfax* and *The Illustrious Client.*)

29. Holmes himself was to use the very same quote (although in its entirety and in the original German) a week or so later during his involvement in *The Sign of the Four.* It is taken from *Faust,* Part I, and reads: *"Wir sind gewohnt, dass die Menschen verhöhnen, Was sie nicht verstehen."* ("We are accustomed to seeing that man despises what he does not understand.") "Goethe," said Holmes, "is always pithy."

30. Curiously, Watson quotes Holmes as speaking the very same words in the opening pages of *The Sign of the Four.* Possibly he referred to it and other published cases when putting together his notes for this one.

31. Again, see *The Sign of the Four.* The reference is, of course, to Miss Mary Morstan, Watson's future bride.

32. See *The Greek Interpreter.*

33. Watson, while serving as an army surgeon in Afghanistan, was severely wounded during the battle of Maiwand and, as a result, was invalided from the service with a pension shortly before his introduction to Holmes in 1881. The precise location of his wound (or wounds) has been the subject of considerable speculation and controversy over the years, because of Watson's own conflicting assertions. At one point he tells us, "I was struck on the shoulder by a Jezail bullet, which shattered the bone and grazed the subclavian artery." (*A Study in Scarlet.*) Later we are told it was not his shoulder, but his *arm*: "His left arm has been injured," says Holmes. "He holds it stiff and in an unnatural manner." But at still another point we find Watson nursing his *leg*: "I had had a Jezail bullet through it sometime before," he writes, later describing himself as "... a half-pay officer with a damaged *tendo Achillis*" (*The Sign of the Four*).

Countless learned essays have been written about this paradox over the years, falling into three general categories: "pro-leg," "pro-shoulder," and "pro-leg *and* shoulder." Clearly the most rational theory is the one first espoused by Mr. R. M.

McLaren ("Doctor Watson: Punter or Speculator?" *The Sherlock Holmes Journal,* Vol. I, No. I, May 1952): "The wound sustained by Watson in Afghanistan was an extraordinary one, the bullet having entered his shoulder and emerged from his leg..."

34. The tea and scones are indeed excellent at the Savoy, but they were not in 1888. Mycroft had anticipated the hotel's arrival on the London scene by a full year (which perhaps accounts for Watson's surprise). Still one of the world's grandest hostelries, the Savoy contained many innovations when it first opened its doors in 1889 (charging a hefty eight shillings a night for a single room). However, it was the Savoy *Theater* that was among the first buildings in London to be illuminated by electricity, not the hotel.

35. See *The Greek Interpreter*.

36. While this particular anecdote may or may not have been true, other stories concerning London's venerable gentlemen's clubs have become legendary, such as the one concerning Lord Glasgow, who after flinging a waiter who displeased him through a window, calmly instructed the club's secretary to "put him on my bill."

37. "Bertie," naturally, was none other than H.R.H. Albert Edward, Prince of Wales, the future King Edward VII. Family members and a few close intimates were permitted on private occasions to call him by the diminutive of his first name.

38. Mycroft had to have been referring to Sir Henry Matthews, Home Secretary in the government of Prime Minister Lord Salisbury. Matthews's ministry had jurisdiction over Scotland Yard.

39. We do not know precisely what position Mycroft Holmes held in government. Presumably he was a member of the civil service, ostensibly an auditor in "some" of the government departments (see *The Greek Interpreter*). But according to no less a reliable source than Sherlock Holmes himself, Mycroft occasionally *was* the British government:

"The same great powers I have turned to the detection of crime, he has used for this particular business. The conclusions of every department are passed to him, and he is the central exchange, the clearing house, which makes out the balance. All other men are specialists, but his specialism is omniscience... in that great brain of his everything is pigeon-holed, and can be handed out in an instant. Again and again his word has decided national policy." (See *The Bruce-Parkington Plans*.)

40. See *The Bruce-Parkington Plans.*

41. Baring-Gould dates Holmes's and Watson's involvement in *The Hound of the Baskervilles* as being between September 25 and October 20 of 1888. If so, the pair would have spent most of September 26 engaged in that case, part of it indeed in Regent Street as deduced by Mycroft, not in perusing the shops, but rather in attempting to chase down the man who was stalking Sir Henry Baskerville. Watson wrote that following that escapade he and Holmes dallied at "one of the Bond Street picture-galleries" before keeping their luncheon appointment with Sir Henry and Dr. Mortimer at the Northumberland Hotel. Afterward, according to Watson in *The Hound of the Baskervilles*, they returned to Baker Street, where, "all afternoon and late into the evening he (Holmes) sat lost in tobacco and thought." But as we now know, at least part of the evening was spent with Mycroft at the Diogenes Club.

Obviously, Mycroft's deductions made from Watson's walking stick missed the mark, but apparently neither Holmes nor Watson had the heart to tell him so.
It is interesting to note, by the way, that the building that housed the Northumberland Hotel still stands at number 11 Northumberland Street. Except it is now known as the Sherlock Holmes Tavern.

42. Salisbury also said that with his mood swings, Lord Randolph had a temperament that was basically feminine, "and I have never been able to get on with women."

43. It is difficult to know what scandal Lord Randolph was referring to, the Prince of Wales was involved in so many of them – including one twelve years earlier involving Lord Randolph himself, a complicated business with comic opera overtones, having to do with a secret affair the prince previously had with another man's wife (the Earl of Aylesford's, a close friend of his), who subsequently was having an *open* affair with Lord Randolph's older brother, George. Randolph, in a naive effort to keep his brother's name out of a potentially messy divorce trial (all of the aristocracy's divorce trials in Victorian England were potentially messy), foolishly went to the Princess of Wales with some letters the prince had written to Lady Aylesford sometime earlier. His motive was to get the princess to convince her husband to bring pressure on Lord Aylesford to call off the divorce proceedings and avoid a major scandal. To no one's surprise but Lord Randolph's, the prince became furious, accused him of blackmail, and challenged him to a duel. The Queen got wind of it and the duel never took place, of course. Instead, Lord Randolph was banished to a government post in Ireland and the prince was banished for a time from his mother's sight (a relief to both of them, according to one observer).

The affair is often held up as proof, if proof be needed, that the true measure of Victorian respectability, among the upper classes, at least, lay not in refraining from extramarital sex, but in engaging in it with discretion. Or, as one member of society put it: "It doesn't matter what you do, as long as you don't do it in the street and frighten the horses."

Be that as it may, Holmes could not have been involved in these goings-on. He was still attending Cambridge at the time and did not start his consulting practice until the following year, 1877.

44. The son Lord Randolph was referring to was no doubt the future prime minister, Sir Winston Churchill.

45. Holmes's earlier statement that he and Watson "are to go down to Dartmoor on Saturday" and the subsequent change in plans are of more than incidental interest. In Watson's published account of the Baskerville case we are told that he did indeed accompany Sir Henry and Dr. Mortimer to Dartmoor by himself. Holmes remained behind, giving the excuse that he was occupied with another matter, and would follow sometime shortly thereafter ("At the present instant one of the most revered names in England is being besmirched by a blackmailer, and only I can stop a disastrous scandal"). It is obvious only now what the other matter really was.

46. *The Adventure of the Creeping Man*, which according to Baring-Gould took place in September 1903. Interestingly enough, Holmes *was* to admit a dependence of a sort upon his friend. In *The Adventure of the Blanched Soldier*, Holmes wrote: "If I burden myself with a companion in my various little inquiries, it is not done out of sentiment or caprice, but it is that Watson has some remarkable characteristics of his own to which in his modesty he has given small attention amid his exaggerated estimates of my own performances." And, he is recorded as saying to Watson (in *The Hound of the Baskervilles*), "It may be that you are not yourself luminous, but you are a conductor of light. Some people without possessing genius have a remarkable power of stimulating it."

47. There is some disagreement as to the date of receipt of this now-famous (or, rather, infamous) letter, which first introduced to the world the sobriquet "Jack the Ripper." Some sources maintain the letter, though dated September 25, was not postmarked until the 28th, while others say the Central News Agency *received* it on the 27th, a day earlier. In any event, its first publication by the press was not until the 30th.

48. Thousands was more like it. Watkin W. Williams, in his biography of his grandfather, Sir Charles Warren, claimed that Scotland Yard was receiving 1,200 letters a day at the height of the Whitechapel murders, while other sources suggest a more realistic figure of about 1,400 a month.

49. That Holmes was an expert in handwriting analysis, and far ahead of his time in that particular science, is indisputable. Jack Tracy, in *The Encyclopaedia Sherlockiana*, lists six separate cases in which Holmes displayed his skill in this specialty to help solve a crime. In *The Reigate Squires* Holmes went so far as to claim the ability to deduce from a man's handwriting not only his character and age, but even the state of his health.

50. Among his other skills, Holmes was a past master in the art of "tailing" (and, of course, was the first to admit it). Witness this exchange between Holmes and Sterndale in *The Adventure of the Devil's Foot*:

HOLMES:	You went to the vicarage, waited outside it for some time, and finally returned to your cottage.
STERNDALE:	How do you know that?
HOLMES:	I followed you.
STERNDALE:	I saw no one.
HOLMES:	That is what you might expect to see when I follow you.

51. In *The Adventure of the Empty House*, Watson was to write: "Holmes's knowledge of the byways of London was extraordinary..." And in *The Red-Headed League*, Holmes is quoted as saying: "It is a hobby of mine to have an exact knowledge of London."

52. While it is true that portions of human anatomy were recovered from the Thames during this period, none of them were ever tied to the Whitechapel killings. A severed arm fished out of the river on Tuesday, September 11, was indeed found to belong to a torso unearthed in the excavation being dug for the new police headquarters building. Dubbed "The Whitehall Mystery" by the press, the affair remains a mystery to this day. (See *Autumn of Terror* by Tom Cullen.)

53. Wrote Benjamin Disraeli of Victorian Britain: "There are two nations between whom (sic) there is no intercourse and no sympathy; who are as ignorant of each other's habits, thoughts, and feelings, as if they were dwellers in different zones, or inhabitants of different planets; who are formed by a different breeding, are fed by a

different food, are ordered by different manners, and are not governed by the same laws... the rich and the poor."

54. Temple Bar, a gate which had obstructed traffic at the boundary of the City for years, was removed in 1878, but the place where it stood continues to bear the name and continues to mark the boundary (and continues to suffer from clogged traffic). Traditionally, the sovereign requires the Lord Mayor's "permission" to cross the line – one of those curious customs the English take to heart, this one going back to a day in 1588 when Elizabeth I entered the City to attend a service of thanksgiving at St. Paul's Cathedral following the defeat of the Spanish Armada.

55. One cannot question the assertion that Sir Henry was a man of some wit. His memoirs were to be subtitled *The Story of Sixty Years, Most of Them Misspent.*

56. There is no way of knowing whether there is any truth to the legend. Mitre Square, in the sixteenth century, was the site of the Priory of the Holy Trinity, and the murder was supposed to have occurred in front of the high altar. According to legend, a woman, kneeling in prayer, was seized from behind and stabbed by a crazed monk by the name of Brother Martin, who then plunged the knife into his own heart – an act, it was widely believed, that put a curse on the place forevermore.

57. Inspector James McWilliam, who headed the Detective Department of the City Police.

58. The Bertillon system, the first "scientific" method of criminal identification, was developed by Alphonse Bertillon (1853-1914) and was based on the classification of skeletal and other body measurements and characteristics. It was officially adopted by the French police in 1888 and soon after by authorities in other countries. Fingerprinting was first used in connection with the Bertillon system as only a supplementary measure; it was not until after the first practical classification of fingerprints by Sir Francis Galton in 1891 that it achieved wide acceptance by criminologists and in time supplanted the Bertillon system altogether. Scotland Yard, in 1901, was one of the first police agencies to adopt the Galton system.

Holmes expressed admiration for Bertillon's system of measurements in Watson's account of the case, entitled *The Naval Treaty*, but while fingerprints played a role in at least seven of his recorded cases, there is no indication that he ever endorsed the idea of fingerprinting criminals as a means of identification. Probably for good reason; as Michael Harrison points out (*In the Footsteps of Sherlock Holmes*), it would be only natural for Holmes to be skeptical of any theory that was intrinsically unproven and unprovable.

The Bertillon system in time became discredited, as did Bertillon himself – he spent years trying to prove that a diabolically clever Alfred Dreyfus actually forged his *own* handwriting in the infamous spy scandal which rocked the French Army at the turn of the century. (All of which goes to prove that Holmes's judgment was not *always* infallible.)

59. Sir Robert Anderson, who was to head the CID, expressed the opinion in his autobiography (*The Lighter Side of My Official Life*) that "an enterprising journalist" was the author of the correspondence. His view was shared by Assistant Chief Constable (and later Commissioner) Sir Melville Macnaghten, who even claimed to know the identity of the journalist responsible (though he never named him). All of this has been hotly disputed, and the authenticity of the correspondence remains in dispute.

Modern handwriting analysis reveals that whoever the author was, he had a "propensity to cruelly perverted sexuality to a degree that even the most casual amateur graphologist could hardly mistake." (See C. M. MacCleod, "Ripper Handwriting Analysis," *The Criminologist*, August 1968.)

60. The now-famous Sherlock Holmes blood test was probably perfected by him in 1881, but did not achieve worldwide recognition until 1887, when mention of it was made in *A Study in Scarlet*. Because the chemistry involved was not revealed at the time, a fierce debate raged among chemists for nearly a century over what chemicals were actually used in the test. The matter was finally (?) put to rest in 1987 with the publication of two learned papers in *The Baker Street Journal*, one by Raymond J. McGowan (March 1987), the other by Christine L. Huber (December 1987). Experiments performed by each of them independently indicated that Holmes must have used one or the other combinations of chemicals mentioned in this passage. Now we know he experimented with both.

61. See *The Sign of the Four*.

62. Nowhere else is it recorded that Holmes ever felt guilty over the acquisition of his violin, but he certainly should have. According to his own reckoning, it was worth at least five hundred guineas (around $2,500 in the dollars of the 1880s), but he purchased it for only 55 shillings, a mere $13.75. Watson wrote that Holmes, "with great exultation," told of obtaining the Stradivarius from "a Jew broker's in Tottenham Court" for that sum, but he didn't say precisely when. (See *The Cardboard Box*.)

63. Arthur Morrison in *Tales of Mean Streets.*

64. Medical accounts of the period indicate that most children in the East End were not only undernourished but physically and mentally underdeveloped, and the infant mortality rate was considerably higher than the national average: Fifty-five percent died before they reached the age of five.

65. The work among the poor performed by the Barnetts in the East End was legendary. In time Mrs. Barnett was to be created a Dame of the British Empire in recognition of her services.

Dr. Thomas Barnardo, known as the "Father of Nobody's Children," was credited with rescuing, unbelievably, over 12,000 of them from the slums.

66. This observation goes a long way toward explaining why Watson's accounts of Holmes's cases are replete with conflicting dates, a state of affairs that has long caused dismay, confusion, and controversy among Sherlockian scholars. Obviously, Watson had a prudent editor and cautious lawyer.

The man credited with being Watson's literary agent and editor, Arthur Conan Doyle, admittedly took a cavalier approach to checking out his facts. Said he: "... It has always seemed to me that so long as you produce your dramatic effect, accuracy of detail matters little."

67. Oscar Wilde's active literary and theatrical career was yet to come, as was the notorious sex scandal involving him and Lord Alfred Douglas, the young son of the Marquess of Queensbury. The affair, which ended up in the courts, ultimately ruined Wilde's reputation and resulted in a prison sentence for him, followed by self-imposed exile to France. However, even at this early period in his life, he had already become the toast of avant-garde London, an arbiter of "good taste," and the acknowledged leader of the so-called Aesthetic Movement.

68. George Bernard Shaw would have been in his early thirties at the time of this meeting. While he had yet to write any of the plays for which he would later become justly famous, he had already begun making a name for himself as a critic and social reformer. It is interesting to conjecture that the idea for his "Pygmalion" may have resulted from this one casual meeting with Holmes – all the *more* interesting when one stops to consider that the only comment Shaw ever made about the great detective was when he was quoted as saying: "Sherlock Holmes was a drug addict without a single amiable trait."

69. Dr. Openshaw was actually with the Pathology Department of London Hospital. He had already confirmed the authenticity of the contents of an earlier package from the Ripper, one sent on October 16 to Mr. George Lusk, the chairman of the Whitechapel Vigilance Committee. It was the other portion of the missing kidney. Accompanying it was a note addressed "From Hell:"

> Mr. Lusk
>
>   *Sir I send you half the Kidne I took from one woman prasarved it for you tother piece I fried and ate it was very nise I may send you the bloody knif that took it out if you only wate whil longer*
>
>   *Catch me when you can, Mishter Lusk.*

70. The "patriotic sentiment" was the initials *V.R.* for Victoria Regina, spelled out by Holmes "in one of his queer humors" with the aid of a target pistol, according to Watson.

"I have always held," wrote Watson, "that pistol practice should distinctly be an open-air pastime; and when Holmes in one of his queer humors would sit in an armchair with his hair-trigger and a hundred Boxer cartridges, and proceed to adorn the opposite wall with a patriotic V.R. done in bullet-pocks, I felt strongly that neither the atmosphere nor the appearance of our room was improved by it." (See *The Musgrave Ritual.*)

71. William Ewart Gladstone (1809-1898), called "the Grand Old Man" by his contemporaries (affectionately by his admirers, derisively by his detractors), was four times prime minister of Great Britain, the leading social reformer of Victorian England, and the dominant figure of the Liberal Party for almost thirty years. A deeply religious and highly moral man ("insufferably self-righteous," was how one critic described him), he had the curious habit of scouring the streets at night for "unfortunate young women" whom, it is said, he would "take home to his wife and lecture."

Queen Victoria, who disliked Gladstone intensely – as much for his politics as for his patronizing manner (she complained that he had the habit of addressing her as if she were a public meeting) – was well aware of his nocturnal activities and suspected him of much worse. But it is unlikely he was capable of energetic murder. He was seventy-nine years old at the time.

72. The fact that the Ripper murders all occurred at either the beginning or end of the month, when the moon was either in its first phase or its last, led to some elaborate theories (some of them from respected scientists of the day) regarding "lunar madness."

73. James Monro, the popular and able former assistant commissioner and head of the CID, had been forced out of office by Warren the previous August.

74. The Queen was extremely upset by the East End murders; her diary during this period contained several entries pertaining to them, and she bombarded Salisbury, Matthews, and other officials with memoranda demanding "the absolute necessity for some very decided action." She even made suggestions pertaining to improved street lighting, better training for detectives, and increased police patrols: "All these courts must be lit, and our detectives improved," she wrote to Lord Salisbury. "They are not what they should be."

75. The Prince of Wales's secretary wrote to Queen Victoria's on one occasion: "I ask again, *who* is it tells her these things?" According to Dulcie M. Ashdown (*Queen Victoria's Family*), the queen was very well informed about her grandson's activities, as she was about most things concerning her large and far-flung family. The Queen felt Prince Eddy "was by no means suited to become king. He had little intelligence, little application, no interest in politics, no firm moral principles to make up for the other defects, and not one vestige of likeness to his sainted grandfather, Prince Albert. To the Queen, he was even more of a disappointment than his father had been."

Mycroft's assessment of him was an accurate one. Stanley Weintraub (in *Victoria: An Intimate Biography*) writes: "Eddy was so backward and lethargic as to be nearly uneducable. He had a reputation for taciturnity, but only because he had nothing to say. He could barely read, had inherited deafness from his mother, had a drooping, vacant face that some women – and perhaps some men – found attractive."

Wrote one of Prince Eddy's tutors to the Prince of Wales in 1879: "He fails not in one or two subjects, but in all. The abnormally dormant condition of his mind, which deprives him of the ability to fix his attention to any given subject for more than a few minutes consecutively rules out any lingering hope that it might be possible to send him to a public school." And in 1880: "Prince Eddy sits listless and vacant and wastes as much time in doing nothing as he ever wasted... This weakness of brain, this feebleness and lack of power to grasp almost anything put before him, is manifested... also in his hours of recreation and social intercourse. It is a fault of nature."

76. This brief discussion between Holmes and his brother is of more than passing interest. Britain's rigid social structure lay at the core of the class struggles taking place in England at that time in its history – class struggles brought about by the extreme social inequities that had always existed but had become more apparent as

the country became more heavily industrialized. It was this to which the East End murders helped call attention.

Even after the reforms of 1884, only one man in five was eligible to vote: England and its Empire were governed by men of the upper classes who, by virtue of their birthright, were trained to rule, just as those of the middle and lower classes were trained to submit to that rule. That members of the aristocracy considered themselves "better" than the middle and lower classes was a premise, interestingly enough, that seemed to be readily accepted by *all* concerned. An Englishman's fate was decided at birth, as it had been since feudal times, and knowing one's "place" was a foregone conclusion.

It was this firm, almost congenital belief in obedience – "absolute obedience," in the words of Mycroft, "to God, the Queen, and one's betters, whoever they may be" – that was the foundation of English Victorian society, a society characterized by Lord Palmerston, who served as prime minister earlier in the period, as being one "in which every class accepts with cheerfulness the lot which providence has assigned to it..."

77. Robert Arthur Talbot Gascoyne Cecil, 3rd Marquess of Salisbury (1830-1903), was Conservative prime minister of Great Britain on three separate occasions: Briefly in 1885, again from 1886 to 1891, and finally from 1895 to 1902.

Salisbury was perhaps the greatest of the many who headed the government during Victoria's long reign (Melbourne and Disraeli notwithstanding). Certainly he was the most highly principled, often opposing his own party in matters that ran counter to his moral views, sometimes to the detriment of his own career. (Disraeli once compared him with "a madman whose delusion it was to believe himself the one sane person in a world of lunatics." Years later he was to call him "the only man of real courage that it has ever been my lot to work with.")

78. Philip Magnus, in *King Edward VII*, says the Prince of Wales formed his own club in a fit of pique in 1869, when the club officers of Whites refused his request to lift a ban on smoking in the morning room. Located at 52 Pall Mall, the Marlborough Club remained in existence until 1952, when rising costs and a declining membership caused it to be torn down to make room for a modern skyscraper.

79. Not surprising, after all, when one considers that the Prince of Wales was more German than English. His father, Prince Albert, was of the House of Saxe-Coburg-Gotha, as was his maternal grandmother, Princess Mary Louisa Victoria (Victoria and Albert were cousins). His maternal grandfather, the Duke of Kent, was the fourth son of George III, and as such was descended from the German House of Hanover.

80. The prince's treatment of his friend Christopher Sykes is well documented. Wrote Louis Auchincloss (in *Persons of Consequence*): "Sykes used to submit, with a frozen impassivity that only more excited the Tudor mirth, while the Prince, amid the yelps of his sycophantic entourage, would pour brandy over his head, burn his hand with a cigarette, or shove him under the billiard table and poke him with a cue."

Sykes is believed to have gone through a fortune entertaining the prince and his cronies: It is said that his sister one day appeared at Marlborough House to inform the prince that his friend was on the verge of bankruptcy, and he was persuaded to clear up the most pressing debts.

81. In those days there were up to ten mail deliveries a day in London.

82. We will probably never know for certain the reasons behind the antagonism between Holmes and the future *King Edward VII*, but there is considerable evidence that Irene Adler had something to do with it. The late Edgar Smith, a preeminent Sherlockian scholar of his day, theorized that "the Hereditary King of Bohemia" in the case involving Miss Adler, *A Scandal in Bohemia*, was in reality the Prince of Wales thinly disguised, and this fragment of discussion between Holmes and Watson tends to support that view. We know that the events dealt with in *A Scandal in Bohemia* occurred in March 1888 (the same month and year, according to Watson in *this* account, that the Prince of Wales visited Baker Street "on a matter of some delicacy and extreme urgency"). And we know that Holmes took an almost instant dislike to "the King" in that affair, going so far as to ignore his hand when it was held out to him at the conclusion of the case.

It may also be that Holmes's hostility was, in part, a reaction to the Prince of Wales's personality. Variously described by those who knew him as "the first gentleman of Europe" and "fat, vulgar, dreadful Edward," the prince evidently appeared to Holmes as being more the latter than the former.

Still, in later years, after Edward ascended the throne, Holmes was to be of service to him yet again, the exact nature of that service remaining unknown, though it was of sufficient magnitude for an offer of a knighthood to have been made as a result. Holmes, as we know, declined it. (See *The Adventure of the Three Garridebs*.)

83. Buckingham Palace did not become the official residence of the reigning monarch until Victoria's accession to the throne. Prior to that time St. James's Palace bore that distinction, and to this day foreign ambassadors are still accredited to "the Court of St. James."

84. "Everyone was there: Tum-Tum, Mrs. Tum, and the five little Tums," wrote the future Lord Darby in a letter describing a wedding he had attended. (See *Edward and the Edwardians* by Phillippe Jullian.)

85. Sir James Fitzjames Stephen (1829-1894) was a noted jurist and legal scholar and the author of, among other works, *The History of the Criminal Law of England* (1883). Unfortunately, he is best remembered for presiding over the trial (in 1888) of the notorious Mrs. Maybrick, accused of having poisoned her husband with arsenic – a trial he so badly mishandled that the police had to be called in to protect him from the public. He was forced to retire from the bench in 1891, diagnosed as suffering from "brain disease."

The younger Stephen, James Kenneth, appeared in every way to be an ideal choice as tutor and companion to the young heir to the throne. He was described as "a man of striking personality" who "fascinated not only the men of his own age but also those of an older generation with his rare physical beauty and his quite unusual intellectual brilliance." Wrote a contemporary: "He was by general consent the ablest of the younger generation... no better choice could have been made."

86. Albert Victor and his younger brother (the future King George V) were sent on an extensive world cruise as midshipmen aboard a naval vessel when still in their early teens. Young George thrived on it (he was to become known as the "Sailor King"); young Albert Victor, a year older, was generally miserable. (See *The Cruise of HMS Bacchante*, 1879-1882 by Reverend John Neale Dalton.)

87. The 10th Hussars, raised in 1715 by King George I (as the 10th Dragoons), fought and distinguished themselves in countless campaigns through the years, including Waterloo, the Crimea, Egypt, and Afghanistan, but achieved the largest measure of their fame as being the regiment of the dashing Beau Brummell, who, in 1806, designed the regiment's uniforms.

88. Most Sherlockian scholars agree that there was not one page named Billy, but two. The first was mentioned in *The Valley of Fear* (which Baring-Gould dates as having taken place in January 1888 and Christopher Morley dates a year later); the second, not until some years later, in *The Problem of Thor Bridge* (circa October 1900) and *The Adventure of the Mazarin Stone* (the summer of 1903, according to Baring-Gould). We know that the second Billy was "young but very wise and tactful." We are told nothing at all about the first in any of Watson's previous writings.

89. Wrote Watson in his only other reference to Johnson: "With the glamour of his two convictions upon him, he had the entree of every nightclub, doss-house and gambling-den in the town, and his quick observation and active brain made him an ideal agent for gaining information. Had he been a "nark" of the police, he would soon have been exposed, but as he dealt with cases which never came directly into the courts, his activities were never realized by his companions." (See *The Illustrious Client*.)

90. Rhyming slang, widely spoken in the East End, was native to the cockney stronghold of Cheapside, and for years it was employed as almost a "secret" language by those who lived and worked within its environs, it being believed that only those "born within the sound of Bow Bells," as the saying went (i.e., the bells of the church of St. Mary-le-Bow), were genuine cockneys and were therefore capable of speaking or understanding it. But over time its use was adopted by non-cockneys as well, becoming a part of the speech of all of London – a colorful jargon of the streets made up of foreign as well as of native words and expressions, doggerel to the uninitiated, but having rich, humorous (and often scatological) meaning to those familiar with it.

91. bushel o' coke – man (bloke)
clubs n' sticks – detectives (dicks)
flag unfurled – man of the world (i.e., of the upper class)
giggle stick – (self-explanatory)

92. "Sweeney" – short for "Sweeney Todd," cockney rhyming slang for the "flying squad" of the Metropolitan Police force, a sort of SWAT team of its day. Sweeney Todd, of course, was the notorious "demon barber" of Fleet Street.

93. Shinwell must have been referring to the now-famed Tower Bridge, which was completed in 1894.

94. There is no longer a Dorset Street (not to be confused with the one near Baker Street) in Spitalfields, having been bulldozed out of existence. In its day it vied with the notorious Ratcliffe Highway for the distinction of being the most dangerous street in all of London. People of the area called it "do-as-you-please street," for police constables were rarely in evidence, being afraid to patrol it alone.

95. Warren had submitted his resignation to the Home Secretary the previous day, and it was promptly accepted without even a pretense of the customary "regret." Curiously, when news of the resignation became known among members of the

department, Warren was visited by a deputation of officers, who informed him, in all sincerity, that "he carried with him the respect and admiration of every man in the force." Eventually returning to active duty with the army, he was to serve in South Africa once again (not without controversy) in command of an infantry division during the Boer War.

96. The pub is still in existence, though in a considerably altered state and with a different name. It is now called The Jack the Ripper.

97. There is some disagreement as to where Hutchinson was standing when he encountered Mary Kelly that night. Some accounts say it was at the corner of Thrawl Street, some say it was near Flower and Dean Street, a short distance away.

98. Dr. George Bagster-Phillips, a police surgeon with twenty years' experience, was more intimately involved with the Ripper murders than any other member of the medical profession, having examined four of the five acknowledged victims (Chapman, Eddowes, Stride, and Kelly).

99. Dr. Thomas Bond, consulting surgeon to "A" Division of the City Police (as well as to the Great Western Railway), who conducted his own postmortem of Mary Jane Kelly, was of the opinion that "one or two o'clock in the morning would be the probable time of the murder." He disagreed with Bagster-Phillips on another important point: Bagster-Phillips, like others, felt the murderer displayed "considerable" knowledge of anatomy and no small amount of surgical skill. Bond, who studied the autopsy notes of all of the victims, and personally examined two of them, was to write: "In each case the mutilation was implicated by a person who had no scientific or anatomical knowledge. In my opinion, he does not even possess the technical knowledge of a butcher or horse slaughterman or any person accustomed to cutting up dead animals."

100. That proved to be the case. The missing key, as well as the method used to bolt and unbolt the door, was subsequently confirmed by one Joseph Barnett, a porter at the nearby Spitalfields Market, who had been living with Mary Jane Kelly up until ten days before her murder.

101. The vast network of underground tunnels, passageways, sewers, and pipelines that threads its way beneath the streets of London goes back to Roman times in many cases. There are even underground rivers (the Fleet River stills runs beneath

Fleet Street, for example), and cesspools of ancient and malodorous provenance, which hover not always deeply beneath the surface, and sometimes make their presence known most inconveniently. (A particularly fetid sewer ran directly under the windows of the Houses of Parliament, as M.P.s discovered to their acute distress during the "Great Stink" of 1858. The sewer in question was the River Thames.)

The first of London's underground rail lines, a marvel of the age, opened to the public in 1863, and by 1875 a joint line of the Metropolitan Railway had been extended to Bishopsgate, while a further joint line was opened to Whitechapel Road in 1884. These were steam-driven, the engines being fitted with special smoke traps and condensers to keep pollution in the tunnels to a minimum.

102. See *A Case of Identity*.

103. See *The Illustrious Client*.

104. The murder actually took place within the boundaries of the Spitalfields district, which did not have its own coroner but came under the jurisdiction of Whitechapel's, Dr. Wynne Baxter.

105. There is a body of suggestive evidence that the hunt for the Ripper during this period was in reality a cursory affair that was not intended to obtain results. The official files apparently lack the same volume of paperwork for this period – investigatory reports and the like – that had earlier been submitted by detectives assigned to the case, suggesting that serious police activity simply stopped.

Most meaningfully, a sharp fall-off in reports filed by Inspector Abberline raises a suspicion that if there was a cover-up, he, quite possibly, was involved in it.

106. Sir William Gull, Bart., Physician Extraordinary to the Queen and Physician in Ordinary to the Prince of Wales and royal family, was noted for his skills as a diagnostician, specializing in paraplegia, diseases of the spinal cord and "abscesses of the brain." He was credited with saving the life of the Prince of Wales in 1871 (receiving his baronetage as a result), when the latter was gravely ill with typhoid. Gull suffered the first of three strokes in 1887 and died in January 1890 at the age of 73.

107. It is a matter of record that on the morning of Saturday, the 10th, the cabinet was summoned to 10 Downing Street in emergency session to discuss the Ripper murders and the wave of fear that had descended upon the capital because of them.

108. Holmes was missing from May 1891 to April 1894 (a period known as "The Great Hiatus" among Sherlockian scholars) and at first was indeed thought to be dead, carried to his death over the Reichenbach Falls in Switzerland by the infamous Professor James Moriarty (see *The Final Problem*). Upon his startling reappearance on April 5, 1894, the public was told that those "missing" three years were actually spent traveling the world (under the assumed name of Sigerson) to such exotic places as Tibet and Persia, Mecca and Khartoum (See *The Adventure of the Empty House*). But the story has always been looked upon with more than a modicum of suspicion, and these new disclosures of Watson's – or rather the suspicious gaps in his notes that suggest new disclosures were made and then suppressed – lead one to question whether Holmes was in Switzerland at all in May 1891. The evidence, though incomplete, strongly suggests what has always been widely conjectured, that it was all mere subterfuge, an effort to deceive the public to prevent it from knowing Holmes's true whereabouts during this period and the actual reason for his absence.

109. This was the opinion expressed in *The Saturday Review*. Not all periodicals were that complimentary in their obituaries of Churchill. *The Outlook* said he represented "the coarser qualities of his race," while *The National Review* called him "swift and dangerous when hard pressed" and "reckless beyond all men's reckoning."

110. Watson, by most estimates, married Mary Morstan in May 1889, at which time he took up residence and established a medical practice in London's Paddington district. But the course of Watson's married life has confounded scholars almost as much as his wartime injury(ies). While he could not possibly have met Miss Morstan earlier than July 1888 (see *The Sign of the Four*), there is evidence that he was already a married man in March of that year, a full four months earlier (see *A Scandal in Bohemia*), and there is an implication that he was married as early as September 1887 (see *The Five Orange Pips*). It would seem, then, that Miss Morstan was his second wife and that the period of mourning between his two marriages was mercifully brief.

But it gets more complex: Sadly, all indications are that the "second" Mrs. Watson (née Morstan) died sometime between 1891 and 1894 (see *The Adventure of the Empty House*), yet we find that the doctor is with wife as late as 1903 (see *The Adventure of the Blanched Soldier*), leaving us with no alternative but to conclude that he was married no fewer than *three* times, in each case, curiously, to a woman named Mary.

While we cannot be sure what his married state was when this discussion took place with Holmes in January 1895, it is certain he was not residing in Baker Street at the time but occupied a residence in Kensington, where he had a practice that was "small" (see *The Norwood Builder*) and "never very absorbing" (see *The Red-Headed League*).

111. The day was forever fixed in Watson's *faulty* memory, for here we come upon yet another of his calendrical inconsistencies. Holmes, as we have already seen, was by all accounts (including at least two of Watson's own), out of the country when Prince Eddy died on January 14, 1892, and could have had no discussion of *any* kind with Watson (see Note 108 above). As is usual with Watson's often muddled dating of things, there is no accounting for the discrepancy.

112. The prince (who had been created Duke of Clarence and Avondale a year earlier) had become engaged, in December 1891, to one of his German second cousins, Princess May of Teck. Unquestionably it was an arranged affair. Wrote Ponsonby, Queen Victoria's secretary: "I am told he don't care for Princess May of Teck, and she appears to be too proud to take the trouble of running after him, for which I rather admire her."

Knollys, the Prince of Wales's private secretary, wrote to Ponsonby: "I think the preliminaries are now pretty well settled, but do you suppose Princess May will make any resistance? I do not anticipate any real opposition on Prince Eddy's part if he is properly managed and is told he *must* do it – that is, for the good of the country, etc. etc."

After Eddy's death, Princess May, who was nothing if not dutiful, allowed herself to be married off to his younger brother, who in time became King George V, while she became Queen Mary. She is best remembered as Britain's wartime Queen Dowager, the mother of both Edward VIII, who was to abdicate and marry a twice-divorced commoner, becoming the Duke of Windsor, and George VI, the father of the current queen, Elizabeth II. Highly popular among the English people (she insisted upon remaining in London during the worst of the bombing in World War II), Queen Mary died in 1953 at the age of 86.

113. The police became interested in number 19 Cleveland Street in the summer of 1889, when it was noticed that the house was frequented not only by certain adult male members of the aristocracy but by an unusual number of delivery boys and telegraph messengers, who appeared to be flourishing a good deal more spending money than their meager wages would justify. Among those named in the scandal was Lord Arthur Somerset, Extra Equerry and Superintendent of the Stables to the Prince of Wales, who was forced to flee the country to avoid prosecution. Prince Albert Victor's name was kept out of it, but only just, by accommodating members of the police raiding party. The officer in charge of the case for Scotland Yard, coincidentally, was Inspector Frederick Abberline.

114. The suggestion here, the hint that Prince Albert Victor might have been done away with, is not as absurd as some might think. There was a subsequent event in England's royal family that removes the idea from the realm of the totally unbelievable and places it into the category of the not entirely impossible: It is a matter of historical record that in 1936, when Albert Victor's brother, King George V, was lying incurably ill, his death was hastened by lethal injections of morphine and cocaine secretly administered by the royal physician. (See *The Sun*, November 27, 1986.)

115. James Kenneth Stephen entered a Northampton lunatic asylum in November 1891 and died there on February 3, 1892, just twenty days after hearing of the death of his former friend, Prince Albert Victor. It is said that he refused all nourishment and starved himself to death.

116. Blunders on his part, Holmes once said, "were a more common occurrence than anyone would think." (See *Silver Blaze.*) "I have been beaten four times," he said on another occasion. "Three times by men, and once by a woman." (See T*he Five Orange Pips.*)

117. As a matter of interest, Sir Arthur Conan Doyle was also of this opinion.

118. The medical examiners who were personally involved in the postmortems of the Ripper's victims were very much at odds over this question. Dr. Rees Ralph Llewellyn was of the opinion that the mutilations of Polly Nicholls were "deftly and fairly skillfully performed." Dr. George Bagster-Phillips stated that whoever removed Annie Chapman's uterus "showed some anatomical knowledge." Dr. Frederick Gordon Brown believed that the murderer of Catherine Eddowes displayed "a good deal of knowledge as to the positions of the organs in the body cavity and the way of removing them." Drs. George William Sequeira and William Sedgewick Saunders disagreed with Brown, expressing the opinion that no anatomical knowledge, other than that which could be expected of a professional butcher, was displayed. Dr. Thomas Bond, an authority in forensic medicine who had conducted the postmortem of Mary Kelly and had made a study of the others, tended to agree with Sequeira and Saunders: "In each case the mutilation was implicated by a person who had no scientific or anatomical knowledge. In my opinion he does not even possess the technical knowledge. In my opinion he does not even possess the technical knowledge of a butcher or horse slaughterman..."

119. Smith's version was one of those which turned out to be inaccurate. The correct one, a copy of which, according to Whittington-Egan, is preserved in the police files, is as follows:

The Juwes are The men That will not be blamed for nothing

120. Who could this mysterious "certain doctor" have been? Many have theorized (and some have even flatly claimed to have "proof") that Sir William Gull, the royal family's physician, and one of the foremost medical practitioners of his day, was in some way involved — either in the crimes themselves or in the cover-up of them.

Mea Culpa

"**H**as anything escaped me? I trust there is nothing of consequence which I have overlooked."
– John H. Watson, M.D.,
The Hound of the Baskervilles

The hand of every writer, as a knowing writer once observed, is guided by those who came before. This book draws heavily on the scholarship of others: First, on the exhaustive studies of a large (and, it would seem, ever-growing) body of indefatigable "Ripperologists" who in the course of their investigations down through the years have left not a stone unturned, a clue unexamined, or a possibility (no matter how remote, implausible, or outrageous) unscrutinized, undissected, and unregurgitated; and, second, on the loving ruminations and commentaries of that dedicated band of brothers known as Sherlockians, slightly dotty all, who, as a result of their scholarly peregrinations and endless debates, have helped to create a myth more real than reality itself.

To all of them, my thanks. It is not too much to say that had not their books happened first, this book quite simply would not have happened at all. They have my respect, my appreciation, and my deepest gratitude.

William S. Baring-Gould
- *The Annotated Sherlock Holmes*
- *Sherlock Holmes of Baker Street*

Vincent Starrett
- *The Private Life of Sherlock Holmes*

Jack Tracy
- *The Encyclopaedia Sherlockiana*

Michael and Mollie Hardwick
- *The Sherlock Holmes Companion*

Orlando Park
- *The Sherlock Holmes Encyclopedia*

Michael Harrison
- *The World of Sherlock Holmes*
- *The London of Sherlock Holmes*
- *In the Footsteps of Sherlock Holmes*
- *Clarence: The Life of HRH the Duke of Clarence and Avondale*
- *London by Gaslight*

Walter Shepherd
- *On the Scent with Sherlock Holmes*

Alexander Kelly
- *Jack the Ripper: A Bibliography*

Tom Cullen
- *Autumn of Terror*

Donald Rumbelow
- *The Complete Jack the Ripper*

Peter Underwood
- *Jack the Ripper: One Hundred Years of Mystery*

Elwyn Jones and John Lloyd
  – *The Ripper File*
Richard Whittington-Egan
  – *A Casebook on Jack the Ripper*
Stephen Knight
  – *Jack the Ripper: The Final Solution*
Terence Sharkey
  – *Jack the Ripper: One Hundred Years of Investigation*
Paul Begg
  – *Jack the Ripper: The Uncensored Facts*
Louis Auchincloss
  – *Persons of Consequence*
William Manchester
  – *The Last Lion*
Stanley Weintraub
  – *Victoria: An Intimate Biography*
Phillippe Jullian
  – *Edward and the Edwardians*
Elizabeth Longford
  – *Victoria R.I.*
James Pope-Hennessy
  – *Queen Mary*
Sir Arthur Conan Doyle, M.D.
  – *The Complete Works of Sherlock Holmes*

Of inestimable help also was scholarship gleaned from the pages of *The Baker Street Journal,* Philip A. Shreffler, editor, and its many contributors; and from the archives of *The Times* (of London) and *The Daily Telegraph,* whose coverage of the Ripper murders remains, quite simply, among the best crime reporting in the annals of journalism.

It would be an act of ingratitude not to mention the services rendered by the librarians of the Berkshire Athenaeum in Pittsfield, Massachusetts, and, most especially, the staff of the New York Public Library's main reading room. Special words of thanks go to Marcia Hanna, Leigh Hanna, and Ted Koppel.

One final observation: In a story based on both fiction and fact, as this one is, it is only natural there be occasional difficulties in separating one from the other. Rest assured that those portions dealing with the Ripper murders and the police investigation of them are as accurate as my reading of the available, often differing, literature has been able to make them.

While it need hardly be said that this is primarily a work of fiction, custom, prudence, and legal counsel require me to do so. Of course, that part of the account relating to the affairs of Dr. John H. Watson and Mr. Sherlock Holmes is wholly factual.

Depend on it.

EBH
The Berkshires, Massachusetts
May 1992

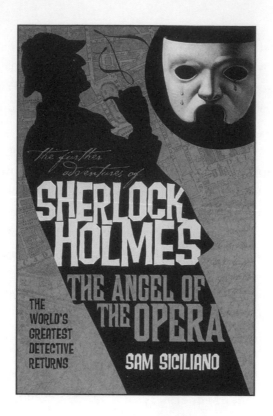

THE FURTHER ADVENTURES
OF SHERLOCK HOLMES
THE ANGEL OF THE OPERA

Sam Siciliano

Paris 1890: Sherlock Holmes is called across the English Channel to the famous
Opera House, where he is challenged to discover the true motivations and secrets of
the notorious Phantom who rules its depths with passion and defiance.

ISBN: 9781848568617

AVAILABLE MARCH 2011

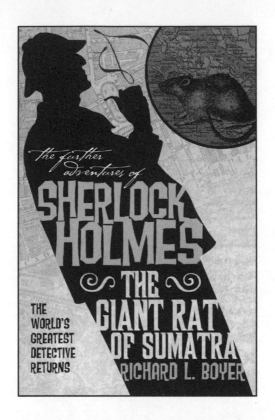

THE FURTHER ADVENTURES
OF SHERLOCK HOLMES

THE GIANT RAT OF SUMATRA

Richard L. boyer

For many years, Dr. Watson kept the tale of The Giant Rat of Sumatra a secret.
However, before he died, he arranged that the strange story of the giant rat should
be held in the vaults of a London bank until all the protagonists were dead...

ISBN: 9781848568600

AVAILABLE MARCH 2011

THE FURTHER ADVENTURES OF SHERLOCK HOLMES

THE SEVENTH BULLET

Daniel D. Victor

Sherlock Holmes's desire for a peaceful life in the Sussex
countryside is dashed when true-life muckraker and author David
Graham Phillips is assassinated. The pleas of his sister draw
Holmes and Watson to the far side of the Atlantic as they embark
on one of their most challenging cases.
ISBN: 9781848566767

AVAILABLE NOW!

THE FURTHER ADVENTURES
OF SHERLOCK HOLMES
SÉANCE FOR A VAMPIRE

Fred Saberhagen

When two psychics offer Ambrose Altamont the opportunity to contact
his deceased daughter, Holmes is hired to expose their hoax. The result
leaves one of the fraudulent spiritualists dead and Holmes missing. Watson
has no choice but to summon the only one who might be able to help –
Holmes's vampire cousin, Prince Dracula.
ISBN: 9781848566774

AVAILABLE NOW!

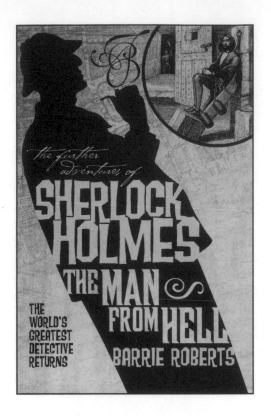

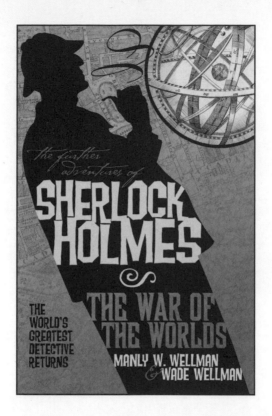

THE FURTHER ADVENTURES
OF SHERLOCK HOLMES
THE WAR OF THE WORLDS

Manley W. Wellman & Wade Wellman

Sherlock Holmes, Professor Challenger and Dr. Watson meet
their match when the streets of London are left decimated by
a prolonged alien attack. Who could be responsible for such
destruction? Sherlock Holmes is about to find out...
ISBN: 9781848564916

AVAILABLE NOW!

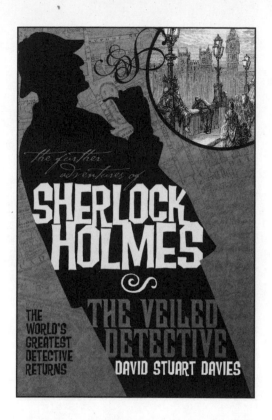

THE FURTHER ADVENTURES
OF SHERLOCK HOLMES
THE VEILED DETECTIVE

David Stuart Davies

A young Sherlock Holmes arrives in London to begin his career
as a private detective, catching the eye of the master criminal,
Professor James Moriarty. Enter Dr. Watson, newly returned
from Afghanistan, soon to make history as Holmes's companion...
ISBN: 9781848564909

AVAILABLE NOW!

THE FURTHER ADVENTURES OF SHERLOCK HOLMES

THE ECTOPLASMIC MAN

Daniel Stashower

When Harry Houdini is framed and jailed for espionage, Sherlock Holmes vows to clear his name, with the two joining forces to take on blackmailers who have targeted the Prince of Wales.
ISBN: 9781848564923

AVAILABLE NOW!